Story Overview

Determined to protect Jackie from evil, Darach Hamilton flees MacLomain Castle without telling anyone his destination. As foretold by Celtic Goddess Brigit, that *should* have made the enemy pursue him. But nothing is as it seems. When he learns the dark demi-god went after Jackie instead, he races to her side only to discover something unexpected. Things have changed. There might be hope for them. Maybe he can finally be with her. After all, he's been dreaming about her for years. The only problem? He already pushed her into another man's arms.

Over a month has passed since Jackie traveled back in time from modern day New Hampshire to medieval Scotland. Since then, it's been a non-stop adventure. Now she's in ninth-century Scandinavia with Heidrek, a Viking set to inherit the throne. A man that Darach is determined she be with despite the unforgettable kiss they shared. Then there's the newfound Claddagh ring on her finger. It is foretold that its stone can only be ignited by the love of a MacLomain. Darach is by birth, the only remaining MacLomain not taken. Yet despite the power the ring's glow could harness, she wants nothing to do with it. Not in light of her terrible secret. One she prays will keep any man from loving her because it will mean their ultimate ruin.

Many revelations come to light when Jackie, Darach, and Heidrek travel through time to keep the future King, wee Robert the Bruce safe. Determined to spare them heartbreak, Jackie refuses both men. Yet one of them ends up invoking unavoidable passion. A timeless draw. One she tries to fight. But some things are meant to be, and Fate has a plan for them all. Epic love. Ultimate war. Inescapable death. Twists nobody saw coming. An ending that will either see Scotland through to what it is today or rewrite history altogether.

Find out how everything unfolds in Passion of a Scottish Warrior, the final installment in the MacLomain Series: Later Years.

Passion of a Scottish Warrior
The MacLomain Series-Later Years
Book Four

By

Sky Purington

Dedication

This is dedicated to my mother-in-law, Nancy.
You touched my life in ways you will never know.
Thank you from the bottom of my heart.

Rest in Peace, my friend.

1943-2015

An Irish Poem

Do not stand at my grave and weep,
I am not there... I do not sleep.
I am the thousand winds that blow...
I am the diamond glints on snow...
I am the sunlight on ripened grain...
I am the gentle autumn rain.
When you waken in the morning's hush,
I am the swift uplifting rush
Of gentle birds in circling flight...
I am the soft star that shines at night.
Do not stand at my grave and cry—
I am not there... I did not die...

COPYRIGHT © 2016
Passion of a Scottish Warrior
Sky Purington

Edited by *Cathy McElhaney*
Cover Art by *Tamra Westberry*

Published in the United States of America

Chapter One

Scandinavia
905 A.D.

"DARACH LET ME go," Jackie murmured against Heidrek's chest. "Just like that, he let me go."

"He did right by you, woman." Heidrek tilted her chin until their eyes met. "Now I will watch over you." His gaze softened. "Care for you."

What had just happened? She still couldn't make sense of it. Not this part of the journey anyway. Like her friends with Broun blood, Cassie, Nicole, and Erin, she had traveled back in time from modern day New Hampshire to medieval Scotland.

Well, at least originally.

Since she first traveled back over a month ago, she had ping-ponged between Scotland and ninth-century Scandinavia. Anything to avoid the evil demi-god in pursuit of not only wee Robert the Bruce but one of the four original Claddagh rings. Apparently the rings were the key to a modern day Broun finding her one true love MacLomain. And as foretold, all of her friends who wore a ring like hers had recently done just that. Fallen in love.

So that only left Jackie.

And Darach.

Despite being in another man's arms right now, they were the only two left that were meant to come together. The only Broun and MacLomain. Yet Darach was determined to see that changed. Which was why he sent her reeling back in time safely within Heidrek's arms.

Not a Scotsman but a Viking.

Jackie was about to respond to Heidrek when two dragons appeared out of thin air. Within seconds, Bjorn and Tait shifted and landed on the dock. They too had returned from thirteenth century Scotland.

She pulled away from Heidrek, anxious to hear what they had to say. "I didn't expect to see you so soon. Is everything okay?" Keep your cool, she preached to herself. Now isn't the time to lose it. "Erin? Robert the Bruce? What happened after we left?"

The last thing she saw before being whisked away in the midst of battle at MacLomain Castle was all hell breaking loose.

"Time passes differently. It has been several hours since the battle. All is well enough," Bjorn grumbled and strode away.

Jackie frowned at Tait. "That doesn't sound promising."

"The demi-god wasn't defeated, but the young king and your friends are safe." Tait shrugged as he watched Bjorn. "Although he ordered me to keep my distance from Erin, it seems my cousin came to love her and struggles with her taking Rònan as a mate."

"That doesn't surprise me," Jackie murmured. She had seen the way Bjorn looked at Erin.

As it turned out, Erin was half dragon so she was more appealing to the Viking dragon shifters. Bjorn and Tait had protected her until now. Her guess was Erin and Rònan had come into their full power, and her ring's gem matched Rònan's eyes. Once that happened, the demi-god couldn't go near it.

That meant Jackie and her ring had become the new target.

"And how are you doing, Cousin?" Heidrek asked Tait. "Is your heart broken as well?"

"I'm fine," Tait assured though a flicker of sadness touched his eyes. "Erin is my friend, and I only wish her the best."

Heidrek nodded. "Good." He clasped Tait's shoulder and met his eyes. "You and Bjorn made me proud. Thank you for protecting your kin so well."

Tait nodded before he headed down the dock. From the get-go, she had been impressed with how much respect the dragon shifters showed Heidrek considering he wasn't half dragon. But he was the oldest and would become king eventually, so it made sense. More than that, he treated them well. He treated everyone well for that matter.

Heidrek sheathed the MacLomain sword Rònan had recently tossed to him and held out his hand, his eyes locked on hers. "Come, Jackie. Let us seek shelter before the storm arrives."

Jackie nodded, took his hand, and eyed the cloudless sky as they walked. While some might ask him why he said that, she knew better. Heidrek might not be a dragon, but there was something mystical about him. His mother had been a powerful seer and his father was a dragon shifter so he was far from simply human.

Though she had been to this ring fortress before, she remained in awe of its sheer size. With dozens of long piers, various sized ships and a large village cozied between a huge wall and massive mountains, it was truly impressive. While she might have spent the majority of her time here indoors caring for Erin who was caught in an unnatural slumber, she managed to get out a little bit. During that time, she got to know Heidrek and his family better.

While Darach continued to avoid her.

Oh, the trouble a kiss can cause.

She vividly recalled the first time she met Darach Hamilton in New Hampshire. He had been teaching Nicole how to fight. Dressed in nothing but faded jeans and black boots, his sweat-slicked muscles glistened in the sun. She sat in her car, hands gripping the steering wheel for far too long as she admired him. And struggled with an unusual feeling of familiarity...almost déjà vu.

After they'd been introduced, he seemed to keep his distance. They talked on occasion and eyed one another. Maybe even flirted here and there but that was it.

Until just before he left.

It had been then, in those last moments before he turned away to leave, that he shook his head, closed the distance, cupped her cheeks and kissed her. It hadn't lasted long. No tongue was involved. But it was the most romantic kiss of her life and had left her breathless.

Yet she knew he regretted it the minute he pulled away.

She saw how disappointed he was with himself.

"You worry over Darach," Heidrek said softly, cutting into her thoughts.

"I do." It wasn't a complete lie. She did. "I wish I understood what was going on. Why he wanted Rònan to give you that blade." Jackie shook her head. "Isn't it supposed to stay with Darach? To help him defeat the dark demi-god?"

Jackie didn't have to wonder why Darach chose Heidrek to keep her safe. It was no secret that she and the Viking had become good friends and that he would do his best to protect her. But why was Darach determined to stay away from her? Was he so opposed to the idea that she might be meant for him?

"Yes, it has been said that the blade can help defeat the evil demi-god," Heidrek said. "But there is a way to keep you and the ring safe. One which does not include you being with Darach."

Jackie eyed him as they walked. As tall and muscled as his dragon kin, Heidrek was remarkably handsome with dark blond hair and pale blue eyes. And like his family, he was every inch a warrior. Yet somehow she knew whatever he spoke of had nothing to do with merely protecting her.

"Darach wants me to be with you, doesn't he?" she murmured. "Somehow he knows a way to break this Broun, MacLomain connection."

"Yes." He never released her hand as they made their way through the crowd and past the fortress gates. As always, he was greeted by everyone. The Viking King might still rule, but it was clear the people looked to Heidrek as well.

While she might genuinely like Heidrek and could admit that she was attracted to him, she didn't like being told who she should be with. Especially when it meant being tossed from one fated man to another. She was angry. Confused. Because none of it made any sense. She just couldn't wrap her mind around it. Why did Darach give her up so readily? Better yet, what gave him the idea that she was *his* to give up in the first place? When she felt her skin tingling in response to her emotions, she tried to suppress them.

Forgive him, Jackie.

Forgive him so that you can calm down.

As if he sensed her disgruntled thoughts, Heidrek pulled her into the stables away from the crowd. He cupped her shoulders as his eyebrows flew together. "Are you well, Jackie?"

"I am," she whispered and inhaled deeply, almost cursing when the normal scent of horses and hay didn't reach her nostrils.

Forgive. But could she?

"You will never be forced into anything you do not want," Heidrek said gently, well aware of her tension, her issues. At least some of them. Where Cassie had gone blind, Nicole was going deaf and Erin, mute, Jackie faced something altogether different. Something that affected her sense of touch and smell.

Two symptoms that would eventually lead to something far worse.

And it was that *something* that only Erin knew about.

12

Or so she assumed. *And hoped.*

It was hard to know for sure who knew what in this land of magic and time travel.

"I hear you saying the words, Heidrek," she managed. "But it feels like Darach expects me to be with you and that you expect the same." She kept trying to forgive them for assuming as much. "And while I appreciate your protection, I'm not a big fan of having others decide my fate."

Born into a wealthy family who owned half the real estate in the Hamptons, she had learned at a young age how pre-planned her life was. In fact, her uncle nearly had her married off before she turned eighteen.

"Darach trusted me to protect you and that is what I intend to do." Heidrek squeezed her shoulders. "If nothing else, we're friends Jackie. Let that fact not make you feel caged but free. I've enjoyed our time together and hope for far more. But that does not decide your fate. Only you decide that."

And that's why she liked this guy so much. He didn't push her. It was yet another reason she supposed the King wanted him to take the throne. Heidrek knew how to handle people.

"Okay," she whispered and met his eyes. "Thank you."

Heidrek held her gaze for a long moment before he nodded and pulled away. When a commotion arose outside, he cocked his head and narrowed his eyes as though he knew precisely what was happening.

"What is it?" she said.

"Something that does not overly surprise me," he said under his breath as he took her hand and led her back out. Jackie's eyes widened when she saw who had arrived.

Grant Hamilton.

Darach's father.

He looked upset as he strode through the village. When his eyes locked on them, he stopped short. "Is he here then? Is my son here?"

"Laird Hamilton," came a deep voice as Naðr Veurr, the Viking King appeared through the crowd. "What ails you, my friend?"

"Darach has vanished." Grant wore a heavy frown as his eyes flickered between Jackie and the King. "I cannae sense him anywhere."

Jackie's frown met Grant's as they joined them. "I thought everything was okay. Wasn't he just at MacLomain Castle?"

"Aye," Grant said. "And in a state. He was last seen on the wall walk with Erin and Rònan. After he left there, he vanished. Nobody can find him."

Her heart leapt into her throat. "Do you think...did the..."

When her words trailed off, Grant's eyes widened. "Do I think what? That he was taken by evil?"

"Well, yes," she started, but the King cut her off.

"Come, Laird Grant, let us go somewhere quiet." His eyes met Heidrek's. "You and Jackie as well."

Grant kept muttering as they followed Naðr deeper into the village until they entered his private lodge. Queen Megan waited and urged them to sit around a fire as they received mugs of ale.

"We have seen no sign of your son or anyone else until Heidrek returned with Jackie," the King said. "What has happened?"

"Bloody hell if I know." Grant took a hearty swig from his mug. Jackie had never seen him like this before. As Laird of the Hamilton clan and the most powerful MacLomain wizard, he was usually far more refined.

"I knew he was upset, we all did," Grant continued. "But Erin convinced me to let him speak with her and his cousins alone. So, I did. I gave them their time." He shook his head, distressed. "Then he just disappears!" Grant took another swig, eyes rounding. "Is he hurt? Has he been taken? I have no idea." His eyes shot to Jackie. "'Tis hard to imagine that he disappeared of his own free will when you're in more danger than ever."

"But I thought..." she started.

"You thought what?" Grant's eyes narrowed. "That my son had the power to keep you and the wee king safe by giving you to Heidrek?"

Jackie's blood chilled at his tone. Heidrek didn't take it much better based on the way his brows drew down.

"Darach did not give me to anyone because I did not belong to him to begin with," she said, enunciating each word firmly but respectfully. "Instead, he told Rònan to toss his sword to Heidrek, and we were pulled through time and ended up here." Her skin started tingling again. *Forgive.* "So please tell me...us, what's going on because we're as clueless as you are."

14

"Aye then, lass." Grant's eyes went to Naðr's. "The demi-god is Keir Hamilton's father. Though it has long been told that Keir was an evil reincarnate, that doesnae seem to be the case. Instead 'twas Keir's da who was reincarnated. Though he went by the name of Innis MacGilleEathain when last on Earth, he was once Eoghan Dubhdiadh, Druid of the South. A powerful warlock who plagued my mentor, Adlin MacLomain's parents in ancient Ireland. He desired the Druidess, Chiomara and stopped at nothing to have her. I've no idea why we were told Keir was Eoghan nor do I know how he became half god. But I do know that there is no worse fate for us."

Jackie could barely breathe. She had been told about Keir Hamilton. A man turned warlock who was determined to take Torra MacLomain as his own and drive Scotland into ruin twenty-seven years ago. A man with a dark heart who the next generation, Grant, and his brethren, had eventually defeated and trapped in a tapestry in MacLomain Castle's great hall. To this day, the man remained locked in a purgatory made of MacLomain and Viking magic.

A place between medieval Scotland and Scandinavia.

"So Eoghan the demi-god attempts to break his son free," the Viking King said. "That is how he's able to track you not only in your time period but here."

"I believe so," Grant said. "'Tis the only thing that makes sense."

Jackie didn't miss the look the king gave Heidrek. It was the one that gave him leeway to speak.

"So all of our people are at risk now," Heidrek said. "Even those at our dragon lair."

"Mayhap," Grant said. "But as it has been from the start, the dark laird seeks the ring." His eyes fell to Jackie's finger. "So I would say since Jackie is here, the fortress is most at risk."

"But what of Darach's convictions?" Heidrek clenched his jaw. "I like the man. I believe in him. Do you mean to say that he is wrong thinking Jackie is safe here? That she is *not* safe with me?"

Grant released a heavy sigh and shook his head. "I think my lad has become less of a warrior and more of a romantic."

"A romantic?" Jackie started, but Heidrek put a hand on her arm and shook his head as his eyes met the King's and then Grant's.

Heck, if she got cut off one more time...

"It is a rare day that a romantic heart gives up the woman he loves to another man." Heidrek's eyes remained locked firmly on Grant as he defended Darach. "We Vikings would see that more as a warrior's heart. Someone who means to protect those he cares for."

Grant shrugged, his expression cautiously reluctant. "Och, 'tis just a thing that we Scots see differently, aye?"

Jackie was used to watching men in power play their games so she made a point of eying the Viking King the entire time. While he might be giving Heidrek the reigns on occasion, he was in charge.

And he wasn't entirely feeding into whatever Grant was up too.

Because Grant *was* up to something.

But what?

"Yes, we come from different cultures so it is always possible that our perspectives are different," the Viking King conceded. "But one thing remains the same. We protect our kin. So what would you have us do seeing how your son is not here?"

"Allow me to take Jackie with me," Grant said. "Let me take her away from here because right now she only puts your people at risk."

"A risk I would take again and again," Heidrek said with more heat than he likely intended.

But the King didn't look his way. He kept his eyes locked on Grant. "It is a noble request, my friend and I appreciate the offer."

Grant set aside the mug. His eyes never left the King's as he said, "But you willnae let her go, aye?"

"I will not," the King confirmed.

"Nor will I." Heidrek's eyes flickered from her to Grant, and she heard the emotion in his voice. "Unless we know she is safe."

"Of course, she will be safe," Grant scoffed. "She will be with me."

Heidrek's eyes narrowed. "And where exactly will *that* be?"

"It doesnae matter," Grant exclaimed.

"But it does."

"Ye dare to question *me*, lad?" Grant's eyes narrowed. "Do ye know how powerful I am?"

Everyone was frowning at this point. Something was seriously off.

Seconds later, black lightning started to sizzle around Grant before he turned into a black mass and spun toward her. No wonder he had been acting so strange.

He was the *demi-god*.

The Vikings sprang into action. A scream caught in her throat when someone spun her and yanked her into their arms. The next thing she knew, her head was tucked against his chest.

"Ye'll not have her," came a deep growl as cool then warm air whipped around her. Colors blurred as she squinted. It didn't take long to figure out who held her based on his scent alone.

Darach.

He smelled like a mixture of cedar and spices heating over flames. Earthy wood smoke on a chilled autumn day.

Whatever was happening around them died in an instant followed by Grant's soft but firm declaration. "I knew if you thought I was the enemy you would come, Son."

Darach pulled away and tried to do something with magic that no doubt would take him out of here, but Grant stopped it.

"What are you running from?" Grant said, his voice desperate as he held Darach back with magic.

Darach clenched his fists by his side as his eyes met hers. She had met a lot of men but none that looked like him. Around six foot five inches worth of broad-shouldered, well-proportioned muscles with an intricate tattoo running from his left shoulder to his elbow, he was the sort of man who stopped women in their tracks. With chiseled cheekbones, a strong jaw, brows that worked at being optimistic and lips that curved toward sin, he was gorgeous. Add in the thick black hair accented with mahogany highlights and watch out.

Then there were his eyes.

Those thick-lashed pale bluish gray eyes that could swallow a girl whole.

"Her," Darach managed to answer his father, but his eyes stayed locked on hers. "I was trying to run from Jackie..." He shook his head, confused by his own answer. "To keep her safe."

Caught in each other's eyes, it took a split second longer than he likely intended before Darach remembered he'd been lured here and his gaze returned to his father. "Let me go."

Grant did the opposite. He grabbed Darach's forearm and came nose to nose. "Dinnae ye ever give me and yer ma a scare like that again, lad."

"You dinnae ken what you've done by tricking me, Da." Darach yanked his arm free and shook his head. "You dinnae ken in the least."

"Then tell me," Grant started but a loud boom cut off his words.

"Bloody hell." Darach's eyes swung to Naðr. "Rally your dragons. Protect your people. I will leave. When I do, you will be safe."

"Darach, what's going on?" she said, but he shook his head sharply, his eyes going to Heidrek. "Keep her here with you, friend. She isnae safe with me." Then his eyes shot to Grant. "You must let me go, Da. Trust me when I tell you 'tis for the best."

"Nothing about remaining in the dark to your plight is for the best," Grant retaliated. "Why are you so convinced that the demi-god will steer clear of Jackie if you do as well?"

"Because I have something he wants. Something easier to take from me than from Jackie protected such as she is." He put his hand in his pocket and frowned before he searched it more intently.

"What is it?" Grant's eyes narrowed. "What are you looking for?"

Darach shook his head, baffled and more concerned by the moment as his eyes shot to her hand. Better yet, the ring on it. "I dinnae ken," he murmured, again fishing around in his pocket. "Where did it go?"

Totally confused, she glanced at her ring and frowned. "Are you talking about this?"

"Och, the bloody gods and their games," Darach muttered and took her hand, peering more intently at her ring. "This isnae right at all."

Suddenly, Darach's expression shifted. Almost as if he heard something.

His eyes flew to Grant. "You need to get us out of here, Da." He gestured at Jackie and Heidrek. "All three of us. Now."

Grant's eyes remained locked on Darach's and she knew they spoke telepathically. What could possibly have Darach wanting her far away from him one second and then with him the next?

The King's eyes went to Heidrek and he frowned. "Why must Heidrek leave?"

Still locked on Darach, Grant's eyes widened slightly as he seemed to understand. "Bloody hell," he whispered. "'Tis a summoning from Adlin MacLomain. How can this be?"

Grant's eyes went to the King's. "You need to trust me when I tell ye Heidrek's journey is with Jackie and Darach for now."

Naðr was about to respond, but Heidrek spoke first, his tone surprisingly stern considering who he addressed. "I will stay with Jackie, my King. I intend to protect her."

Though clearly displeased, Naðr eyed Heidrek for a long moment before he gave a curt nod. "You must follow your path. But do not forget that there is one laid out for you here as well. One that includes my kingdom and you ruling it someday."

"A future I embrace, Uncle," Heidrek assured. "I will return once I know Jackie is out of harm's way."

The King nodded. "Then go, Nephew, but travel safely."

Heidrek nodded as his hand slipped into hers. For a split second, she almost felt guilty and pulled away. But why should she feel guilty? Because of Darach? They might have shared a brief kiss, but he hadn't been around to offer her the amount of comfort Heidrek had. He may have had his reasons but in all actuality, that didn't change a thing. She barely knew him. So she squeezed Heidrek's hand, thankful if nothing else for the support and friendship he offered.

"Now, Da." Darach's hand slid into hers as well. "Get us where we need to go."

Okay, so this was a little weird.

But 'weird' soon took a backseat to that edge of fear she always experienced when magic unleashed around her. Now she squeezed both of their hands, grateful when they came close and protected her against what Grant threw at them.

It felt different.

More powerful.

Wind whipped and the crackling fire at the heart of the Viking lodge swirled away only to be replaced with higher flames and screaming. Though they kept her safely between them, she heard the metallic ring of Heidrek and Darach unsheathing their swords. Yet she soon realized as she peeked out from beneath their arms that the fire she saw was at the heart of a tall, square building and the screaming was people celebrating.

"Well, what do we have here," said a tall, handsome young man with black hair and light blue eyes.

"More followers then, m'Laird?" someone said.

"We can only hope." He grinned and cocked his head, his eyes meeting Jackie's despite the men cocooning her. "Someone from the future, aye?"

"Bloody hell, Da did it. We made it," Darach murmured. "'Tis Adlin MacLomain."

Chapter Two

Scotland
The Original Highland Defiance
845 A.D.

"YE CANNAE APPEAR out of nowhere and expect a blade willnae be at yer throat."

Darach stilled and peered down at the young lad with the tip of a small blade held against his hip. He might be standing in front of the great Adlin MacLomain, but he still said, "Ye do know that ye've got the blade nowhere near my throat, aye, lad?"

The boy with big brown eyes glared up at him. "Aye, Mister, but my other will be after I use this one."

"Och, enough, William," Adlin said with a chuckle. "He is a friend. They all are."

Like Heidrek, Darach stepped away from Jackie but didn't release her hand. Though it seemed clear they were safe enough, looks could be deceiving.

"Where are we exactly?" Darach asked.

Adlin cocked the corner of his lips. "At my Defiance. But not for much longer. We leave on the morn."

Darach knew they needed to be sent back in time to locate Adlin when he was young, but wasn't sure exactly where that would land them. "So you know who we are?"

"Enough so." Adlin's eyes went to William. "'Tis time to make our guests welcome. Go fetch them some whisky."

Unsure, the boy eyed them. "Truly?"

"Aye, lad."

William sighed, narrowed his eyes one more time at Darach then headed into the crowd.

Adlin's eyes remained on the three of them, not cautious in the least but kind. "Might you introduce yourselves then?"

Darach was surprised that he said "you" instead of "ye." Something that MacLomains hadn't started doing until the first Broun lass traveled back in time. But then again, this was Adlin. The arch-wizard of the MacLomain clan. Immortal until the day he fell in love and started to age. Not only that but he was conceived by Chiomara the Druidess, and Erc, King of the Dalriada, in fifth century Ireland only to be delivered by the gods to Scotland a full grown man.

A man who started his legacy and clan right here at the Highland Defiance.

"Aye, of course. I'm Darach." He gestured at Jackie. "This is Jackie." Then he nodded toward the Viking. "And that's Heidrek."

A twinkle lit his eyes when Adlin looked at Heidrek. "A Viking ancestor then." He smiled. "'Tis good to have you amongst us, friend." His eyes went to Darach. "You as well my distant offspring." Then his gaze settled on Jackie as he approached.

Neither Heidrek or Darach released her hand when Adlin stopped in front of her, his eyes even kinder than before as they held hers. "And you. A Broun, aye?"

Jackie nodded, her eyes darkening even more with emotion.

"You've no need to be frightened," Adlin said softly, his eyes flickering between the men before again landing on her. "Not with such brawn lads to keep you safe."

Jackie pulled her hands from the men and stood up taller. "I can keep myself safe."

Adlin eyed her for a long moment before he nodded. "I am sure you can, lass."

But they all knew she couldn't and Darach felt a tinge of guilt about that. He had worked tirelessly to make sure Nicole could fight but turned Jackie away whenever she asked to be taught as well. He just couldn't do it. He couldn't risk following a path that might lead to one of the many dreams he'd had about her coming true. Dreams he'd had for years. Ones he never would have imagined held any truth until he first laid eyes on her in New Hampshire.

"You've been here before, aye?" Adlin asked Jackie.

Darach bit back aggravation when Jackie's eyes went to Heidrek before she spoke. A need to ground herself in this reality. But how could he blame her when he had pushed the two of them together?

"I did. With Bradon and Leslie. Friends of mine," she said. "But it looked a lot different."

"How so?"

"It was abandoned." Her gaze drifted upward past a set of stairs that wound themselves along the walls until they reached the ceiling far overhead. "And the ceiling was in rough shape."

"Aye," Adlin whispered, his sad eyes following hers. "'Tis a shame that."

"You summoned us, m'Laird. But what era have we landed in?" Darach kept his voice respectably soft. "What is happening with our MacLomains?"

"Summoned you?" Adlin shook his head. "Nay. 'Twas the magic of one of my gods. I sensed it around you when you arrived."

That wasn't surprising. Brigit and her games.

Adlin eyed the Defiance for another moment before one sort of sadness replaced another. Even so, his voice and eyes were light when he responded. "Due to circumstances beyond my control, we MacLomains will travel south on the morrow and start a new life elsewhere."

Darach felt his answer as if the weight of all his ancestors landed on his shoulders. They had returned to the time when Adlin left his origins in Scotland behind and set out to start a new life in Cowal. All because those in the area could not accept that he welcomed people of both Christian and Pagan faith under his roof. This era, like most in the past and even the future, weren't ready to accept that multiple faiths could coexist.

And though it seemed strange to say considering the clans' comradery in the future, Darach murmured, "Because of the MacLeods then."

Jackie's eyes shot to him in surprise. As far as she knew, the MacLeods were stout allies of the MacLomains. And her closest friend, Erin, had just ended up with one of them.

"Aye," Adlin whispered, eyes a little distant before he gathered himself. "But 'tis not for ye to worry over right now." He held out the crook of his elbow to Jackie. "Come, lass. Might you join me and mine in celebrating our last night here?"

"I don't understand." She slipped her arm into Adlin's. "Why are you celebrating considering you're leaving?"

23

That was the last he heard before Adlin walked her into the crowd. Soon after, young William returned and held out mugs with a scowl. "For ye both then."

Darach and Heidrek took the mugs and nodded.

"Pft," William scoffed with disdain as he crossed his arms over his chest and eyed Jackie as Adlin showed her around. "'Tis poor of ye both to let a lady wander off with someone ye just met."

Heidrek cast an eye at the lad. "Then might you go make sure she is safe?"

William cocked an eyebrow at him before muttering, "I suppose somebody ought to," and darted into the crowd.

Heidrek and Darach took a swig from their mugs and kept their eyes trained on Jackie. Neither said a word at first likely because they had come to a point they hadn't anticipated.

Being with Jackie at the same time.

Jackie.

Jacqueline.

A lass who was no longer part of his dreams but flesh and blood. And hell was she beautiful with her long, thick, pale blond hair. A slender but voluptuous figure. Full breasts, a small waist, slightly flared hips and long, long legs. A face so delicate and well-proportioned he was shocked men weren't tripping over themselves to get to her.

And her eyes.

Those eyes.

Made for sin, they were such a dark shade of brown they almost appeared black. Almond-shaped, thickly lashed, they were liquid destruction designed to steal a man's soul. Eyes like hers didn't let go once you gave into them.

That's why he kept his distance. Save that one kiss.

That one, life-altering kiss.

A kiss he wished he could repeat a thousand times. A million.

His whole damn lifetime.

"Why did you give her to me, Highlander?" Heidrek said softly. "She is not only the kindest but the most beautiful woman I have ever met. It makes little sense."

It would if Heidrek knew what Darach did about the ring. "I meant to keep her safe."

"Meant." Heidrek's eyes swept to Darach. "So do you mean to pursue her now?"

Darach stiffened. "I still mean to keep her safe."

"As do I."

"Then she will be well protected."

"So it seems."

Though the idea truly troubled him, Darach intended to honor his promise to the Viking if Heidrek still desired as much. "As I told you before, I know a way to switch the power, the passion that might lie betwixt her and me because of the ring."

"Passion," Heidrek said so softly he barely caught it. "Is such a thing something a mortal man can so readily control?"

"Aye and nay." Darach took another shallow sip and watched his surroundings closely. "With the right amount of magic, anything is possible."

"I would think only the gods possess such power," Heidrek said. "And you and I do not worship the same gods."

Heidrek had no idea how close he skirted to the truth. Their eyes met briefly before they continued to keep a close eye on what was going on around them. Both were in a whole new world and neither trusted it.

Eventually, William sidled up next to them with a dagger tucked by his side and disbelief in his voice. "I dinnae think ye've a ballock betwixt ye letting your lass roam as she does."

The boy couldn't be a day over ten but acted years older.

"I trust Adlin MacLomain," Darach said. "Do ye not then?"

"Och." William shrugged. "He's nice enough but nice enough doesnae mean ye've got a lad figured out, aye?"

Darach and Heidrek perked their brows at his response. What sort of youngling thought that way?

"You speak as though you have lived a life far longer than you have," Heidrek said.

"'Tis just simple logic." William shook his head. "Have ye no logic of yer own then?"

"William," a lass hissed as she took his hand. "Enough, lad."

More bonnie than most with flaxen hair, she nodded at Darach and Heidrek. "Please forgive, William. Like ye, he is new to this place."

When his eyes caught hers, Darach felt an odd sense of familiarity. "Aye, lass."

Their eyes held for a moment before a tall Highlander with light brown hair joined her. His eyes locked with Darach's as he wrapped an arm around the woman's waist. "My apologies if William caught ye unaware."

This time, the sense of familiarity was stronger. Much stronger. But why? Darach shook his head and tried to speak, but nothing came out.

"All is well." Heidrek nodded at the couple who must be William's parents.

"Come, lad. Let us give the newcomers some peace, aye?" the man pulled William and the woman after him.

Darach was almost tempted to follow before Adlin reappeared without Jackie. His eyes were merrier than they should be considering all that was on the horizon.

"I've provided Jackie with a chamber so that she might wash up." Adlin's eyes twinkled as they went between the two men. "Space is limited, so I'm afraid you must refresh in the same chamber."

Darach and Heidrek not only frowned but voiced their opinion at the same time.

"Nay," Darach said. "'Tis unseemly."

"No," Heidrek said. "Not until she belongs to me."

When Darach's eyes shot to him, Heidrek only shrugged.

"Then dinnae bathe." Adlin waved a hand by his nose as he eyed them. "But dinnae expect she will want either of you near her otherwise."

Darach and Heidrek's eyes flickered to each other again, unsure. Adlin rolled his eyes and pointed upward as he walked away and threw over his shoulder, "'Tis not a matter of laying with her, lads. She could use your company and bathing is best for all."

After Adlin left they continued to eye one another and pretend to drink.

"'Tis unseemly," Darach reiterated.

"She does not belong to me yet," Heidrek said.

Silence fell between them as the celebrations grew rowdier. Men chased women and lust blossomed in darkened corners. Though tempted to find a way to her without Heidrek knowing, Darach did his best to remember he was trying to push them together. So he finally said, "'Tis unwise of us to leave her alone."

"It is." Heidrek's eyes went to Darach's. "She is unsafe."

"Without us defending her, how else could it be?"

They nodded and made their way up the curving stairs. Never had a stranger building been constructed than the Highland Defiance with its oddly placed arrow-slit windows and lack of balustrade. It had long been a joke in the MacLomain clan that Adlin might be a mighty wizard but not the brightest when it came to architecture. Why else would he have designed his first masterpiece so poorly?

When they reached the top, Darach called down the narrow hallway leading to the only empty room in the place. "Jackie, 'tis us...may we join you?"

"Um, give me a minute please," she replied, and water splashed.

"Take your time, woman," Heidrek said. "Adlin wanted us to remain close so we are here."

Though the men kept their eyes on the crowd, Darach knew Heidrek was as tempted to catch a glimpse of her as he was.

"It's all right to come in now," she finally called out.

Good thing there was just enough space for two to walk down the hallway or he and Heidrek might have battled it out to arrive first. Yet for all their rush to get there, both froze at the doorway.

He had never seen anyone lovelier than Jackie as she stood with her back to the fire. Though simple in design, the dress she'd been given was an off-white shade that warmed her creamy complexion and accentuated every curve to perfection. Her freshly scrubbed skin glowed and her sultry eyes flickered in and out of the torchlight.

"Hey there." Her eyes went from Darach to Heidrek before sort of settling between them as she turned slightly and tugged at the back of her dress. "Label this awkward but I need someone to help me tie this."

"I will help," both men said at once and stepped forward.

Her eyes rounded and she shook her head. "I don't think it takes four hands to get this done."

Darach bit back a sigh. If he meant for the two of them to be together, he better let Heidrek do it. Because if his hands dusted her smooth flesh, that might be the end of all his noble intentions. So he nodded at the Viking and stepped back.

Heidrek wasted no time and soon tied her sashes with enough expertise that it was obvious he'd had his fair share of women. Despite himself, Darach couldn't help but watch Jackie a little closer than intended. A lass's body language gave away a lot, especially when a man was so close to her…touching her.

Though her head was bent and slightly tilted, she didn't seem flushed. No gooseflesh rose on her skin. His magic tested the air around her. There were no heat fluctuations or movement based on tremors or shudders of pleasure.

He was only slightly surprised when Heidrek stilled and his eyes narrowed on Darach. The Viking sensed his magic. Though Darach had no idea how much power Heidrek possessed, his mother had been even more powerful than his father so he imagined the lad had inherited some gifts. That he could feel Darach's magic—the element of air—said much. Out of the four elements, it was the most difficult to track because it shifted so frequently.

"Thank you," Jackie murmured, her eyes on Darach as Heidrek finished tying up her dress and stepped away.

For a second, he got the feeling she sensed his magic as well. All of the Brouns were witches, but as far as he knew, Jackie had displayed no signs of power yet except being able to communicate with Erin when she was in the Otherworld.

Heidrek crouched beside the tub and ran his hand through it once before he stood. His eyes met Darach's. "The water is warm again. Bathe next Highlander. I will keep Jackie company."

Darach's eyebrows perked. So Heidrek could control the element of water as well?

The corner of the Viking's lip inched up ever-so-slightly as he winked at Darach then took Jackie's hand. "Come, woman. We will go watch the celebrations while the Scotsman sees to himself."

"Sounds like a plan." She offered Darach a smile as she passed.

He frowned as they went to the end of the hallway and sat on the edge overlooking the crowd. The Viking was all about spending time alone with her first. Which was for the best…right?

Darach undressed and bathed as quickly as possible. The room was much like he remembered except now it had furnishings. Hexagonal in shape, a keyhole-shaped window was the only thing that allowed in fresh air. A large, four-poster bed with sheer hangings was its centerpiece along with a small table and a few chairs.

He still wondered precisely why they were meant to be here at such a time. Though one would never know as much by looking at it, this building, better yet the stone that made up the window, was one of the most powerful places in Scotland. A portal of sorts that would lead to other Defiances throughout the country.

A change of clothes had been left on the bed. Darach smirked as he put on a tunic, wrapped a MacLomain plaid and pulled on boots. It looked like Heidrek would be wearing a plaid as well.

By the time he joined the other two, they were chuckling at something and their shoulders rested against one another's. He suppressed a surge of jealousy and smoothed his expression as he plunked down on Jackie's other side and gestured at Heidrek. "Your turn to bathe, Viking."

Heidrek nodded and left but not before he squeezed Jackie's hand and smiled.

"'Tis good you two are getting along so well," Darach said. "He's an admirable man."

"I agree." Her eyes returned to the crowd and an uncomfortable silence settled between them. He knew on some unconscious level that she was upset with him and he didn't blame her. It was wrong of him to have kissed her then made himself scarce.

"Jackie," he began, keeping his voice soft. "We should talk. I need to explain some things."

Though she didn't look at him, her words were blunt and to the point. "Why don't you start by explaining why you kissed me then avoided me afterward?"

Unfazed by her directness, he told her the truth. Some of it anyway. "I kissed you because I wanted too. Because I couldn't help myself." It took everything he had not to tell her about his dreams. Though she tensed, he continued, trying to remember all the words he rehearsed for this very moment. "I shouldn't have…" He shook his head, tongue-tied. "Not when I knew I could put you in jeopardy."

"Why can't you tell me what's going on?" Her eyes shot to him. "A kiss is just a kiss, Darach. We're by no means together and I can't see it heading that way." She shook her head. "It won't head that way. We're from two separate worlds."

"Aye, lass," he murmured, but her firm declaration upset him. He should be grateful. This is what he wanted. Her safety.

"I think it would be best if we forget the kiss ever happened and focus on getting along," Jackie said. "It's obvious the MacLomain, Broun connection doesn't necessarily apply to us. That you know something I don't." She cocked her head. "What happened back at the Viking fortress? What was supposed to be in your pocket?"

If he could only forget that kiss. How sweet she'd tasted. The softness of her skin. There would be no forgetting it. In fact, he was fairly certain he'd vividly recall that kiss far into the future.

"Darach?" she prompted. "Your pocket?"

He sighed, not sure how much he should say.

"Please tell me." Her eyes pled with him. "Does it have to do with why you want me to be with Heidrek?"

"Aye," he whispered. "It was supposed to stay with me. A lure. A means to trick the demi-god and keep him in pursuit of me, not you."

"I don't understand." She frowned. "He wants my ring. What could possibly be more important?"

"The real ring," he murmured. "Given to me by Brigit, the Celtic Goddess of Divination, shortly after Erin traveled back in time. The one you wore was a replica." His eyes fell to her ring. "Until now mayhap."

Her brows flew together and her frown deepened as she eyed her ring. "You mean to tell me I had a fake one on before?"

He took her hand and ran the pad of his thumb over the ring. "Aye."

Magic wasn't needed to sense the ripple of awareness that tore through her at his touch. She pulled her hand away and clenched her fist on her lap. "So you don't know for sure if this ring is a fake or not."

"Nay, but I'm guessing 'tis real because the ring in my pocket is gone." His eyes never left hers. "The magic used to make the false one was too great for me to know the difference."

"I can only assume your father and Torra couldn't tell the difference either."

He shook his head. "Nay."

She pressed her lips together and her eyes returned to the celebrations. "What about Adlin? Isn't he supposed to be the most powerful wizard known to Scotland?"

"Aye," he said. "I think that's why 'tis likely Goddess Brigit wants us to be with him now."

"Goddess Brigit? That's unbelievable," she said softly, her eyes a little distant. "I studied the Celtic deities and always found her the most intriguing. It's said that she was born at the exact moment of daybreak. She's considered a triple goddess. They say she has three sister selves with distinct roles. Lady of Healing Waters, Goddess of the Sacred Flame and Goddess of the Fertile Earth or fertility in general. She brings the Flame of Inspiration, the Flame of our Creative Consciousness."

"You know a lot about her," he said, surprised.

"I read a lot," she said. "And despite what Nicole says, the vast majority of it isn't romance." The corner of her lip tilted up. "Not that I don't enjoy a good historical romance on occasion."

"What made you want to read about Celtic gods?" He found it curious considering everything that was happening.

"I don't know." She shrugged. "They just drew me more than most deities."

It occurred to him how focused he had been not only on his dreams but on her appearance…how little he really knew about her. He had suspected her intelligence from the beginning but wondered what existed beyond her careful facade. Because there was more to her beneath the mask she had learned to wear so well. Someone else beneath those tempered smiles and soft spoken words.

"What else are you interested in," he started before Heidrek reappeared and ended the conversation with his appearance alone.

"Oh my God," Jackie whispered staring up at him.

Darach scowled. Who knew a Viking could cut such a fine figure dressed as a Scotsman? It wasn't right.

Heidrek held his hand out to her. "Might I escort you to the celebrations, Jackie?"

She grinned and took his hand. "Absolutely."

It didn't escape Darach that Jackie did not glance back to see if he followed. Again, there was no blaming her. There might be an attraction between them, but she wasn't the sort to let that rule her.

Instead, it seemed she was more than willing to go in the direction Darach had pushed her.

Toward Heidrek.

"Ah, there you are!" Adlin exclaimed when they reached the bottom. He eyed all three with approval. "You clean up well."

His eyes met Heidrek's. "Why dinnae you take the lass for a turn to the pipes, aye?"

Heidrek nodded and pulled Jackie after him.

Adlin handed Darach a mug of whisky and gestured that he follow him. While honored to be in the company of the great MacLomain patriarch, his eyes trailed after Jackie. Hell, was he envious of the Viking.

"Stop looking as though all is lost," Adlin said when they stopped at the outer edge of the dancing crowd. "You've followed the path laid for you admirably, lad."

Darach's eyes went to Adlin. "Though ye didnae summon us, ye know quite a bit, aye?"

Adlin shrugged, a mischievous glint in his eyes. "I know what the Celtic gods tell me." His lips thinned. "The ones that arenae evil that is."

"And how many are evil outside the obvious?"

"Och, like with any religion, the Celts have their fair share." Adlin sipped from his mug. "Tell me more of this dark demi-god ye face and the beauty, Brigit, determined to help you."

Darach filled him in on everything, all the while getting the sense that Adlin already knew most of it. If anything, his patriarch was trying to get a sense of how his offspring saw things and how they intended to deal with it. He covered everything from the Broun lass's disabilities to how Keir Hamilton's father, the evil demi-god, had gradually been shifting from a black cloud to a man. He also mentioned Brae Stewart's role in it and her twin brother, Cullen's part, a Scotsmen turned angel. He didn't leave out that the *Genii Cucullati*, three shadowy Celtic spirits, were in league with the demi-god as well.

"The *Genii Cucullati*." Adlin rubbed his chin in contemplation. "Stealers of the soul. They tend to frequent births. Interesting ally for the evil you face."

"Aye," Darach agreed. "Have you any thoughts on it?"

"The *Genii Cucullati* would only ally themselves in this if they had something to gain. Something well worth their while."

"And what do you suppose that is?"

Adlin mulled it over before he sighed. "'Twould have to be the chance to steal an important soul, indeed. One that would give them far more leverage in the realm of Celtic gods."

Darach frowned, more and more uncomfortable. Where was this leading? "What sort of soul is that important?"

"One they've likely been chasing for a long time," Adlin murmured.

Before Darach could respond, Adlin swiftly redirected the conversation. "Tell me about your communications with Goddess Brigit."

Darach knew she was the infamous goddess who supposedly saw Adlin to Scotland to begin with. "She came to me in a dream and gave me a Claddagh ring."

Adlin nodded, his eyes trained on Jackie as she danced with Heidrek. Too closely with Heidrek in Darach's opinion. But again, that was good…right?

"The ring Brigit gave you was the real one, aye?" Adlin said. "And until now, Jackie wore the replica."

"Aye." His eyes met Adlin's. "So you think Jackie wears the real one?"

"'Tis without doubt," Adlin said.

Renewed worry for her flared. So did hope.

Hope he shouldn't feel because he would honor his word to Heidrek.

"'Tis admirable that you meant to keep her safe, that you wanted her to find love when you desire her so much." Adlin quirked a brow. "Now things have changed and she wears the right ring. One that could bind her to you. Yet Heidrek is here as well. That is interesting, aye?"

"'Tis something all right," Darach grumbled. "So mayhap the ring willnae lead a Broun to a MacLomain this time."

"Aye, mayhap 'twill be a Hamilton instead." Adlin chuckled and eyed him. "So you are son to a man who will inherit more of my gifts than most. Son to the current MacLomain arch-wizard. A MacLomain turned Hamilton."

Darach nodded. "I am son to Grant Hamilton, a man you will care for verra much. Someone you will mentor."

Adlin's wise eyes never left Darach's face. "So tell me, why dinnae you want to become chieftain of the Hamilton's?"

Darach knew better by now than to be surprised by the wizard's uncanny insight.

"I've not a drop of Hamilton blood in me," he muttered under his breath before he could stop himself. "I am a MacLomain."

"Hmm. So you willnae tell me yet." Adlin rubbed his chin again. "A puzzle of sorts then." A smile split his face. "I always did love a good puzzle."

Honestly, he was surprised Adlin did not already know. But then, strangely enough, Darach's da didn't either. He was about to speak when he spied Jackie and Heidrek. The Viking held her close. And she seemed just fine with it. Jaw clenched, he refocused his attention elsewhere.

"He isnae a real Scotsman, is he? His accent is all wrong," William said as he leaned against a post and shook his head.

"Who?"

William frowned at Darach. "Dinnae be so daft." He gestured at Heidrek. "Ye've no ballocks in the least letting yer lass dance with him."

Darach snorted. "And what fault do you find with my friend?"

"He's not like us." William glared at Heidrek before his eyes met Darach's. "A Sassenach then, aye?"

English? He shook his head. "Nay, lad."

"Then what is he?" William crossed his arms over his chest. "Because he isnae Scottish and I dinnae trust him."

"And here I thought I was the one ye took issue with," Darach muttered.

"Och, I do," William said. "Mainly because ye've no ballocks."

"William," a woman chastised. The same lass who had claimed him earlier joined them. Her eyes met Darach's. "My apologies." She shook her head. "My lad doesnae know his manners."

"I am not yer lad," William grumbled and strode away.

When Darach glanced at Adlin, he'd vanished.

"My name is Lilas Thomson," the lass said softly. "Again, I am sorry for William's behavior. Life has not been kind to him."

Darach figured as much. "What happened to him?"

34

Lilas hesitated, her eyes searching his before she apparently saw what she was looking for. "His parents were killed in a raid."

"Och." He frowned, well aware of Scotland's history and the havoc tearing the country apart. "Vikings or Sassenach?"

"It doesnae matter," came a deep voice as the man who had been with Lilas earlier appeared and pulled her close, a wary eye on Darach.

Lilas made introductions. "This is my husband, Dougal."

"Nice to meet ye both. I am Darach." He gestured at Heidrek and Jackie and gave their names as well.

Darach again had that strange sense of familiarity. Bizarrely enough, Jackie's eyes locked on them from across the room as though she felt the same. Odder yet, they eyed her with equal interest. Because of his superior hearing, Darach could hear the couple whisper to one another.

"She seems so familiar," Lilas said.

"Aye," Dougal said. "They both do."

What was this draw between the four of them? Maybe Adlin knew. But when his eyes swept the room, the MacLomain wizard was nowhere to be found.

"Look at William now," Lilas murmured to Dougal.

Darach almost grinned when he saw what the lad was up to. He had approached Jackie and Heidrek. Whatever he said soon had the Viking handing her off to William.

"He has a way with the lassies," Dougal said proudly.

"So it seems," Lilas responded. "Takes after his Da he does."

"I'm not his Da." But there was no mistaking a wee bit of fatherly pride in his voice.

"Nor am I his Ma but we are in spirit."

Darach's lips curled up as he watched William hold Jackie at arm's length but kept his eyes locked on hers.

"Look at him, aye?" Lilas said.

"A true gentleman." Dougal nodded with approval.

"He'll grow up to be a fine lad."

"Aye."

Darach offered a brief nod to Heidrek as he joined them. Call it whatever you want, but he was damned glad to see Jackie out of the Viking's arms. He and Heidrek remained silent as they drank and watched Jackie dance with William then several others.

35

"Might we dance?" came a soft voice.

Darach tore his gaze from Jackie only to find a comely lass in front of him, her doe eyes more brazen than most as they swept over him. He was about to say no when Adlin joined them. "Aye, he will, lass. My lad doesnae need to watch any longer. Go, enjoy her company Darach. It'll do ye good."

If there was one thing he couldn't do, it was dispute Adlin MacLomain. So he slid his hand into hers and joined her on the dance floor. Though she tried to sidle closer, he kept her at arm's length and made idle conversation. "'Tis nice to meet ye, lass."

"Aye, 'tis," she murmured, squeezing closer as the crowd grew merrier. "Yer brawn ye are."

Darach did his best to keep her wandering hands at bay, but she was fast.

"Let us say farewell to our home properly!" Adlin cried to a crowd that only grew thicker. "More pipes!"

If ever a great hall—or large chamber—could explode with merriment, it did now. He'd never felt such energy vibrate in the air. An energy born of people who were saying goodbye to one life but had faith that the next would be so much better.

The crowd pressed closer as did the lass in his arms. So close that he took a step back. They spun once to avoid another couple.

Then again.

And again.

Until she let go and another fell into his arms.

Someone far more favorable.

Chapter Three

JACKIE SHOOK HER head as she looked into Darach's eyes. Being in his arms was the last place she needed to be. Yet the crowd pushed them closer and the man she had been dancing with vanished. She swallowed hard when his arm wrapped around her waist and twirled her away from a couple that stumbled by them laughing.

The pipes trilled.

The crowd was wild.

And she was tight against Darach.

Not a good place to be. Or was it? She swallowed again and kept her arms down because if she lifted them, what would she touch? The sides of his muscled torso...his strong forearms...his wide shoulders?

"You dinnae need to keep shaking your head no," he murmured. "I willnae..."

When he trailed off, she realized that he had no idea what he would or would not do. Besides the arm that he wrapped around her waist, his other hand didn't touch her at all.

His head was bent near hers, his lips so close to her ear that she could feel his hot breath down the side of her neck. Chills and heat raced over her simultaneously as she tried to sift through her feelings.

Push away. Touch his chest and push away.

But again, if she touched him...what then? Would pulling away still be an option?

The pipes seemed to trill louder, and the fire in the center of the room sparked higher as the celebrations became a boisterous background to the quiet she suddenly felt on the inside. A strange silence made up of her heartbeat and the indentation where his neck met his collarbone. She inhaled deeply and turned her face inward, chasing his scent and heat.

She barely felt the slight touch of his hand on the back of her head as she nuzzled in, desperate to get closer to...something. It almost felt like a memory. One just out of reach. Lips open, she flicked her tongue, eager to sample. Eager to capture his scent. Curious what it tasted like.

Only when he whispered, "Bloody hell, lass," did her eyes snap open and she realized what she was doing. By that time, it was too late. He tightened his hold, dug his hand into her hair, tilted back her head and met her eyes. Their lips were inches apart when he whispered, "What are you doing to me?"

Jackie had no idea. What *was* she doing to him? What was he doing to her? She'd never felt anything like it. So much. Almost too much. Yet it felt like something not entirely real. As if she recalled snippets of a dream.

Their lips drifted closer, eager but tentative.

Wanting but unsure.

His eyelids drifted down. So did hers.

There…almost there.

"Och, bloody hell!" he growled and jerked away.

Confused, Jackie blinked until she saw the blade against Darach's side.

William glared. "Ye dinnae know how to respect a lass, do ye?"

She had to give him credit. Darach didn't lash out at the boy. One who apparently nicked him in the thigh enough that blood trickled down his leg.

"It's fine, William, he's not hurting me," she tried to assure the boy.

William peered up, eyes narrowed. "What is yer next move because it best be a good one."

Darach stilled, eyes locked on the lad. "'Tis safe to say my next move will take me away from Jackie, aye?"

William's eyes narrowed even more. "'Twill lest ye want me to cut ye again."

"That wouldnae be good," Darach relented. "And here I thought ye wanted me to grow a pair of ballocks and dance with the lass. Now if ye'll remove the blade, I'll step away."

William eyed him for another moment before he nodded and stepped back.

Jackie jolted in surprise when the air chilled and almost seemed to crackle as Darach pulled away. Not only that, she swore she felt a slight suction. As if the very air fought against them separating. Their eyes shot to each other. What was that?

"'Tis one thing to dance with a lass, another to take advantage of her when doing it," William reprimanded. "Now ye best keep a proper distance, Mister."

"Call me Darach."

William frowned at him. "I will be watching ye, Mister," then he vanished into the crowd.

Jackie sensed that Darach wanted to continue dancing with her but thought better of it not because of William but because of what had happened between them. Something he clearly seemed determined to avoid. This, of course, only renewed her aggravation. His *apology* for kissing her then avoiding her. As far as she was concerned, that only happened when a man truly had no clue where his heart lay. But did she want his heart? Or even Heidrek's for that matter? Who was she kidding letting either of them too close when there was no hope.

Still, every once in a while it was nice to pretend.

To fantasize.

With a heavy sigh, she brushed by Darach and made her way toward the entrance. What she wouldn't do to have Erin here. Somebody she could talk to who understood all the barriers she faced. While it was likely her friend would only grow aggravated with her for not enjoying the company of these men, they both knew there was a good reason. Nothing could come of it because in the end she'd only end up hurting them.

How else could it be considering Jackie was dying?

Not wanting to think about it right now, she went outside and breathed in the cool air. The small, fenced-in courtyard was fairly quiet considering most people were inside celebrating. Torches spit and a random horse whinnied from the stables. It was nice to be away from the crowd.

While she enjoyed the way both Scots and Vikings celebrated, she had never been a huge fan of parties. Probably because of all the stiff, formal affairs her uncle had hosted when she was young. Though people were far different here, she still felt a level of discomfort. One she just couldn't break free from.

"Are ye there then, lass?" whispered through her mind.

Surprised, Jackie smiled, headed for the stables and replied within the mind, *"Eara?"*

"Aye, lass."

Sure as heck, she found Eara two stalls down once she entered the stables. Eara was the last of the four horses that had mysteriously appeared at the barn in New Hampshire right before Jackie and her friends arrived at the old Colonial. Every other horse had merged with a former MacLomain wizard thanks to ancient Viking magic.

Thus far, all had been related to the Scotsman each of her friends had ended up with. Either a mother or grandmother. Which made Eara a complete mystery because Darach's grandmother, Coira, had already merged with Niall and Nicole's horse, Vika. According to those of the Next Generation of MacLomains, especially Grant, there was no way Eara was somehow merged with Darach's mother, Sheila. And Sheila agreed wholeheartedly.

So *who* had merged with Eara?

"It's so good to see you!" Jackie entered the stall. "How on Earth did you get here?"

Jackie had first heard Eara speak within her mind when she traveled back in time, but she swore they had been talking for far longer than that. Strangely enough, it wasn't all that different than how she felt dancing with Darach. Flickers of something she couldn't quite put her finger on. Flashes of memories. Maybe even dreams?

"I dinnae know how I arrived here, lass," Eara said. *"One moment I was at MacLomain Castle. The next, I was here. Adlin found me in the woodland and made sure I arrived safely."*

"Ah." Jackie kept smiling as she stroked Eara's muzzle, admiring her light tan coloring and white blond mane. "So when are you going to tell me who you really are?"

Until she met Erin, she had never been around horses. Even then, she felt uncomfortable. Fearful. But not with Eara. Not in the least.

"'Tis not for me to tell you who I am, I'm afraid," Eara murmured into her mind. *"Ye know ye must wait until the time is right, just like your friends did."*

"But wouldn't it make things easier to tell me now?" She met Eara's eyes. "Maybe if we knew who you were we could better prepare ourselves for what lies ahead."

Eara only neighed, shook her head and stomped her foot. Just then, Jackie got an eerie feeling that someone was watching her. Goose flesh dotted her skin and the hair stood up on the back of her neck. Almost afraid to look, but acting on instinct, she glanced over her shoulder and gasped. A tall man in full armor, with a helmet, faceplate, and a long brown cloak shimmered just beyond the stall door. His form was ghostly and transparent as his eyes locked on her hand…more so, her ring.

"I've missed ye so much," he murmured before his eyes flickered to hers, concerned. "Are ye well, lassie?"

An Irish lilt?

"I…wha…" she started and blinked several times as a wave of familiarity washed over her. As soon as she felt it, it vanished. One more blink and he was gone. Instead, Darach stood in his place with a look of concern on his face.

"Are ye well, lass?" he said…repeated.

She blinked a few more times. What the hell was going on? Was this part of the magic that was Scotland or was her condition worsening?

Jackie frowned and turned her attention back to the horse. "I'm fine. Thanks. You don't need to be out here."

"We were worried about you," Heidrek said, joining Darach. "It is not a good idea for you to be without protection."

"I'm fine, guys," she said. But was she? Truly? She felt like she was losing it.

"You should come eat." Darach came alongside the horse and stroked Eara's neck. "When did she arrive?"

"Recently," Adlin said as he entered the stables. He wore a grin as he joined Heidrek at the stall door and eyed Eara. "'Tis good that the horse arrived when she did. Now she can travel with us on the morrow."

Jackie made a point of keeping her eyes averted from Darach's as their hands ran along either side of Eara's muzzle. She didn't want another awkward moment like they had when dancing.

"I will be calling an end to the celebrations in a wee bit," Adlin said. "The three of you should make your way to your chamber. Food and drink awaits."

Jackie's eyes shot to Adlin. "But there's only one bed."

"But 'tis a big bed, aye?" Adlin shook his head and chuckled as he left, calling back, "We leave early. Best get your rest whilst you can. 'Tis the beginning of a journey unlike any other!"

"Adlin's right," Darach said. "We're about to embark on a journey that will make all MacLomains envious." This time, she couldn't help but meet his eyes based on the excitement in his voice. "We travel to what will someday be MacLomain land. Better yet, MacLomain Castle."

"How far is it from here?" Heidrek said.

As always, once her eyes locked with Darach's, they held. "Far South. Several weeks' journey."

"Then we should rest," Heidrek said firmly as his hand slipped into Jackie's.

"He's right," she murmured and tore her gaze from Darach's. She gave Eara one last pat and then left.

As tactfully as she could, she pulled her hand free from Heidrek's and headed back toward the Defiance. More people filtered around the courtyard so she knew Adlin was slowly winding the party down. When she entered the building, the crowd had thinned considerably. As she headed upstairs, she wondered exactly how this was going to work…because she wouldn't be sleeping in bed with either Darach or Heidrek.

An array of food was set out on the table in their chamber and several pitchers and mugs. Darach filled a mug with water and handed it to her. "I know you dinnae drink alcohol, but I could manifest some tea if you like."

"No, thanks," she said. "Water's fine."

"Are you sure?" Darach said. "It might calm your nerves."

"My nerves are just fine." But they weren't around him, and he damn well knew it.

"Suit yourself, lass."

Soon, the three of them were enjoying an amiable enough meal. The bread was warm and soft. The seafood fresh. Even the water tasted better than it did back home. Their conversation stayed light. The men talked about the era in which they'd arrived. How different it was from their own.

Jackie got the impression they were just talking to talk. Easy, safe conversation. Anything to get through the meal and avoid all the turbulent emotions they were feeling. At least her and Darach.

Heidrek seemed rather relaxed. Eventually, everyone finished eating, and her sense of discomfort grew as she eyed the bed.

But it seemed she had no reason to worry as Darach slid down against the wall on one side of the room and Heidrek the other. When she frowned, the Viking nodded at the bed. "Did you think we meant to sleep in it with you, woman?"

"We'd never do that," Darach added. "You've nothing to worry over, lass."

While grateful, she frowned at them. "So you guys are going to sit on the floor all night?"

"We are warriors," Heidrek grunted. "This floor is more comfortable than some places I've slept."

"Aye," Darach agreed and nodded at the bed. "Sleep, Jackie. We will protect you."

"I can protect myself," she nearly said, but the truth was she'd be lying. She had already seen the power of their enemies. But, more than that, she'd seen Nicole and Erin fight. She knew how well they could use a weapon. And she had no clue how to do the same. None at all.

She nodded and was about to climb into bed but stopped when an idea occurred to her. Maybe she could play on their sense of needing to see her comfortable or safe to get what she wanted...what she needed. So she slid down onto the floor at the end of the bed and settled in to rest.

Heidrek frowned. "What are you doing?"

"Going to sleep."

"You're not sleeping there." Darach frowned as well. "'Tis too cold, lass. Get into bed."

"I'm fine right here." She closed her eyes. "If you guys can sit on the floor then so can I."

"Nay," Darach said at the same time Heidrek said, "No."

"Why not?" she murmured. "It only seems fair."

"Jackie, get into bed," Darach said softly. "Please."

"No."

Jackie waited patiently as a tense silence passed. She could be more stubborn than most when put to the test.

"Go to bed, lass," Darach repeated, his voice a little firmer.

"No."

43

A longer stretch of silence passed before they fed right into her hands.

"What will it take to get you into bed," Darach finally growled.

Jackie cracked open an eye. "I'm not sure what you're talking about."

"Aye, but you do." Darach sighed. "What do you want, lass?"

She opened the other eye and met not Darach's but Heidrek's eyes. "I want to learn how to fight."

"'Tis a bad idea," Darach grumbled. "You're not built for it."

What did he mean by that? She might not be as toned as Nicole and Erin, but she did Yoga and Pilates and tried to stay fit.

"Hence, me asking Heidrek and not you, Darach," she said flatly, eyes never leaving the Viking's. "Will you teach me how to fight, Heidrek?"

"I tried at the fortress but you would not," he started, but she cut him off, not wanting him to share her reasons.

"I'm ready now, and I want to learn."

Jackie clenched her jaw and refused to look at Darach. The only reason she had said no to Heidrek was because she was still determined that the Scotsman teach her. Likely because she felt she needed to prove some sort of point to him. That she could do it. That she wasn't the helpless blond he seemed to be making her out to be. I mean, seriously, why would he teach Nicole but not her? Then Erin went into her strange Otherworld sleep, and Jackie lost focus.

No more.

"I disagree with Darach. It does not matter a person's build," Heidrek said. "If you want me to teach you to battle, it would be my pleasure."

A flicker of excitement rushed through her. "Really?"

Heidrek nodded. "It would give me great pride to do so."

Darach mumbled something, but she tuned him out. "So I have your word that you'll train me?"

"Yes, but only if you get into bed," Heidrek said.

"You got it." She shot a triumphant grin at Darach as she got up. "But I have a small stipulation."

"I can only imagine," Darach muttered, his frown deepening.

Jackie ignored him and pulled everything off the bed except a pillow and blanket then gave the rest of the bedding to them. "If you're sleeping on the floor, I want you to be as comfortable as possible."

Some women might have invited them to sleep on the bed as long as they behaved but she knew it would be a bad idea. Yes, an attraction simmered between her and Heidrek but something far more dangerous festered between her and Darach.

She still had no idea what to make of her time dancing with them. When Heidrek pulled her close, she felt warm and flustered. When Darach did the same, she about burned up and lost herself.

Either way, she wasn't the sort to play men against each other. She had enjoyed a healthy sex life back home. She dated. Never committed. Because God knows they were likely in it for her inheritance. A trust fund she couldn't even touch. Nonetheless, life was simpler after her uncle left the States to travel the world. Things were uncomplicated. Just the way she wanted it…had wanted it for a long time.

Now? In light of recent revelations from her doctor, it was more uncomplicated than ever.

It was only a matter of time.

Jackie pulled a blanket over herself, closed her eyes and wondered what would come of all this. Why had she been able to protect Erin when she was trapped in the Celtic Otherworld? Because somehow by being with her, she had healed her friend from what should have been certain death. More than that, she'd flitted in and out of that gray place to do so. Yet she felt no fear.

Rather, courage.

She had no clue why, considering it was so horrible. But when she was there with Erin, keeping her prone body the safest she could, she felt strong. Ready. For what, though?

"To be with me again," whispered through her mind. *"To realize what a fool ye were for turning from me to begin with."*

When Jackie opened her eyes, it wasn't to the room at the Defiance but to the Otherworld. A place made of jagged mountains and tall, lifeless grass. Where a winding stream ran dry and trees were barren. A sharp cliff rose nearby, and the ocean rolled black and oily in the distance.

She turned and froze as a tall, dark haired man approached. With a long black cape crackling with flames, his dark intensity nearly made her sink to her knees.

"Who are you?" Jackie whispered, but she was afraid she already knew.

"How could ye forget me?" He stopped within feet of her, his Irish lilt gravelly. "When I have not forgotten ye for even a day. What we had."

Jackie shook her head. Somehow he was familiar. "I don't understand."

"Of course, ye do not." His eyes fell to the ring, and disgust flickered across his face. "If ye take off that *thing* ye will remember me. Eoghan Dubhdiadh, Druid of the South." His eyes locked on hers. "Ye will remember the love of your life."

Jackie shook her head in denial as the sense of familiarity grew.

"'Twas a good trick the imposter pulled keeping the real ring from ye, but now the truth can be laid bare. A dark truth that has been kept secret." His eyes went from the ring to her face. "Take it off and remember what ye have so long forgotten because the real ring had not yet touched ye."

"No," she whispered, terrified by what she might discover. "I won't." She shook her head and backed away when he took a step forward. "Leave me alone. Release me from this place."

"Why would I release ye?" he growled, his eyes never leaving hers as he took another step forward. "When 'twas our place all along?"

Jackie staggered back a few more steps, still shaking her head. "No."

Patience hanging on by a thread, his voice deepened. "Come to me lassie, for I willnae stop until I get ye."

"Nor will I stop until I know she's safe," came a loud declaration.

A split second later, the armored warrior she saw before came thundering forward on Eara.

"No!" roared the dark man as he lunged at her, his black cape billowing in the wind.

Too late. Jackie was scooped up into the warrior's arms, and they were racing toward the cliff. Oh, this couldn't be good. When she tried to look over her shoulder, the man held her tighter and made it impossible.

"Stop!" she cried. She might be scared shitless of the dark man but plummeting to her death didn't sound much better. Close. Closer. Super close. *"Please, stop!"*

Too late.

They flew over.

Terror-stricken, she screamed.

"I've got you, Jackie," came a distant, worried voice. "Wake up, lass!"

"No, no, no," she repeated as wind rushed by her and the ocean rose up. "God, *no!*"

"You're safe, I've got you," came the same voice. *"Please* wake up, Jaqueline."

Instead of crashing into the ocean, everything vanished and the world went still.

Very, very still.

The next thing she heard was the steady beat of thunder. It took several moments to realize that thunder didn't beat. A heart did. One inside a warm chest.

Jackie's eyes shot open, and she pulled back.

"Shh, calm down," Darach said gently, holding her shoulders as their eyes locked. "You had a nightmare, but you're okay."

She blinked rapidly and tried to get her bearings. She was still in the room at the top of the Highland Defiance. Dim daylight filtered through the keyhole window and she sat on Darach's lap. Heidrek was next to them, a blade drawn as though he meant to defend her from something unseen.

"Bloody hell. I knew if I put the three of you up here I'd get to the bottom of things," Adlin said as he appeared at the door. His wise eyes fell on them. "Now I know precisely why you were sent to me and what we must do if we've any hope of saving the MacLomains."

Chapter Four

IT SEEMED ALL the tales told around campfires since Darach was a wee bairn were true. Adlin was not only meddlesome and evasive but cryptic. He refused to explain why they were here or what he meant when he said I know what to do if we are to have any hope of saving the MacLomains. But he refused to tell them *what* that was. This had Heidrek scowling fiercely. Not soon after, Adlin declared that they were leaving, and to ready themselves.

"I'm sorry," Jackie mumbled before she scrambled off Darach's lap and looked anywhere but at him.

"You dinnae need to be sorry, lass." Darach came to his feet and looked at her with concern. "Are you all right now?" He poured some water and handed it to her. "Here. Drink."

Her eyes flickered to his then away before she took the cup and murmured, "Thanks."

He and the Viking had slept in shifts so that one of them always kept watch. Darach had been sleeping when it happened.

When his nightmare blended with hers.

That was the only way he could describe it.

One moment everything was dark, the next it was gray. Mountainous, dead, and lifeless, the land around him appeared desolate and unearthly. As he rode Eara, only one thing lit his way. A light. Life.

Jackie.

When he saw the massive cloud fluctuating in front of her—the demi-god—he thought nothing of rushing to her rescue. Then he thought nothing of letting Eara take over as they flew off the cliff and toward the water...toward death. As though it wasn't the first time he had done it with her.

Then, unlike Jackie, he awoke with no fear.

Calm, prepared for her distress, he held tightly and gently coaxed her out of the nightmare.

"Are ye well?" came a concerned voice. "We heard a commotion and wanted to check on ye."

Darach was surprised to see Lilas and Dougal at the door. Lilas had her eyes trained on Darach and Dougal's were on Jackie.

When Heidrek frowned at them, Dougal stood up a little straighter and eyed the Viking. "We dinnae mean any disrespect 'twas just…"

When her husband trailed off, Lilas said, "'Twas just that we thought someone was hurt. It didnae sound good in the least."

"Och, nay," Adlin muttered as he returned and shooed them out. "All's well enough. Ye two just confuse things." His eyes met Dougal's. "We leave soon. Ye keep a close eye on yer wife and wee William, aye?"

"I dinnae need watching over," William declared, scooting past the adults until he took up position in front of Jackie. He held a dagger and eyed everyone with a frown as he spoke to Jackie. "How fare ye, lass? I would have gotten here sooner, but my legs are far shorter than theirs."

Heidrek's eyes narrowed. "Not that much shorter."

Adlin sighed. "The lad slept at the top of the stairs determined to protect Jackie when you two failed."

Darach chuckled. They had known the lad was out there. "No faith then?"

"None at all." William looked between Heidrek and Darach. "Ye've yet to prove a bloody thing to me when it comes to this lass."

"Jackie," she said softly. "My name's Jackie."

"When it comes to *Jackie*," William corrected himself.

"I'm fine, William." She peered over his shoulder and met his eyes. "I just had a bad dream is all. But thanks for having my back."

William's brows snapped together in confusion. "Right now I'm protecting yer front." He spun and peered behind her, dagger at the ready. "Does yer back need protecting too?"

"No." She lowered his wrist, a warm smile on her face as she met his eyes. "It's just an expression. I'm really okay. All of you did a great job protecting me."

"Aye?"

She nodded. "Yes."

William eyed her for a long moment before he stepped away.

"Come, William." Lilas held out her hand. "Adlin means for us to leave now."

"Aye?"

"Aye." Adlin nodded at William. "Go with Lilas and Dougal now. They love ye."

William contemplated everyone for another long moment before he obeyed. Meanwhile, Adlin eyed Jackie, Darach, and Heidrek. "It seems none of you even took off your boots last eve. 'Tis good enough I suppose." He gestured for them to follow as he ushered William and his parents down the hallway. "Darach and Heidrek, 'twould be best if you take Jackie's hand as soon as possible."

Though Darach and Heidrek frowned at each other, they were smart enough to realize if the arch-wizard said something, they better listen. What neither expected was how soon Adlin meant. They had just reached the landing when the wizard flung his arms in the air and started chanting.

Darach was shocked by the amount of people squeezed into the room below and going up the long, winding stairs. Stairs that allowed more to stand on them because there was no balustrade. Darach and Heidrek didn't just hold Jackie's hands but pulled her between them as Adlin began chanting.

"Now I plead, let my people flee. Now I plead, let my people be free. *Obsecro, domine mi et fugientibus consulite. Obsecro, domine mi liberi populi.*"

Light poured from the keyhole window, down the hallway, until it washed over them and spread down the stairs into the crowd below. The narrow windows seemed to help direct it. At first warm and welcoming, it soon turned blinding. Consuming. Yet there was no fear as the floor dropped out from beneath them.

No, there was only a feeling of joy.

Change.

Redemption.

It felt like he stood at the edge of Heaven.

When the light faded, Jackie still stood between them and all the people who had been in the Highland Defiance stood in a forest. Darach didn't need to use magic to know they stood on the outer edges of what would be MacLomain land.

"Where are we?" Heidrek said.

Adlin smiled as the last of the white light and fog faded into the woodland. "Almost home." His eyes slid to Heidrek. "Not yours I'm afraid."

"Sonofa-fn'bitch," a woman exclaimed. "A little warning would've been nice!"

"I thought you were trying not to swear around the kid," a female responded within the mind.

"She was, but she sucks at it," came another feminine voice.

"I was… oh shoot, I mean *son-of-a-gun."*

Darach couldn't help but grin. He knew those voices.

"Nicole? Cassie?" Jackie pulled free and peered around as the last of the fog drifted away. "Erin?"

"Right here," Erin said before she came out of nowhere and wrapped her arms around Jackie. *"Hell, woman, you had me worried."*

Because she was mute, Erin only spoke within the mind.

Soon after, Nicole and Cassie were right there hugging them as well.

All three of her friends had faced a life-changing disability. Not for the first time, he wondered what Jackie's was. Though tempted to ask her friends, he knew better. They wouldn't tell him, only urge him to ask Jackie. Something he lacked the courage to do and he couldn't figure out why.

Darach didn't realize how tense he had been until Niall, Rònan and Logan were in front of him. Until they embraced and locked arms and shook hands like Scotsmen. His cousins were here. His kin. His lifeblood. The men who had trained alongside him to protect wee Robert the Bruce.

"All of you are here," Darach murmured, grateful.

"Aye," Adlin said before he turned his attention to the people and raised his voice. "'Tis time for us to journey forth and start our life anew. 'Tis time for us to find the unity we sought at the north of Scotland, our home." The wizard breathed deeply, and Darach got the impression he met every woman, man and child's eyes in that single breath. "Though not all of ye were born of the MacLomains, ye are now one. Ye are my kin. Ye chose a life not dictated by others but one chosen by ye. Yer own destiny. A religion and life of yer own choosing."

"We've a few days travel then I will show ye where we will build." Adlin gestured in a forward direction. "I will show ye where our castle will be." He stood up taller and smiled. "Would ye like that? Will ye continue to follow me?"

"Aye!" rose up, echoing through the forest.

Adlin nodded. "Aye, then." He grinned broadly and rubbed his hands together in anticipation before he pointed in a southerly direction. "'Tis time to start walking then."

As the people moved on, Adlin turned to the MacLomain men and eyed them with approval. "'Tis good to meet more MacLomain kin."

Darach made introductions. Though Niall and Rònan had come across Adlin briefly in the Otherworld, he was an old man so he didn't yet know them. Naturally, Adlin offered no explanation for them being there but strolled off once he knew who everyone was.

As Darach walked with his cousins, Logan, the current MacLomain chieftain, eyed Heidrek and spoke telepathically. *"So how goes it with you and the Viking?"*

Rònan laughed into his mind. *"How do you think?"* His cousin winked at him. *"Like I had to, he's got to deal with competition."* Then his voice grew serious. *"We've been worried about you, Cousin. What are you not telling us? Are you truly well?"*

"*I am.*" Darach's eyes flickered to Jackie. *"'Tis just complicated."*

"'Tis been complicated for us all," Logan said. *"And now you know our stories. Might you not share what's happening to you so that we can help?"*

"Aye," he said then shared everything except his dreams.

"Well, one thing is for certain." Rònan nudged him closer to Jackie. *"You willnae figure out who belongs with who if you dinnae spend time with the only Broun left."*

"Hey!" Nicole batted at Rònan when he kept nudging Darach and she had to move.

Erin stepped away gracefully and rolled her eyes, muttering with a grin, *"Dragons."*

Logan took Cassie's arm and redirected her until Darach and Jackie were alone.

"They're not discreet," Jackie mumbled.

"Nay," Darach agreed. "How are you doing? Any better since you awoke?"

"Yes." She nodded but didn't meet his eyes. "Better now that my friends are here."

"Aye." While tempted to take her hand, he didn't. Instead, he said something he wasn't convinced of in the least but hoped would calm her. "All will be well now that they're here."

"Here's hoping," Jackie whispered before her eyes flew to his and her voice grew stronger. "Do me a favor?"

"Anything."

"Don't say what you think I *want* to hear but what I *need* to hear."

"Och, I didnae," he began, but she veered away and walked with Erin. Disappointed, he cursed under his breath. Mayhap he could have handled that better. She was going through a lot and evidently needed honesty right now.

Heidrek came alongside. "I need to understand where we are going and my part in it. Have your kin shared anything I should know?"

"Nay." Darach frowned. "None of us have any idea why we're here."

"Yes you do," Heidrek said. "At the very least you're here to watch MacLomain Castle be built."

"True." He shook his head. "But I dinnae know why. What purpose does it serve considering what we're facing now?"

Heidrek said nothing for several long minutes. "Is MacLomain Castle not like my Viking fortress? A place where everything that matters most to our people first took root?"

Darach nodded with pride but felt a flare of guilt as well. Why didn't he have as much pride in his own castle? In Hamilton Castle? But he knew all too well. He despised its beginnings. He despised that his Da was imprisoned there for fourteen winters. "Aye, I've pride in MacLomain Castle though 'tis not my home as the Viking fortress is yours."

It seemed the Viking sensed his disgruntled thoughts and surprised him with his acuteness.

"So where does your heart truly lie?" Heidrek asked. "At MacLomain Castle or with your own castle?"

Darach meant to respond, but the words died on his lips because he didn't know the answer.

"If you do not know where your heart lies, what hope have you in protecting your people?" Heidrek wondered.

Though tempted to say he knew exactly where his heart lies, Darach remained silent. He wanted to tell the Viking to go back where he belonged. To leave this alone. But he had more respect than that so said nothing.

"Why does Heidrek keep staring at my lass?" Rònan growled into Darach's mind. *"Does he not know we're mated?"*

He glanced at the Viking only to realize Rònan was right. Heidrek's eyes weren't on Jackie but trained on Erin.

"As you know, I havenae been around much lately," Darach said to Rònan. *"Have Heidrek and Erin met before today?"*

"Nay," Rònan said, troubled. *"The only time they were around one another was when you gave both your sword and your lass to the Viking at MacLomain Castle."*

"She isnae my lass," Darach murmured.

"Yet," Rònan said. *"But I see the way you look at one another."* He kept grumbling, *"He needs to get his bloody eyes off my lass."*

"Stop being jealous, Rònan." Niall joined the conversation. *"Erin loves you, and you're mated. You dinnae need to be threatened by the Viking."*

"As if you wouldnae be just as jealous if he was looking at Nicole like that," Rònan retaliated.

"I think you numbnuts forgot we Brouns can hear your telepathic conversations," Nicole said into their minds. *"Including Erin...and Jackie!"*

Jackie could hear their thoughts? *Hell.* Since when?

"Yup." Erin shook her head without looking back. *"And Rònan knows exactly how I feel about insecure dragons."*

"Och," Rònan muttered aloud before he strode forward, flung Erin over his shoulder and kept walking. *"Now the bloody Viking can eye my arse instead of yours, aye?"*

Erin sighed then grinned at Rònan's backside. *"Well, it is an ass well worth eying. Love the kilt but we need to get you back into leather pants one of these days."*

Rònan slapped her backside and chuckled. *"Only for you, me wee dragon."*

Heidrek frowned at Rònan's odd behavior but said nothing.

"I think 'twould be wise if everyone remembers that Heidrek is our ancestor and show him more respect," Logan cut in.

Darach met Logan's eyes and nodded. Where Niall and Rònan were close, he and the MacLomain chieftain shared the same bond. They often thought alike. And right now, he knew Logan was absolutely right. More than that, though they assumed otherwise, there stood a good chance Heidrek could hear them. If he could control both water and air, there was a lot more to this Viking than they all previously thought.

Though he shouldn't be, Darach was caught off guard when the air shimmered and Grant appeared with the wee Bruce. His father sighed with relief when he spied Darach. "Och lad, 'tis good to find you here."

"Where else did you think I'd be?"

"'Tis hard to know for sure lately," Grant said softly when Adlin turned and locked eyes on him and Robert.

"Adlin." Grant fell to a knee and lowered his head. "'Tis so verra good to see ye again, Mentor."

Darach sensed the magic Adlin unleashed at Grant as he approached and felt him out.

"Ye've great magic about you." Adlin stopped in front of Grant. "A magic ye've learned to harness well through exemplary training." A grin blossomed. "My training to be sure."

"Aye, old friend."

"Rise." Adlin kept smiling as Grant stood. "I can see inside ye, lad and 'tis much ye've done for our clan despite such a grave start to your life."

"'Twas a start needed to ultimately defeat an old enemy," Grant said. "One who's kin has now returned and is a far greater threat than his bairn ever was."

"Aye." Adlin's eyes narrowed. "Eoghan Dubhdiadh, Druid of the South. An old enemy indeed and one before my time."

Darach frowned when he felt the turbulence in Jackie's mind at the mention of the druid. Not only he but Adlin glanced her way. He was somewhat surprised when she shifted closer to him and fear flashed in her eyes.

"What is it, lass?" It seemed perfectly natural to slide his hand into hers and squeeze…to try to offer comfort.

She frowned and took several deep breaths. Something had her terrified. Something he needed to understand.

Adlin eyed her for a long moment before he walked over and held out his hand. "Might you hold my hand for a moment, Jackie?"

She started to shake her head until Adlin said, "Please, lass. 'Twill only be for a moment."

Darach felt Adlin's persuasive magic. So did Jackie it seemed because she took his hand. The wizard's eyes slid shut for a moment before they opened and he whispered, "Och, lass. You cannae feel my touch, aye? Nor can you smell the loch's salt on the wind."

What? A terrible sense of foreboding rolled through him.

Jackie clenched her jaw as a variety of emotions flickered across her face. Sadness. Defiance. Courage. Bitterness. But more than anything?

Acceptance.

"All right, that's enough," Erin growled. At some point, Rònan had put her down. Within seconds, she was beside Jackie with her eyes narrowed on Adlin. No, make that her dragon eyes. Pale purple and fierce. Pure threat laced her voice. *"You best step away right now."*

"Erin," Rònan warned as he came alongside. "''Tis not your place, lass."

"My place is defending my friend." Erin's eyes never left Adlin's. *"Take your hands off her and we're good."*

Why was the lass reacting so strongly? The situation didn't seem to warrant it. When Adlin's eyes narrowed, Darach knew they had a problem. Their arch-wizard might be jolly enough when he needed to be but no one ordered him to do anything. And if one thing held true above all, Adlin was far more powerful than Erin.

"It's okay, Erin," Jackie interjected, clearly sensing that things were escalating quickly. "Really."

"I don't know that it is." Erin's eyes stayed locked with Adlin's. *"You're pretty arrogant, aren't you?"*

"Oh shit," Nicole muttered as she and the MacLomain men moved closer. None would dare harm Adlin but then again, no one would hesitate to protect Erin. She might be Rònan's, but she was theirs too. All the Broun lasses were. One way or another, they were a team.

"Stand down, Dragon," Heidrek growled. *"Now."*

Erin's eyes shot to Heidrek.

So did everyone else's.

Not only did the Viking's eyes shine pale blue but a tattoo that hadn't been there before started to glow on the side of his neck. A dragon. Though his stance remained non-threatening and he held no weapon, Erin's eyes widened, and she stepped back. Rònan's gaze was just as intense on Heidrek. He'd never seen such a look on his cousin's face.

Half awe, half respect.

"What *are* you?" Rònan whispered. "Because you are not a dragon but…something else."

"What I am is none of your concern right now." Heidrek's eyes went to Adlin. "Forgive the woman. She has only just started to learn how to control the beast within."

Darach's shock only intensified when Erin gave no sharp response. Instead, she kept her eyes trained on Heidrek as though it were impossible to look elsewhere. If he wasn't mistaken, she was *obeying* him. What was more interesting? Rònan said nothing but kept his eyes trained on Heidrek not with defiance but with continued respect.

"There is nothing to forgive," Adlin replied to Heidrek but looked at Erin. "Might we all have such a fierce protector as this lass."

Apparently finished with addressing Erin, Adlin turned to Grant. "What tangled webs we weave, aye?" He shook his head and grinned before his eyes at last landed on Robert. He lowered to a knee, took the lad's hand and bent his head. "My name is Adlin MacLomain. 'Tis a great pleasure to meet ye, wee one. Know that I will always remain devoted to ye."

Of course, Adlin knew who he would someday be.

Robert stood up a little straighter. "Many thanks, Adlin MacLomain."

Adlin nodded and stood, his eyes returning to Grant. "Well, you'll not likely enjoy where you must travel next, friend, but there is only one way to better ken your enemy and get out ahead of him."

Darach didn't like the sound of that.

Grant frowned. "I dinnae ken."

"Nay." Adlin sighed. "I dinnae suppose you do."

"I can well see why I mentored you." Adlin clasped Grant's shoulders. "Not only do you possess great magic but a goodness despite all you faced in your past. I only just met you but already I am so verra proud."

"Thank you," Grant said with an edge of wariness in his voice.

"No need to thank me. If anything you might be disliking me for a wee bit," Adlin said softly. "But the answers you seek can only be found at the verra beginning."

Grant's brows lowered sharply when he seemed to see something in Adlin's eyes. "Och, nay. Dinnae…"

His words were drowned out as wind whipped through the forest and fog came in so fast that Darach couldn't see his own hand within seconds. But he knew exactly where Jackie was. So he reached out and pulled her back against him.

"What's going on?" she said, a slight tremor to her voice.

"Time travel," he said. "'Twill be okay, lass."

"Nothing okay has come out of time travel so far," she whispered. "Except my friends finding love."

He appreciated that she focused on the positive, but he had an awful feeling about where they were heading. "Whatever happens, you're not alone. I'm right here beside you."

And he was as the fog burned away and their new location was revealed. What he saw made the blood in his veins freeze.

It seemed he wasn't alone.

"Bloody hell, nay," his Da said. "It cannae be."

Chapter Five

Hamilton Castle
1240
Nearly three years after Grant MacLomain was kidnapped.

JACKIE'S EYES WIDENED at the beautiful gothic style castle beyond the woods and a strange shiver of awareness rippled through her. "Where are we, Darach?"

"Home but not," he whispered.

"What does that mean?" she started to say, but Grant interrupted them.

"We need to get somewhere safe now."

It appeared they hadn't traveled through time alone. Not only were Heidrek, Rònan, Erin, Nicole, and Niall with them but little Robert and surprisingly enough, young William.

"Now!" Grant roared into their minds.

If there was one person no one questioned it was Grant. Niall scooped up Robert and started after Grant with everyone close behind.

All but William that is.

"Lad, ye must come with us," Darach said. "There's nothing but danger here."

"Where am I?" William ground his jaw, his eyes wide as he clenched a blade. "Where did Lilas and Dougal go?"

"Ye'll see them again," Darach assured. "But not if ye dinnae come now."

Jackie knew Darach was going to need help. As it turned out, Heidrek came to the same conclusion because he had remained behind.

William frowned at Darach. "I dinnae believe ye."

"I don't blame you. He's questionable at times," Jackie kicked in, her brows arching. "But do you know who I *do* believe?"

"Who?" William asked.

61

Jackie nodded into the woods. "Grant. He's a really good person, and if he says we're in danger, then we are."

"Aye?" William's eyes narrowed. "Then why are ye not running after him?"

"Because I'd rather stay where you are and get hurt than leave you behind."

"Och, nay." A tremble rippled through William as his eyes stayed on hers. "So ye really think ye are in danger?"

"I think we all are."

William assessed the situation again before he declared, "Then I must see ye out of harm's way, Jackie. My weapon is at yer back."

Jackie nodded. "Thank you." She looked at Darach. "Lead the way."

Relief flickered in his eyes as he grabbed her hand and they raced after the others. They didn't run for more than ten minutes before they came to a large boulder that was half surrounded by trees and half on the edge of a cliff overlooking the ocean. Darach braced on the edge and urged her to go pass him. He meant to protect her from falling.

"Shoot," she murmured, eying the long drop.

"'Tis not that bad." Darach squeezed her hand. "Just move along." His eyes held hers. "I willnae let you go over, lass."

God, she hated heights. But she hated seeming like a wimp more, so she ignored her tingling skin and allowed him to help her shimmy over.

Once safe, she waited as Darach held out his hand to William. "Come on, lad."

Incredulous, the boy eyed the long drop. "Nay!"

"If you are set to be a warrior then be one," Heidrek grunted from behind. "Go now."

William's eyes shot to the Viking. "I dinnae need to listen to ye. I saw what ye did earlier. Yer no Scotsman but an unnatural beast."

"Am I then?" Heidrek grinned, dark promise in his eyes. "Then you are no longer in a position you wish to be in." The Viking moved fast and flung William over his shoulder.

Darach joined Jackie as William cursed the whole way. By the time Heidrek set the boy down, he was in a state...of pure embarrassment, she'd say.

"Bloody hell," William declared, scowling as he frowned at the Viking.

"If you meant to protect Jackie, you should have thought nothing of your own fears," Heidrek informed him before he strode after the others.

"Bloody hell," William repeated, still scowling as he eyed Jackie. "I would have followed ye readily if given half a chance." He glared at Heidrek's back. "But I was made to look the fool instead."

"I would say ye made yerself look the fool," Robert said.

Jackie bit back a grin, not surprised in the least that the little King watched William closely.

Incredulous, William's eyes rounded on Robert, who stood a few inches shorter. "Who are ye to say such a thing, ye wee piece of..."

Robert straightened and looked down his nose at William as he interrupted him. "I am Robert the Bruce, son to Sir Robert VI de Brus, 6th Lord of Annandale and Marjorie, Countess of Carrick." He puffed up a bit more. "I am none other than the Earl of Carrick and the future King of Scotland."

"Is that so?" William appeared less than impressed as he looked Robert over. "I dinnae care in the least who ye are. Show me ye can use a blade then mayhap all yer fancy titles will be worth something."

Robert's hand went to his waist where no blade could be found. Pride and frustration crossed his face.

"Aye, that is what I thought." William rolled his eyes and strode into the cave after the others, throwing over his shoulder. "Yer all bluster, lad."

"Am not," Robert started but stopped. He might be young, but a new wisdom lit his eyes. One born of the adventures he'd had since meeting Jackie and her friends. "I'm learning to use a blade and am always willing to learn from those who know how to wield one better."

William stopped. He didn't turn but tilted his head sideways. "Aye?"

"Aye," Robert said.

"Do ye mean ye'd be willing to learn from me then, High-and-Mighty?"

Robert nodded. "Aye."

63

William paused for a long moment and contemplated. Jackie bit her tongue when Robert appeared torn and eager at the same time. The boys needed to work this out on their own.

"Then I will teach ye more when we've the chance," William said at last.

"Aye, many thanks," Robert said. "Have ye a full name then?"

"Nay, 'tis just William." But they all heard his soft words as he walked away. "At least till ye've earned my respect. Then ye might get the rest."

Robert waited until William was out of earshot before he released a hefty sigh and frowned. "I handled that all wrong, aye?"

"Nay, ye did just fine," Darach said.

"I agree." Jackie smiled and crouched in front of him. She had spent quite a bit of time with Robert at the Viking fortress when Erin was in her unnatural slumber. "It's good to see you again, Little King. That was pretty scary at MacLomain Castle when Erin almost died, and I vanished. How are you doing?"

Her chest tightened when he blinked back moisture and gave her a wobbly smile. "I am well." His eyes trailed to where William had been. "Well enough I suppose."

"Hey." Jackie squeezed his shoulders. "Look at me."

When he did, she said, "You've done really well. William's just been through a lot, okay?" She held his gaze. "Just like you have, Robert. You dealt with him perfectly and it's going to be okay."

"I dinnae think I dealt with him well at all." His frown deepened. "'Tis clear he's but a few winter's older and already a fierce warrior. What does that say about me? What does that say of how well I will someday lead Scotland?"

Jackie cupped his chin. "Do you remember what we talked about at the Viking fortress when you joined me at Erin's bedside that last time? When you were struggling to understand why that Viking boy wouldn't play with you?"

"Aye," he murmured. "Ye said I must remember that there's a reason behind everyone's actions. That I should search out that reason before judging them. It turned out he was just shy."

"It's good you discovered that rather than continue to think he was mean," she said softly. "Because nobody is what they seem when you first meet them. More than that, it sometimes takes a while to figure out who they really are."

"Aye," Robert whispered. "And 'twas your advice that helped me just now with William."

Jackie smiled. "Good."

"We should go," Darach said. "The further into the cave we get the better."

She gave Robert a quick hug then gestured at Darach. "Looks like you need to lead the way again."

"Aye, then." His eyes met Robert's. "It can get a wee bit treacherous. Watch my footing closely, lad."

Robert nodded.

Darach's eyes met hers. "Stay close to us, aye?"

"Of course."

Darach wasn't kidding. Though sunlight streamed from multiple crevices overhead, the path downward grew steeper and the rocks slicker with a fine sheen of sea spray. The wind whistling through cracks and the ocean crashing against the rock created a haunting echo that well-suited the eerie cave. She stayed close behind Robert, ready to grab the back of his tunic if he started to slip. By the time they made it to the bottom, it was so dark she could barely make out Darach's silhouette.

"I'm surprised one of you wizards doesn't use magic to light the way," she mentioned.

"Nay." Darach moved slower and made sure they stayed behind him. "'Tis not a good idea to use magic around here. Not right now."

They didn't go that much further before light increased, the cave widened and they came to an exit that overlooked a good sized area. It appeared to be a lightly forested meadow completely surrounded by cliffs. A valley lush with greenery and colorful wildflowers. Though the echo of crashing waves could still be heard, it only added a mystical feel to the place as spray twisted with sunlight far overhead but never touched the ground.

"Oh, wow," she whispered. "This is astounding."

"Aye," Robert agreed, his eyes as wide as hers.

Jackie took his hand, and they followed the others to a group of pine trees that offered ample protection.

Grant gestured to the women. "Please gather wood. We can burn a fire here. The smoke will remain unseen." Then he looked to the men. "There are inlets and small caves throughout this area. Hunt, so we can eat. Then I will explain where we are."

"*With all due respect, I hunt not gather,*" Erin informed, eyes intent on Rònan. "*Let's go make some spears from sticks and catch lunch, dragon.*"

Nicole snorted. "Yeah, I'm sure that's all you two will be doing."

"*You should talk, preggie,*" Erin shot back before she grinned and left with Rònan.

Meanwhile, Niall continued muttering under his breath about Nicole being in yet another unsafe situation. Jackie didn't blame him considering her pregnancy.

"I'll be fine," Nicole assured and kissed him before she said, "Go hunt with the guys. I'll pick up sticks with Jackie."

Jackie got a distinct feeling that was the last thing Nicole wanted to do. Her friend knew how to use a weapon and wanted to join the hunters. She bit back yet another surge of irritation. She didn't want to be so dependent on others to protect her. It stunk, and she was just about over it.

Heidrek looked at Darach. "Go hunt. I will stay with Jackie."

"I can protect Jackie and the bairns just fine," Grant said. "Both of you go."

"Well, I am no bairn," William announced and started striding after Erin and Rònan.

"Nay." Grant shook his head. "Ye'll stay here and help gather wood, lad."

When William kept walking, Grant's voice deepened. "Ye dinnae want to test me. Ye willnae like the results."

Grant's tone of voice stopped William in his tracks. She didn't miss his reddened cheeks when he glanced at the men walking by to go hunting. Poor kid. Pre-teen years sucked...especially in this day and age.

"I know Grant is mighty, but I could use the extra protection," Jackie piped up. "Besides, I think you and Robert have a much more important job making sure Nicole and I stay safe."

"I'm with Jackie," Nicole agreed. "We need you two to protect us."

"Aye, then, I will defend ye both," Robert declared and tucked a stick into the side of his pants as though it were a sword.

William looked at him as though he was daft. "Did ye not hear the other lass? Ye need to sharpen a stick before it can be any sort of weapon."

Robert eyed his stick. "Do ye know how to sharpen one, then?"

"Aye, who doesnae?"

Nicole frowned. "Hey, be nice." Her eyes narrowed. "Who are you again?"

"His name is William." Jackie gave him a pointed look. "And I'm sure you didn't mean to sound condescending, right?"

"Condescending?"

"As though you were better than Robert."

"No more than he did when we first met," William said. When Jackie frowned, he sighed and looked at Robert. "Do ye want me to show ye how 'tis done then?"

"Aye." Robert nodded. "Please."

"Everyone does their fair share," Grant interjected. "First ye lads help gather wood then William can show ye how to whittle a stick."

"Aye, then," the boys said and got to it.

Nicole eyed Jackie. "How are you doing, Sweetie? Rough stuff back there at MacLomain Castle. We were all super worried about you."

"I'm all right." Jackie felt bad for wishing Erin had stayed, and Nicole had gone hunting. She loved them both but could have used some time alone with her best friend. "How are you feeling? Any queasiness yet?"

"Naw, I'm fine." Nicole's eyes met hers. "Seriously, Jackie. You seem a little off. Not to say this whole adventure hasn't done that to all of us but..." She shook her head. "I dunno. What's going on with you and Heidrek? You spent a lot of time with him at the fortress. Then Darach pretty much vanished...anyway, are you and Heidrek hooking up or what?"

"I'm not sure." Jackie shook her head and wished to hell they weren't having this conversation. "I don't think I'm hooking up with anybody."

"Uh huh. I get the denial thing," Nicole said. "The same thing happened with Niall and me."

Jackie had heard about their adventure in great detail, and though she was thrilled Nicole was happy, she wasn't particularly up for hearing it yet again. Therefore, she redirected the conversation. "So do you think you two will get married?"

"Maybe." Nicole shrugged. "I suppose you think we should seeing how I'm pregnant."

Jackie sighed. "I didn't say that."

"You didn't have to," Nicole said. "I can hear it in your voice."

"You didn't hear anything in my voice." Jackie picked up more sticks. "I just know your ring shines for him so that evidently makes him your true love."

"It does," Nicole agreed. Then she surprised Jackie. "So yeah, though I think marriage is overrated, I'll probably tie the knot with my brute."

Jackie looked at her. "Yeah?"

A small smile hovered on Nicole's lips. "Yeah."

"Good." Jackie smiled. "I'm happy for you."

"You are?"

"Very. I like Niall."

"Aw." Nicole scuffed her boot and grinned. "I'd give you a hug if I didn't have an armful of sticks."

Jackie kept smiling. "Me too." She nodded toward the pines. "Come on. It's getting chilly. Let's go get a fire started."

Not long after they got a fire going, Nicole pulled one of Niall's tunics out of a satchel, put it on, sat against a tree stump and dozed off. The boys were wandering around looking for the perfect rocks to whittle with. So, that left her and Grant.

And Grant, it seemed, had an agenda.

"How do you fare, lass?" While he appeared genuinely concerned, she sensed something else in his demeanor as their eyes met across the flames. Though she knew he was unsettled that they had traveled here, there was more to it.

"I'm okay." Though Grant had spent very little time getting to know her at the Viking fortress, his wife Sheila had. She only stayed for a few weeks, but it was more than enough time for them to connect.

Jackie liked her. A lot. But then Sheila was easy to get along with...much like her son when he wasn't avoiding her. As far as she could tell, Darach definitely inherited his mother's personality. They were easy-going with a likable nature. At least that's how Darach seemed in New Hampshire. She didn't have much to go on after that.

Then again, there had been rumors at the Viking fortress that hinted at another nature entirely. Rumors that spoke of him getting together with a girl there before Jackie showed up.

So *after* their kiss.

Grant's eyes fell to her ring, his words soft. "It has changed, has it not?"

She looked at her ring. "Apparently so."

"Perplexing." Grant threw a few more sticks on the fire.

Something about his tone set her on edge.

While her upbringing demanded that she respect her elders, Jackie was in no mood for unfair judgment. Not after the past few months not only dealing with a shitty prognosis at home but here with all of its confusion and unrest. "No disrespect, but have you got a problem with me?"

Grant wasted no time getting to the point. "How do you feel about Heidrek?"

Heidrek? What did he have to do with her wearing the real ring and...then it occurred to her. The ring was supposed to bring her and Darach together, yet Heidrek was here too.

Grant was protecting his son.

Well, that was fine and good, but she wasn't having it, especially after the way Darach had treated her. So she looked him dead in the eyes. "Considering your son kissed me then ditched me, I'm fairly certain how I feel about Heidrek is none of your business."

Grant's brows perked. "Darach kissed you?"

"Don't look so surprised." She frowned. "Yes, he kissed me in New Hampshire then made himself scarce."

"So you didnae start something with Heidrek at the fortress despite knowing your ring likely meant Darach was your true love?" Grant said. "An attraction betwixt you and the Viking that would have caused my son to give you to Heidrek because he thought 'twas the right thing to do?"

Jackie kept frowning, just as perplexed as Grant. "No, Heidrek and I are friends...good friends. I like him a lot. And just to be clear, no man gives me to another. I take offense to that statement."

"Aye." Grant twisted a blade of grass, his eyes a little lost as he stared at her. "My apologies...on several fronts it seems."

Emotions turbulent, she tried to ignore her numb skin. *Forgive, forgive.*

69

Grant focused more intently on her. "Och, lass."

He knew. But then she figured everyone suspected something after Adlin's reaction to her.

When Grant started to head her way, she shook her head sharply. "Please don't. I'm fine."

He sat slowly, his eyes never more intent, his words far softer. "You're unwell."

"No," she denied. "Just overwhelmed. It'll pass."

"Adlin sensed it," he murmured, studying her face. "Tell me, lass. What disability do you face?"

Jackie was relieved that they weren't using magic here. That way Grant couldn't figure it out. Because if anyone outside of Adlin had the power to do it, Grant would be the guy.

But she knew she had to give him an answer. "It's a sensory thing. Mostly I'm losing my ability to smell."

God, that sounded weak.

"Smell?" Brows furrowed, his pale grayish blue eyes grew especially intent. It was disconcerting how much Darach looked like his father. Jackie strongly suspected he would be able to pass for Grant's twin when he was older.

"Yes," She shrugged. "I know it's minor compared to what everyone else is going through, but you'd be amazed how much you miss the smell of maple bacon frying. Or turkey at Thanksgiving." She twisted her lips. "If you lived in the twenty-first century that is."

Now Grant eyed her with that look of wisdom she was getting used to. He didn't believe she was telling the whole truth, but he wouldn't press it.

So though tempted to say, "Really, it's true, just my sense of smell," she kept her mouth shut.

Thankfully, Erin and Rònan reappeared and the conversation ended. Her friend had several dead rabbits tossed over her shoulder and a dewy, content sheen on her face that told Jackie she'd been doing far more than hunting. Erin no sooner tossed down the carcasses when everyone else returned.

Darach and Heidrek had small bucks over their shoulders.

Niall had a handful of birds.

Erin snorted. *"Wow, Niall. Way to hunt."*

"Their meat is bland," Niall said, not riled in the least by the taunt as his eyes fell on a still slumbering Nicole with affection. "My lass's stomach will be able to handle it better."

Jackie's eyes shot to Nicole. So she had lied about being sick. Wasn't that something. The friend she once knew would have made sure everyone knew she had morning sickness and how awful it was.

Grant eyed the bucks. "Too much meat. One will have to be disposed of." He frowned at Darach and Heidrek. "'Twas poor of you to kill more than we needed."

"*I told them as much,*" Erin muttered. "*Men and their dick sizes. Never ending battle. Primitive bullshit.*"

Jackie's cheeks burned when she realized what Erin was talking about. They were trying to outdo each other. But why? She almost felt stupid for thinking it when their eyes flickered to her before returning to each others with a definite dare as to who would forfeit their kill.

Drawn by the commotion, the boys returned.

"I am hungry," Robert declared. "I will eat at least one of these bucks."

By instinct, Jackie's emotions flared, and she headed that way when he did. Something about a child touching a dead animal didn't sit well. "No, don't touch them until they've been cooked."

"Nay, lass." William stepped in front of her. "'Tis not for a lady to be around such things."

Jackie shook her head and smiled. "It's okay." She ignored the numbness spreading through her, stepped around William and stood beside the dead deer, angling so that Robert wouldn't come closer. "This isn't for kids." At least not to her way of thinking. She nodded at the fire. "It needs more sticks. Like Grant said, we should all pull our weight."

"Aye, then." Robert sighed and turned away.

She was about to step away as well when a strange tingling started around her ankle. At first, she thought it was just sensation returning until Erin said, "*What the hell?*"

Jackie yelped when the deer at her feet twitched, and its head shot up. She barely had a second to process what was happening before Darach and Heidrek pulled her back, and the deer leapt to its feet.

Not dead but very much *alive.*

71

Its eyes met hers for a long moment before it darted off.

Stunned, Jackie could only watch it go. What the hell just happened? Because it couldn't possibly be how it seemed…could it?

"I dinnae ken," Robert said. "Was that deer not to eat?"

"Nay, lad. The other is," Grant said softly. "'Tis time to sit and enjoy our food. Then we will all talk."

"I think we should talk now." William's wide eyes went to Jackie before he sank to a knee and lowered his head. "I dinnae know which god ye are but thank ye for sparing a life that gave no nourishment."

"Och." Grant sighed. "Then ye will eat later, and we will talk now."

When he flicked his wrist, both boys fell to the ground gently, sound asleep.

"I thought you shouldn't use magic here," she whispered.

"'Twas just a wee bit and Da is talented enough to keep others from sensing it," Darach explained.

Jackie had to wonder if he hadn't used a wee bit already to look inside her mind.

For whatever reason—mostly because Jackie figured she was always on her own wavelength—Nicole bolted upright when the kids hit the ground. With a wide yawn, she peered around until her eyes landed on Niall and she offered a sleepy smile, mumbling, "I'm hungry."

"Aye, lass." Niall went to her. "Soon."

In the meantime, Grant and Darach laid the boys down on a plush bit of grass and covered them with blankets. Good thing everyone arrived with satchels because she, Darach and Heidrek had nothing.

"Everyone sit," Grant ordered. "'Tis time to talk."

Jackie heard him but felt more numb than ever. Her emotions were high, and her limbs were freezing up.

Heidrek took her hand. "Come sit, woman."

Her eyes went from his face to their entwined hands. She couldn't feel a thing.

"Come, 'tis okay." Darach slid his arm around her lower back. "Let's sit."

Relieved that she could feel *him*, more so that her legs seemed to be working, she welcomed Darach's help to a stump. Though he seemed slightly confused, Heidrek sat on her other side without commenting.

Everyone else joined them around the fire.

Grant eyed the flames and seemed to get lost in them before he spoke. "Though 'tis hard to know where I should begin, 'tis likely best to begin with where we are." His eyes met Darach's. "As you know, we're at Hamilton castle, *our castle*, though 'tis earlier in our era. 'Tis when I was but a few years older than young William is now. The year I was finally released from Keir Hamilton's dungeon and allowed to roam beyond the castle walls."

Jackie slid her hand into Darach's when he tensed.

"'Twas in this valley that I found occasional sanctuary while I was imprisoned, whether figuratively or literally," Grant continued. "'Tis a place Keir Hamilton knew nothing about. A place of unusual magic. And 'tis a place that will keep us safe whilst we're here."

Darach's hand clenched hers and his frown only deepened. "I dinnae ken, Da. Why did Adlin send us here?"

"I suspect because he wants me to ken something about Keir Hamilton that I couldnae recognize at such a young age," Grant said. "We must all be vigilant because there's something to be learned here that will help fight Keir's father…that will help destroy the evil determined to take the wee Bruce, use the ring and change Scotland."

"'Tis an unkind mentor that sends his apprentice back to the days that haunt him most," Darach murmured, his tone dark, his words unforgiving.

"And 'tis an equally unkind mentor who wouldnae do anything to help his kin see more clearly," Grant said. "Remember that son. Remember that there is *always* a bigger picture and if you but look you will see it."

Jackie clenched her jaw when Darach's eyes narrowed. Though he was talking about Keir Hamilton and the future of Scotland, she heard something else in Grant's advice. Something that had more to do…with her?

"All aside," Grant continued. "We are safe here. On the morrow, we will venture out and see what we can learn." His eyes went to the children. "I cannae fathom why they've been sent on this journey, but a few of us will stay behind to watch them at all times.

Because Robert cannae under any circumstances be subjected to Keir Hamilton."

There was no missing the vehemence in Grant's voice. The pure anger of someone who remembered all too well how poorly a child could be treated.

Before any could respond, Grant's eyes landed on Heidrek. "Though we need to ken many things whilst here, let us begin with you."

Heidrek nodded. "What would you like to know, Shaman?"

"You made Erin back down from confronting Adlin. And had Rònan bowing to your will as well." Grant's eyes held Heidrek's "What are you? I've never seen anyone who can control a dragon shifter."

Erin and Rònan's eyes remained locked on Heidrek, eager for an explanation.

But Heidrek never lost eye contact with Grant. "I am something different. Something that allows me to hear all of you speak within the mind."

"All right. But what precisely are you?"

"What I am does not matter."

"It verra much does." Grant's eyes went from Jackie to Heidrek. "If you mean to keep her safe."

Heidrek's hand slid to the blade at his waist. "I know how to keep her safe."

"Aye," Grant agreed. "But we all saw that you have a way of doing it without a weapon. So again I ask, what *are* you?"

Heidrek eyed Grant for a long moment before his gaze slid to Erin and Rònan. Jackie was surprised by the slight glow of their eyes—a flicker of dragon neither expected—before he gave his answer not to Grant but them.

"Amongst other things, I am a Dragon Seer."

Jackie didn't miss the slight shift in Grant and Heidrek's posture.

Though they didn't draw them, both put a hand on their weapons at the same time. This, naturally, made the MacLomain men do the same.

"Impossible," Grant hissed softly. "They are but myth long before your time. And markedly vulnerable to darkness."

"Not anymore." Heidrek slowly removed his hand from his weapon as he eyed each and every man. "I cannae say if there are others, but I am one. And though my mother turned to darkness, I will not."

"But you control dragons," Grant said. "That is a verra powerful and unique form of magic. A type that can weaken even the strongest of human minds. And a weak mind is easier to corrupt."

"Then we must hope my mind is stronger than most."

"Indeed." Grant cocked his head. "So why are you really here?"

"You were there. Because Adlin summoned me. Not only that but your son requested it, and I agreed. I mean to protect Jackie and I desire…" his eyes went to Jackie but drifted to Erin. When Rònan's eyes narrowed, Heidrek's gaze returned to Grant. He shook his head, his eyes again flickering back to Erin. "I desire Jackie, but something has changed."

Rònan clenched his jaw, his hand still on his weapon. Even so, he was obviously unsure of his next move based on the odd sort of worship in his eyes when he looked at Heidrek.

Erin took it out of everyone's hands when she clenched Rònan's thigh and narrowed her eyes on Heidrek. *"I'm not available so you better get your shit together fast."*

Heidrek bowed his head before his eyes met Rònan's. "I am no threat, Dragon. I am but a brother."

"What sort of brother, though," Rònan wondered, the dragon in him defiant though the man clearly wasn't. "When ye arenae a dragon?"

"Born to a seer and dragon-shifter, I am what I am," Heidrek said simply. "I share a kinship with dragons that is hard to explain. I think as you think. Beneath the Viking King's tutorage, I have become stronger and wiser. Now something new calls to me…" His eyes again went to Erin. "Something has changed."

Erin's brows shot together as she plunked down on Rònan's lap and kept a you-better-understand-who-I'm-with look on her face. *"Well, I'm not sure how I can help you,"* she patted Rònan's chest, *"because I'm with him."*

Heidrek's eyes went to Grant. "I will not harm you and yours."

Grant's gaze stayed locked with his for several moments before he finally spoke. "I dinnae think you will, lad, but I will be watching you verra closely regardless."

After Heidrek nodded, Grant turned his attention to Jackie. "Now let us get to what weighs most on our minds."

Jackie felt Grant's stare as though her life had narrowed down to a single pin-prick point.

Darach's arm again snaked around her lower back, his gaze never leaving his father. "Take care how you go about this, Da."

Grant's eyes met Darach's before they settled on the fire. "Either I tell her, or you do, Son."

Upset, Jackie frowned at Darach. "Well, somebody needs to tell me and sooner rather than later. What's going on? Why did that deer run off? I can only assume it wasn't all that injured to begin with."

"Nay, 'twas dead, lass," Darach said softly as his eyes connected with hers. "It seems you have a gift nobody expected but mayhap explains why you were able to keep Erin safe when she traveled to the Otherworld."

"Just tell me," she prompted when he paused. "I have the right to know."

Darach nodded, but she could tell he was worried about how she would react.

"It seems you have the power not only to keep death at bay but to resurrect not only people but animals," he said. "'Tis a rare and special gift, lass. I've never known another to possess it to the degree you do."

Impossible. Chills raced through her only to be replaced by tingling then numbness. "What exactly do you mean by *degree*?"

"I mean that while Aunt McKayla and Lair have the ability to heal, I cannae say they've ever brought anyone back after they've passed over," he said. "And that it was a deer, something you had no emotional attachment to, makes it more profound."

"I see," Jackie murmured as she tried to suppress her fear. "Any thoughts on why I'd be able to do such a thing?"

Grant shook his head. "Verra few in history have possessed such a gift." His compassionate eyes met hers. "As tales foretell it, she who can resurrect must first stand on the brink of death herself." His disgruntled eyes went to Darach. "And she can only ever be meant for he who would chase her into the afterlife with no chance to return."

Chapter Six

LOST IN THOUGHT, Darach finished the last of his meat and continued to eye the fire. Erin and Jackie had gone off to talk a while ago with Rònan and Heidrek trailing at a distance. Darach had wanted to speak with Jackie alone, but she refused, saying she needed time with Erin. So here he sat, confused as hell and trying to come to grips with what his father had implied.

Jackie was sick…possibly even dying.

And by the looks of it, only Erin knew because Nicole wasn't doing well at all. Grant wouldn't answer any of her questions, saying it was Jackie's place to tell her. So now she paced with a disgruntled Niall alongside as he tried to convince her to calm down. That it wasn't good for the wee one.

"Was it necessary to say such around so many?" he mumbled to his father. "'Tis a poor time for everyone to be so upset."

"Aye," Grant said, clearly upset as well. "Adlin wouldnae have responded to her as he did if he didnae want her secrets known. More than that, 'tis a truth that needed to be revealed so that we all better ken what lies ahead."

He kept looking to the woodland, hoping Jackie would return.

"You mean so that *I* would better ken what lies ahead." Darach narrowed his eyes. "So that I might have all the facts before I continue pursuing Jackie. Do ye truly think I would let my own potential death stand in the way of my feelings for the lass?"

Darach understood his father was upset that the prophecy said her true love would die. And while he didn't blame him for his concern, he'd rather his Da find it in his heart to approve rather than dissuade.

"Ye willnae *potentially* die if ye end up with Jackie, Son. 'Twill be a definite, unavoidable thing." Pain ran deep in Grant's eyes. "Ye arenae a father yet so ye dinnae ken how I feel. How much pain losing ye would cause. And though I want ye to find the kind of love I have with yer mother, ye cannae fault me for trying my best to give ye fair warning…to hope mayhap yer heart will lead ye in another direction."

"It cannae. It willnae." He met his father's eyes and finally came clean. "I've been dreaming about her for years, Da."

Surprise flashed across his father's face followed by concern. "Why didnae ye tell me?" His frown deepened. "Yer my son. I've been inside yer mind and never sensed these dreams."

"I didnae tell ye at first because I didnae want ye to worry. Eventually, she became more to me and for lack of a better explanation, I started feeling possessive of her. There were times I wanted to tell ye and my kin but 'twas impossible. She became a secret I couldnae seem to share." He frowned. "Now I wonder if Goddess Brigit had something to do with that."

"Goddess Brigit?" Grant's brows lowered sharply. "I dinnae ken."

Darach had assumed he did by now. Evidently not. So he shared her part in everything.

"Well, this certainly gives me a better sense of direction," Grant muttered.

"I'm surprised Adlin didnae mention as much."

"I could say the same about you, Son." Grant frowned. "Adlin told me the ring had changed and little else. He didnae mention one was a replica." He shook his head. "Between that bit of information and your dreams, 'tis becoming far clearer why ye gave her to Heidrek." His voice dropped an octave. "'Twould have been good to know before I accused her of betraying ye."

"Och, da!" He scowled at his father. "Ye didnae?"

"Aye, I did, and she put me in my place for it." Grant shrugged when Darach kept scowling. "I'm a parent watching out for my bairn. 'Tis really your fault for not sharing things with me sooner."

Darach sighed and shook his head.

"So ye continue to feel just as strongly about Jackie?" His father searched his eyes. "Are ye certain 'tis not just a false sense of commitment based on the dreams?"

"Nay, what I feel for her has only intensified. 'Tis verra real."

"Let me ask ye this then," Grant said. "If she continued to wear the duplicate ring, would ye still be on the run? Would ye still be willing to give her up?"

"Without hesitation," Darach said. "I'd do anything to keep her safe."

His Da eyed him for a long moment. "I believe ye mean that son." He tilted his head. "So 'twas truly risky to kiss her then, aye? Because God knows, a kiss can change everything."

"Let me guess?" Darach arched a brow. "Ye learned as much when Jackie put ye in your place?"

"Aye, lad," Grant said. "And 'tis safe to say she was as upset with ye as she is with me at the moment."

"No doubt." Darach shook his head. "'Twas foolish of me." He sighed. "Had the demi-god suspected how strongly I felt, it could have caused a great deal of harm."

"Aye." Grant continued to eye him as Darach looked at the fire. "Tell me how ye learned to switch the passion of the ring."

"Och." Darach's eyes shot to his father. "How did ye know about that?"

"Adlin." His father gave him a pointed look. "He was concerned and wanted me to look into it."

"'Tis of no importance now." He frowned. "Even if I didnae want her, I wouldnae do such a thing to Heidrek in light of recent revelations."

"Nay, I dinnae suppose ye would." Grant considered him. "So tell me how the passion is switched."

"'Tis naught but an incantation that calls on Brigit's intervention. 'Tis she who has the power to switch the passion," Darach said. "After all, 'twas she who created the rings."

"Indeed." Grant's eyes narrowed as he pondered. "A Celtic goddess who is clearly playing games seeing how the real ring is now on Jackie's finger. What happened to the replica?"

"I dinnae know." Darach shook his head. "One moment 'twas in my pocket, the next 'twas gone."

Darach again eyed the trees. Where was she? They'd been gone too long.

"Interesting," Grant murmured. "Somehow I imagine this all ties into ye avoiding becoming chieftain. How so, Son?"

He should have known his father would lead the conversation in this direction. Yet one of his long-standing reasons for not becoming laird had just become a moot point. "It doesnae matter now, Da...it doesnae matter in the least."

"So 'twas something to do with Jackie?"

"Partly," he conceded.

Yet there was another part. One his father had long speculated and reiterated now.

"And partly because ye still remain bitter that I ended up staying at Hamilton Castle despite my youth there," he said softly. "Ye shouldnae blame it on our people. 'Twas not their fault."

If only it were that simple. Though tempted to say they weren't technically *their* people by blood, he wasn't in the mood to go down that same tired road. Right now he wanted Jackie to return so he could make sure she was all right.

Restless, he stood and squeezed his father's shoulder. "We'll talk more of this later. I need to walk and clear my head."

"Son?"

"Aye?"

His father's eyes were more troubled than ever when they met his. "Ye know that no matter what comes of all this I love ye… and that I'm verra proud of ye."

"Aye, Da, I know. I love ye too," he murmured before he left.

It didn't take long to find Rònan and Heidrek. They were chatting in a narrow rock corridor that led to what he suspected was a smaller glade. He remained shocked by Heidrek's recent revelation. Not only about being a Dragon Seer but by what the Viking implied after that.

That he was no longer pursuing Jackie.

While some might speculate it was because she was sick, Darach knew better. Whatever happened had more to do with Erin and like Heidrek said, recent changes. Changes that had to do with dragon blood.

"Cousin." Rònan frowned as Darach joined them. "How fare ye?"

"I've been better." Darach frowned as well. "How is Jackie?"

"Upset the last we saw of her," Heidrek said. "She has been speaking with Erin for some time."

He nodded and clenched his jaw. If anyone could tell her exactly what she needed to hear it was Erin.

Rònan eyed Darach. "From what Erin's told me, Jackie is verra strong of mind, Cousin. She will be all right. We will make sure she is."

"And how will we do that?" Darach bit out. "With our brawn? Our weapons? Our battle skills? Because if I understood Da's implication correctly, nothing of this world can help her."

Ronan leaned against the rock wall, hung his head and remained silent.

"You're right. It seems unlikely anything of this world can help her, but perhaps something not entirely of this plane can." Heidrek held out the blade that Ronan had so recently tossed to him. "I cannot in good faith keep this. It is meant for he who not only intends to keep Jackie safe but love her with his whole heart."

Darach's eyes narrowed. "And that man isnae ye then?"

"No." Heidrek shook his head, eyes a little sad. "Though I had hoped otherwise, it cannot be."

Darach's eyes went to Ronan. "Is this because of Erin?"

"Aye." Ronan's eyes went from Heidrek to Darach. "He doesnae want her for his own but senses another affiliated to her. Someone he must meet before he commits to any other."

So he was meant for another lass?

Once he knew they didn't have a problem in regards to Erin, Darach nodded at Heidrek and took the sword. Relief washed over him the moment he held it.

It had been no easy thing giving up this blade.

"Who is this person affiliated with Erin?" he asked.

"I do not know." Heidrek appeared unsettled. "Someone part of her lineage. Someone connected to her dragon blood."

Darach's brows perked. "So someone from the far future?"

"Yes."

"Aunt McKayla has been rambling about visions of late," Ronan said. "Stories she wants to write about our Viking Ancestors' kin and lasses from the future. When Erin is available, we'll talk more with her about her family. See if there's anything we should know."

"Ah." Darach's eyes connected with Heidrek's. "So ye willnae be pursuing my lass anymore? Just like that, ye can shut off your attraction to her? Because dinnae tell me it wasnae there."

"*Your* lass then?" Ronan echoed, but he heard the approval in his voice.

"My attraction to Jackie was there. It still is," Heidrek said without hesitation. "But to ignore the call of my dragon is to deny who I am. *What* I am. And I would never turn my back on such a thing despite how much I cared for a woman. If I did, then I would not be worthy of accepting the Viking King's crown someday."

While Darach appreciated his honesty, he would rather the Viking had lost interest in her altogether.

"If nothing else, Jackie is my friend," Heidrek continued. "And I will not leave her until I know she's safe from harm."

Darach was about to respond when Erin appeared.

Where was Jackie?

Rònan pulled Erin against him and kissed the top of her head. His voice remained respectful and soft. "How does Jackie fare, lass?"

"She's hanging in there." She sighed. *"Learning that she can resurrect isn't really fazing her all that much. At least not yet."* Her eyes went between Darach and Heidrek. *"I think what's bothering her more right now is the part about the guy who loves her facing death."* Erin pressed her cheek against Rònan's chest and wrapped her arms around his waist. *"Can't say I blame her."*

By the look on Heidrek's face, Darach would bet Jackie already had two men who loved her. One was just convinced he had to walk away.

"Where is she now?" Darach asked.

"Around the bend. She needed some alone time," Erin said. *"Don't worry, it's a dead end, and she's well protected."*

Darach headed that way.

"I said alone time," Erin called after him, but he ignored her.

The last thing she needed was to be alone.

More than that, he needed to see her.

To know she was all right.

He found her in an area no larger than a small courtyard. Covered in grass, a few small pines grew up the walls, and she sat in a tiny alcove carved into the rock. Her eyes were closed as she rested her cheek on bent knees. It was impossible not to sense how sad she was.

"Jackie?" he said softly. "Are you okay?"

Her eyes locked on him before she sighed. "Thanks for checking on me but I need a little time to…" She shook her head and rested it back against the stone, emotion evident in her voice. "I just need some time to process things."

"Aye, lass." But she wouldn't be processing them alone. He set his swords aside and sank down against the wall beside her. "I willnae bother you. Nor will I leave you here by yourself."

"Seriously, I need time alone," she murmured.

"The last thing you need is to be alone." He crossed his legs, leaned his head back and shut his eyes. "I willnae say a word. Just allow me to…" Emotion thickened his voice. "Just allow me to be here. Let me watch over you."

Please let it be okay because he couldn't stand to be anywhere else right now.

A long silence passed before she said, "The words 'watch over you' usually imply that the one doing the watching has their eyes open."

"I'm a wizard." The corner of his lips hitched up. "That means I can watch over you with my eyes closed."

"Even when you can't use magic?" she mocked.

He was relieved to hear an edge of humor in her voice. So he looked at her. Head still resting back, she was watching him.

Their eyes locked for a long moment before he spoke. "I willnae pressure you to tell me a thing, Jackie, but you should know something now. Though I might not have acted like it so far, I'm your friend."

"I'm glad you said that," she whispered. "Because I could always use another friend." Before he could respond, she kept going. "But just a friend and nothing more." Pain flashed in her beautiful brown eyes. "I won't subject any man to what your dad hinted at. Not you or Heidrek or anyone else." Her voice grew firm. "I'm officially off the market."

Unlike his cousins, he had spent a lot of time in the twenty-first century and understood her terminology. She refused to be with any man. No one would die because they loved her.

But it was already too late.

Because he had fallen in love with her before they ever met.

Nonetheless, now wasn't the time for any of that. Now was the time to give her exactly what she asked for. What she needed.

Friendship.

"Then you're off the market." He grinned. "That makes this far less complicated, aye?"

Her eyes narrowed for a moment before she nodded once. "Actually, it does."

Darach kept grinning. "Now that we've settled that, can I stay and keep you company?"

"As if you wouldn't have anyway," she said.

"True," he conceded. "But at least now mayhap we can talk? Mayhap I can do what I should have from the start and get to know you better?"

"Hmm." Jackie kept eying him. "I don't know." She made a show at considering it before she relented. "I suppose it wouldn't be the worst thing ever having a little company right now." She shrugged. "And getting to know each other better."

Before he could speak, she held up a finger, voice stern. "As long as you realize I'm standing my ground. Friends. Nothing more."

"Friends and nothing more," he agreed.

"I mean it."

"As do I."

"Yeah?"

"Definitely."

Darach knew by the way she kept studying him that she didn't believe him. Not entirely. But it seemed she wanted to connect more than anything else. And he didn't blame her. If he were sick, he would want to connect with people too.

Anything to hold onto his humanity.

"So who would you like to talk about first? Me or you?" He issued his most charming smile. "Because I imagine we're both verra interesting."

The corner of her lip twitched. As though she wanted to smile but fought it. "Why don't we start with you?" She rolled a pebble between her fingers. "Who is Darach Hamilton? I know you've avoided becoming laird and that you're on the go a lot. Like everyone else, I figure the two are related. That's about all I know of you outside of our brief time in New Hampshire."

Darach pondered how much he should say, but in the end found himself telling her more than expected.

"I've been a handful for my parents from the beginning." He offered a small smile. "I started walking far later than I should have because of my magic. Whilst I dinnae remember it all that well, Da says 'twas because I'm a wizard of air, and unfortunately my gift ignited when I was learning to walk." He chuckled. "There's nothing quite like a wee bairn getting caught in air currents when they're trying to stand. From what I hear 'twas comical."

There was a soft smile on Jackie's face when she said, "I can only imagine. You poor thing."

"Och, nay," Darach scoffed. "Once I got the hang of it, I was just fine. I didnae suffer the same sort of strife again until years later when I began to learn how to battle and deal with weaponry."

Her eyebrows perked. "Uh oh."

"Uh oh is right." He shook his head. "Whilst I thought I was in control of my magic by then, 'twas not the case. All went well enough when I used wooden swords. However, when I swung my first metal sword, everyone realized fast that the weight and mayhap the element of metal made a difference."

Jackie scrunched her nose, amusement in her eyes as she leaned forward. "What happened?"

"I remember the day well as I'm sure most of my clan does. Ma and Da were there. It was high noon, and the sun was bright. The weather was bonnie. There was nothing but a light breeze. One that all should have heeded I suppose." Darach wiped a hand over his face and shook his head, remembering. "When I swung the sword, it rippled the air in a way nobody anticipated. Chickens flipped, and feathers went everywhere. The head cook happened to be passing through at the time and tripped when she couldn't see. Regrettably, she was carrying a tray full of porridge and ale."

He offered her a sheepish look. "Caught in the wind currents I created, the porridge ending up all over the lad I was set to fight. Good thing it had already cooled off. Worse than that, a mug of ale sat overturned on Da's head. He was dripping wet, his outfit a sodden mess. 'Twas most unfortunate considering several lairds from neighboring clans had just arrived."

Jackie put a hand over her mouth, eyes merry as she mumbled, "You're kidding me?"

"Nay." Darach shook his head and smiled. "While Ma did her best to save the day and greet the clansmen properly, she did it through a good run of tears she was laughing so hard."

"Oh, God." Jackie's chuckle turned into a bubble of laughter. "I can totally see it. Your mom would've got a kick out of that."

85

"Oh, she did." Darach chuckled too, pleased by the light in her eyes when she spoke of his mother. "I know 'twas Ma's influence that had Da setting aside that mug and grinning at me before he turned his attention to the chieftains and welcomed them with a wide smile."

"What makes you think it was your mom's influence?" Jackie cocked her head. "Your Dad might run a little serious at times, but something tells me he would've responded that way even if your mom wasn't there."

"Mayhap," Darach murmured. "'Tis hard to know with Da."

"So it seems." Jackie perched the pebble she'd been fiddling with on her bent knee. "But I think he's just that way because of his beginnings. A lone soldier." She kept her knee level and removed her hand so the pebble stayed in place. "I think when people find out at a young age that they've got to act a certain way to maintain their mental stability, their simple humanity, it sort of sticks with them. It forms who they are."

Darach eyed her. "You can relate to my Da?"

"Maybe." Jackie kept her eyes trained on the pebble and her knee steady. "I can understand getting through ones circumstances, and learning to play the cards you've been dealt. Of making the most of a bad situation. I can relate to being grateful that I had a roof over my head and that even with the bad, there's good to be had if you just stick it out."

Darach wanted to ask a thousand questions.

He wanted to understand what put that haunted look in her eyes outside of the obvious.

"Your dad's a good guy. Powerful," she murmured. "But that's not what he wants you to take from knowing him."

Irritation flared just beneath the surface, but he tempered it. Jackie didn't need that. But what did *she* know of his father? Nothing he hadn't already figured out...or so he assumed.

"Da was tortured and imprisoned in the castle I'm to call my own. That I'm to become laird of," he said. "Outside of the obvious, understanding what he wants and doesnae want from me hasnae always been easy to figure out."

"I don't know. I'd say he wants you to be happy." Her eyes met his. "And to keep an open line of communication with him."

He knew what she was getting at and supposed he ought to address it and clear the air. "I'm sorry Da got upset with you about Heidrek. He didnae have all the facts and was looking out for me."

"Oh, I knew what he was doing." She gave him a pointed look. "So does he have all the facts now?"

"Aye, lass." He returned her pointed look. One that had everything to do with her revealing that they'd kissed. "Even more than I would've told him it seems."

A little smirk curled her lips and she shrugged before she scooped the pebble off her knee and started fiddling with it again. "Tell me about your life after you got the hang of magic. You're not married. That's a little surprising all things considered."

He could only imagine what she meant by that. Mayhap his upcoming title and how that might appeal to a lass?

"Nay, not married." Though hard to do, he tore his eyes from her face and focused on the pine nearby. What should he say now? The truth? Lies? How much was acceptable? In the end, his gut told him to keep giving her exactly what came to mind. "I really liked a lass once, but it didnae work out for the best."

"You really liked just *one* woman?" He heard the tempered humor in her voice. "I find that hard to believe."

Darach knew she was hedging toward rumors of him and the Viking lass but kept things where they needed to be. In a genuine part of his past. "I thought myself in love with her. So on the eve of my seventeenth birthday, I asked her to marry me."

"Really?" She eyed him with interest. "That sounds serious."

"Everything seemed so serious back then, including the lasses," he said. "She was the first one I kissed, and I wanted to do right by her."

Jackie bit her lower lip and met his eyes. "Really?"

"Aye." He nodded, realizing too late that he was walking into something that he couldn't turn back from. "I was raised that a kiss was important and that a lad didnae give one unless he felt strongly. Da always said a kiss was not to be taken lightly." His last words trailed off on a murmur. "That it could change your life."

A heavy silence lingered between them until Jackie spoke. "And what did she say when you asked her to marry you?"

"Aye," Darach whispered. "She said yes."

Their eyes held. "Yet you're not married."

"Yet I'm not married," he confirmed. Though tempted to look away he didn't.

"And why is that?"

If she only knew. But to tell her would reveal the depth of his feelings and risk her friendship. Because if she realized how strongly he felt and for how long, she would push him away.

"Because I knew my love for her wasnae genuine," he said. "So I broke off the betrothal."

Besides perking a brow, Jackie's face remained emotionless. "So you broke her heart."

All he wanted to do was explain why. That everything inside him screamed that it was wrong because he loved another. A phantom. Because of that phantom, a woman he had only dreamed of, he disappointed his father. He did something he shouldn't have because he was eager for a kiss.

Her kiss.

Not the lass he was with but the one he'd dreamt of.

Jackie.

It was her lips he imagined when he pulled that lass into his arms. It was her lips he imagined melting beneath his. What else was a teenage boy to do but propose marriage? Especially when his father was watching him so closely.

"Aye, I broke her heart," Darach finally said.

A long, somewhat awkward silence stretched between them before she finally spoke. "You were young. I suppose we all make mistakes when we're too young to know better."

"Aye," he agreed softly, never more grateful for her understanding…or at least her take on it considering the information he'd provided.

But he should have known better than to relax.

"So what's your deal now?" Her eyes met his. "You kissed me after you made it clear that you wanted Cassie, maybe even Nicole, and then you ended up with a Viking girl."

So she knew about his interest in Cassie.

Bloody *hell*.

He could only imagine the comments his cousins would make if they were here now.

"I was attracted to Cassie," he admitted. "She's a kind soul."

What he couldn't tell her was what he figured out after the fact. Her friend reminded him of the lass he dreamt of. Her soft nature. Her sharp intelligence. But at the heart of it, he suspected it was because Cassie was the first Broun who traveled back in time and his soul sensed another was coming. One that meant far more.

Jackie.

"Cassie is a good person," Jackie agreed. "And Nicole?"

"A good person too," he said. "But I wasnae attracted to her beyond friendship. We're too different."

She seemed a bit overly concerned about his attraction to other women. He repressed a smile. That could only be a good thing. And gave him the opening he had been waiting for.

"As to the Viking lass? Nothing happened betwixt us." He held her gaze. "I made sure it seemed like that so you thought I wasnae interested in you. So that you would turn from me. So that I could keep you safe."

"Ah," she murmured. "Seems sort of pointless considering that you intended to push me into Heidrek's arms anyway."

There *was* that.

Something he wished he could undo but tried to keep in mind that at the time he thought there was no other choice.

She kept eying him with a speculative look on her face. One he hoped meant she was beginning to realize that she shouldn't turn from this. That she shouldn't push him away. Instead, she said the last thing he expected.

"I suppose I ought to come clean too," she murmured. "Seeing how I ended up kissing Heidrek."

Chapter Seven

JACKIE FELT AWFUL for saying it but she was determined to push Darach away. He would not die because of her.

"And was it a good kiss?" he murmured with a heavy frown.

"It wasn't bad."

A short silence passed before he inhaled and nodded. "That's good..." He seemed to struggle with the words as his brogue thickened. "'Tis good ye and Heidrek had time together."

She should tell him it was just a kiss on the cheek but she couldn't. Not if it helped turn him away. Because despite agreeing to be friends, it was becoming more and more clear how much he cared about her. Just look at the lengths he had gone to in order to keep her safe.

"So I've told you something of myself," Darach finally said without looking at her. "Might you not share something of yourself now?"

"You really want to hear about my life after what I just told you?"

"Of course." His eyes at last turned her way. "You sharing a kiss with the Viking has nothing to do with you and I becoming friends, lass."

She should have known better than to hope it would.

"True." God, her youth was nothing worth talking about but something about the way he relaxed and offered a small, genuine smile, made her start talking. And she said far more than intended.

"My parents died when I was young. A boating accident off the Canary Islands."

"I'm sorry, lass." He frowned. "That's terrible."

"It is." Jackie sighed. "They were amazing. Fun. Unlike my uncle. He became the...prominent figure in my life."

"So you didnae get along with him?"

"No." Jackie shook her head and tried to keep the intensity from her voice. "Never." She tore her eyes from his again and focused on the pebble in her hand. "He wasn't really the sort who should've inherited a child."

"Why not?" Darach's brows flew together. "I cannae imagine you being all that difficult to raise."

Jackie quirked the corner of her lips. "Let's just say he was more interested in money than kids."

"I dinnae ken."

"My parents were rich. Really rich." Jackie shrugged. "When they died my uncle inherited their estate." She shook her head. "No, he became the executor until I was old enough to inherit it. But that meant he had access to the funds...most of them in the end it seems."

Darach shifted a little closer, interest piqued. "And what did he do with those funds?"

"The better question is what didn't he do with them?" she muttered. "He spent a lot and I wasn't allowed to touch a dime without his permission." She frowned. "The estate paid for my college education, but like a fool, I spent more time going after various degrees than actually settling down and getting a job. A career. I was so frustrated that my uncle was squandering my parent's money that I didn't realize I was too."

"Och, it couldnae be easy losing your parents so young, lass," he said. "And I dinnae think you necessarily squandered their money. "'Tis good to be educated, aye?"

"Thanks for the vote of confidence but I'm already twenty-seven." She shook her head. "It's foolish of me not to have a steady job by now." Jackie gave up on trying to balance the pebble on her knee and tossed it aside. "I almost copped out once to gain access to my inheritance."

"How so?"

How much should she tell him? Better yet, why on Earth had she led them into a conversation that urged her to share how much they had in common one way or another? But when their eyes met, it seemed she was as willing to share as he was.

"I agreed to marry," she said. "As it turned out, my parents were really old-fashioned. I couldn't access my entire inheritance until I got married. As stipulated in their will, they wanted me to find the kind of love they shared before I searched for happiness with something as materialistic as money."

"Wise parents." He shifted even closer though they still sat a good four feet apart. "So you were betrothed?"

"Yes."

"And what came of that?"

"I ended up doing the right thing."

Darach slanted his head and narrowed his eyes. "Are you married then?"

Offended, she frowned. "What do you think considering I kissed you?"

"I think things can happen in the heat of the moment. Especially when a man kisses you and not the other way around," he replied honestly.

He moved even closer.

Leave it alone. Don't take his bait.

But take his bait she did.

"I kissed you back, Darach and you know it." She picked up another pebble and focused on anything but him. "That said, if I was still engaged then that would've turned me into someone I wouldn't be very proud of."

He didn't miss a beat. "So you're no longer engaged?"

"No," she whispered. "I broke it off a long time ago."

Another bout of silence fell as he pondered her statement. "Why?"

"Because I was doing it for all the wrong reasons," she said. "Because I didn't love him. And worse than that, he was hand-picked by my uncle. That meant they likely came to some sort of agreement that would've kept my money from me. More so, they were of the same ilk. Men who like power, luxury, and prestige. Men who expect women to behave a certain way. I'd spent most of my childhood conforming to be the perfect doormat. The opposite of everything I used to be. But at least I had a roof over my head. Because my uncle threatened to put me in foster care more than once."

Jackie shook her head. "I didn't want to continue living like that." She sighed. "But as it turns out, it's been a hard mold to break."

Darach's eyes held hers for a long moment before he nodded. "'Tis a good reason to end a betrothal."

"I never should have agreed to it to begin with," she mumbled.

"Aye," Darach murmured. "It seems we've both done things for the wrong reasons."

Her brows perked. "I don't think what you did was for the wrong reason. You kissed her and I assume slept with her, so thought you should marry her. That's honorable, especially in this day and age. Sounds like you were trying to do the right thing."

Darach shrugged and offered no response. When he rested his arm on the ledge by her foot, her eyes fell to the tattoos wrapped around his bicep and forearm. Amazed she had shared so much and eager to take the focus off of her, she nodded at them. "What's up with your tattoos? It makes sense that Rònan has them because, well, he's *him*." She grinned. "Yours don't really fit a medieval Scotsman."

Darach glanced at his arm and grinned. "You dinnae want to know the reason behind them."

She sat forward and wrapped her arms around bent knees. "I wouldn't have asked otherwise."

"Aye?"

"Yes."

Darach sighed. "'Tis nothing to be proud of."

Caught by the sheepish octave of his voice, the corner of her lip turned up. "Now you *have* to tell me. Why'd you do it?"

"To keep a lass," he murmured softly.

"What?" She leaned closer. "I didn't quite catch that."

"Och." Darach shook his head and met her eyes. "I did it to keep a lass."

"The one you were meant to marry?"

His brows flew together, and he frowned. "Nay." Then he sighed again. "To keep one who had her eye on my cousin."

"Which one?"

Because seriously, none of his cousins were as good looking as him. At least not in her opinion.

"Rònan," he grumbled. "He has a way with lasses. Dragon blood and all."

Jackie bit back a smile. "Are you serious?"

His frown deepened. "Aye, lass."

"So you ended a betrothal to one woman only to tattoo yourself to gain the attention of another?" Jackie smirked. "For real?"

"Aye, 'twas real." He gestured at his arm. "Obviously."

"You know that's not what I meant." She swung around until she sat next to him. "I'm surprised you did something like that to win over a girl."

"'Twas wrong that she ended up with him considering our history," he retaliated.

The minute he said it, she knew he regretted it. "And what was your history?"

"It doesnae matter," he muttered.

When he started to stand, she grabbed his hand and shook her head. "Obviously, it does. Who was she to you?"

Darach scowled and sat back. "Like I said, it doesnae matter."

"God, stop it." She tilted her head until their eyes met. "If we're going to be friends, I'd like to think we can be honest with one another."

Darach started to talk then clamped his mouth shut. So she squeezed his hand and propped her brows. "I won't judge you any more than I hope you judged me."

"Yet I didn't learn all that much about you," he mentioned. "When I would like to know more."

"And you will," she assured. "Once you tell me what happened."

"'Twas just a wee bit of confusion that Rònan and I have since worked out."

"Okay," she said. "I'm listening."

"Clearly."

"Just tell me. Please." Jackie narrowed her eyes. "Who was she?"

He seemed to rally his courage before he met her eyes. "'Twas a lass who reminded me of someone I often dreamt about."

"All right. I suppose I get that." She shook her head. "Why didn't you want to tell me?"

His eyes held hers for a long moment. He was holding something back.

"What is it?" she murmured.

When his eyes dropped to her lips, she worked to keep her breathing steady. What had she been thinking when she moved so close to him? This couldn't happen. *They* could not happen. She refused to risk his life. But damn, it was hard when everything inside her screamed to close the distance.

To kiss him again.

Just one more time.

"Och, lass," he whispered before he dragged his eyes away and stood. "If 'tis friendship you want, then 'tis friendship I will give."

Friendship.

Right.

"And as your friend, allow me to teach you how to fight." He held out his hand. "You need to know how to protect yourself."

He was changing the subject. But considering what he offered, she decided that was okay for now. So she let him pull her up. "I thought you didn't want to train me. What changed?"

"My perspective," he said. "I was wrong for avoiding this. It only makes sense that you learn how to defend yourself."

She wondered if it had anything to do with him knowing she was sick. She wasn't fooling herself after what Grant had shared.

Everyone knew she was dying.

Maybe this was Darach's way of keeping her around a little longer.

"The first thing you should do before engaging anyone in battle is be aware of your surroundings," he said. "What's near you. A tree? Bushes? Slick surfaces? Rock ledges? All will matter as you begin to move."

"Why?"

"Because they can be used against you as easily as you can use them against the enemy. Say you're fighting at dawn." He gestured at a patch of grass. "'Tis likely dew will make that slippery. Beware of such when fighting. For beginners like you, avoid it at all cost. For seasoned warriors like myself, I'd purposefully use it because I fight just as well on difficult surfaces. Therefore, I often lure my opponents to those areas to give me more of an advantage."

"That makes sense." Jackie nodded. "So no treacherous surfaces for me then." Her eyes went to the pine. "What about trees, shrubs and rock ledges?"

"If 'tis a sunny day, any tall object can act as a barrier against direct sunlight. If the sun's at your back, keep the tree there too. Make sure the enemy can see you well, and then shift. The light will blind them, and that's more than enough time to drive your blade home."

"True," she said. "What about bushes and ledges?"

"Bushes can hurt. Drive your enemy back into one and you've afforded yourself another opportunity to injure them," he said. "As to rock ledges and walls, never let yourself get cornered on or against one. Where I would draw them there to kill them or drive them over the edge, it would be a mistake for you to try the same."

Jackie ignored the fact she was heading toward death anyway and kept his advice in mind. Her eyes widened when he tore off a strip of his plaid.

"Do you trust me?" he asked.

"I'm working on it," she said honestly.

"May I cover your eyes?"

"But I thought you were going to teach me how to fight?"

"I am."

She eyed the fabric and shrugged. "All right, I suppose."

"The next thing you need to learn is how to become aware of your surroundings without the use of sight." He stepped around her and tied the strip over her eyes. "Everything counts in battle and considering you're dealing with magic, you never know where you'll end up."

"Okay," she murmured, overly aware that he still stood close behind her.

"Dinnae speak but listen. Become aware of every sound. The wind and what direction it comes from. Where there might be water. Is it trickling like a stream or rushing like a river? Are waves lapping or crashing in a loch or ocean?" He shifted away. "Pay attention to the sound of my footsteps. What am I walking on? Rock, dried pine needles, leaves or broken twigs. All can help you locate my position."

"Listen to where my voice comes from," he continued from somewhere off to her right. "Is the wind carrying it away from you so I might be closer than I seem?" He spoke from her left. "Or does the wind carry it to you and I'm further than I seem?"

"'Tis crucial that you pay attention to every little detail," he continued. "There's nothing more effective than tracking your enemies as you fight. It not only keeps you safer but gives you the element of surprise. You can plan how you're going to attack them while fighting another. The more practiced you become, the more lethal."

Though tempted to say it sounded complicated, she wanted to learn. That meant being a good student. So she nodded. "Got it."

"Tell me, have you ever felt the presence of someone without actually seeing them?" he asked, his voice a ways out.

"Like when someone stands too close behind me in line?"

"Exactly like that," he replied. "Honing that skill can make you a great warrior. The air around you becomes displaced when someone's near you. Though you dinnae realize it, there's a slight temperature change. On some level, you pick it up. 'Tis the feeling you get when the hair seems to stand up on the back of your neck. Or when gooseflesh rises on your skin."

"Oh wow, okay," she murmured. "Interesting."

"Now do what I've taught you," he said. "Focus on your surroundings."

"Okay." Though she wore a blindfold, she still closed her eyes. Funny how unaware of everything she actually was considering she'd been here for a while. So she went absolutely still and started to focus on wind, sound, and sensation.

"I still feel the warmth of the sun on my face and know it's setting in the west. That means the wind is out of the north," she murmured. "Though there's a pine nearby I didn't realize there were several more in the eastern corner of this glade. They have a distinct sound. Not the rustling of leaves but more of a swish when the needles rub together."

Jackie focused more intently. "The crash of waves is louder so the wind is increasing." She cocked her head. "So is the whistling in the cave." Head tilted back, she inhaled deeply. "The air is growing more oppressive, the sea salt thicker. I'd guess inclement weather is coming in."

No sooner did she say it when a distant rumble of thunder rolled across the sky. Jackie smiled. She could *do* this. Excited, she focused even harder. "There's tall, dry grass somewhere. So dry. It almost crackles as it bends in the wind."

She was about to say more but became aware of something else.

A slight shift in the air around her.

Heat.

A presence in front of her that wasn't there before.

Gooseflesh rose as she reached out and made contact with a hard chest.

Darach.

"I never even heard you approach," she whispered. Maybe she wasn't so good at this after all.

Half a breath later, warm, weapon-roughed hands cupped the sides of her neck, and his lips were on hers. Though she knew she should pull away, it was impossible. It was the kiss back in New Hampshire all over again but a hundred times more intense. Maybe because she was so in-tuned with everything right now or simply because he kissed so damn well.

When he slanted his lips more firmly over hers and the kiss deepened, she groaned. He tasted so good as his tongue twisted around hers and the kiss intensified. Just when she was thoroughly drowning in it, he pulled away.

Startled, she tore off her blindfold.

Both breathed harshly as their eyes connected.

"I'm sorry, lass," he whispered, his brogue thickening. "Ye were just so bloody tempting."

Before she could respond, he turned away. "If you'd rather Heidrek teach you at this point, I ken."

Get upset. Agree. Push him away. How could they ever be friends if this sort of thing kept happening? How could she keep him safe?

But if so many years of education had taught her nothing else, it was how to spot a great teacher. And Darach definitely was. So instead of saying what she should, Jackie said the opposite. "I want you to keep touching...I mean teaching me," she stuttered and shook her head. *Hell.*

"Then I will," he said softly. He hesitated a long moment before he turned and his eyes met hers. "But only under one condition."

"What's that?" she whispered, trying to find her voice.

"That you know the truth."

Chills raced up her spine. "What truth?"

"One that might make you change your mind about me," he said. "Especially considering you desire nothing more than friendship."

She narrowed her eyes. "Just tell me, Darach."

His eyes held hers for a long moment before he spoke.

"You are the reason I broke off my engagement," he said softly. "And you're the reason I got my tattoos."

Chapter Eight

"I DON'T UNDERSTAND," Jackie said. "Those things happened when you were young."

Darach was about to respond when Erin telepathically called out, *"Hey, you two. Grant sent me. A storm's coming. You need to return."*

"We'll be right there," Jackie replied, her eyes still locked on his. "What are you talking about, Darach? You didn't know me then."

"Nay, now," Rònan said as he joined Erin. "The storm can affect magic. You're only safest in the main glade."

Troubled, Darach's eyes shot to the sky before they returned to her. "Come, lass. We need to go."

She might want answers but knew better than to doubt Grant. "Then talk as we walk because I deserve an explanation."

"Aye," he agreed as they headed for Erin and Rònan. The last thing he wanted to do was speak of this in front of his cousin. "But mayhap 'tis best left for when we're alone?"

"No, now." She nodded at them. "Thanks for coming to get us."

He knew she was upset. That she felt like she had been lied to. Which, in a vague sense, she had been.

"Sure." Erin's eyes narrowed between Jackie and Darach. *"Everything okay?"*

"Yes." Jackie kept walking. "Darach and I just need to talk."

"Okay," Erin said carefully. *"Want us to hang back?"*

"Nope," Jackie said at the same time Darach said, "Aye."

Rònan's brows perked. "Mayhap we should."

"No." Jackie shook her head. "Erin's my best friend so she can hear whatever Darach has to say." Her eyes went to Rònan. "It kind of sounds like you should hear this too."

Jackie might come across as delicate and soft-spoken most of the time, but right now she was anything but. As he suspected, beneath her tempered façade lay another lass entirely. One determined to take control of her own life. One who was angry and had become very good at hiding it.

He understood that more than most.

So as they walked, he laid his heart on the line. "I've been dreaming about you for years, Jackie. Since I was old enough to desire a lass."

She stopped and turned wide eyes his way. "What do you mean, dreaming about me? Like someone who reminds you of me?"

"Nay." He shook head. "'Twas verra much you." Though tempted to remain vague, he just couldn't do it when pinned beneath her curious gaze. "There were so many dreams. Some were snippets of places I dinnae ken. Others were moments here on Scottish soil. Then there were different dreams altogether." He cleared his throat. "More intimate ones."

"Och," Rònan said under his breath. "Mayhap we should give them their privacy after all, Erin."

Erin put a hand on Rònan's arm and shook her head.

Jackie cocked a brow at Darach. "How intimate?"

"A kiss…or two…" He sighed. "Mayhap several. But nothing more. We never laid together."

Jackie pressed her lips together. "So what's this got to do with you breaking off your betrothal then tattooing your arm to steal back a girl from Rònan?"

Rònan muttered something indiscernible.

Darach shook his head, his frustration suddenly rising. He didn't like laying bare something he had kept close to his heart for such a long time. And though he knew full well she didn't deserve his frustration, he couldn't help but narrow his eyes.

"Have ye any idea what it feels like to dream of a stranger for so long? To taste a lass's lips but wish it were another's? To feel her skin and wish it were another's? To want someone so bloody much knowing she can never be yers?" He frowned and continued walking as he tossed over his shoulder, "I broke off my engagement because she wasnae ye. And I disliked Rònan because he stole a lass that reminded me of ye."

Always aware of the air shifting around him, he knew they were all frozen in place, stunned. So be it. He was tired of the lies. Tired of keeping secrets.

"Bloody hell, Cousin." Rònan strode after him.

Though the lasses soon followed, they hung back.

"You should have said something," his cousin grumbled as he joined him. "'Twould have made things so much clearer. I never would have…"

Darach cut him off. "Of course, you would have. We were young." He kept scowling, his anger still simmering beneath the surface. "Nothing I said back then would have made a difference. You took what you wanted."

"But I never would have," Rònan started.

"Aye, ye *would*," Darach interrupted and spun on him, eyes narrowed. "Ye thought nothing of others but only of yerself. If it were otherwise, ye would have questioned my tattoos."

"*Guys?*" Erin said, her voice distressed.

"Ye got the bloody lass back," Rònan said. "So why are ye still upset?"

Darach came nose to nose. "Because ye felt the need to take her to begin with."

Erin's voice grew a little more intense. "*Um, guys?*"

"I didnae feel a need. Ye all but pushed her at me!" If one thing always held true, Rònan could only repress his dragon for so long. He blinked once, twice, before his eyes started to glow and the dragon tried to surface.

"*For fuck's sake,*" Erin growled. "*You two need to snap out of it. Now. Because we've got big problems.*"

Ensnared by the urgency in her voice, their eyes went to where she pointed. The sky wasn't just darkening with storm clouds but something else altogether. Flashes of light bubbled across the horizon as a long dark shadow undulated overhead in the distance. The demi-god was here. Darach didn't hesitate but tossed Jackie over his shoulder and spoke to everybody within the mind. "*Time to go.*"

No one needed to be told twice.

They moved.

While Rònan and Erin kept running, Darach's feet grew heavy until it felt like he was walking in an anti-gravity environment.

"Oh no," Jackie murmured. "You shouldn't have touched me. You should've left me."

"Bloody hell," Darach muttered as they were dragged backward.

Rònan and Erin stopped and ran back to save them, but it was too late. They were sucked away until everything vanished. The next thing he knew, they were standing behind a cottage on the outskirts of Hamilton Castle.

"Shh, lass. Dinnae say a word," Darach whispered as he slowly lowered Jackie to the ground. When her eyes met his, he put a finger to his lips and shook his head.

"How are we here?"

It took him several moments to realize she spoke within his mind. He knew she could do it with Eara but had no idea she could do it with humans. Darach set aside the rush of lust it caused and replied, *"I've no bloody clue."*

When he heard a familiar voice, he took her hand and pulled her after him until they crouched behind the cottage. *"Say nothing aloud, lass, all right?"*

She nodded, her eyes wide as Darach carefully pushed aside a plank a fraction so they could look inside. *"My Da is in there."*

That is, his father when he was around fourteen winters. Darach bit back emotion at how gaunt he looked. How obvious it was that he had been abused.

"God, look at him," she whispered into his mind. *"So young."*

Darach nodded, grateful she said nothing more, that she refrained from pitying him. Yet it was this—his father's history with this clan—that made Darach so bitter.

Grant sat with a few others around a fire.

"I cannae tell ye how good 'tis to see ye out and about more, Grant," a young man said. "We didnae think…"

When the lad broke off, emotional, Grant shook his head. "All's well now, Bryce." He squeezed the lad's shoulder, his eyes as steady as his voice. "I am out more regularly now, and things will get better."

Bryce? A man Darach now called uncle? His father's best friend and first-in-command?

Bloody *hell*.

"Och, but Keir's abused ye something fierce." Bryce's eyes glistened. "We've heard yer cries of pain from the dungeon these long years."

"Aye, ye heard them," Grant agreed softly. "But ye'll hear them no longer." He met the eyes of each and every man sitting around the small fire. "I am well." He gave them a reassuring smile. "As are ye if yer still drawing breath, aye, my friends?"

When several sighs resounded, his Da continued. "Dinnae seem so down. Yer all as strong as I am."

"Are we?" one of the men said. "When we exist beneath slavery and tyranny?"

"Aye," Grant said. "'Tis because of that ye are strong. 'Tis because of that ye willnae ever give up." His eyes swept over them, the set to his jaw firm. "We will survive this together. And we will find strength in each other. No man need go it alone."

Darach released a shallow breath. He'd never realized how rallying his father had been considering his circumstances. If he had been ripped from his kin then imprisoned for years, he would have been furious and bitter.

"Ye've a more forgiving heart than most, Grant MacLomain," came a soft voice.

Grant's eyes went to a lass tucked in the corner.

Darach squinted but couldn't make her out.

"Might ye give us some time alone," Grant asked those around the fire.

"Aye," they murmured and left.

When Bryce paused, unsure, Grant nodded. "'Tis all right. No harm will come to your sister, friend."

His sister? Aunt Kenzie? It couldn't be.

When Darach shifted forward, Jackie put a hand on his arm. *"Aren't we supposed to stay put?"*

"Aye," he whispered as he watched his father eye the fire without moving. He had never seen such sadness.

"Ye know I willnae hurt ye, lass," Grant murmured, never looking from the flames as he blinked away the moisture in his eyes. "Might ye not join me where 'tis warm?"

A long moment passed before he whispered, "Just a wee bit o' warmth. Do ye not remember what that feels like then?"

"Nay," the lass whispered. "'Tis not something that I am allowed verra much."

"Then come share my fire," Grant urged. "Come warm yerself."

"Will ye be wanting something in return?" she murmured. "The laird's made sure my virginity remains intact, but I'm schooled in other methods of pleasure now."

Darach felt like the ground dropped out beneath him. He had heard whispers that Aunt Kenzie had once been a whore, but he refused to believe it. And his Da had always said she was anything but. That she was a fine and noble lass who had been beneath Keir's rule as well but came out better for it. She'd been spared the horror because she was a lass. Never once had it occurred to him that his Da might have been protecting her honor. What a fool he'd been. What else would the enemy have done with a woman?

As the skinny lass with straggly hair shifted closer to the fire, his fears were confirmed. "God, no, Aunt Kenzie," he whispered.

Jackie squeezed his hand and remained silent.

"Nay, I'll not be wanting a thing from ye, lass." Grant remained perfectly still, as though dealing with a frightened animal. "Sit wherever ye like and warm yer bones."

Kenzie nodded and shuffled closer to the fire until she knelt and warmed her hands, a cautious eye still on Grant. While his aunt might seem timid, a bit of the woman she would become came through as she eyed his father. "Yer a brave sort considering all the harm done to ye." Her eyes narrowed. "Why?"

"'Tis because of all the harm done to me that I'm brave, lass," Grant said. "I might not be able to stop him from beating me, but he'll never destroy what matters most. My soul. 'Tis where my greatest strength lies." His eyes met hers. "Though it might not feel that way now, ye've the same strength. 'Tis the will to survive. 'Tis untouchable."

"I know nothing of strength," she murmured. "I do what I must to keep food in my stomach."

"And that is yer will." He pulled some bannock out of his pocket and handed it to her. "Embrace it. Harness it. Let it be yer shield. And someday, I promise ye, 'twill become an intricate part of who ye are."

She took the bannock and nodded. "Ye speak brave words for someone behind bars for so long. 'Tis an odd place to rally such strength."

"As odd as the place from which I ask ye to rally yer courage from." Grant held her eyes. "But rally we must if we're to survive."

"Is that all we can hope for then?" she murmured. "Survival?"

Grant hesitated as though he sensed something. He shook his head and gave her a pointed look though he said, "Aye, but as I said, survival is found in strength. And we both know Keir needs us to stay strong for various reasons. And m'laird would want me to rally ye always."

His father was showing her one thing while saying another.

That meant he feared Keir might be listening. Based on what he knew of the evil Hamilton laird, that was very likely. He once heard that Keir could see through Grant's eyes via dark magic. Whether or not that bond had been forged yet wasn't worth risking.

Though tempted to approach his father, Darach knew better. They *must* stay out of sight.

No sooner did he think it when none other than Keir Hamilton appeared. While his father had told him what the man looked like, there was no mistaking the dark laird. Evil all but slithered off of him and black sizzled in his aura. When Jackie's eyes widened, Darach didn't take any chances. He pulled her close and put a hand over her mouth. A shiver rippled through her but she remained still.

Honestly, he was shocked Keir didn't know they were there already.

But then he wasn't exactly sure how they got here to begin with unless the demi-god brought them. Yet that made no sense.

"Ye see how good I treat ye, lad?" Keir murmured, eying Kenzie over. "I've had not only this one's life, but virtue saved for ye if, of course, ye become my best warrior." His eyes narrowed. "Ye will always do my bidding, aye?"

Grant eyed Kenzie with lust then fell to a knee and lowered his head. "Aye, m'laird. Always. And yer too kind for saving such a comely lass for me."

It took all of Darach's willpower not to draw his blade and rush Keir for putting his father in such a submissive position. Yet even as he fought his fury, a part of him understood his da was merely playing a part. Right now he was doing what was necessary to keep Kenzie safe.

He had always taken issue with his father embracing the Hamilton clan when he was by birth a MacLomain. Why would he do that when they weren't blood? When they were part of such a nightmare? But, now he was starting to see another picture. One that bespoke a clan that had become who they were *because* of his father. One that Grant didn't feel obligated too but truly loved and cared about from the very beginning. Clansmen that clearly felt the same way about him.

While Darach loved the Hamilton's, he suddenly felt a new sense of pride in them. A better idea of the hardship they had endured. And what they were witnessing now was early on in Keir's reign so that said much about the duration of their suffering.

"Aye then, 'tis good ye see the right o' things," Keir murmured, looking down his nose at Grant. "Mayhap ye'll not make a home of the dungeon much longer. Ye've 'til dark to exercise yer legs and get back to the castle." He grabbed Kenzie by the hair and yanked her after him. "Until he gets his turn at ye, ye'll find other ways to earn yer keep."

Darach pulled his hand away from Jackie's mouth as the room fell silent. When Grant finally lifted his head, a tear slid down his cheek and fury ravaged his features. There it was. The emotion he knew his father *had* to be feeling all those years.

When Darach's eyes met Jackie's, hers were damp as well. He cupped her cheek, thankful for her compassion before his eyes were snagged by what drifted overhead toward the castle. Heavy raindrops started falling, and the wind whipped up, but it had no effect on the cloud. On the evil demi-god. Keir's father.

Jackie's eyes shot to the sky. *"Why isn't he coming after us?"*

He swore the stone on her ring flickered black, but a blink later, it was normal. Then that strange suctioning sensation they experienced back at the glade started happening again. *"We're being pulled somewhere, lass. Dinnae even speak within the mind unless I speak first, aye?"*

"Okay," she said, a tremble in her voice as he pulled her even closer.

Within seconds, everything around them vanished, and something else appeared. Complete darkness except a pinhole of light a few feet away. Darach pressed her head against his chest and stroked her hair so she wouldn't panic. He didn't use magic but took a moment to sense his surroundings. The cold stone. The drafty breeze that came off the Atlantic. The wafting cobwebs.

It didn't take long to figure things out.

They were hidden in a very narrow hallway that ran behind the rooms on the third floor of Hamilton Castle. The light they saw was coming from the corner chamber. A room his father had long sealed off because it was once Keir Hamilton's.

Darach was grateful Jackie wasn't the hysterical sort and followed quietly when he pulled her after him. The hole in the chamber wall was only big enough for one of them to look through. He gestured that he would be looking through it and she nodded.

When Keir entered the room, a fire sprang to life on the hearth beneath a creepy looking altar. Endless black candles dripped wax in long, dark tendrils down the mantel.

How were they here without Keir knowing? Why were they supposed to see this? Because one way or another, the demi-god seemed to be pulling them along. *Almost* as if he didn't know he was doing it.

Keir sank to his knees and peered up at the altar. "Our plans are long set in motion, father. I will get my dragon. I will have Torra MacLomain. When I do, ye shall have yer rings." He bent his head. "Then might they lead ye to the ring that brings ye to yer love."

When Jackie tensed, he squeezed her hand in reassurance and continued focusing on what was happening. He knew from his Da and the Next Generation of MacLomains just how much Keir had wanted Torra. As far as Darach knew, he never had any interest in the Claddagh rings. If anything, he didn't want their power igniting against him.

Yet it seemed he'd had an ultimate goal beyond Torra.

At least one of the rings. And the only way to get it was to have the power of Torra MacLomain at his disposal. But for what? To manipulate time to find the ring that would lead him to his lost love? Really? And what did Robert the Bruce and altering Scotland's history have to do with it?

His eyes narrowed when smoke from the fire shifted and started to blend with something pouring in from outside. The demi-god. He was surprised when Jackie began trembling even though she couldn't see a thing. So he pulled her against his chest and kept stroking her hair as he continued to watch.

"Father," Keir murmured, head lowered.

"Aye," whispered on the wind and blew the candles out. After that, there was nothing but silence. Almost as if the demi-god wasn't there.

"Aye, I hear ye," Keir said. "Once I get the dragon, and we get the rings, ye will. Then we will be unstoppable."

The fluctuation of power in the air that usually accompanied the demi-god wasn't there. Everything felt calm. *Too calm.* That's when Darach realized what he was looking at. Not a demi-god but a wraith. An echo of a man who had once walked this Earth. An inkling of what he would someday become. Until then, he was but a spectrum that continued to haunt his evil son.

Eoghan Dubhdiadh.

The ghost of a Druid.

As he watched the wraith twist and undulate around Keir, he got the sense the Druid poured darkness into his son. Almost as if he was sharing his evil. That's when it occurred to Darach. This might be why they thought Keir was Eoghan to begin with. Perhaps he carried a part of his Da's taint within. If these odd visitations between father and son had been going on for years, God knows how much of Eoghan's dark essence churned within Keir.

Yet as they all knew, the demi-god had still managed to keep his own soul.

"Aye, Father." Keir lowered his head and repeated, "Ye find yer ring, ye find yer love."

Darach frowned when Jackie pressed tighter against him. What the bloody hell was going on?

"Son?" whispered through his mind.

"Da?" Darach shook his head when he heard his father's voice. *"Nay, stay clear of me..."*

Too late. Once Grant locked onto them, he and Jackie were whisked back to the glade. It took several moments to adjust to their sharp transition. Rain poured and night had fallen. Everyone was there. Erin came up and put her hand on Jackie's back. *"Hey, hon..."* She cocked her head and tried to make eye contact. *"Are you okay?"*

Jackie shook like a leaf and pressed against him so tightly he knew she wasn't going to get over it anytime soon. She was terrified.

"I've got her." Darach swung her into his arms and started toward the fire. "I need warm blankets. I know she doesnae drink but whisky too if we've any."

"Aye," Niall and Rònan said at the same time.

Meanwhile, Heidrek walked alongside with his blade drawn and his eyes scanning their surroundings, not convinced in the least she was safe. Hell, Darach wasn't even convinced after what just happened. The only thing that lent him comfort was his father's lack

110

of concern as he muttered, "You're putting white hair on my head far too fast, lad."

Even once they sat around the fire and Jackie was on his lap tucked against his chest, she still trembled. Erin crouched beside them, held a skin to her lips and said, *"I know you've stayed away from this since your prognosis, but I think we're beyond that at this point."* She gave her a stern look and ordered, *"So drink up and calm down, Sweetheart."*

When Jackie started to shake her head, Erin narrowed her eyes. *"This isn't up for debate. A little booze isn't gonna put you under."*

"But," Jackie whispered.

"No 'buts'," Erin said. *"You nursed me back to health. This is my way of returning the favor."*

Jackie's trembling subsided a wee bit, and her voice grew a little stronger. "I spent a month taking care of you. A sip of whisky returns that favor?"

Erin grinned and winked. *"Just drink already."*

"Fine," she murmured and took a quick sip.

"More," Erin ordered.

"Bully," Jackie whispered before she took a deeper gulp.

"Sure am." Erin offered a comforting smile and sat beside them. Nicole sat on their other side.

Erin squeezed Jackie's hand and whispered, *"Can you feel this?"*

When Jackie nodded, he frowned. It was the same thing Adlin had asked before. Something to do with her illness.

Jackie didn't drink any more, but the trembling *did* subside. The children were sleeping, and the adults remained quiet as they waited for her to adjust. She eventually loosened her grip on him and pulled away. He made sure the blanket stayed around her shoulders as she sat between him and Erin.

Her eyes went to his father first, and though she might be coping with what had just happened, they lit with compassion. "I," she started then stopped as her eyes shot to Darach's and she shook her head.

He understood. She didn't want to be the one to share the first half of their odd adventure. So he did. Whether or not his father intended it to be a secret or not, it needed to be told. When finished, he inhaled deeply and met his father's eyes. "You made me bloody proud, Da. I knew 'twas a verra difficult road for you, but I never saw it as anything other than harm done to you." He shook his head. "And whilst there was certainly harm done, you rallied our clan..." His voice caught. "Including Aunt Kenzie and Uncle Bryce."

Pain flickered in Grant's eyes but also that same strength Darach had seen in his Da when he was so young. Though his father's eyes might be moist, his words were strong. "Whilst I would have preferred to be with you when witnessing such a thing, I'm glad you took from it what you did." His eyes went to Jackie. "But that isnae what has you so upset. When you're ready, please share, lass. Though 'tis hard 'tis important."

"Aye." Darach's eyes met Jackie's. When she nodded, he understood. She wanted him to continue.

"What pulled us from here wasnae Keir or even the demi-god as we now know him. It couldnae have been. We were too protected. Too unknown." He shook his head. "As though we were dragged along without intention."

Grant narrowed his eyes. "Not by Keir but by the demi-god, Eoghan Dubhdiadh?"

It didn't go unnoticed that Jackie took another swig of whisky.

"Aye." Darach nodded. "But he was merely a wraith of the druid he once was." Then he shared his speculations on Eoghan's dark influence over Keir.

"'Twould verra well explain why it was thought Keir was Eoghan," Grant murmured, troubled. "And but proves yet again how truly evil the demi-god is that he would use his own offspring in such a way." He frowned. "Though I speculate Keir was dark enough to begin with."

Everyone fell silent as they pondered the news. The only thing he hadn't shared was Jackie's intense reaction or those final words that seemed to put her over the edge. And while tempted to blurt it out, he wanted to speak with her alone if it made her more comfortable. Because, for whatever reason, that last bit sent her into sheer panic.

But it seemed she was ready to speak.

"There's more," she whispered then cleared her throat. Her eyes scanned everyone before they landed firmly on Grant. "Something I think might be important."

"Aye, lass?" Grant said softly...patiently.

"What Darach hasn't told you yet is what Keir said to Eoghan." She took a deep breath. "He told his father that if Eoghan found the ring, he would find his lass."

"Well, that's interesting." Grant's eyes narrowed. "But why does that bother you so?"

Though he got the sense she wanted to bolt, Jackie sat up straighter, kept her eyes trained on Grant and said the last thing Darach expected.

"Because I'm fairly certain I'm the woman he's talking about," she said. "I think we were in love."

Chapter Nine

HAD SHE REALLY just shared that? Should she have? By Grant's reaction, yes and far sooner. By Darach's reaction, probably not.

Nobody said a word.

Silence stretched.

Then Nicole in typical Nicole fashion murmured, "Well *shit*, I never saw *this* coming."

Grant's eyes flickered from Darach to Jackie, voice firm and none-too-pleased. "What do you *mean*, lass?"

Erin nudged Jackie's skin of whisky. "*Another sip isn't gonna kill ya.*"

Heck, even before her diagnosis she wasn't a big drinker, but the look on Darach and Grant's faces might just change that. So she took another sip.

"Back at the Highland Defiance, when we were with Adlin." God, she was going numb, and it had nothing to do with whisky. Forgive. Forgive. When Erin squeezed her hand, she felt nothing. When Darach's leg touched hers, she felt it.

What *was* that?

Why did she always feel him?

But right now wasn't the time to be curious. Right now they needed to get to the bottom of things. So she continued.

"Back at the Defiance I had a nightmare," she explained. "I'm pretty sure I was in the Celtic Otherworld. It was gray, lifeless, so much dead grass."

"That sounds about right," Rònan said.

"There was a man there," she said. "He had a long black cape." She shook her head and made a motion with her hands. "It almost seemed like flames came off of him."

Grant didn't let stunned silence settle long before he nodded. "Go on."

"Okay." She took a deep breath and continued sharing, something she probably should have done sooner but had thought it was just a nightmare...hoped it was.

"He seemed to know me." She glanced at her ring. "He said if I took off this ring, all would become clear."

"But that makes no sense." Darach frowned. "You got upset when Keir spoke of Eoghan finding the right ring. Wouldn't that imply that you needed to wear it?"

"No, Son," Grant whispered. "Not necessarily."

"What do you mean?" Darach asked, upset. "I dinnae ken."

"I think the demi-god wanted me to put the ring on so that he could find me." Jackie swallowed. "Because when he saw me in the Otherworld, he wanted me to take it off. He wanted me to remember." She shook her head, her gaze falling to the fire. "Something that happened between us in…"

When she struggled to say the words, Grant continued, "In another life, aye?"

"In another life?" she croaked. "I hope not…maybe."

But how could that be? Yet Darach had to be thinking the same thing as her. No wonder Brigit kept the real ring from her. Especially if it was a beacon for Eoghan.

Grant's eyes shot to Erin. "Tell her what you learned about you and Rònan. Tell her what can happen."

Erin frowned, clearly upset as she shook her head. *"It can't be the same sort of thing."*

"Erin?" Jackie asked, confused by her behavior.

Erin ground her jaw and met her eyes. *"Rònan and I are not only dragon mates but soul mates."*

Jackie offered a small smile. "That's great but what does that have to do with this?"

She barely felt Erin's hands when she took hers and searched her eyes. *"Rònan and I met before. In another lifetime. To be dragon mates we needed to be soul mates first. So, what Grant's trying to say is that you're likely reincarnated."* She shifted closer, still frowning. *"He's implying that you might have lived another life."* Erin shook her head. *"One with the demi-god. Because your souls obviously know one another."*

Jackie had no idea what to think of that.

What to make of it.

Yet when she went to shake her head no, she couldn't. Instead, all she could do was stare at the fire. And remember how *real* it had all felt. The Celtic Otherworld. Her surroundings. Home but not.

116

"I don't love him," she whispered as her eyes met Grant's. "I don't know him."

"I dinnae think you do," Grant said softly. "Not in this lifetime anyway."

Bile rose in her throat.

Did they *all* think she was in love with the enemy in another lifetime? In love with someone evil?

"That's why you said I shouldnae have touched you when the demi-god first passed over, and we were pulled to the cottage," Darach murmured. "You were afraid you shared some sort of connection."

Jackie nodded. Though tempted to drink more whisky, she wanted to keep a clear head. "I guess I did," she murmured. "I'm sorry. I should've said something sooner."

"Nay." Darach squeezed her hand. "*I* should have." His eyes stayed with hers. "Jackie, I shared some of that nightmare at the Defiance with you. I was riding Eara determined to save you from the demi-god. And I did. I think. I scooped you up, and Eara raced over the cliff. It felt like something I had done before. *We* had done before. I awoke before you, calm...knowing you would be upset."

Jackie's heart slammed into her throat, and she shook her head. "No, it was a man in armor with a brown cape." She struggled to swallow. "The same one I thought I saw…"

"Where?" he whispered when she trailed off.

Struggling to remain calm, she continued. "In the stables at the Highland Defiance. The same knight appeared. And like the demi-god, he had an Irish accent. He said it had been so long since he saw me. Then asked if I was well? He seemed so...sad. As though he really missed me." Her eyes met Darach's. "But a second later, you stood in his place. Exactly where he had just been."

A stunned silence fell again before Grant finally spoke.

"Bloody hell," he said. "It seems you're caught in some sort of love triangle that has withstood the ages, lass." His eyes locked with Darach's. "Mayhap before ye were a Scottish warrior, ye were an Irish warrior, lad."

Darach and Jackie's eyes rounded on him.

"Holy *crap*," Nicole whispered as Erin murmured, *"I'll be damned."*

"You mean to say Jackie and I likely knew each other in another lifetime?" Darach's brows lowered. "That we may have been in love?"

"Stranger things have happened," Grant said, troubled.

Jackie got the sense Grant wanted to say more, but didn't. Good thing, because she could connect the dots. While it might seem romantic that she and Darach came back together, it also meant his son was somehow interlocked through time with a monster. And based on what the demi-god said, it could have very well been a love triangle.

Which made her sick to her stomach.

Not because of Darach, of course. He seemed to be the only saving grace in what might be a very dark history.

"I need to process this," she whispered, trying to ignore the numbness. "I need time alone."

"Aye." Grant nodded. "There are small caves nearby. As long as you stay in one of them, you'll be safe." His eyes went to Rònan and Erin. "You two go with her."

"I will as well," Darach said.

"Nay." Grant shook his head. "We need to talk."

"Och," Darach muttered and frowned before his eyes met hers. "Will you be all right, lass?"

"I have no idea," she murmured. When she stood, Nicole did as well.

"I want to come with you guys too." Her eyes pleaded with Jackie's. "Please? I need to know you're okay."

"I am," she assured, and though she couldn't feel a thing, she squeezed Nicole's hand. "I know you're worried about me. I'll be okay. I swear. I just need some alone time."

"You're not okay in the least." Nicole's eyes grew moist. "Why didn't you tell us you were so sick?"

"Because," Jackie started and shook her head, wondering how much she should say. But the look in Nicole's eyes tugged at her heartstrings. "Because I didn't want you to feel like this. I didn't want you to be sad. I wanted things to stay normal between all of us before our disabilities changed everything."

"But you're not facing a mere disability," Nicole whispered.

"There's nothing *mere* about any of your disabilities," Jackie argued but kept the distress out of her voice. "Right now, I'm all right. So let's just take things one day at a time, okay? Please don't treat me differently. That's the last thing I want."

Nicole searched her eyes for a long moment before she muttered, "Fuck," under her breath and wiped away a tear. Her eyes shot to the sleeping boys. "I mean fudge." She released a heavy sigh and pulled Jackie in for a hug, murmuring, "Okay, I get it. No special treatment."

Jackie closed her eyes and tried to ignore that she couldn't feel Nicole at all. Thankfully, Erin hooked arms with her as they walked away. She might not be able to feel her best friend, but something about her presence bolstered her strength. And, believe it or not, that helped her work through her numbness.

They didn't go too far before Rònan led them down a narrow hallway into a small cave. Only a small waterfall caused by rain runoff spilled down the rock in the corner but kept going into some unseen outlet so the cave remained dry. He dropped an armful of wood in the center, flicked his wrist, and a fire ignited.

His eyes met Erin's, and he nodded before leaving. She knew he wouldn't go far. He would never travel far from Erin if he didn't have to.

Erin pulled a blanket out of her satchel and laid it on a patch of grass before she gestured for Jackie to sit next to her. She said nothing at first but wrapped her arm around Jackie and urged her to rest her head on her shoulder. She didn't cry. Not really. Maybe an errant tear because she was so sad…and scared.

After a good ten minutes, Erin finally spoke. As Jackie knew she would, her friend cut to the chase. *"Well, everything's out in the open now. Not just your illness but shit you didn't anticipate. The way I see it, only one question remains. And it's a damn important one."*

Jackie sat back. "What's that?"

Erin met her eyes. *"What are your feelings toward Darach now?"*

"The same as they've always been." Jackie focused on the fire. "I like him."

"Uh huh." She knew Erin's eyes remained on her face. *"You just 'like' him then. Nothing more?"*

"I don't know him well enough to feel anything more."

"You're bullshitting me." Erin nudged her shoulder. *"In fact, I'm pretty sure you were less than honest with me when we spoke earlier."*

Jackie shook her head and kept her eyes on the fire.

"Hey," Erin said. *"Look at me already and tell me you were straight with me about him earlier. I wanna see the truth in your eyes."*

Knowing full well she wasn't getting out of this, her eyes met Erin's. "There's something that happens between me and Darach that doesn't happen with Heidrek. A strange sort of compulsion."

"Compulsion?" Erin's eyes perked. *"Like he enchants you?"*

"Kind of." Exactly. "It's intense. Different. More than simple attraction. I haven't felt anything like it before so I assumed it was because he's a wizard." She shook her head. "Now I know it might be because..." she cleared her throat, "because we might have lived another life together."

"You mean, been in love before."

"I mean lived another life," she reiterated. "Besides, Heidrek is still a possibility."

"Actually, I don't think he is." Erin shook her head. *"It seems he's not pursuing you anymore."*

Jackie ignored the sense of relief she felt. She cared about Heidrek, but sparks didn't fly with him like they should. "What do you mean?"

Purple flared in Erin's eyes. The dragon sensed Jackie's reaction. *"I'm glad to know you're not crushed."* She shrugged. *"Apparently, he feels that he's connected to one of my relatives."*

"One of your relatives?" Jackie frowned in confusion. "But you don't have any...that are blood-related anyway."

"I know. It's weird. And I tried to tell him that," Erin said. *"No blood relatives so no possible dragon-shifters in the family."*

"Strange," Jackie murmured. "So could he be talking about the cousins you moved in with after your dad died? Friends of the family. Maybe he's not interested in dragon-shifters in the least."

"Oh, he's all about the dragon blood," Erin assured. *"Or so it seems."* She cocked a grin at Jackie. *"You've met a few of my cousins. Can you imagine any of them being half-dragon? Comical. Especially the two I put up with the most. With the one, it'd be like*

throwing fireworks on flame. With the other, introducing a psycho to sanity."

"You must be talking about Cybil and Samantha." Jackie chuckled. "Samantha was excitable and always causing havoc. And Cybil was the endless dare-devil who put you to shame when you were kids. You had a few other cousins too," she reminded. "Big family."

"Ugh, don't remind me. I can't believe my Dad's best friend had five daughters." She shook her head. *"Insanity nowadays...or in our day that is."*

"Your dad's best friend. AKA, your uncle."

"Fine, my uncle," Erin relented. *"And Cybil didn't put me to shame,"* Erin groused. *"I kicked her ass repeatedly."*

"That's not how I hear it." Jackie grinned. "Sounds like she won a lot of competitions between you and…"

"All right, buzz kill," Erin interrupted. *"Enough about Cybil. She's part of my past."* Her friend eyed her. *"And right now, we're talking about your present."*

"I'd rather not."

"But we are," Erin said. *"Things might not be as bad as you think. When I first met the demi-god, he tried to tell me that we were meant to be together too. So don't overthink the whole soulmate, lived-another-life-together-thing."* Her eyes held Jackie's. *"The guy's an evil dirt bag. He'll say anything to get a hold of one of the rings."*

"True," she relented. "But I had such a strong sense of familiarity. The same feeling I had when I first saw Darach."

"I felt that way with the demi-god, and now we know why. Maybe he's pulling the same sort of trick on you. Maybe he visited you in your past, and you just don't remember."

"Maybe," she started, but her words faded away when Darach ducked in out of the rain.

It felt like the cave became a million times smaller.

Erin's eyes flickered from Darach to Jackie. *"Why don't we finish this conversation later?"*

"What?" Jackie said within the mind. *"No, wait."*

But it was too late. Erin was gone, and Darach plunked down beside her. Though tempted to bolt, she was made of stronger stuff than that. They needed to talk...to make sense of things. Yet despite her best intentions to remain calm, he had a way of making her heart race.

Yet she didn't go numb.

He handed her a skin. "I brought water."

"Thanks." She took a swig, grateful for anything that delayed the inevitable. He eyed the fire with a firm set to his jaw as though debating how to handle the conversation.

"Any chance you brought whisky too?" she said.

His eyes met hers. "Aye?"

"Yes." She offered a small shrug and a half smile. "I wasn't going to drink anymore, but a sip or two might help calm my nerves. It's be a rough day."

"Aye," he agreed as he pulled a skin out of his satchel and handed it to her. "But something tells me 'twill not be as hard as days to come."

"I think you're right." She took a sip before handing it back. "Again, I should have told you and Heidrek about my nightmare at the Highland Defiance right away. It might've helped somehow."

"No need to be sorry. I should have told you I was part of your nightmare too." Darach sighed. "Trust me, I'm more at fault considering I ken magic. I knew it was unusual. I just…"

When he trailed off, she said, "What?"

Darach's eyes slid to hers, looking somewhat guilty. "My reasons for not sharing earlier arenae exactly admirable."

"No?" she said, grateful she didn't sound half as breathless as she felt. If she intended to keep him at arm's length, she needed to stop being flustered by simple conversations.

"Nay." He shook his head, brogue thickening. "Somehow I saved ye in the Otherworld. When I did, it became something we shared even if you didnae know I was there." He shrugged. "'Twas a connection betwixt us. Something I had over Heidrek."

"Ah," she murmured, heat warming her skin at his possessive tone.

"Something's been weighing on my mind," she said. "I was going to speak to you earlier about it, but I was trying to get over the shock of learning I could resurrect. And of course dealing with the fact that if someone loves me, they die."

"'Tis a lot to try to come to grips with," he agreed.

"It certainly is." She eyed her ring. "Anyway, I've been mulling over what you told me at the Defiance about this ring. I should have reacted differently. Been more thankful." Her eyes met his. "You were trying to act as some kind of decoy, right? That's why you avoided me...and why you pushed me toward Heidrek?"

He nodded. "'Tis all right, lass. You were trying to ken a lot. But aye, I did my best to stay away from you and keep all of the attention on myself." His eyes went to the fire. "That's why I never should have kissed you. It might've caused the demi-god to take a greater interest in you. And that might have proven the end of everything."

"How so?"

His eyes returned to hers, emotion evident. "Because I would have given him the ring to keep you safe."

"No," she whispered, unable to tear her eyes from his as she shook her head. "You would have done the right thing. You would've protected the ring and Robert before anything else."

"That's where you're wrong," he murmured. "At first, I thought mayhap I was strong enough. That I would do what was right no matter what." He shook his head. "But I've never been so wrong. If all the dreams werenae enough, every glimpse I caught of you in Scandinavia and Scotland only made things worse." His brogue thickened. "Lass, I loved ye before I even met ye. Now that I have, the feeling has only grown stronger."

Her heart leapt into her throat. He could not love her. Not if what Grant said was true. She wouldn't allow it.

Before she could respond, he said, "I think that's why the real ring ended up back on your finger. Brigit must have realized things werenae going according to plan."

"This is crazy." Her eyes dropped to the ring. It looked the same as it always had. "Dreams aren't real. So you don't really know me. That means you can't love me, Darach." Her eyes went to his. "What if your Dad's right about me? Do you *want* to die? What good would that do anyone?" She shook her head. "It would hurt everyone who loves you and those you're determined to protect."

"I dinnae care about dying. Now that the ring has returned to your finger I intend to protect the lass who wears it. Therefore, protecting the king. The only difference between my cousins and me is I already know where my heart lies. They didn't. " Darach's brows

123

drew together. "This isnae something I can merely stop feeling because I wish it."

Jackie had no idea how to respond to that except to make him see logic. Anything to keep him away. She held up her hand. "Its stone doesn't glow your eye color. That's kind of telling, don't you think?"

"I think like all the rings before it, 'tis fickle and will glow when 'tis ready." His eyes narrowed. "But I can promise you this. No bloody ring will change the way I feel."

Yet she saw trouble flicker in his eyes. Not self-doubt but something else.

"So it seems both you and the demi-god dislike the ring," she murmured.

When he clenched his jaw, she knew her statement explained his troubled look.

"What is it?" she said.

Darach arched his brow in question.

"Is there something else about this ring I should know?" She frowned. "Something you're not telling me?"

"Nay." He shook his head. "Nothing more than my dislike for its control over so much."

"I don't know," she said. "These rings have found my friends some amazing men. Supportive guys who love them. That's pretty impressive."

"Aye," he agreed. "And I'm happy for them." His eyes searched hers. "But they need naught be the only ones to find such love, Jackie. Such support."

"It can't happen between us, Darach," she reiterated as her chest tightened.

His hand slid into hers. "Because you're dying?"

"Yes," she breathed and tried to pull her hand away, but he wouldn't let go. "Another thing I should have shared earlier. I should've told both you and Heidrek that from the beginning." She cursed the tremor that rippled through her. "And now that I know whoever loves me will die as well, it's a definite that no guy's getting close to me."

"'Tis too late," he said softly. "I'm already close to you."

When she started to shake her head, he cupped her cheek and locked eyes with hers. "I've been in love with you for a long time,

124

Jackie." He cupped her other cheek. "Nobody can change that. Not an evil demi-god. Not even your own denial."

She licked her lips, shocked when she didn't go numb as fear ripped through her. Amazed that she could still feel him.

Pull away. Don't let this happen. He'll die.

"You think you love me," she whispered. "But you don't know me...at least not in this life."

All her good intentions became a distant whisper of warning when he closed his mouth over hers. Possible reincarnation meant nothing as their lips parted and his tongue met hers. As it had been at the Highland Defiance then in the small glade, she suddenly felt as though she were outside herself.

As if she drifted in another place.

Nothing about the way they came together made sense, but she still wanted more. So much more. He called it love. She called it lust. Because what else could it be? A heavy need blossomed between her thighs. A driving desire that had her digging her nails into his forearms and moaning when an intense ache spread through her body.

"Lust not love. *No* love," she half whispered, half murmured over and over when he brought her to the ground and ran his lips down her neck. She tried to push him away, but it was a weak effort as his hands began stroking everywhere. Clothing didn't seem to matter in the least.

"Oh, God," she mouthed, but nothing came out as he seemed to measure her body in ways no other man had. She bit the corner of her lip when he stroked, cupped, massaged, pinched, then kissed his way over her breasts, worshiping them so thoroughly he had her groaning.

All the while, his hands were on her waist, circling, pressing, searching in an erotic fashion that had her squirming. It was as if a dozen hands touched her at once. When she peered down, she realized he must be using magic. Manipulating the air. Because his hands weren't everywhere that she felt sensation.

"What?" she gasped before his lips closed over hers again and his whispered words blew through her mind.

"I cannae help it, lass. Ye have a way of drawing out my magic."

Magic he probably shouldn't be using. "Oh!" She arched against him as pressure built everywhere. Her arms, neck, chest and lower back. Outer thighs. Ass. Inner thighs.

Then upward.

Closer.

So close to where she needed it most.

Teasing.

Tempting.

"Don't love me," she managed to rasp before his lips again closed over hers, and all good reason fled. Gone. Lost. Completely vanished. He tasted like warm sugary male. He smelled like every good memory she'd ever had.

Somewhere way, way in the back of her mind she knew she was putting him in harm's way.

That this was wrong.

Harmful.

Lethal.

Yet their lips pressed tighter, eager to fit more securely, determined to somehow meld. Their tongues tangled and lapped and sought. Desperate, they struggled to get closer as they tore at each other's clothes. She was so caught up in passion it never occurred to her that she no longer laid on a scratchy blanket but soft, warm grass.

Stop *now*, she preached to herself. Nothing good can come of this.

But nothing connected as she felt him against her.

Over her.

Pressing down.

His arousal.

Their lips only separated long enough for them to yank at one another's clothes. He bent so she could pull his tunic over his head. She paused so he could pull down the front of her dress.

Then they were on each other again, eager to feel and taste flesh. She kissed, nibbled then laved his tattoo, wanting to claim it as her own. Meant for her. Meanwhile, he pulled her nipple into his mouth and sucked hard. When she cried out, he offered no mercy but yanked her skirt up and trailed a hand up her thigh until he made his way to…

"Hell!" she cried when his fingers found what they were looking for.

Any hope at stopping this was long gone when he rubbed his palm against her clit, pressed a finger deep inside and sucked her other nipple into his mouth. She cried out, and by instinct, reached between his legs, grabbed him and groaned. He was rock hard. Large. She squeezed instinctively.

"Bloody hell," he growled close to her ear. "Bloody *hell*."

Jackie felt like a blasted virgin as she kept squeezing without doing anything else in the least to pleasure him. It was as if this was the first time she'd touched a damn penis. In truth, though? It was the first time she had actually felt one in a while. A man for that matter. Because once she got excited, everything went numb.

But she felt Darach. Every last inch of him.

And she was beyond excited.

This felt amazing.

Yet she knew what would feel far more amazing. They both knew as their eyes locked then their lips crashed together again. He didn't have to love her. She would make sure he didn't. Later. After.

Because there was no stopping what was happening.

Not in a million years.

Or maybe just lifetime after lifetime.

Her skirt was still wrapped around her waist when he finally covered her completely and his hard flesh touched hers. She moaned with relief and anticipation.

It felt like she had waited for this for so long.

To feel the weight of his body.

To hear the heaviness of their breathing, quick and desperate for each other.

She wanted this over and over, again and again. It was like a memory she had forgotten but somehow better because she remembered. Every inch of his body felt like a new place to explore. Every sound she drew from his lips something she hadn't heard in far too long.

"Och, I missed ye," he whispered against her skin, neck, cleavage.

Jackie didn't care what he meant because somehow she related.

She had missed him too.

So much.

For a second she thought her ring flickered but was too consumed by him to glance at it again. Breathing became more and more difficult as he kissed her everywhere and spread her legs with his muscled thighs. She felt like she was caught somewhere between the warm sensation of coming home and the exciting sensation of something new. Sweat. Passion. A need for this endless feeling.

Almost a sense of peaking before an actual orgasm.

Her body rippled. It was as if he were already in her. As if she was already part of him. There was no making sense of it. Not until their eyes met. Then only one thing translated.

Now.

"Jackie," he whispered before he thrust.

Her insides seemed to burst wide open. Welcomed. She arched and cried out with pleasure, barely aware he swirled away yet stayed there at the same time. Discombobulated, she tried to hold onto to him, but it became more and more impossible.

What was going on?

"Awaken, Gwendolyn." Someone shook her shoulders. "Ye as well, Devlin."

Jackie gasped when her vision finally cleared. The cave was gone. In its place, rolling green hills and a clear blue ocean. Lush trees blew in a warm wind. A beautiful woman knelt in front of her. Beads and pale gold ribbons were interwoven within her many blond braids. She wore a white gown with a rope of gold cinched around her slender waist.

"I know you," Jackie whispered.

"Of course, you do," the woman said. "I have been your sister Chiomara since the day you were born."

Chapter Ten

Ireland
484 A.D.
Where it all began...

WHERE DID JACKIE go? What the hell just happened? One moment he was in pure euphoria, deep inside her, the next she was ripped away. He blinked and peered through slits at a blue sky.

"Bloody hell!" He sat up and tore off his helmet. Relief flooded him when he spied Jackie. But why were they clothed? Eyes wide, she shook her head as she put a hand over her mouth and stared at him.

"What?" He frowned as he eyed their foreign surroundings and the woman crouched nearby. "Where are we? What's going on?"

"Did you both take a bump to the head, then?" The woman shook her head, disappointment on her face as she eyed him. "I know ye are First-in-command of my father's army and his favorite, but he would ill favor ye indeed if he found ye lying in a field with my sister, Devlin." Her voice lowered to a whispered hiss. "I've done my best to keep this attraction betwixt ye two secret. Now this."

Jackie's eyes were still wide as she finally removed her hand and whispered, "He really *is* you."

When Darach looked at her in confusion, she gestured at him and spoke within the mind. *"Look at your clothes. You're...my Irish knight!"*

Darach looked down. "Bloody hell!" he repeated and stumbled to his feet. He wore wool trousers, light armor including a bronze chest plate and a dark brown cloak. "I dinnae ken."

The woman frowned at Jackie. "Gwendolyn, you need to get home and prepare." Her eyes met his sharply. "And my father will be expecting ye to be by his side when Eoghan arrives."

"Eoghan?" he said into Jackie's mind, finally taking in the enormity of not only their surroundings but her appearance. Though she still looked the same, she was dressed similarly to the lass who now confronted him. He fingered one of her tiny braids. *"I think mayhap we've done a wee bit more than just travel back in time, lass."*

"You think?" Jackie said, a hint of sarcasm in her voice. *"Before you woke up, I learned a few things. Besides the whopping realization that Chiomara's my sister, it seems I'm about to marry a well-known demi-god named Eoghan. Except it sounds like he's just a Druid right now."* Her eyes widened. *"An actual Druid!"* She sighed. *"On an up note, Chiomara apparently can't hear us speak telepathically, and though we think we're speaking English, we can't be. Either way, she understands us. Or vice versa. I have no idea. Magic I assume."*

Darach was about to speak, but she said, *"Another thing?"* She held up her hand. *"My ring's gone."*

He took her hand and frowned at her bare finger.

"Enough of that." Chiomara batted Darach's hand away. "Go do what ye must, soldier, whilst I care for my sister."

Dumbfounded, Darach stared after them as they walked away. Was that truly Chiomara the Druidess? She who would marry King Erc and birth Adlin MacLomain? She had to be. But as far as he knew she didn't have a sister.

While tempted to further explore his surroundings, he figured it would be wisest to follow them. If for no other reason than he had no idea where to go. The only thing he did know was that he and Jackie were Gwendolyn and Devlin in another life. And they clearly were not of the same rank. Nor were they supposed to have feelings for one another. Worse than that, Eoghan was her intended.

Darach shook his head as he walked.

It had long been told that Eoghan wanted Chiomara, so this was some untold part of family history. Just like her having a sister. A frown settled on his face. He had a bad feeling about this beyond the obvious.

"Oh, wow," Jackie murmured into his mind. *"Look at all this."*

They had just topped the hill to a sprawling community overseen by a quaint castle. The community seemed happy enough as they sold wares from their carts. He had no sooner passed through the gates when a buxom lass was on either side, wrapping elbows with him as they grinned.

"Every time Druidess Gwendolyn wanders off ye do too," one complained with a well-practiced pout.

"Ye know ye cannot have her, aye, laddie?" the other said, batting her lashes. "A druidess can only live a solitary life or be meant for another druid."

Darach gave no response, not sure in the least how *Devlin* would respond and not willing to risk it. He merely offered a small smile.

"So will ye join me this eve after the celebrations?" the first lass implored, brushing the side of her breast against his arm.

"Mayhap after he has a go at me," the other informed and winked at him.

When Jackie tossed a look at him over her shoulder, he offered a sheepish grin and shrugged. She rolled her eyes and allowed Chiomara to pull her into the crowd. A crowd that grew so thick she was soon stolen from his sight. It was a good thing that they could speak within the mind, or he would have been a lot more uncomfortable. As it was, it took almost more strength than he had not to toss her over his shoulder and leave.

Anything to put distance between her and Eoghan.

"I dinnae like this, lass," he murmured into her mind. *"Keep talking to me so that I know you're well."*

"I will...when I can."

"When you can?" He scowled. *"We just lay together."* Darach shook his head. *"You know how I feel. Being ripped from what we just shared is hard."*

"Or meant to be," she whispered.

"Och, lass," he started but was soon intercepted by another warrior.

When the man made a curt motion with his hand, the lasses on Devlin's arms sighed and sauntered off.

"The men are ready at the castle, Sir. A bath awaits your pleasure," he said, his eyes locked with Darach's. Devlin clearly garnered enough respect that the bits of grass stuck to his armor would not be mentioned nor even glanced at with disapproval. The other possibility? Maybe Devlin made a habit of napping in the grass. Perhaps he was lazy. But no. That was obviously not the case based on the endless nods of respect not only from the villagers but fellow warriors as he passed by them.

Darach nodded his thanks when the man led him to a cottage then left. A round, wooden tub full of steaming water waited as well as a change of clothes. It appeared he wouldn't be wearing armor tonight.

"Thank the bloody hell," he muttered as he started to remove the uncomfortable stuff.

He narrowed his eyes when someone said, "Sir, allow me to help ye."

A teenage boy melted out of the shadows and started pulling at the strappings on his armor. He had a squire? Interesting.

"Thank ye..." When he perked a brow at the lad, hoping he would provide his name, the boy shook his head in confusion.

There was only one way to handle this. Play dumb.

"It seems I took a bump to the head earlier," Darach explained. "Might ye remind me of your name?"

"Of course, sir." The lad lowered his head. "I am Úistean."

"And how long have ye seen after me, Úistean?"

"Several turns of the moon now, sir." He kept his head lowered but peeked at Darach. "Going on twenty-four fortnights now."

"That long." Darach perked his brows. "Are we friends yet then?"

"Ye are kind to us all, sir." Úistean tilted his head and spoke over his shoulder. "Taggart, go fetch more water for our good sir."

"Aye," came a soft voice and yet another lad he didn't realize stood there exited.

As soon as he left, Úistean transformed. While still respectable, he seemed far more relaxed as he pulled off Darach's chest plate. "Ye were gone longer than usual with her this time, sir. If ye are not careful, people will wonder more than they already do."

"Her?"

Úistean gave him a knowing look as he continued to help Darach. "Were ye not yet again with Druidess Gwendolyn?" Before he could respond, the lad sighed and shook his head. "I have done as ye've asked and spread rumors to the contrary but the way ye two look at each other in passing does no' help your case."

"I cannae imagine it does," Darach murmured. "Have ye been protecting us for long then?"

Úistean's brows furrowed and he inhaled deeply as he eyed Darach. "'Twas a good bump to the head, aye?"

"Aye." Darach rubbed his head. "'Twas bad."

"As far as I know ye've been sneaking off with Druidess Gwendolyn for many fortnights now. At least twelve." He shook his head. "But it could have been far longer for all I truly know."

At least half a year? Darach well understood that. Had he actually been in Devlin's shoes, he would have done the same.

"So what can I expect this eve?" He breathed a sigh of relief as the last of the armor was removed. He could only imagine why he would have been wearing it out on a secret rendezvous with Jackie...or Gwendolyn.

"Nothing ye will like, sir."

When the lad tried to help him unclothe, Darach shook his head.

"So Eoghan is to marry Gwendolyn?"

Úistean nodded. "And I have not heard good things about him." His voice lowered to a whisper. "'Tis said he practices the dark arts."

If Úistean only knew.

Though he dismissed Úistean, the lad paused at the door. "Might I say one more thing, sir?"

"Aye."

Úistean's eyes met his. "Everyone cares a great deal about ye. Do not challenge this Eoghan over a lassie that can never be yours."

Darach nodded, and the lad left. He was about to undress when he spied something in his pocket. Upon closer inspection he realized it was a handkerchief with the letter G sewn into the corner. Fleeting images flashed in his mind of a warm summer day. Green leaves flipped in the wind overhead as he kissed Gwendolyn. Then she pressed this into his hand. A token of her love for him.

He told Jackie about it and heard the warmth in her response. *"That feels familiar somehow. I sense that it was a wonderful day but can't really grasp onto anything solid about it."*

"Aye," he agreed.

By the time he sank into the water, he was more troubled than ever. Why were they here? What was the purpose of this? He didn't need to experience another life with Jackie to confirm his feelings for her.

"But it wouldn't hurt to see what happened, eh?"

He closed his eyes and inhaled deeply at the feel of her in his mind. Now that he was alone, all he *could* focus on were those moments stolen from them. How she had felt in his arms. The look on her face as he pleasured her. The sweet, eager taste of her lips. The way she spread her legs wider when he…

"I don't know what changed between us since leaving Scotland," she murmured, *"but I assume you meant to think about all that sex stuff, not say it into my mind."*

"Och," he muttered but couldn't help grinning *"It seems you might be in my head a wee bit more than before."*

"So it seems."

He smiled wider when flashes of *her* thoughts flickered through his mind. How aroused she still was. How eager and unfulfilled she still felt because they didn't get a chance to finish what they started. Regrettably, her next words quickly diminished his growing erection.

"So I was thinking," she said. *"If I'm Chiomara's sister in this life, and she mothered Adlin, and he's your great-great however many times removed grandfather, wouldn't I technically be your great-aunt several, several times removed?"*

Hell, he was starting to hate time travel. In more ways than one.

"I think mayhap the bloodline would be thinned enough," he began.

"Just kidding." He heard the smile in her voice. *"It turns out we're foster sisters so not blood-related at all."*

Darach eyed his withered cock with renewed hope and a matched grin in his voice. *"I dinnae think joking is your strong point, lass."*

In truth, he was somewhat amazed either of them could find humor considering the circumstances. But he was glad they could. And he was grateful to learn more about her regardless of where they were. Because she was right about one thing. He didn't know her as well as he would like to. Yes, he knew he loved her. It was almost ingrained. But what if she were right? What if it was only because of their previous lives? He understood how that might seem less substantial. It wasn't built on moments they had lived together in this one.

Naturally, she sensed his thoughts.

"You understand where I'm coming from now," she said.

"Aye, lass," he murmured. *"Mayhap I do."*

"Good." Her voice grew curious. *"So where are you?"*

"Bathing. Where are you?"

"Bathing."

His brows perked. *"Aye?"*

"Yup."

"Are you alone?"

"I am. Hmm." A grin warmed her voice. *"Though tempted to pick up where we left off earlier, that probably wouldn't be the best use of our time."*

"I disagree." He smiled. *"I think whatever you have in mind is likely the best use of the time we have left."*

He cringed as he said it because it occurred to him it would revert her back. Not so much to her eventual death but his if he loved her.

"But seriously," she said, going where he knew she would. Away from intimacy or the risk that came with love. *"What's been happening with you since we went in separate directions?"*

Though he'd much rather return to the kind of talk that would appease his renewed erection, he filled her in and kept the conversation light.

"So we've...I mean Gwendolyn and Devlin have been sneaking around for some time?" she said.

"Aye," he said. *"And I get the feeling that they...we, havenae been all that discreet."*

"Yeah, I'm getting the same sense from what Chiomara has said." She paused for several moments. *"But I also get the feeling that she supports me. That she likes you...I mean Devlin."*

"'Tis good I suppose," he murmured, not entirely sure any of this was good in the least. *"Did she talk more of Eoghan? Of your relationship?"*

"A little." He sensed the tension in her voice. *"Enough."*

"What is it?" he said.

"Just..." Jackie again hesitated. *"It sounds like Eoghan has been 'courting' me for at least four months."*

"That long then," he murmured.

"Why, how long have Gwendolyn and Devlin had a thing going?"

He frowned. *"Longer."*

135

"Well, not anymore if what Chiomara says is correct," Jackie said. *"Because Eoghan doesn't sound like a real nice guy."*

"Then why are you...I mean why is Gwendolyn marrying him?"

It was odd talking about another woman who had apparently looked identical to Jackie.

"Sounds like it's pre-arranged," Jackie said. *"Gwendolyn marries a druid from the south and Chiomara will eventually marry a druid from the north. That's how their father wants it to be. To seal in the power around his land."*

"Interesting," Darach said.

"But it gets even more interesting," Jackie said. *"It seems Chiomara has had her eye on another for a long time. Someone she can't have."*

"Who?"

"Erc Breac, King of Dalriada," she said. *"The guy who rules over all these lands."*

"King Erc. He who fathered Adlin."

"Exactly."

Darach narrowed his eyes. *"'Tis perplexing, all of this. Aye, lass?"*

"Better than any novel I've ever read, romance or otherwise."

"I dinnae like it much." He wished she was here, that he could see her. *"Please stay safe. Dinnae do or say anything that might..."*

When he trailed off, she continued. *"Shift the air against my favor?"* He was never more grateful to still hear a smile in her voice. *"Don't worry. I won't do anything that'll lead to a mug of ale upturned on anyone's head...figuratively speaking."*

"Aye, lass." While tempted to tell her he loved her because it felt right, he refrained and nodded thanks to Taggart when he returned and poured more warm water into his bath. *"Listen to everything Chiomara tells you. Every detail matters."*

"I know," she said. *"If it makes you feel any better, what you're asking of me isn't all that different than what I've been doing my whole life."*

He rubbed a bar of soap between his hands. *"No?"*

"No." There was an octave of resolution in her voice. *"Heidrek knows. And I started talking to you a little bit about it. I dealt with this sort of thing a lot. Listening to my elders. Watching the power*

games they played. I'm better than most at paying attention to my surroundings and the way people manipulate each other."

Power games? Manipulation?

And *Heidrek* understood.

Darach scowled, fighting back jealousy when he recalled that she'd kissed the Viking. He shouldn't be dwelling on such trivial things but focusing on protecting her from Eoghan. Irritated with himself, he set aside emotion and focused. On her. On what mattered most.

Before he could respond, she said, *"Chiomara's back. I need to go."*

"Aye," he whispered. *"I will see you soon enough."*

And he better. Frowning, he finished bathing and dried off. When young Taggart stepped forward to assist him, he shook his head. "Thank ye, lad. I can manage. Please leave me."

Within minutes, he was dressed in wool trousers, a finely spun deep blue tunic and boots. Darach was no fool. The clothing meant Devlin was not only first-in-command but considered family. Blue dye cost money. Only those in high favor would be afforded clothing with such color. Even his boots were a rich, supple leather.

Once fully dressed, he tucked Gwendolyn's handkerchief in his pocket, wrapped a leather belt for weapons, pleased with what had been shined and provided. Only then did he realize the blade meant to kill Eoghan was long gone into the future. A life separate from this.

But Darach—like his kin—was nothing if not a survivor. And a ruthless killer if given half a chance. A chance he could only pray he got with Eoghan.

Even if it meant it could change their entire future.

Despite his dark thoughts, he truly appreciated the weaponry. Four daggers. All of which he strapped to his body. A double-edged axe. He managed a smile as he imagined what he could do with that. His smile broadened as he strapped it to his back alongside a gleaming broadsword that someone not only polished but sharpened to perfection.

That only left one thing. The dark brown cloak. Clearly Devlin's signature piece of clothing. That which proclaimed him first-in-command. Darach swung it over his shoulders and left the cottage.

137

"This way, sir," Úistean said, coming to rapt attention before he led Darach forward.

"Ye dinnae go far, aye lad?"

"I never have," Úistean informed.

The closer they got to the castle the scarcer people became. While some might speculate they were respecting the man marrying one of their grand mistresses, he knew better.

This village was frightened.

Though a fraction of the size of Hamilton Castle, it was by no means small with a single moat and drawbridge. The only difference was wear. It was in need of repair. Finances. That became clear as he took in the run down stables and cookery. The horses wandering about were ill-shod and the people's clothing while not threadbare were barely thick enough considering the cool, moist climate.

Darach worked to keep a frown off his face as he eyed the castle's stonework while climbing the stairs. Like his, this castle was close to the sea. That meant never-ending vigilance when it came to updating the masonry. Stone wore more so beneath the wind and sea. It was man's job to see to its survival.

Thoughts of castles and their upkeep faded when he walked into the great hall and laid eyes on Jackie. Perched on a dais beside a dour-faced man and Chiomara, she had never looked more beautiful. Her hair was braided with ribbons and tiny beads. Her dress was long, flowing, satiny white, and tied at the waist with a silver rope.

"Bloody hell," he whispered, astounded.

When their eyes met, his pure awe seemed to magnify. Her gaze filled him with a mixture of emotions. Immense love. Great misery. Untouchable longing.

Change.

So much change his throat closed and it was hard to keep walking.

Then he knew...somehow knew. They were living out a moment Gwendolyn and Devlin had lived. A moment that would change their lives forever.

No sooner did he think it than someone came in behind him.

Walking with a swift, crisp gait, a reed-thin man stopped in front of the dais. With a quick flourish of his hand and worship in his eyes, he announced the arrival of the man who had just entered. "I present my Lord, Eoghan Dubhdiadh, Druid of the South."

Chapter Eleven

JACKIE FROZE THE second she saw him. The man from the Celtic Otherworld just walked into the hall. Living. Breathing. *Alive.*

Eoghan Dubhdiadh.

She had never felt such terror. Such absolute fear.

"Jackie, 'tis all right," Darach said into her mind. *"He cannae hurt you as long as I'm here."*

She tried to respond, say something, but it was impossible.

Eoghan was *real.*

And clearly arrogant as he approached the dais and looked down his nose at the man who was her father. "Lord Sithchean of Ulster," he declared. "Will ye give your daughter, Gwendolyn of Ulster, to me so that ye might have the power of the South behind ye?"

Though shivers raked her at the dead look in his eyes, she didn't go numb with anxiety. No, she felt the bite of her nails as she dug them into her palms. In fact, she felt everything here regardless how off the charts her emotions were.

Eventually, she managed a whispered response to Darach. Short and to the point. How she felt about him going anywhere near Eoghan. *"Please don't. Stay away."*

And she meant it. This guy was pure evil. The idea of him going after Darach made her throat clench and mouth go dry.

"I gave ye my word, Eoghan Dubhdiadh," the man by her side said. "And so it will be."

Not only Chiomara but many others lowered their heads and murmured, "So it will be."

Eoghan eyed her 'father' for a long moment before his gaze settled on her. It felt like every bad thing she had ever experienced dwindled down to this single moment.

One that was going to change everything.

"Please." Lord Sithchean gestured at the tables laid with food. "Might we feast first?"

Eoghan eyed her and her father for several long moments before he offered a brief nod and headed their way.

139

"Ye will be fine," Chiomara whispered with reassurance.

If there was one thing she'd learned, it was that her 'sister' was in her corner. It was clear based on their time alone that they loved each other a great deal.

"I only want the best for you," Chiomara had murmured as she knelt beside Jackie's tub earlier. "Ye need to survive, sister."

"What does that mean?" Though Jackie already pretty much got the gist of it. "I should marry Eoghan without complaint?"

"Yes." Chiomara squeezed her hand and met her eyes. "Forget these feelings ye have for Devlin. Father will never allow it. And if Eoghan finds out, 'twill make his evil wrath so much more vengeful." Her eyes pled. "'Tis evil, sister. That which can cause harm we cannot comprehend."

Jackie meant to say it would be okay, that she would never put them in harm's way, but something else came from her mouth. Something she imagined Gwendolyn once said.

"What sort of life are any of us to lead if we give into Eoghan Dubhdiadh? If we give in to evil so that it might save our people for one more day? Because trust me, a bargain struck like this will see no satisfying end. 'Twill want more, again and again through the centuries."

She was torn from thought when Eoghan sat beside her. Teeth clenched, she focused on remaining calm. And only one person could do that for her here.

Darach.

Or Devlin.

Jackie sipped her mead and watched him. As befit his station, he sat at the head of the table closest to the dais. He wore no armor now. God knows, he didn't look any less intimidating with his wide shoulders and tall, muscled body. She couldn't help but notice his various weapons. They almost seemed part of him. As if he was born knowing how to wield each and every one

When his eyes met hers, she knew he would protect her at all cost.

"Eat and act as normal as you can," he murmured.

"I'll try."

"Don't try. Do. I'm right here, and dinnae intend to go anywhere."

She had never heard the particular octave he used in her mind. A new sternness. But she wasn't fighting it. Darach was all she had here. All that made sense. Outside of her 'sister' Chiomara. A woman who would apparently mark the beginning of so much when she conceived Adlin MacLomain.

Eoghan leaned close and murmured in Jackie's ear, "Ye look very becoming, lassie. But 'twill be good to finally get ye out of those clothes...to make ye mine at last."

Jackie offered him a tight smile. When their eyes connected, she saw three distinct things. Possessiveness. Lust. Obsession.

It was that last one that sent shivers up her spine.

This man would stop at nothing to have her. Actually, Gwendolyn.

A terrible sense of foreboding rushed through her when her eyes returned to Darach. One way or another, he would end up in Eoghan's direct line of fire. She just *knew* it. Almost as if magic warned her.

That's when she realized.

She felt what Gwendolyn once did. It was easy to forget that all of these moments had already been lived. That she and Darach were simply passengers on a ride that had already run its course...that somehow led to the future.

Chiomara and King Erc.

Eoghan's eventual desire for Chiomara.

It was all so strange considering their current circumstances.

When Eoghan pulled her hand onto his lap, dangerously close to his groin, bile rose in her throat. Food untouched, Darach's eyes narrowed on them. Not something he would normally do considering how dangerous things were. No, like her, he was partially a puppet to his other half. Devlin. And both, it seemed, were acting out a play they couldn't control.

"A toast," Chiomara declared and held up her cup. "To a marriage that might see all flourish."

Though Jackie knew Chiomara did it to distract Darach, it didn't work. Instead, he and Eoghan's eyes narrowed on each other. People raised their mugs, but Eoghan interrupted them before anyone could respond.

"I can think of no better way to toast my upcoming betrothal than to see a good battle." Eoghan's pinky finger slowly twirled around the rim of his goblet as he eyed Darach. "Lord Sithchean, your first-in-command against mine. After we eat. Before I'm married. I know just the spot."

"Of course," Lord Sithchean said.

"A fight to the death."

"But you can no' mean that, good Druid." Her father shook his head. "Not on such a blessed day."

"Blessed indeed." A sly smile came to Eoghan's face as his eyes narrowed further on Darach. "We shall call this a sacrifice to the gods so they might show favor to our union."

"But surely death is not such a way to mark our," Jackie began before she was cut off.

"There is no better way to begin our life together than to spill the blood of he who looks at ye with such desire," Eoghan hissed.

Her stomach flipped and though tempted to look, she kept her eyes from Darach.

"He wants you dead," she said into his mind. *"He knows about Gwendolyn and Devlin."*

"That doesnae overly surprise me," he responded.

"No." Jackie sighed. *"It sounds like Gwendolyn was very opposed to this marriage. That she had strong feelings for Devlin long before they started sneaking off together."*

"How long?" Darach said, an edge of surprise to his voice, likely because she hadn't shared this yet. She had learned about it after their last conversation.

"Probably early teenage years by the sound of it," she murmured. *"According to Chiomara, Gwendolyn never loved another."*

"Och, my dreams," he murmured and rested his forehead against his palm. To most it appeared he might be upset over the upcoming battle, but she knew better. Images started to flicker through her mind. Dreams that finally made sense. More so to her because she knew what she looked like when she was younger...the same way Gwendolyn had.

Maybe around the age of twelve, they laughed as they jumped into a river, hand in hand. Then they were a little older. Maybe fourteen. This time, they raced through the woods. She tripped. He was on the ground seconds later, cradling her head, worried she was hurt. At that moment, looking into each other's eyes, something more than friendship sparked. They didn't kiss. Not yet. But soon enough other dreams filtered through her mind.

Far more intimate ones.

But none were so intense as the one where she wore a wreath of flowers on her head. A dress of white. Vows were made beneath a lush green oak tree. They were in a glade surrounded by mountains cut through by a bubbling brook that led to a cliff overlooking a wide expanse of ocean. That's when she gave him the handkerchief.

Darach and Jackie's eyes shot to each other.

"Oh my God," she said. *"Gwendolyn and Devlin got married without anyone knowing."*

"Aye," he said. *"And it happened in an area that we now call the Celtic Otherworld."*

"I tire of tasteless food," Eoghan declared and stood abruptly, yanking her after him. "I wish to see a quick defeat in battle then marry my bride."

All Jackie could think about as Eoghan pulled her after him was what he had said when they'd been in the Otherworld. How he'd implied it was *their* spot. Her terrible sense of foreboding only grew stronger as he led her out of the castle. His warriors suited him well. They were just as dark and ominous as they fell into step behind them.

She suppressed renewed fear when she saw who led them. The man who could only be Eoghan's first-in-command. Bald and rugged, he was as tall as Darach and ferocious looking. His boulder-like shoulders were broad, and veins bulged over heavy muscles. The bear of a man wore a never-ending snarl.

"Dinnae fret," Darach reassured. *"I've fought larger and meaner than the likes of him."*

Somehow that didn't make her feel any better. Nor did the way everyone lowered their heads and backed away as Eoghan led her through the village. Fear permeated the air. It had mothers tucking their children behind their skirts and dogs tucking their tails between their legs as they crouched and whined.

"I don't like this, Darach," she said as Eoghan pulled her after him. *"I've got a really bad feeling."*

"Worry naught, lass. 'Tis just your surroundings making you feel that way," he said. *"All will be well."*

She frowned as Eoghan led her past the gates and up a hill. *"Remember what I said about telling me what I want to hear?"*

"Aye, that you dinnae like it."

"Exactly."

"Well, you've little choice, lass," he murmured. *"Because I'm telling you what needs to be said...for both our sakes."*

Jackie pressed her lips together. While frustrated, she understood. He was as honest as he could be under the circumstances. Something he might not have done even a day ago if it spared her from worrying. Oh yes, she understood his reasoning. More than that, she had begun to realize that it was genuinely difficult for him to be anything but a nice guy. He saw no reason for her to be upset when he could take the weight on himself.

She tried to remain focused on Darach as Eoghan and his entourage led her through the forest toward a special destination. Thankfully, though she was terrified, it wasn't all that hard to keep her mind on Darach. On the glimpses of his dreams. The life they had shared here. One that gave her a deeper understanding of how close they had been. Maybe that didn't count toward what they shared now, but it was...something.

Something she couldn't ignore or pretend didn't happen.

Jackie was so caught up in thought that it took several moments before she realized where they eventually ended up. How far had they walked? The hills were more mountainous and the landscape so familiar that she froze.

"It can't be," she whispered.

"Aye," Eoghan murmured. "'Tis our place. Where I first laid eyes on ye and will ultimately marry ye."

"God, Darach," she whispered into his mind. *"This can't be happening."*

But it was.

They had just arrived at the Celtic Otherworld.

Except it looked far more welcoming. Birds chirped. A light breeze blew, rippling leaves on hundreds of trees. Yet one stood apart from the rest. She recognized it instantly.

A young oak.

It was the same one that would eventually become decrepit and shrunken in the Otherworld. The one she nursed Erin back to health beneath. One she knew Nicole and Rònan had once sat under. More than that, it was the one she and Darach...no, Gwendolyn and Devlin got married beneath.

A marriage that nobody ever knew about.

Was it even valid?

Yet the minute she thought it, her chest tightened and her breathing grew choppy. Gwendolyn took her commitment to Devlin very seriously. Then why hadn't she said something? Why had she let it get this far?

But as she watched the way Eoghan and his men took over everything and felt the darkness surrounding them, she began to understand. Gwendolyn might have fallen in love with and married another man, but she wasn't willing to risk the safety of her people for it. People who were clearly in harm's way if she didn't marry this monster.

Eoghan threw up his arms and declared, "Let our first-in-commands battle here. Let this be a fight for the ages."

A roar arose from both Eoghan and Lord Sithchean's warriors as everyone formed a huge circle, half on one side of the stream, half on the other. Eoghan's man tore off his armor and tunic. Darach pulled off his cloak and tunic before he leapt the water, turned, crouched and bent his head.

"Remember what I taught you, lass," he said into her mind. *"Become aware of everything around you. The direction of the wind. The landscape. Pay attention to it all so that you might see clearer when it matters most."*

"He looks like a mean bastard, Darach," she said, her stomach in knots. *"I think you should open your eyes."*

His opponent chuckled as he unsheathed his blade and swung it back and forth, his steely gaze never leaving Darach.

"Are you aware of your surroundings, Jackie?" he whispered into her mind.

What? *"Are you serious?"* She grew more and more anxious as Eoghan's warrior's started chanting. *"I'm pretty sure it's all about you right now, Darach."*

"Nay." He lowered his head even more, almost as if he was disheartened by what was to come. *"Right now is about us. Our survival. Close your eyes. Tell me of your surroundings. If you were in my position, what would matter most?"*

"This should be bloody good," Eoghan said with a sneer. "Look, your Da's warrior already knows his end comes soon."

"Do it, Jackie," Darach reiterated. *"You're close enough. Close your eyes and tell me what's happening around me. Tell me what can be used."*

Oh, the man! Was this really the best time for a lesson? Frustrated, cornered, she scowled.

"Dinnae be mad, just focus," he said. *"Now."*

"Stand, Darach." She frowned as she watched his opponent pace the opposite shore, a mere fifteen feet away. *"Fight him!"*

"Let Eoghan enjoy the defeat he thinks he already has and tell me of my surroundings," Darach said. *"Once you do, I will continue to teach you how to fight."*

Darach's opponent flexed his muscles as he swung a sword in one hand and an axe in the other.

"Prove to me you're worth training. That you are a lass who can fight like Erin and Nicole."

Her eyes narrowed. God, he was stubborn. For sure, she was worth training. So she closed her eyes, exhaled…and focused.

The wind blew her hair back. The sun had been setting to her right. So the wind came out of the north. It blustered then dwindled then picked up. No storm was coming. The trees barely moved save the ones she stood near. They were caught in a slight but shifting wind. She tilted her head.

Mountains.

They created a wind tunnel.

Eoghan's man took a step. It sounded far away, but she knew it was close.

"Verra good," Darach whispered, sensing her thoughts. *"What else can you tell about his step?"*

She almost opened her eyes. *"That it's damn close!"*

"Nay, Jackie," he growled, so serious she stopped short. *"What else?"*

Pissed off, she kept her eyes closed and tried to focus. His enemy had just walked on the rocks next to the stream, he was ready to lash out, then…nothing…why nothing? What gave no sound…what became silent…

"He's at the edge of the river!" she said. *"The ground is soft."*

"Aye, verra good. Now watch," Darach said calmly. *"And whatever you do, dinnae respond. Keep a level head. I'll be all right."*

Her eyes shot open. What did he mean by that? She soon found out.

Darach never lifted his head but whipped a dagger that caught his nemesis in the thigh. The man fell to his knee, growling as he yanked the blade free. He tossed his head back and laughed before he whipped a dagger. Darach shifted his shoulder just in the nick of time. She almost flinched but schooled her reaction.

Darach stayed put and slumped more, as though he was the one already defeated. Eoghan bought into it and preened.

"I could have killed him already but I would rather everyone underestimate me," he said. *"This also allows more opportunity for you to learn."*

"I'd rather you kill him now," she muttered. *"I can learn later."*

"'Tis always best to assume there willnae be much more time, lass," he said. *"'Tis best that you learn as much as you can now whilst there's battling to be had."*

Jackie kept scowling, but it was apparently pointless to argue with him.

"Under the assumption that I'm an easy target, several more are about to make their move," he said.

"I thought this was supposed to be one on one," she said.

"Och, nay," he murmured. *"A man like Eoghan isnae honorable. He meant this to be a quick slaughter. 'Tis something you should always keep in mind when dealing with your enemy. 'Tis unlikely they will keep their word."*

Two men moved in Darach's direction.

"Always assess the various threats coming at you and plan accordingly. The one on the right wants Eoghan to notice him so he'll make a show of it. It's the one behind him that could be trouble. He has a steady gaze and cares nothing for what others think," Darach said as the first two men he mentioned rushed at him. *"Then there's a third. The real first-in-command."*

What? She had no chance to question him before he continued.

"The axe is a more cumbersome weapon to carry while fighting so I'll use it first and take down my immediate threat. The man who

cares nothing of what others think." He reached his arm over his shoulder then whipped an ax. His target fell.

"A dagger is easier to aim and can take down opponents quicker. Just hold it loosely by the hilt, don't think, just aim and throw." He whipped one at the guy trying to impress Eoghan then spun and whipped another. It lodged in a man's shoulder. *"That's the real first-in-command. I'll get back to him in a moment whilst that dagger does its job and weakens his sword arm."*

All the while, Eoghan looked more and more frustrated.

Darach pulled his sword, leapt the stream and used the edge of the blade to splash water in the big guy's face. The man who was *supposed* to be first-in-command. Momentarily blinded, he never saw what was coming until Darach's blade was through his neck.

Her father's men cheered.

Eoghan cursed, his expression only growing more thunderous as Darach pulled his blade free, leapt the water again and went after the real first-in-command. A slight man who barely came up to his chin.

"Size doesnae matter in the least," Darach said. *"As you'll soon find out."*

Darach wasn't kidding. Despite his injury, the little guy moved with matched speed and agility as they crossed blades. Fast and furious, they drove at each other, spinning, leaping, thrusting. They fought so quickly she barely kept up with Darach's moves. Yet she didn't miss how graceful he was. How could she *ever* hope to fight like that?

"You set your mind to it and practice hard," he responded. *"I will teach you well, lass."*

Jackie pushed her sadness away at the determination in his voice. How convinced he sounded. Because they both knew she didn't have that kind of time. And neither would Darach if Eoghan got his way.

Though they fought ferociously, it soon became clear that Darach had been wise to whip the dagger into the man's shoulder. It was just enough to slow him down and leave him vulnerable when the lethal swipe came and opened his throat. Furious, Eoghan growled as the man fell to his knees in front of Darach.

"Darach," Jackie warned as black started to crackle around Eoghan. *"Watch out. Eoghan's not too happy."*

But Darach was far too busy fighting off several more men who lunged at him. Why didn't her father's men—well, Gwendolyn's father's men—help? But deep down she knew. If they did, not only their lives but those of their families would be in jeopardy.

Eoghan raised his arms and started chanting.

"No, stop," she cried, but it was too late. He had summoned evil.

Jackie didn't think but leapt in front of Eoghan before he brought his wrath down on Darach. Regrettably, she caught the full impact of his fury. She was hit so hard her feet left the ground and she landed on her back. Pain burned and ripped through her chest.

Inescapable, blinding pain.

"Darach, I'm scared," she whispered as she stared up at the blue sky and something warm trickled from the corner of her lips. *"Everything's going numb again."*

From far, far away she heard both Darach and Eoghan's roars of denial. Then she heard Chiomara scream. Yet even that drifted farther and farther away as darkness descended.

And her last breath rattled from her lips.

Chapter Twelve

"JACKIE? CAN YOU hear me?" Darach had never felt such fear...such pain. Not just his own but what Devlin once felt. *"Dinnae leave me, lass."*

Enraged and terrified, Darach took down one last man willing to rush him despite what had happened. By the time he made it to Jackie, her head rested in Chiomara's lap and a wide, black burn scarred her chest. Head bent, the druidess remained unnaturally quiet and still as Darach fell to his knees beside her moments after Eoghan.

She couldn't be dead.

She just couldn't be.

"Ye did this," Eoghan seethed at him. "She was always mine. Never yours."

"Nay," Chiomara said softly, her eyes slowly rising to Eoghan. "She was always Devlin's and ye bloody well knew it." Her eyes narrowed. "Her blood will forever be on your hands, druid. Ye did this when ye forced Gwendolyn to be yours. When ye threatened our people if ye could not have your way."

Horrified, Eoghan stared at Jackie and shook his head. "Nay, I will not let her go." He flung his head back, closed his eyes and started chanting. "I call on Balor, God of Death, give me this lass and I will belong to ye for all eternity."

"Nay," Chiomara cried before she flung her head back, closed her eyes and started chanting. "I call on Brigit, Goddess of Divination, to protect my sister's soul from evil. For this, I will forever do your bidding."

Wind whipped and immense power fluctuated around the druids. Darach pulled Jackie onto his lap. "I've got you, lass," he whispered in her ear, his brogue thickening with emotion. "I'll never let ye go." Then it was Devlin speaking. "I'll find ye life after life till we can be together again. He will *never* have you."

Yet even as he said it, he knew it was being taken out of his hands...out of Devlin's.

151

The grass around Eoghan started to die as he continued chanting. Determined to keep Jackie free of his taint, Darach lifted her and staggered against the wind-driven magic toward the oak. More and more land died as the wind grew colder. By the time he sank down against the tree with her on his lap, their surroundings had begun to look eerily familiar.

The riverbed went dry. Leaves turned brown and fell from their limbs. Even the ocean seemed darker and more sinister.

Everything was turning into the Otherworld.

A place, it seemed, solely created for and by this event.

Darach pulled her closer as dark clouds started to twist over Eoghan. Yet something else happened as well. A golden light formed around Chiomara until a beautiful, glowing woman materialized.

"Ye called on me, child," the woman said. "Ye wish me to save your sister's soul."

"Aye, Goddess Brigit." Chiomara lowered her head. "In exchange, I will do anything ye ask of me."

"Anything?" Brigit kept her gaze steady. "'Tis a great feat ye ask of me, Druidess. One that will require sacrifice."

"Anything at all," Chiomara reiterated. "My sister has watched over me and protected me when others would not. I will do the same for her."

Brigit considered her for a moment before her eyes drifted to Darach and Jackie. A blink later, she stood in front of them. He was unprepared for the emotion that blew through him when her eyes locked with his. While he knew it was the goddess's power, he also realized it was a reflection of what existed inside him. His feelings for Jackie. "Such love ye have for this lass, warrior," she whispered. "Timeless. Enviable. Worth repeating."

The dark cloud grew thicker and thicker over Eoghan.

"Come here, Druidess Chiomara," Brigit said as she made a fist then rubbed her fingers together. Bright light glowed then faded as she crouched. The Goddess took Jackie's hand and slid a ring on it.

The ring.

Jackie's Claddagh ring.

"This is the first of its kind and will protect your sister in the afterlife," Brigit murmured to Chiomara before her eyes met Darach's. "She will find ye again in other lives as will the ring when 'tis meant to be. 'Twill help protect her against evil. But so too will it make her a beacon."

Dumbfounded but grateful, he whispered, "Thank ye."

"As with any divine spell, there must be a price paid. A sacrifice." Sadness filled her eyes. "Hers will be to forever die young as she did in this life. A repeated cycle to keep the balance."

Darach felt her revelation like a punch to the gut. No wonder Jackie was sick.

Brigit's eyes went to Chiomara. "Though ye will remember very little of what happens here today, ye must sacrifice as well. Great darkness comes to assist Eoghan and we must remain one step ahead. For at least this lifetime, I will redirect the druid's passion for Gwendolyn so that he desires ye instead and does not pursue your sister right away."

"Aye, Goddess," Chiomara said. "Of course."

"When I leave here, ye shall travel the land of Eire and begin helping others," Brigit said. "Ye will become well known as a great Druidess."

The dark cloud had nearly twisted into the shape of a man when the oak died. But not before its last acorn fell into the goddess's hand. "As I now deem foretold by the *others,* ye will someday be called to the circle of stones beneath the oak. That oak will be the offspring of this acorn and well-aged indeed. Like every oak born of it, 'twill be a Tree of Life. There ye will come together with Erc Breac, King of Dalriada."

When Chiomara's brows perked, Brigit held up a finger of warning. "'Twill be but one coupling only before Fionn Mac Cumhail delivers something to ye. When asked, ye will give them to me. Do ye understand?"

"Aye." Chiomara murmured a prayer. "'Twill be as ye wish, Goddess."

Brigit was about to say something else when the ground trembled.

Balor had arrived.

"Ye will answer for this Brigit!" he roared seconds before the Goddess flung up her arms and a bright light blinded Darach. Then it faded only to be replaced by images twisting around him. The dead oak at his back then a gnarly oak overseeing five standing stones, then the oak growing up the side of the mountain in Scotland. Next came the oak in front of MacLomain Castle then the oak in front of the Colonial in New Hampshire.

Then all went dark.

Silent.

"Wake up, Son. Ye *must* wake up now."

"Da?" he tried to say, but nothing came out. He felt heavy, weighed down…lost.

"Follow the sound of my voice," Grant urged, distressed. "And find your way back to me, Darach."

"Aye," he managed to whisper as he trailed after his father's voice. Strong magic kept drawing him further and further out. As it did, the darkness finally faded away. The moment he was able to, he searched out Jackie. She was still in his arms, on his lap, with her cheek pressed against his chest.

"Jackie?" Fear gripped him as he tried to figure out if she was breathing, if she was alive. "Speak to me, lass."

"Shh, Darach," Erin whispered. *"Your dad's bringing her back."*

Only then did he realize they had returned to the small cave off the glade. Not only were Grant and Erin there, but Heidrek and Rònan. His cousin gripped his shoulder in support but remained silent as Grant held Jackie's hands and kept chanting with an intense look on his face.

Suddenly, Jackie gasped and arched.

"Bloody hell," Darach murmured and kept a firm hold on her. "I've got ye, lass."

She blinked rapidly and inhaled several more times before her eyes shot to him. "What happened? Where are we?"

"We're back in the cave." His heart hammered as he rubbed her arms. "You're okay. Alive."

Jackie felt her chest where Eoghan's burn mark had been. "I don't understand…how…"

When she trailed off, Grant spoke. "Erin had a vision out by the fire. She was with you in the Celtic Otherworld. She saw Jackie attacked by Eoghan then nothing more."

"When we got in here you two were like this but…" Erin cleared her throat and cocked the corner of her lip. *"Let's just say the four of us saw more of you both than you'd probably like."*

Jackie's cheeks reddened as she peered around at the clothing tossed around on the cave floor. "Oh, *God*."

Erin looked at Darach. *"You can thank your dad for flicking his wrist and getting you both dressed so quickly."*

Darach nodded at his father who appeared more troubled than ever.

"I've been in your minds and know everything that happened," Grant said. "I think 'tis best that we try to find Fionn Mac Cumhail and share this information. For he delivered the three original rings to Chiomara. Those that were given to Brigit when the time was right." His eyes fell to Jackie's ring, and he shook his head. "It has long been rumored that a fourth ring was created for Chiomara. But I've never heard that she had a sister and the ring was hers. A ring more powerful and dangerous than any other."

He was about to say more when it flickered.

"Och," Grant murmured as both black and light bluish gray swirled within the stone at its center. "I dinnae like this in the least."

Everyone stared at it, confused.

"I thought I saw it flicker black when Jackie and I were at Hamilton Castle," Darach said.

Jackie's eyes met his. "And I thought I saw it flicker bluish gray before we ended up in Ireland."

"Black to represent Eoghan's eyes," Grant said softly. "Bluish gray to represent Darach's." His frown deepened. "An unnatural love triangle tainted even further by Balor, the Celtic demonic God of Death. A demon verra slighted indeed when Brigit gave Gwendolyn that ring and a soul escaped his clutch." He looked at Jackie. "Your soul, lass."

"Now I better ken why the *Genii Cucullati* are assisting the demi-god," Grant continued. "They gain great respect and power by aiding the demi-god's master, Balor. As close as a god can get to the Celts' version of Satan."

"Damn," Erin murmured. *"This just keeps getting crazier and crazier."*

"Are you telling me that the devil is after my soul?" Jackie whispered.

"'Tis verra possible," Grant said gently and squeezed her hand. "But ye've got quite a powerful champion in Brigit." He shook his head. "We will figure all this out soon enough. Right now we must

155

focus on the here and now. I just used a tremendous amount of magic to get you back safely. And I suspect the ring senses Eoghan when he's drawing closer." He stood. "That means Keir Hamilton likely knows we're here and time is verra limited."

He no sooner said it when Niall spoke within their minds. "Trouble comes!"

Grant's eyes met Darach's. "Stay with the lass and protect her. Regain your strength. We will return soon."

"No, I'll stay," Erin said. *"It seems to me you're gonna need all the wizards you can get."*

"And at least one of them needs to stay with Jackie," Grant said. "She's far too vulnerable. Though you and Rònan cannae shift here, you're a strong warrior, Erin. Come with us."

Erin nodded before she looked at Jackie. *"Sit tight. It'll be okay."*

"Yeah, go. Protect Robert and William," she said, voice stronger than he expected. "We're right behind you."

The second they left, Jackie rested her cheek and a shaky hand against Darach's chest, whispering, "I just need a sec. I feel like I just ran ten marathons in a row."

"You did one way or another." He stroked her hair, so damn grateful she was alive. "You gave me a good scare, lass. I've never been so bloody frightened."

Jackie took several deep breaths. "Honestly? Me neither. That was terrifying."

"Aye, murder is."

"No, you misunderstand," Jackie whispered before she met his eyes. "I wasn't scared of dying. I've been ready for that for a while now." She shook her head. "What scared me was that *you* almost died."

His heart leapt at the emotion in her voice. "But I didnae."

"But you will if you love me." Her eyes grew moist. "And I don't think I can go through that again."

"I don't think either of us has much choice," he said softly. "Because I cannae stop loving you. Even if I could, I wouldnae."

"Damn it, Darach," she whispered. "You're so stubborn."

"Nay, just human." He brushed a tear from her cheek. "We're in this together whether you like it or not."

"I don't. Not at all." She crawled off his lap. "Love shouldn't mean death."

"People love then die all the time." He leapt to his feet and helped her when she stood. "'Tis inevitable. If our time comes sooner than most, so be it."

"Aren't you the optimist." She leaned against him as she tried to regain her balance. "My time is coming no matter what. Yours doesn't have to."

"This is an argument you'll never win," he said, overly aware that she trembled from weakness. "So why waste any more time speaking of it?"

Her eyes met his. "Because I can be just as stubborn as you, Darach Hamilton."

He grinned. "We'll see."

Her eyes narrowed and her lips thinned. "You're impossible."

"Aye."

"I still can't believe you gave me a fighting lesson when you were in so much danger," she complained.

"Did it keep you distracted?"

Her eyes widened. "You know it did."

"Then 'twas the perfect time to teach you." He winked. "It kept your mind off your fear and you learned a thing or two."

Jackie grumbled to herself, shook her head then refocused.

"We need to get out there," she said. "They need our help."

"There is nothing you can do in your current state."

"You don't know that."

"I do."

"I can stand just fine on my own," she murmured and stepped away.

When her knees buckled, he wrapped an arm around her lower back and pulled her against him. He only meant to stabilize her, but when her hand met his chest and her eyes rose to his, he knew the tremor that rippled through her now had nothing to do with what they'd been through. No, it had to do with right here.

Right now.

Stark desire.

"We need to help them," she whispered as her eyes fell to his lips.

"But ye cannae," he whispered back as his eyes fell to hers as well.

Heat fluctuated between them. A need that had no place here when a battle might rage beyond. Yet they pressed closer, caught in the magic of being together. Caught up in being *them* again, not two star-crossed lovers from ancient Ireland. He had nearly closed the distance and kissed her when a yelp then whinny echoed through the cave.

Jackie frowned. "What was that?"

When a low growl resounded, he positioned himself in front of her, cursing when he realized he had no weapons.

"Hell," he murmured as a huge black wolf lumbered into the cave. Blood dripped steadily from its chest as it bared its teeth and kept growling.

"Dinnae move or say a word," Darach said into Jackie's mind.

"It's injured badly."

"Aye, and 'tis not happy about it."

"We've got to help it."

"We do?"

"Of course!" He heard the frown in her voice. *"It's scared and injured."*

"And nearly my size," he pointed out. *"'Tis one hellishly large wolf and we have nothing to defend ourselves with."*

"We have your magic in a pinch."

Darach frowned. *"Aye, but I get the sense this wolf has a certain familiarity with magic."*

"Then we're going to have to risk it," Jackie said.

"Where are you, Wolf?" someone yelled from outside.

The wolf swung its head back moments before it sunk to its haunches.

"Oh shoot," Jackie murmured.

Darach grabbed her arm when she headed that way. "Wait, lass."

"There ye are," came a voice before young Grant rushed into the cave and fell to his knees beside the wolf. "Och, laddie, nay."

When Darach whispered, "Bloody hell," Grant's eyes shot to him.

Their gazes locked.

There was nothing quite like meeting your father when he was still a teenager. When Grant leapt in front of the wolf and whipped out two daggers, Darach put his hands in the air, shook his head and spoke softly. "We mean ye no harm, lad." He nodded at the wolf. "We only meant to help yer beastie. Nothing more."

When Grant took a few steps toward them and made ready to whip a dagger, Jackie shook her head. "No. Please. Darach's right. We mean no harm."

He cringed at the use of his name. That couldn't be good.

"Who are ye and speak fast," Grant ground out.

"We're friends. And I might be able to help your wolf." Jackie nodded at the wolf. Though his head rested on the ground, he still managed a weak growl.

"Och, lass," Darach said into her mind. *"What are you doing?"*

"I resurrected the deer," she said. *"Maybe I can help the wolf too."*

"You could get hurt."

"It's not about me."

"Actually, 'tis," he reminded.

"So you'd have me ignore it?" she said. *"When there's a chance I could help?"*

Darach contemplated the wolf. Its eyes had slid shut, and its breathing was labored. He felt Jackie's emotions blow through her as if they were his own. The overwhelming need to help.

Though he didn't want her anywhere near something so dangerous and unpredictable, he was beginning to realize how similar the two of them were. If they had the ability to protect and help, nothing could stop them. Nothing *should* stop them. Especially not someone who claimed to care about them...love them.

"Again, who are ye?" Grant's eyes skirted with worry between them and the animal as a gurgling sound rattled in the wolf's lungs.

"We're friends. And your wolf's almost out of time," Jackie said. "Please let me try to help him."

"Scratch that." Darach was surprised by how quickly Jackie jerked out of his grasp and hurried toward the wolf, muttering, "There's no more time."

He was even more surprised when her eyes rounded and she said, "Grant, watch out behind you!" When he glanced over his shoulder, she whacked his wrist and his dagger went flying.

159

Stunned, Grant went after her with his other dagger. Darach swiftly confiscated the blade before he knocked Grant's legs out from beneath him and brought him to the floor. Before the lad knew what hit him, Darach had him pinned as Jackie fell to her knees beside the wolf.

Grant struggled, but he was going nowhere.

"'Tis bloody strange holding my Da down like this, lass," Darach grumbled into her mind.

"I'm sure. Sorry about that." She ran her hand down the wolf's fur. *"Thank you."*

"Are ye sorry then?" he said, more distraught than ever as Grant spat out an endless stream of curses. *"Because ye dinnae seem it in the least."*

"That's because I'm trying to fix a dead wolf and have no clue how," she said. *"Any idea how I should do this?"*

"Och," Darach muttered aloud. "Nay."

Suddenly, Grant stopped struggling and whispered, "Dinnae leave me, Wolf. Yer all I've got."

Jackie's sad eyes went to Grant before they returned to the wolf and she placed a hand on his head. Darach rippled at what she felt...or *didn't feel*, as he experienced everything she went through. She was anxious about the wolf's survival and how important he was to Grant. The more her anxiety rose, the more numb she became. First her lips, cheeks, neck, then it started to spread everywhere.

He had never felt anything so alarming.

Yet Jackie kept an even expression and her hand on the wolf. As Grant struggled with grief, her anxiety only grew. The need to make things right. Then a tingling started in her hand. Just a spark at first but it soon warmed and became far more. Something he couldn't put definition to. Something that humbled him to his very core.

Seconds later, the wolf jerked.

Done with holding Grant down, Darach moved fast and pulled Jackie away from the wolf.

Grant staggered forward and fell to his knees as the wolf jerked again then leapt to his feet. His eyes locked with Jackie's just like the deer's had when she brought it back to life.

"Ye did it, lass," Darach whispered and pulled her against him, determined to protect her though he knew the wolf meant her no harm.

"We must go," Grant declared as he strode into the cave with everyone following.

While he thought there was no stranger moment than first connecting eyes with his father as a teenager, he was wrong. Nothing was odder than his father locking eyes with his younger self.

His Da stopped short, and young Grant froze.

Though there was a good chance young Grant had no idea who he looked at, his father absolutely knew based on his shocked expression. If that wasn't enough, the wolf shook, tested his limbs then all but pranced toward Da before he stopped short and looked back toward young Grant.

The wolf was as confused as they were.

Truth be told, the wolf was as confused as everyone there.

"The beastie seems undecided, does it not?" Robert said as Erin tucked him by her side.

"Can't really blame the beastie," Erin said, eying them.

"We've got to," his Da said, eyes wide on his younger self, "Go." He shook his head. "I think...now."

"Aw, you were such a little hottie." Nicole nudged his father, a wide smile on her face. "All long gangly limbs and big beautiful eyes."

"Och," his Da muttered and frowned. "Go. We need to go."

"Aye," Darach agreed.

But how did they do that?

It seemed his father was taking matters into his own hands because he flung his hands toward young Grant and started chanting first in English then Latin. "Take this memory from thee. Let your mind be free. Might your wolf protect you until you choose anew. *Accipe memoriam, ex te. Sit animum tuum sit. Lupus vestri custodiat donec de novo eligere."*

Magic started to swirl around them but not before he saw the look on his father's face. The tender, nostalgic way he gazed at the wolf.

"Where are we going?" Jackie said into his mind. *"What's happening now?"*

"I have no idea but 'tis my Da's magic so dinnae be frightened."

Yet she was and he didn't blame her. Since she first traveled back in time she had been whipped every which way through time and experienced living another life. It was frightening by anyone's standards. He pressed his hands over her ears and tried to relieve the pressure but knew she felt it regardless. When the magic finally abated, it was daytime and they were surrounded by woodland.

Adlin leaned against a tree with a broad grin on his face. "Welcome back." His eyes went to Grant's. "I take it ye found the answers ye needed?"

"Aye." Grant frowned as he accounted for everyone. "I dinnae ken why ye could not just share such with me."

"But I did."

"*Without* shifting us to my castle."

"Och, nay." Adlin started into the woods and gestured for them to follow. "As ye well know, there's a reason behind my methods. Everyone needed to have their own experiences so that ye can all move forward and be better prepared for what's to come."

Grant's eyes met Jackie's. "Thank you for saving my wolf, lass. You have no idea how much that means…meant. He eventually ended up with my brother Malcolm and was named Kynan."

"My pleasure," Jackie murmured.

Grant squeezed her hand then went after Adlin. "I ran into myself," he informed. "And 'twas bloody odd to say the least."

"Aye." Adlin nodded. "'Tis indeed." He cocked his head. "And how did you deal with it?"

"Well, I cast a spell of course. And though I know it worked, I think mayhap 'tis clear now why I was so compelled to name my son Darach." Grant tossed a sidelong glance at Darach and Jackie. "The wolf's life being saved would have impacted me greatly even through a veil of magic. If I had a name to relate to the experience, I would have thought highly of it." He cocked a brow at Jackie. "Did you say Darach's name around my younger self, lass?"

"I might have. It was pretty tense back there." She shrugged and slid a sweet but somewhat smug grin Darach's way. "Nice to know I played a part in naming you."

He couldn't help but grin in return. Things might be rougher than ever, but she seemed to be doing okay. Better somehow. But then she *had* just come back from the brink of death, so maybe she was just grateful to be alive.

"I like the idea that you played a part in naming me." He slid his hand into hers. "'Tis something no other MacLomain couple can claim, aye?"

"So you're a couple now?" Erin piped up.

"No," Jackie said as Darach said, "Aye."

Nicole chuckled. "That sounds familiar."

"You left this when you went to check on Jackie earlier." Heidrek handed Darach his sword.

Darach took it and nodded, fairly amazed that he left it behind. Then again, he'd been incredibly worried about her at the time.

"Remember well, son, that worried or not, you cannae protect her without that blade," Grant said.

Darach nodded. His father was absolutely right. He couldn't afford to make the same mistake twice.

"Where are Logan and Cassie?" Niall looked at Adlin. "They were with you last time we were here." He peered around. "As were many others."

"Logan and Cassie returned to the future," Adlin said. "A wee bit o' time has passed since ye were here."

"How much time…" Erin's words trailed off as they exited the woods and stepped onto a wide meadow.

All were speechless as they stared.

Made of wood, not stone, MacLomain Castle was nearly built.

Chapter Thirteen

DARACH WAS TRULY humbled by what he witnessed. There was no greater honor than to see such a thing. MacLomain Castle at its birth. A place that would oversee so many things in the years to come. Touch so many lives. Be considered 'home' and offer safety and protection to countless people.

"'Tis bloody beautiful," Grant whispered.

"Aye." Adlin beamed. "Everyone's done a wonderful job on it."

"I always assumed ye built it with magic," Grant said.

"Now, lad, ye know better than to assume." He and Grant started walking. "'Twas best to let my people work together to build it so even though most reside in cottages, they know this castle is as much theirs as 'tis mine."

"That's verra good," Grant said.

"Your parents are here and look forward to seeing you, William," Adlin said.

"They are no' my parents," William grumbled but took off for the castle with Robert right behind.

"Okay, girl time." Erin looked at Jackie. *"Come catch Nicole and me up on everything that's happened."*

"Except the part about you getting naked with Darach." Nicole grinned as they started walking. "We all know about that already."

Darach shook his head and sighed.

"You're lucky that's all that came out of my lass's mouth," Niall commented.

"True enough." Darach's eyes narrowed on Rònan and Heidrek. "So how much *did* you see of Jackie?"

"Very little," Heidrek said.

"Next to nothing," Rònan agreed.

Liars. But there wasn't much he could do about it.

"What happened back at the glade?" Darach asked. "Did you battle Keir Hamilton?"

"Nay, he hadn't arrived yet. Just a few of his warriors," Niall said. "One that clearly saw the wolf as a threat."

"'Tis too bad." Darach frowned. "I would have liked a chance to fight Keir."

"Aye," his cousins agreed.

"Tell us what happened to you and Jackie before Grant woke you from that unnatural slumber," Rònan said. "Because it had both Erin and Grant verra upset."

"No doubt." As he shared what happened, all grew troubled.

"I had hoped we could somehow find a way to save Jackie from her illness," Heidrek said softly. "But now it seems inevitable."

"Aye," Darach murmured. "All we can do is make the best of the time we have left."

"'Tis sad that." Rònan's eyes met Darach's. "But I dinnae know that I would give into Fate so easily. It sounds like you've shared other lives together but none like this. None with all four rings involved. And if we have learned nothing else from meeting our Broun lasses 'tis that unexpected things happen often."

He appreciated Rònan's optimism. How supportive he seemed despite Darach's recent behavior.

"Thanks, Cousin." He clasped his shoulder and met his eyes. "I owe you an apology for growing so upset with you at the glade. 'Twas poor of me."

"Nay, all's well," Rònan said as they continued walking. "I would have been just as upset had our roles been reversed. It couldnae be easy desiring a lass for so long yet never finding her beyond your dreams." His eyes locked on Erin. "I couldnae imagine."

"But now I've found her," Darach said. "And I dinnae intend to let her go."

He felt the emotions his cousins were careful not to show. Though they well understood finding true love, they didn't like the idea of losing him because of it. Or Jackie for that matter.

Clearly eager to lighten the mood, Niall cocked a grin. "So you were an Irishman then, aye, laddie?"

Rònan chuckled. "Now that would have been something to see."

Niall chuckled as well. "'Twould have been a sight, indeed."

"Is Adlin not from Ireland then?" Heidrek's brows perked and a smile ghosted his face as he eyed them. "Would that not make all of you Irish?"

"Born on Scottish soil," Rònan grumbled. "Makes me Scottish."

"Aye, verra Scottish," Niall agreed. "Though always thankful enough for my Irish ancestry."

"And is your mother not from the future, Niall?" Heidrek continued. "And of many other nationalities?"

Rònan nodded and eyed Niall. "I've heard it told that your Ma's father was from Italy. Makes sense considering your looks."

"There's nothing wrong with a wee bit o' Italian. And what of yours?" Niall's eyes widened. "You've clearly something else in your blood besides Scot and Irish."

Rònan shrugged and offered him a crooked grin. "Nay. Even my grandma from the future was originally born in Scotland."

Darach chuckled and shook his head. "I think Heidrek tries at humor but is better at starting battles."

Heidrek shook his head. "Humor has never been my strong point."

Rònan grinned at him. "We'll get you there, friend. For surely some of your dragon kin have a sense of humor." He scowled. "Besides Tait that is."

Darach tuned out their conversation when he felt Jackie's surge of happiness. He soon learned why when Eara trotted over the drawbridge and headed in their direction. Now that he had spent time in Ireland and realized Devlin had been the warrior who rode the horse into the Celtic Otherworld, he was starting to have his suspicions as to the horse's identity.

Who else could she be but Chiomara?

He joined Jackie as the horse came alongside.

"'Tis good to see ye both safely returned," Eara said.

"It's so good to see you again as well," Jackie said. *"I was worried when you didn't come with us."*

"Aye," Darach said. *"We missed ye."*

"Aye, it seems I cannae follow ye everywhere," Eara said. *"But 'twas not so bad spending time with Adlin MacLomain."*

"I would think not." Darach tested the waters. *"Especially if he is your son."*

The horse neighed and flicked him with her tail before trotting back toward the castle. *"Guess all ye like but ye'll not get my identity quite yet, Darach Hamilton."*

"Well, what fun is that?" Darach murmured aloud and continued walking with Jackie.

"What, don't you like a little mystery?" Jackie teased.

"Sometimes," he relented, tempted to say he'd had enough of it. He wanted all the facts so he could figure out how to save her. But he didn't say any of that and risk taking the soft smile off her face. Instead, he chose to flirt. "What about you, lass? Do you like a wee bit o' intrigue then?"

She slid him a look. "Sure, a little mystery is good."

Was she flirting too? A grinned blossomed. "Then I'll be sure to be as mysterious as possible."

"No, you won't." She chuckled. "I think you've had enough of being mysterious and keeping secrets." Her eyes went to Heidrek as they walked over the drawbridge. "Now there's a guy full of mystery."

"Are you trying to make me jealous then?" He took her hand. "Because 'tis working."

She eyed their hands but didn't pull away. "And you only grow more persistent when jealous, huh?"

"Aye." He eyed her. "You seem changed, lass. Happier somehow."

"I am." She shrugged. "I'm glad we're here." Her eyes met his. "And in our own bodies again."

"Me too." He got the sense that wasn't the only reason, though. She seemed more open now.

"I remembered a lot of Gwendolyn's memories, especially with Devlin," she said softly. "She reminded me a little of how I used to be. Fun. Spirited. Less contained."

Darach looked at her in question. "So you're glad we had that experience in Ireland?"

"In some ways," she said. "It sort of feels like I reconnected with a piece of my soul."

"You did," he said. "And I'm happy that you found something favorable in it."

"I am too." Her eyes went to him. "What about Devlin? Did he enlighten you at all?"

Only that he was more determined than ever to be with her. But he didn't say that because he liked their easy conversation.

"Aye." Darach grinned. "He confirmed that I'm a damn good fighter in every lifetime."

"Was that all?" Jackie quirked her lip. "Because based on Gwendolyn's memories, Devlin rivaled you in other areas too."

His brows shot up. "Did he then?"

"Mm-hmm." When her eyes drifted to him, lust quickly replaced flirting as her emotions mixed with his. Neither thought of what they might have done in a previous life, but what they so recently did in this one. Better yet, their mutual lack of fulfillment when climax was so close but ripped away.

He wanted more of her.

All of her.

And soon.

"Not a good idea," she whispered. Yet her eyes stayed with his.

"'Tis a verra good idea," he whispered.

"It won't help matters."

He shifted and willed away his ill-timed erection, grumbling, "I think 'twill verra much help matters."

Jackie bit back a grin as her eyes dropped to his groin.

"Looking in that direction will only get ye beneath me all that much faster, lass," Darach warned, unable to stop his brogue. "That I can assure ye."

Her eyes widened before she finally looked elsewhere. "Say no more."

Only then did he take the time to appreciate the vastly different courtyard. Though the cookery, stables and warrior's quarters were where they had always been, everything was wood and designed differently. Naturally, there were far fewer people and the place had a renewed energy that it lacked in the future. But then this was just the beginning for Clan MacLomain without the added centuries of warfare that would not necessarily weigh it down but change it somehow.

The castle innards were even more astounding. Jackie explored with her friends as he joined his kin. Though some smaller tapestries were hung, the larger ones were years away from gracing these walls. Like all MacLomain men, Darach stopped and stared up at the barren space where the great Viking tapestry would one day hang.

"'Tis a bloody odd sight," Rònan murmured.

"Aye," Niall agreed.

Heidrek stood beside Darach and crossed his arms over his chest as he considered the wall. "It will be an impressive tapestry that hangs here one day. A good likeness of my uncle. And it will serve its purpose in connecting our people." He paused. "But seeing the lack of it here now allows me to see renewed possibilities."

Darach frowned. "What do you mean?"

"Someday Keir Hamilton will meet a bad end in that tapestry. Something that must happen because our timelines cannot change," Heidrek said. "He must always be trapped between Scotland and Scandinavia. Between our people."

"Aye," Darach said. "True."

Having clearly heard the Viking, Grant and Adlin joined them.

"And such must happen until that timeline runs out," Heidrek continued. "We focus on what is in front of us and what must be and forget that there is an era in which things can change. A place where we can choose to end the timeline before your nemesis does."

Arms crossed over his chest as well, Grant eyed the blank wall and clearly saw the same possibilities. Ones that Darach and his cousins had yet to figure out. "Bloody hell, ye mean to bait the beast."

Adlin had a wise look on his face as he eyed Heidrek. "And the reasons become even clearer why a Viking ancestor has joined you on your adventure."

"Bait the beast," Darach murmured, focused on one word.

Bait.

Only one person could possibly compel not only Eoghan but Balor, his demonic overlord.

The lass that got away.

Jackie.

"Nay." Darach shook his head. "Dinnae even think it."

His father's eyes met his. "We will talk about this more once I've had time to mull it over." He squeezed Darach's shoulder. "And nothing will be decided without Jackie's approval."

"How can you even consider it, Da?" he whispered.

"Because there are so many lives at stake and the future of Scotland," he said softly. "As it should be for all determined to keep our king and country safe, *everything* must be considered."

"Not this." Darach shook his head. "We'll find another way."

Their eyes held for a long moment, equally pained, before Adlin interrupted. "Though the castle isnae completed, there are plenty of chambers ready and available. I've already had some made up.

Everyone should adjourn and rest up so that we might celebrate tonight. After all, we will be completing MacLomain Castle."

This caught everybody's attention.

"Aye, then." Adlin smiled, his jolly nature temporarily abating Darach's distress. "Whilst most of it has been built by the determined hands of its clan, even they agree 'twould be best if the final touches are completed with MacLomain magic. Scottish wizards," his eyes went to Heidrek, "and Viking ancestors."

Grant squeezed Darach's shoulder one more time and murmured, "We will talk more later." His eyes went to Jackie, who was heading upstairs with her friends. "Enjoy the night with your lass, Son. 'Tis bound to be more special than most."

He couldn't help but recall his father as an imprisoned teenager more concerned about the welfare of his friends and even perfect strangers than he was of himself. Even to this day, his da carried a great weight on his shoulders being their arch-wizard. So though he rebelled against the idea of putting Jackie in harm's way, he wouldn't argue with his father right now. This was a night to be enjoyed and cherished by all. A night that would not only see the completion of MacLomain Castle but time Grant could once more spend with his beloved mentor, Adlin.

"All right, Da," he said softly. "Ye enjoy the night as well."

Yet as he sat in a steaming tub of water an hour or so later, his thoughts kept returning to what Heidrek implied. What he knew his father and Adlin approved of. Jackie being put in harm's way to lure evil. Something he knew she would do without hesitation if it helped.

"You're overthinking it," she whispered into his mind.

Darach's frown deepened. Of course, she heard his thoughts. Which meant she had followed everything. *"'Tis impossible not to."*

"I suppose." Yet she didn't sound upset in the least. *"But I'm pretty sure you told your father you would relax and enjoy tonight."*

"I implied it," he said. *"No promises were made."*

"I see." Her voice grew softer. *"So what are you doing?"*

"Bathing."

"Me too."

A wry grin tugged at his lips as he remembered their time as Devlin and Gwendolyn bathing in Ireland. *"I suppose if there's one way to distract me, 'tis telling me that, lass."*

171

"I thought as much."

"I can just imagine how you look at this moment all wet and...clean." He tried to clear his throat to continue but only ended up coughing.

She chuckled. *"Dirty talk isn't really your thing, is it?"*

Dirty talk? Is that what she wanted? Darach eyed his raging erection. *"It can be verra quickly."*

"I don't know," she said, unsure. *"Either you're a natural, or you're not."*

"Oh, I'm a natural," he assured. *"Hence envisioning your full breasts all wet and..."* He swallowed, unable to push more words into her mind as he imagined all the things he wanted to do to them.

"All wet and what?" she prompted.

"Wet...nipples," he stuttered, picturing one in his mouth. *"Erect."*

"Erect?" she said, voice husky. *"My nipples or your cock?"*

Darach had been to the twenty-first century enough. He understood its women. He understood Jackie. Or maybe not. No, it seemed he was meeting another side of her entirely.

One he liked *immensely.*

"Darach," she purred. *"You're awful quiet considering I'm about to touch somewhere I'd bet you'd rather touch."*

Images flashed through his mind. Her hand sliding down her smooth stomach. Her thighs spreading. A low moan as she slid her fingers between her legs.

"Bloody hell," he growled and swung out of the tub. Enough with this 'dirty talk.' He wanted more than that. Right now. And she was only a few chambers away. He didn't bother drying off, just wrapped a plaid around his waist and headed out the door.

Only to stop short.

Dressed in a gown of light satiny gold and so damn beautiful his breath caught, Jackie leaned against the railing across from his door with a devious grin on her face. "Hey there." Her eyes trailed down his body. "You might want to get dressed." She licked her bottom lip. "Or a little more dressed than that."

"You werenae in your bath then?" he said, eyes wide.

"Clearly not." She grinned. "Just having some fun. Trying to lift your spirits."

"Aye, you did that, lass." He took a step toward her and gestured at his billowing plaid. "And lifted something else as well."

"I can see that." Her eyes narrowed, and she sidled sideways when he moved in her direction. "It was all in good fun." She ran her hands over her skirts. "Look at me. All ready to go."

"Aye, ye better be ye little tease," he declared and leapt at her.

"No!" she squealed and took off.

"Get back here!" he roared, not caring in the least if they gained the attention of the entire great hall. Bagpipes sprang to life and people laughed as he flew after her. She only made it as far as the end of the walkway before he caught her and pulled her into a small alcove hidden from sight.

"Look at me," she cried. "My hair's all done up. I'm dry."

"Aye, ye've never looked more bonnie," he agreed as he walked her back against a wall. Before she could utter another word, he cupped her cheeks, pressed close and kissed her hard. The second their lips connected, everything else fell away. The kiss deepened and their tongues twisted.

He slid his hands into her hair and pressed his thigh between her legs, eager to further ignite the burning need she already felt. More than eager to fill that need, she clenched the sides of his torso as the kiss intensified and they struggled to get closer.

"Oh, *Jackie? Darach?*" called an all-too-familiar, irritating singsong voice. "Where *are* you?"

"Nay," he murmured against her lips. "Dinnae respond."

"I won't if you won't," she managed before their kiss deepened again.

"I know you guys are here somewhere," Nicole chimed, drawing closer. "We all saw your mini-show. Before it becomes a grand finale, you need to come downstairs. Adlin's request not mine."

Jackie tore her lips from his and pressed her forehead against his chest, muttering, "Of all people why did they send Nicole to look for us?"

Darach groaned and rested his chin on her head. "'Twould be my guess that she volunteered." He inhaled the scent of her hair and did his best to will away his arousal. "Though she seems to be mellowing with pregnancy, am I wrong in saying Nicole likes to be at the center of most dramatic situations?"

"Not wrong in the least." There was a smile in her voice. "So I suppose this is a dramatic situation?"

"Aye," he breathed. "At the verra least." He pulled away and tilted her chin until their eyes met in the dim light. "We'll be finishing this as soon as we have the chance, lass."

"I don't know," she said. "It seems like Fate keeps getting in the way."

"Not this time." He kissed her again. Softly. Gently. Not with just his lips but something deeper. His heart.

"Ah, there you are!" Nicole declared.

Jackie allowed the kiss to go on for another moment before she pulled back, and met his eyes.

"Yup, here we are."

"Big night." Nicole grinned as they finally turned in her direction. They must have looked equally displeased because she shrugged and gave them an apologetic look. "Listen, I think the whole yelling, screaming I-don't-want-you-but-really-do sex display was great but big things are happening." She looked at Darach and pointed over her shoulder. "Things having to do with this castle that I know you're not gonna wanna miss."

Honestly, lying with Jackie sounded better than anything else, but he knew Nicole was right. What was happening below stairs was important.

"We're coming." Jackie stepped away from him and tried to adjust herself. "Just give us a minute."

Jackie knew how important this was. She understood. How could she not? They were so inside one another's minds now he was shocked her ring didn't shine brightly with the color of his eyes. But no. Right now it was dull and lifeless. He pushed aside any thoughts of it twirling with both black and blue. Because he'd be damned if Eoghan would ever have her...or be her bloody true love.

"Okay. You sure?" Nicole eyed them up and down. "Because you both seriously need to pull yourselves together."

Jackie touched her disarrayed hair and peered down at her damp dress with dismay.

"We'll be down shortly." He pulled Jackie after him and winked at Nicole. "Thanks, lass. See you there."

Before Jackie could grumble more about her appearance, he pulled her into his chamber, shut the door and put a finger to her lips when she started to talk.

"Dinnae say a word." He touched her dress, murmured a chant and dried the fabric in an instant. "And before you thank me, remember that you asked for this."

"I had no intention of thanking you." She fluffed her skirts and scowled. "And I'm pretty sure I never asked for it."

"Oh aye, you asked for it." He whipped off his plaid and grabbed another. "You just didnae expect me to act on your dirty talk so quickly."

When Jackie went silent and thoughts of desire bombarded him, his eyes shot to hers. Her lips were parted. And based on the angle in which he stood, it was hard to tell if her gaze was locked on his arse or his cock. Mayhap a bit of both.

"You're," she started and held up a finger, "it's," she shook her head, "good." Then she clenched her hands behind her back as her eyes sort of drifted over him. Finally able to say a solid stream of words, she mumbled, "You're naked, Darach."

"I am," he agreed, realizing it was the first time she had seen him like this. When they laid together, it had been so quick and passionate there was little time to appreciate one another's body. He grinned. "Would you like me to remain this way?"

"Yes," she breathed then shook her head. "No." She looked away and started fiddling with her hair. "We should go."

He'd much rather throw her on the bed and forget about finishing MacLomain Castle. He wanted to rip that dress in half and see *her* naked. But she was right. They should go. This night was too important.

So he wrapped his plaid correctly, pleased to see a MacLomain brooch. He pulled on tall black boots, and a sleeveless tunic. Though he knew she was determined to avert her eyes, Jackie watched him every step of the way.

By the time he stood in front of her, ready to go, she had a far away, lost look on her face. So he cocked his head and tried to meet her eyes. "Are you ready, lass?"

She sighed, her eyes floating to his. "I doubt it." She frowned and touched her hair. "It was so well arranged. Not so sure it is anymore."

"Do you really care?" He touched a strand. "You're bloody bonnie, lass."

"I do." Her eyes met his. "I should." She licked her lips. "Tonight's important...for your clan that is."

"Aye," he whispered, realizing she wasn't referring to his clan at all but something else altogether. Something so unexpected, his heart twisted into his throat. She was talking about him. Her.

Them.

She wanted this.

Lust, yes, but mayhap more.

Mayhap risk.

Almost as if she'd been cast beneath a spell, he sensed the guilt she suddenly felt about her desire. About putting him in danger. So when she started to shake her head, he cupped her cheek and stopped her. "You're allowed to want this, lass."

"No," she whispered, eyes moist. "I'm not."

He could try to convince her but knew it would make this small window of opportunity grow smaller. So he ran his fingers through her soft hair.

"What are you doing?" she whispered as her eyes drifted shut.

"Fixing it," he murmured, so tempted to close his lips over hers that it took immense strength to remain focused. "Hair like this should always be down."

"Most people like it better up," she said softly, her eyes on his lips. "They say it looks more professional."

"Professional? Mayhap. But better?" He pulled the pins out. "Nay."

"I should look a certain way if I'm going to represent," she started, but he interrupted her.

"Represent what?"

When she frowned, he tilted up her chin and made her look at him. "Represent what, Jackie?"

"This," she said. "*Us.*" Her brows shot together. "I should look put together. Your dad and Adlin should know I'm up for any challenge."

Darach pulled back as though he'd been slapped. "What do you mean?"

Jackie raked her hands through her hair, notched her chin and headed out the door. "If Heidrek has a plan to use me as bait to save everyone, I intend to do it."

He should have known she was still contemplating that.

"Ye'll do no such thing," he declared as he followed her.

"I will." She headed downstairs. "I've made up my mind."

"Bloody foolish mind," he growled, right behind her. Nobody was in the great hall. Everyone had gone outside. "You're not thinking straight."

"I'm thinking straighter than ever."

"Nay."

"I am."

"You're not."

"Just leave me be, Darach," she said before muttering under her breath, "Forgive, forgive."

"Jackie," he said.

"Just come on."

"You're only saying this because you think you're dying."

"No, I *know* I am." Jackie spun on the last stair, glared at him and pressed her temple. "I have a tumor in my frontal lobe. It's growing fast. In my case, it seems to be affecting my sense of sensation and scent first. Especially when I get upset." She pulled her shoulders back. "It's inoperable. I'm dying. That's not going to change." Her eyes narrowed even further. "And don't you dare pity me."

She spun and strode away, saying as an afterthought. "Even if you do, I forgive you. Forgiveness is the key."

"Always the key," she kept muttering before she exited.

Though it felt like a mace hit his knees and an axe caught him in the chest, he tried to follow but had to stop to let what she said sink in. No battle wound had ever felt so crippling.

He knew she was sick before, but now it somehow felt worse. Hell, even despite a Celtic goddess saying this was her plight life after life, nothing had quite gotten through until now.

There would be no saving her.

Jackie was going to die.

Chapter Fourteen

JACKIE WAS SO busy trying to escape Darach, that she didn't realize what was happening until she was halfway across the courtyard.

"*Look at this.*" Erin grabbed her arm and pointed up. "*I've seen amazing things since traveling back in time, but this takes the cake.*"

Jackie was only vaguely aware of her surroundings, she was so upset. Adlin, Grant, Rònan, Niall, and Heidrek were lined up and clearly doing something with magic. She glanced up at the castle and saw bright lights surrounding the top.

"*Pretty amazing, huh?*" Erin said. "*I get the feeling all they're waiting for is Darach because…*"

"Ye thought to say something like that and walk away, lass?" There was no time to vanish further into the crowd before Darach scooped her up and stormed back toward the castle. "'Twas poor of ye."

The crowd fell back as the magic intensified.

"Put me down." She struggled. "Don't you see what's happening? You should be helping them with the castle."

"I see what's happening," he growled, walking through the maelstrom of magic and back up the stairs. "Yer a bloody coward."

"You're being an ass, Darach." She kept struggling, but he was too strong. "Your family needs you."

"They'll have to wait." He broke through the curtain of magic and entered the great hall. "Because we need to talk."

"No, we don't." She arched hard and he, at last, let her down. "Everything's been said that needs to be said."

"Nay." He blocked the stairs before she could go up. "Talk to me, Jackie. 'Tis obvious you're in pain."

"Actually no," she quipped as she headed for the fireplace. "Pain is typically the *last* sensation I feel."

"Aye, and now I know why." He followed her. "Why didn't you just tell me from the start?"

"Tell you what?"

"That you were so sick," he said. "*What* you were sick with."

"Because it didn't matter."

"But it does."

I tried but the words always died on my lips. "It really doesn't matter." She stopped in front of the fire. "Incurable is incurable."

"Aye, but sharing so others can help you through it would have been good."

"I shared with Erin," she said. "That was enough."

"Nay." He shook his head. "It wasnae enough. You should have leaned more on your friends...on me."

"You?" She cocked her head. "The guy who avoided me without telling me why? You're the last person I felt I could lean on. Not to mention I barely knew you." Jackie ground her jaw. "Besides, I didn't want this." She gestured between them. "How you're treating me now."

Darach shook his head, the pain in his eyes almost more than she could handle.

"I'm sorry...I didnae mean to..."

Shit, this was hard. Too hard.

"I know," she murmured and looked at the fire. Anything to avoid the pity in his eyes.

"'Tis *not* pity," he said, his voice low and firm as he sensed her thoughts. "'Tis anything but."

"Oh, really?" Angered by what had to be a lie, she met his eyes. "Then what *is* it?"

"Sadness," he answered honestly, both aloud and within her mind.

"Because of my tumor?"

"Of course," he said. "But more than that." He took her hand. "Mostly because you were so afraid to share what was happening with you. Not only with me but everyone else. I felt what happened to you when you got overly upset about the wolf. The numbness you experience. 'Tis not easy, lass. You're verra brave."

Brave? That's about the last thing she felt. It was strange knowing he had experienced how numb she went. It was an unexpected connection she hadn't anticipated. Still, she wished they weren't having this conversation. That she was anywhere but here.

"No." She yanked her hand away. "I don't want any part of this."

"Of what?"

"You!" Jackie trained her eyes on the fire. "And this shit you're pulling."

"I've never heard you curse."

Her eyes shot to his. "Excuse me?"

"Curse." He took her hand again. "You typically dinnae do it."

"Actually, I do when I'm provoked."

"And I'm provoking you?"

"You know you are."

"Nay." He reeled her a little closer. "If anything, you're provoking yourself."

"No." She frowned. This time, when she tried to pull away, he didn't let go. Regardless, she was on a roll. "You knew I was sick, Darach. Now you know why. Let's just leave it at that. There's nothing more to say."

"But there *is*." He pulled her closer. "You need to know that what you shared doesnae change how I feel." The way he looked at her made every nerve ending come alive. "I want you." His gaze seemed to intensify. "I love you, Jackie."

"You need to get over it," she whispered. "You just think you do because of our other life."

"More than just one," he murmured. "Remember, we've lived other *lives*. All with the same outcome. You die young. But that doesnae stop me from loving you."

"Right." She knew full well what had happened after she died in Ireland. "At least this time you have a choice, Darach. You *know* I'm sick. Why get so invested?"

"I have no choice. Not since the moment I laid eyes on you...since I started dreaming of you." He pulled her against him and cupped his hand behind her neck. "Your illness makes no difference. I'd love you even if we only had a day left together."

As their eyes held, it finally sunk in. He truly meant every word. And he was stubborn. So there was no turning from this. No pushing him away. He loved her, and that wasn't going to change.

Yet the question remained, did she love him?

That was something she had religiously navigated around because she didn't want to put his life at risk. Maybe, just maybe, the rules changed as to him dying if his love wasn't returned. And maybe her saying as much would push him in the opposite direction.

"I don't love you," she murmured, surprised by how difficult it was to say.

"You dinnae have to, lass," he whispered, kissing her cheek, then earlobe, then the tender area beneath her ear. "Even though I suspect you do."

"No," she denied. But as usual, he managed to weaken her resolve with either the right words or the way he looked at her...or touched her. Though she meant to push him away, she ended up clutching his tunic when he pressed her back against the side of the mantle, braced a hand above her head and closed his lips over hers.

A long, low rumble caused by what was happening outside echoed through the castle and the fire flared on the hearth.

"'Tis powerful magic," he murmured into her mind as the kiss grew more passionate. *"Good magic."*

Though she knew he referred to everyone else's magic at work, he was implementing his too as he touched the mantel. Because she was somehow entangled within it, she felt his power seep into the wood. It swirled through them and the castle itself as his other hand rode her thigh. She groaned when desire rushed through her. Sensations intensified as their tongues twisted. It almost seemed like she felt not only what he did to her but what she did to him.

There was no way to know how long they stood there touching, stroking...needing far more. All she knew was that he had taken the fight right out of her and replaced it was something else entirely. Blatant need. Desperation. Impatience.

She needed relief.

They needed relief.

"I cannae wait any longer, lass," he groaned. "I want ye too bloody much."

There was no denying it. She was too far gone. So when he swept her into his arms and headed upstairs, she wrapped her arms around him and buried her face against his neck. Yet again, she had failed miserably at keeping him away. Perhaps if they slept together and finished this time, his interest would wane. Perhaps hers would.

Or it would grow stronger.

They were so desperate by the time he laid her down on his bed that they didn't bother to take off their clothes. Their lips connected as he yanked up her skirt and his plaid and settled between her thighs. When he filled her with one, long deep thrust, she arched, gasped and exploded.

Three thrusts later, he joined her.

He locked up against her, pressed his forehead to the pillow and released a strangled groan and shudder. She tried to hold onto him but couldn't as heat blasted through her and spasms rippled outward until her toes curled.

"Bloody hell, I'm sorry, lass. 'Twas fast," he finally whispered. "Ye just felt so damn good. And we didnae finish properly before."

"Really good," she whispered, unable to say much else. It was good all right. Amazingly so.

Their eyes met as thoughts he likely didn't want her to hear brushed her mind. He hadn't slept with anyone since she and her friends had shown up in New Hampshire. Since he laid eyes on her. And for a man like Darach, that had to have been difficult.

His lips curled slightly. "A man like me?"

She grinned. "You strike me as the affectionate type."

"Mayhap." He dropped a soft kiss on her lips as he worked at pulling her dress down. "I know you like the mysterious type. So what of affectionate types?"

"I think it's fairly...obvious," she gasped as he squeezed one nipple and sucked the other into his mouth. The man seriously knew how to use his lips, tongue, and teeth.

"I'd like it to be *more* obvious," he murmured as he pulled her dress down further, exposing her stomach and hip bones. She had no idea what he meant until he continued exploring with his tongue and hands and magic. Everywhere he touched seemed to invoke a different sound. It became very clear that he made love like he battled, creatively and with more finesse than most. And it became even clearer that he knew a woman's body as well as he knew how to wield a weapon.

The light trail of a rough finger had shivers racing everywhere. A press here and there on different points of her hipbone shot pleasure straight to her core. A swirl of his tongue in her bellybutton combined with a few fingers trailed down her side made her womb clench in anticipation.

By the time he yanked off her dress entirely and made his way between her legs, she was starting to feel a little wild. Free almost.

She'd always been a fan of sex but had never felt it like this even before dealing with ill-timed numbness.

New sensations.

Soul deep pleasure.

What made it even better was that she knew he felt the same.

This was a first for them both.

"Oh, God," she groaned as he worked the flesh between her legs. Before he could get too far, she shook her head and panted, "No." Then she yanked at his clothing, eager to remove it. "Both of us."

His brows perked with interest when he realized what she was after. "Och, lass, I like the way you think." She never saw a man remove his clothing so fast. Seconds later, she was on top and his mouth was between her legs.

Better yet, hers was between his.

After that, it was pure, unfiltered pleasure.

So much pleasure.

Because of their mental connection, she knew exactly what he liked and vice versa. Not only that, she thoroughly enjoyed every second of pleasing him. The sounds he made. The way he tasted. After another shattering climax found them, she lounged on top of him.

"*So* good," he murmured, massaging her backside as he trailed a finger up and down her spine.

"Mm-*hmm*." Limp, sated, her eyes were closed, and her cheek rested on his thigh.

"More," he growled.

Jackie yelped when he tossed her onto her back. Before she had a chance to react, he flipped her onto her stomach.

"Insatiable," she mumbled into the pillow, grinning.

"Aye," he agreed. "When it comes to you." His lips came close to her ear. "On your knees, lass."

A shiver of awareness shot through her when he flicked his tongue against the side of her neck.

"No energy to," she breathed.

"Nay?" His tone had grown suspiciously soft.

"No."

She heard the grin in his voice. "Oh, I think there is."

Her eyes rounded, and laughter erupted when he started tickling her. "Darach!" She tried to wiggle away but played right into his hands when she came to a knee to move forward. Taking advantage, he gripped her hips and pulled back, which brought up her other knee.

"There ye are," he murmured before he thrust deep.

Laughter turned to a long moan, and she dropped to her elbows. He felt so incredible. Astounding. And he hadn't even moved yet. Instead, he seemed to be enjoying the view as he caressed her ass and hips. She had never experienced a man who touched and massaged so much during sex. It was wonderful. And yes, *affectionate*. He made her feel worshiped and adored while at the same time thoroughly lusted after. Tender mixed with animalistic.

The more he didn't move but touched her, the crazier she felt.

She needed more.

Friction.

Now.

"Darach," she pleaded, her voice husky.

"Aye, Jackie?" he said a little too sweetly as he wrapped a hand around and touched her clit.

"No fair," she said through clenched teeth. "Just *move* already."

"But you wouldnae move for me when I asked you to," he reminded. "So you'll wait until I'm ready."

"Will I then?" If he could tickle her into submission, then she could force the same from him. So she rolled her hips and rocked back and forth.

They both groaned as he cursed under his breath, gripped her hips again and took control. After that, she drifted away on pleasure. Far, far away. This time, he lasted considerably longer, his energy admirable and bone weakening. Several orgasms tore through her as he moved at varying speeds. Sometimes fast and deep. Sometimes slow and even deeper.

She eventually sank, her body putty in his hands. It was then as he rolled her onto her side and spooned her from behind that it grew far more intimate.

Loving.

He tilted her head and kissed her while touching between her legs again. He did everything so masterfully that mini-orgasms rolled through her in crests that built one on top of the other until she hit a plateau. One that kept her trembling.

It almost felt like her body waited for him.

As if their flesh worked in harmony separate from their minds.

When he wrapped his arm around her waist, pulled her tight against him and his breathing became harsher, she knew he was close. Something about that, the raw pleasure he felt, pushed her right off the plateau and seemingly straight out of her body. He released a deep chested groan and locked up tight against her. The feeling of him throbbing deep within only heightened her own acute ecstasy and she struggled for breath.

She had no idea how much time passed as she drifted somewhere multi-dimensional. At some point, she ended up on her back with her eyes closed. When she finally opened them, Darach was propped on an elbow, gazing at her.

She almost felt bashful. "How long have you been watching me?"

"For a while." He ran a finger along her jaw. "You're hard to look away from."

Her gaze got caught in those eyes of his. "I could say the same."

"Ye married me in at least one other life," he murmured as he ran the pad of his thumb over her chin, the look in his eyes tender. "Marry me in this one, Jackie. I want ye to be mine in the eyes of God before I lose ye again."

"What?" Her heart leapt. "You know I can't do that."

"But you can." He cupped the side of her neck. "'Tis what people do when they're in love."

"I'm not in love," she whispered, but even as she said the words she knew something had changed. That she felt things for him that she never had for another. Intense things that she suspected might very well be love. Yet he didn't need to know that.

"I'm inside your mind," he said softly. "You cannae keep such from me."

Right. She needed to remember that.

"I don't believe in love at first sight or that you can be in love with someone so quickly." Her eyes searched his. "It's supposed to take years to develop through compatibility and shared interests." She frowned. "So maybe what I'm feeling now is because our past lives are getting in the way."

"Mayhap some of it but not all." He again explored her jawline with a lazy finger. "If you havenae noticed, true love tends to happen quickly and often betwixt Brouns and MacLomains. Love that lasts straight into the afterlife." He dropped a soft kiss on her lips. "You just need to accept and enjoy it. Not overthink it."

Could she really, though? Wasn't that selfish considering he was doomed?

"Nay," he murmured. "I have chosen my own fate. 'Tis inescapable. The only selfish thing you could do now is to deny me when we both want this so much."

Jackie narrowed her eyes. "Are you trying to manipulate me?"

"That depends." Darach grinned. "Is it working?"

"Maybe." But now wasn't the time to analyze his tactics. The sound of bagpipes had started to drift up from the great hall. "We should go downstairs and join the celebration. This is a once in a lifetime opportunity. And you don't want to miss it."

"Aye," he agreed. "More so because of what we've shared."

She didn't respond, though she agreed. "Let's go back down."

He looked at her for a long moment before he relented. "If that's what you wish."

Jackie was shocked by her thoughts. Because what she *really* wanted was to spend the night in bed chatting…and playing. More than that, she realized she wanted a chance to have a life with him. A chance to create memories together. It might be hard to know how compatible they would be, but she sensed he was easy-going enough that he could manage her bluntness. But then he wasn't one to hold back either. And she strongly suspected that spark between them would work.

He had a way of chiseling away at the persona she had created long ago, and she liked it. Somehow it felt as if the 'real' her was surfacing. Someone who used to smile more. Who wasn't contained and careful. The person she had nearly forgotten existed.

Someone he truly liked.

Neither said a word as they dressed but she felt his emotions as much as he felt hers. Turbulent. Conflicted. Jackie bit her lip and eyed him when it was time to tie up her dress. She had help from a servant before.

Her heartbeat quickened when he finished tying his boots and stood. God, he was handsome all done up in Highland regalia. Even the tattoos worked. Or maybe the muscles. Definitely both. And she had never really been into either. She'd always been more into scholarly guys in suits.

Not anymore. Not at all.

A small grin curled his lips, no doubt at her thoughts, but he made no mention of it as he stepped behind her and started tying her laces. "I've wanted to do this since you needed your dress tied at the Highland Defiance."

"Yet you let Heidrek do it," she murmured and shivered at his proximity.

"Aye." His voice grew husky. "'Twas good that you didnae feel then what you feel now."

She bit back a smile. "I didn't realize you were paying such close attention."

"Sure you did." Darach pulled the strings just a smidge tighter than necessary, plumping up her cleavage even more. "There." He wrapped an arm around her and pulled her back against him. "Perfect."

She narrowed her eyes and tilted her head. As suspected, he was eying her chest. "Enjoying the view?"

"Verra much so."

"What about my inability to breathe because the dress is so tight?"

When he brushed his thumb across the underside of her breast, her breath caught. "You dinnae quite breath correctly around me anyway." He grinned and winked as he pulled away. "But if you need it loosened, let me know."

"I need it loosened."

"Aye then." He tucked two fingers into her cleavage, yanked her against him and kissed her. She had nearly melted against him when he stepped back and grinned again. "See, your dress is loosened yet your breathing still isnae quite right."

Jackie scowled and eyed her dress. "Good thing you didn't rip it."

Darach continued to eye her breasts. "'Tis too bad, really." He wiggled his fingers. "But as you've recently learned, I'm verra good with my hands."

She snorted, then chuckled at the unladylike sound. "Come on. Let's go."

Darach held open the door. "After you."

"Thank you."

He took her hand, and they walked down together. As she guessed, the celebrations were well underway. What she hadn't anticipated was the crowd quieting as all eyes turned their way.

"*Um,*" she said into his mind. "*What's going on?*"

"*I dinnae know.*" That same grin was back. "*Mayhap you've too much cleavage showing after all.*"

"*Seriously,*" she said. "*Did you tell someone you proposed?*"

His brows shot up. "*Now why would I do that unless you said yes?*"

"*I'm starting to learn that with you anything's possible.*"

"There you two are!" Adlin declared, emerging from the crowd with a wide smile. "Everyone's been anxiously awaiting your return."

Jackie and Darach looked at him in confusion as they arrived at the bottom of the stairs.

"Aye?" Darach said.

"Aye," Grant said, joining them with an impressed look on his face as he gestured across the hall. "After all, my son and his lass created MacLomain Castle's great mantle."

Chapter Fifteen

IT TOOK DARACH a moment to realize what his father meant as his eyes landed on the huge mantel over the main hearth. The very mantel he and Jackie had leaned against earlier. Where before it had been wood with no design, now it was stone with several intricately carved faces. It had always been the heart of this castle. The most magical spot.

"Bloody hell," he murmured. "I dinnae ken."

"Come, join us in front of the fire." Adlin beamed. "And I will explain."

Darach and Jackie received mugs of whisky and made their way through the cheering crowd.

"All right, my friends," Adlin announced to the clan once they arrived in front of the fire. "Let's give this fine couple some time to admire their handiwork. Back to celebrating!"

"It didn't even register earlier that this wasn't here yet." Jackie's eyes were wide as she studied the mantle. "It looks different than it does in the future. Fewer faces."

Her friends joined them as well as his cousins.

"That is because many have yet to be born, lass," Adlin said. "You do know what this mantle is, aye?"

"Not really except that it's magical."

"'Tis verra magical," Adlin agreed. "'Tis also a portal between here and the afterlife for those of the MacLomain clan."

"Oh, wow," she murmured.

"That's what I said," Erin kicked in. *"Unreal."*

"And you helped create it, Jackie," Nicole added, a wide smile on her face. "That's incredible."

"I think that face up in the corner looks a lot like me," little Robert announced, joining them.

"Why would ye be on a mantle meant for MacLomains?" William scowled as he came alongside. "Are ye of their blood then?"

"Nay, but I've a king's blood," Robert pointed out.

William crossed his arms over his chest. "So that makes ye able to grace any mantle in Scotland, does it?"

"Hey, you two." Jackie crouched. "Good to see you again."

They smiled, both clearly smitten with her as Robert said, "Good to see ye too, Jackie."

They weren't the only ones taken with her. He noticed far more men eying her than before. But then she had a new glow about her. One *he* put there.

Yet it was more than that.

The person he had sensed beneath was slowly surfacing. She was less refined and more open somehow. It seemed everyone noticed because Rònan and Niall had a perplexed expression on their faces as they watched her. Even Erin and Nicole seemed to be studying her with interest. And while some of it likely had to do with the mantle, he knew it wasn't just that.

"Enough lads," Lilas said as she smiled at them and started to shoo William and Robert off. "Let yer elders talk amongst themselves now."

Yet again, he had a strong sense of familiarity when he looked at the lass. It appeared Jackie did too because her eyes lingered on Lilas as she hugged then bid the boys goodbye.

"So tell us, Adlin…" Darach took Jackie's hand when she stood. "I contributed some magic whilst touching the mantel but how did Jackie and I end up creating it? I for one am not nearly that powerful."

"Nay, you arenae," Adlin said softly. "But you *and* Jackie together are."

"It took the perfect mixture of things to create this mantel," Adlin continued. "The magic of air is one of the most unique. 'Tis constantly changing and shifting. Combined with the power to resurrect and the intense emotions that fluctuated betwixt you two at the time, a doorway was created betwixt worlds." He kept smiling, immensely pleased. "One made *by* MacLomains *for* MacLomains."

"You mean to say that Jackie and I created this mantel alone?" Darach shook his head. "That the rest of you truly had nothing to do with it?"

"Aye, 'tis precisely what I am saying."

"Okay, no offense but this is a lot to wrap my mind around. Nothing I'm overly ready to…" Jackie started but stopped and shook her head. "Even if what you're saying is true, one thing doesn't add up." She frowned. "You said it was created by MacLomains. I'm *not* a MacLomain."

"Och, but you must be for this mantle to have been created," Adlin assured. "It can be no other way."

Grant's eyes never left Jackie's, his voice soft. "Do you *want* to be a MacLomain, lass?"

Darach was shocked. Did his father want him to marry Jackie? Even knowing what would eventually happen to his son because he loved her?

"I'm not sure what you're getting at," she murmured.

"I think you do." Grant's eyes went from Darach to her. "My son is by blood a MacLomain. Marry him and you become one too." Grant tilted his head. "Did he not propose to you?"

"What?" Erin and Nicole said at the same time.

Jackie's eyes narrowed on Darach. "Did you seriously tell your father?"

"Nay, I did." Adlin grinned. "'Twas impossible not to sense the verra first proposal made in this castle."

She inhaled deeply and shook her head. "We created the mantel without being married so I'd say everything worked out."

"Well..." Adlin shook his head, and his grin fell away. "'Tis verra likely the mantel will lose its power if things dinnae go as they should."

"Aye, true enough," Grant agreed. "Magic can be verra odd indeed."

"Nothing says I won't marry down the line." Her eyes narrowed on Darach, clearly aggravated by the direction of the conversation. "And you'll be lucky if it's to you after this."

At least she wasn't thinking of her illness anymore. Darach shot her a crooked grin, not fazed in the least by her denial. "If not me, then who?"

"Maybe another MacLomain."

"Another?" His eyes went from his cousins to her. "In case you havenae noticed, they're a wee bit taken."

"I wasn't referring to your cousins." She crossed her arms over her chest. "I'm sure there are other single MacLomains floating around somewhere."

He chuckled. "None like me, lass."

"So you say."

He winked and eyed her over with purpose. "So I know."

"Oh, listen to you two." Nicole grinned at Jackie. "I didn't know you had it in you, sweetie. I thought what happened upstairs might've been a one-time deal."

"Aye, 'tis certainly something betwixt these two, something powerful that created our mantel." Adlin was back to grinning. "And allow me to clarify, Jackie. It cannae be just any MacLomain but the one you made the magic with."

Darach couldn't help but toss a few erotic reminders of what they did earlier into her mind. "Aye, magic indeed."

The corner of her mouth twitched in amusement. "I'm not marrying you."

"I think you might."

"Never going to happen."

"But 'twould be verra good if it did," Adlin said. "And it just so happens we've a holy man here this eve."

"See, 'tis meant to be." Darach grinned and set aside their mugs. "Marry me, lass."

"'Twould make me and your Ma verra happy if she would," Grant said.

Jackie's eyes rounded on Grant. "Since when?" She frowned. "And I can only guess what Sheila thinks about this."

Grant smiled. "Aye, I think you should marry my son." He looked over Jackie's shoulder and pointed. "And if you dinnae believe me about his Ma's opinion then ask her yourself."

They turned as his mother appeared through the crowd, smiling.

"Ma!" Darach gave her a big hug. "When did you get here?"

"Hi, sweetheart. A little while ago thanks to Adlin." She hugged him tight before she pulled back. "I hear you've been busy."

He kept grinning. "Aye."

Her eyes held his as her smile widened. "You look happier than ever despite all you've been through."

"Aye," he said. "I am."

"Brother?"

Darach's eyes shot past his mother to his sister. "Lair!" Laughing, he gave her a big hug and spun her around. "I cannae believe you're here as well."

Lair smiled softly. "Like Ma said, thanks to Adlin."

Where he shared his mother's temperament of being more open and lighthearted, Lair was more like their father with a careful nature and quiet wisdom.

"Jackie." His mother embraced her. "So good to see you again."

"You as well."

Sheila pulled back and took Jackie's hands. "I take it you're feeling more awkward than ever right now."

"Just a smidge," Jackie murmured. "But I'm definitely glad to see you."

Lair hugged her next before his mother took Jackie's hand. "Mind if I steal you for a few minutes?"

"Actually, I'd welcome it."

"Great." His mother led Jackie into the crowd.

"This is awesome," Nicole said the minute they left.

Darach looked at her in question.

"Do I need to spell it out for you?" Nicole grinned. "Jackie's totally into you. She's totally gonna marry you." She shot Niall a look. "I told you Jackie had a thing for Darach all along. It's meant to be."

"I agree." Erin nudged Darach. *"I've never seen her act like this before. What you two have is real."*

"Act like what exactly?" he said, happier by the moment.

"Free. Alive. There's no other way to explain it," Erin said. *"She's become good at hiding from life. Building barriers. Rehearsing her response to every question asked of her. She was so guarded and isolated from what was real that I was starting to wonder if she'd break out of it before…"*

Erin cleared her throat and shook her head. *"Like Rònan did for me in more ways than one, you're pulling Jackie out of her self-inflicted shell."* Emotion was evident in her voice. *"And I'm damn glad to see it."*

"Aye," Niall and Rònan said at the same time.

"She definitely seems to be changing," Rònan said. "More likable. Her true self. The woman she's truly supposed to be."

When Erin shot him a look, Rònan shrugged. "'Tis true and I told you as much. She wasnae all that approachable before."

"Well, she seems verra approachable now." Niall's eyes narrowed. "Despite being with your mother."

Darach wasn't surprised to see far too many men hovering near her, eager for her to look their way. Jackie was remarkably beautiful as it was. Yet now with her new glow, she was drawing more men than he would like.

"You do not need to worry, friend," Heidrek said, having recently joined them. "Your family is right. Jackie desires you and no one else."

He nodded. "Thank you, Heidrek. On many counts." Curious, he said, "One of which was helping complete this castle. I didnae realize you possessed such magic."

"Actually, 'tis Heidrek's addition to this castle that will someday make that Viking tapestry a conduit betwixt our people," Adlin said. "Yet another reason I imagine he's here."

"So it seems." Darach again nodded his thanks to the Viking. He still wondered at the extent of Heidrek's power but now wasn't the time for more questions.

"I like Jackie, Brother," Lair said softly. "She balances ye well."

Darach smiled at his sister. "Ye think so?"

"Aye." She made a tipping motion with her hand, and a smile ghosted her face. "Yer verra off balance but 'tis interesting to watch ye both even things out. Something I suspect ye'll do for years to come."

"Years to come," he murmured, trying to push her illness to the back of his mind.

"Aye." Lair squeezed his hand. "Years to come, Brother. If ye but believe it. The power of the mind is forever stronger than that of the body."

Their eyes held. Very few were better healers than his sister so he took her words to heart. "Aye, then."

"Aye, then," she repeated and whispered, "Dinnae give up faith."

"Oh, here she comes. I wonder how the 'mom' talk went," Nicole said, smiling.

"Based on her expression, I'd say Sheila smoothed things over." Erin nudged Darach again. *"So don't mess this up."*

What did she mean by that? He would have scowled at her if he wasn't so busy admiring Jackie. He hadn't meant to propose to her, but yet, he couldn't help himself. She felt so perfect in his arms. Everything about her drew him. From her body to her mind. And it wasn't becuase of his dreams or their previous lives. It was simple. He liked her, nay, *loved* her, for who she was now.

She was repressed but open. Blunt though she tried to be tactful. Strict, though at heart, playful. Watching her bloom and change was like watching a moth morph into a butterfly. And he wanted to be with her every step of the way. He wanted to know the woman she was and the one she would become. So when the idea of asking her to marry him popped into his head, it felt absolutely right.

Unquestionably right.

"Did you just compare me to a moth?" she said into his mind.

"A moth?" he said innocently as she joined him. *"Och, nay. Hearing my thoughts is a tricky thing sometimes. Hard to ken on occasion."*

"Liar," she whispered aloud.

Just having her close again made his heart warm. She could deny him all she wanted, but he wasn't giving up. "Will you marry me?"

"No."

He smiled when her heartbeat increased. She *wanted* to say yes but was fighting it. More so than ever.

"Now who's the liar," he whispered. "You want it as much as me."

"I don't."

"You do."

"There's no point," she said, but he sensed a change in her since speaking with his mother. "And you know it."

"I know no such thing."

She was breaking.

Time to be more persuasive.

So he took her hand and fell to one knee, his eyes never leaving hers. "There stands a verra good chance many of us will die soon, and you and I are at the top of that list. I dinnae care. And 'tis clear I didnae care in any life prior." Darach took her other hand and squeezed. "You're worth the risk, Jaqueline. I would rather love you and die then turn from this to save myself." He searched her eyes and meant every word. "Because there would be nothing left to save."

"Of me?"

"No, of me." He frowned. "Are you not following?"

"Barely." She twisted her lip. "You run a little sappy."

"Sappy?"

"Overly emotional," Niall started but stopped short when Nicole elbowed him.

"I know what sappy means." Darach shrugged and squeezed Jackie's hands again, making no apologies. "When it comes to you, aye, I'm verra sappy."

"I can see that." Her eyes narrowed. "And I'm not a moth."

"Not anymore."

"There'll be no marriage in our future," she confirmed.

"Aye, there will be."

She shook her head. "No."

"Aye."

"How's your knee feel?" Her eyes flickered from the floor to him. "The rushes look thin."

"My knee is fine," he said. "I'm a hardened warrior."

"That's used to fighting on his knees?"

"Aye." He shook his head, confused. "Nay."

She leaned a little closer. "I think all your blood must've rushed from your head to your poor knee because you don't seem to be thinking clearly."

"I've never thought more clearly."

"Really, Son?" his father murmured, a smile in his voice. "Because you seem to be running a little daft right now."

He frowned. "I dinnae ken…"

"She said, in the *future*!" Nicole blurted. "Even I caught that."

"What does the future have to do with anything," he started but trailed off as it occurred to him and his eyes shot back to Jackie.

Right now, they were technically in the past not the future.

She would marry him here not there.

A soft smile curled her lips. "A little play on time travel. Get it?"

She *joked*. The vixen. But he liked it. Hell, he would probably love the devil himself right now.

He narrowed his eyes. Two could play at her game.

"Did you just make a mockery out of my proposal?" He frowned on purpose. "Something so serious?"

It seemed she had no intention of being baited. "I certainly did." Her eyes narrowed. "Did you propose down here in front of

198

everyone again and again so that I would feel guilted into saying yes?"

"I certainly did."

Their brows perked at the same time.

"You're awful," she murmured.

"As are you," he murmured.

"I think I might actually love you," she whispered.

"Old news," he said. "So you'll marry me?"

"Yes, but I probably shouldn't make it this easy."

"This has been *easy?*"

Jackie grinned. "Yup."

"You better run, lass," he growled into her mind as his heart soared. *"Because I mean to do all sorts of things to punish you for putting me through this."*

She grinned at his threat. *"Did I ever mention I ran track in college?"*

"Nay," he managed to get out before she darted off.

"Oh no, you don't." He chased after her. "Come here my wee bride!"

The crowd parted, laughing as he flew after her.

"You're not married yet!" Adlin declared and rushed after them with everyone in tow. "Somebody find the holy man!"

Hoots and hollers echoed as everyone cheered but one voice managed to rise above it all.

"Oddest damn proposal *ever*," Nicole cried. *"Love* it!"

Darach didn't care what happened behind him. Only what happened in front. And that was Jackie. *"You're fast but not that fast."* She didn't get far before he tossed her over his shoulder and booked it up the stairs. They could marry later. Right now he wanted to celebrate another way entirely.

She laughed. "Your legs are longer than mine."

He laughed as well, curious. "What made you change your mind, lass?"

They were being pursued so he raced past his chamber.

"Good advice."

"From my Ma?"

"Yes," she said. "She's pretty amazing."

"She really is."

And God, he was going to thank his mother a thousand times over.

"Where are we going, Darach?"

"I have no bloody clue." He headed up another set of stairs. "The castle is different."

"And built by the wizards chasing after us." She kept chuckling. "So good luck going anywhere they can't find you."

Though he thought he was running to another set of chambers, he wasn't. They ended up on a wide wall walk with dozens of burning torches. Stars glittered across the sky.

A dead end.

"Och," he murmured as he lowered her but kept her close. "We've nowhere else to go."

"Apparently not," she said softly as her eyes met his. "It seems I'm done running, one way or another."

"Aye?" He cupped her cheeks. "Because I'll keep chasing you if that's what you need."

They both knew what he was talking about. And it had nothing to do with love or proposals. No, it had everything to do with her not wanting him to die because he loved her. If she needed him to keep pursuing while she kept saying no, he would do it until his last breath.

"No," she whispered. "It's time for you to catch me...for us to have this."

"Found at last!" Adlin said.

Darach grinned at her. "I can toss you over my shoulder and head back down."

She smiled. "I'm pretty sure no matter where we go, they'll follow."

"Is it true then, Jackie?" William said as he and Robert clambered onto the wall walk with her friends and his family. "Are ye marrying him?"

"Darach," he provided.

"Are ye then, Jackie?" William repeated.

"I am," she confirmed.

William eyed Darach up and down. "Are ye sure, lass?"

"Definitely," she said.

"Och, 'tis fine that," Robert exclaimed, a wide smile on his face. "I approve."

"Ye would," William muttered.

"As should ye," Robert declared, shoulders back and voice firm. "Darach is a fine and noble Scotsman."

William eyed Robert. "Ye would stand up for him then?"

"I would," Robert said. "He has been kind to me. More than that, he cares for and would protect Jackie with his life. There is nothing more honorable."

"Aye," William agreed, still contemplating Robert before his eyes turned to Darach. "So ye've grown a pair of ballocks and will treat her as ye should?"

Darach would make no mistakes with the lad this time. He withdrew his sword, knelt on one knee, held out his blade on two spread palms and lowered his head. "Upon my sword, I swear that I will always protect Jackie, body and soul."

He didn't have to look up to know William was contemplating this carefully. "'Twas not the best display ye showed in the great hall," he said. "Ye seemed a wee bit...overeager."

"He has you pegged," Jackie said into his mind with a chuckle.

"Love can make men do foolish things." His eyes met William's. "But I can assure ye, great love is always worth it. And a lass like Jackie, more worth it than any."

"Ye mean that?"

"Never more so."

Their eyes held for a long moment and he wondered why he knelt before this lad. Why it felt so important. No matter, anyone who stood up for a lass's honor so well would always be worth kneeling before and respecting.

"Then ye have my blessing," William finally said as he backed away.

"As have ye mine," Robert said.

"Then a hug please," Jackie said as she crouched.

Robert grinned and flew into her arms. She squeezed him tight and murmured something in his ear before he darted off.

"I wouldn't mind one from you too, William," she said.

"Och, nay." William bowed. "Many thanks but 'twould be unseemly, m'Lady."

"Jackie."

"Nay." His eyes went from Darach to Jackie. "Ye are a lady and should be addressed as such."

"That's very sweet of you to say." She nodded and stood. "Thank you, William."

"All right then," Adlin said as a man with brown robes joined him. "Might we have a wedding then?"

Darach's eyes met Jackie's. "Might we?"

Their eyes held as she whispered, "Yes."

So as the torches dimmed and stars brightened, a scrap of MacLomain tartan was wrapped around their wrists. Though they were the last couple to come together of his generation, they were the first to marry. And while they likely had little time to enjoy it, nothing had ever felt more right when at last the vows were said, and he kissed her.

Nothing else mattered as he wrapped his arms around Jackie. Not their other lives. Not even the ring that still didn't glow.

Just them and this moment in time.

He heard the congratulations and felt the slaps on the back but nothing really got through as their eyes stayed with one another's.

"I want to…" she murmured into his mind, leaving the statement without end.

But he knew.

"Aye, lass," he replied before he swept her into his arms and they left it all behind. There was no memory of bringing her back to his chamber, only of the way she looked standing in front of him. Pale blond hair flowing down her back. Skin glowing. Big brown eyes eager.

His *wife*.

Everything he had ever wanted.

He took his time undressing her, cherishing every inch of flesh as though it was the first time he saw it. Its smooth, satiny texture. The way goosebumps rose in the wake of his touch. They didn't bother with the bed but fell to the fur in front of the fire.

"Jaqueline," he whispered as he pressed her hands to the floor and sunk into her welcoming heat. They groaned as she wrapped her legs around him and took him deeper. Then they slid and writhed against each other as they struggled to get closer…merge.

"Darach," she whispered as they rolled until she was on top and ground against him. There was no more beautiful sight than her hands pressing against his chest as her head fell back, her eyes closed and she swayed over him.

Though tempted to grab her waist and take control, he wanted her to have this. How they felt together. When she rolled her hips and slithered her body against his, any momentary willpower snapped in half.

He grabbed her arse and thrust hard.

Then it became a mad wash of near violent sex.

Like they did with words, they challenged with their bodies. Thrusting. Shifting. Taking. Giving. He had no clue where she began and he ended as they went far beyond sex and lovemaking to something different.

Closer.

More explosive.

Sweat-slicked, energized, he rolled his hips and kept thrusting. By the time he found his way to release and had her arms pinned over her head, a roar was on his lips and a scream on hers. The sex was so bloody good. The second it ended he wanted it again.

They must have dozed off because the next thing he knew daylight flooded the chamber and she was tucked by his side, sound asleep. Darach flicked his wrist and the blanket on the bed was wrapped around her. Pulling her tighter against him, he inhaled the sweet scent of her hair and closed his eyes.

"We must leave soon, Son," his father said into his mind. *"Trouble comes and it cannae come here."*

Darach pressed his nose into her soft hair and tried to ignore his father, tried to ignore that though he might finally have his lass where he wanted her, she wasn't truly there at all. She might be his wife now, but there was still someone out there that wanted her just as much...or *something*. Something so dark and evil that he knew his father was right. They shouldn't be here anymore.

He was about to respond when he felt some sort of shift. Fear. Sadness. His magic responded to something, but he couldn't quite figure out what.

Soon enough, he understood.

"We're leaving now, back to our own era," Grant said into his mind, just as upset. Yet it seemed his father knew exactly what had happened. *"Eoghan couldnae find us so he's bringing us to him. Hamilton Castle is under attack."*

Chapter Sixteen

"LASS, WAKE UP. We must go." Jackie's eyes shot open at the urgency in Darach's voice. With a flick of his wrist, both of them were dressed.

"What's going on?" She had never seen him so upset as he strapped on his weapons. "Talk to me, Darach."

"My castle's under attack," he growled. "My people."

"Oh, my God," she exclaimed. Any sleepiness she felt vanished.

"'Tis bad. Da and Adlin are moving us fast." He yanked her against him as magic swirled out of nowhere. Darach pressed her cheek against his chest and spoke within the mind as everything vanished and that familiar suctioning sensation began. *"Be prepared for anything. I dinnae know exactly where we'll end up. It could be in my castle or in the thick of battle."*

"Don't worry about me. I'll be okay," she said. *"Just focus on your people, all right?"*

"I am." He kissed the top of her head. *"You are my people too."*

Colors whipped and blended around them before the pressure and suction vanished, and screams rent the air. They were in the courtyard of Hamilton Castle, and it was insane. Loud. Chaotic. And even though the gates were closed, it was clear the battle wasn't going well. Enemy warriors had somehow cleared both portcullises, and some were making it over the battlements. Darach shoved her behind his back and whipped a dagger at one who had just made it into the courtyard.

"Protect Jackie and the wee King," Grant roared at Darach. "Get them into the castle."

"Aye." Darach nodded as he pressed a dagger into her hand, scooped up Robert, withdrew his sword and told her to stay close. Complete chaos reigned around them as more of the enemy made it into the courtyard, and the demi-god's shadow fluctuated on the horizon. The spirits of the *Genii Cucullati* screamed like banshees as they swooped and attacked.

205

As far as she could tell, her friends and all of Darach's cousins were here. Rònan, Erin, and Torra had just shifted into dragons and launched into the air. Heidrek followed Grant up to the tallest battement while Niall and Nicole helped protect her and Robert as they rushed toward the castle.

Yet too many were infiltrating. They were in serious trouble. Darach was trying to fight off warriors with Robert still in his arms. But their numbers were overwhelming.

"Put him down, Darach," she said, her voice far calmer than she felt. "I'll get him into the castle."

He sliced a man's throat. "Nay!"

More and more rushed him. While plenty of Hamilton warriors surrounded them and Niall and Nicole fought valiantly, it wasn't enough.

Jackie focused on remaining calm. In fact, she did as Darach had taught her and paid close attention to her surroundings. What building was closest if they couldn't make it to the castle. How many enemy warriors were between here and there.

Clearly sensing their position was too precarious, Darach shook his head and set Robert down. Though there was no time for their eyes to connect, she felt his faith in her. *"Go, lass. Get him to safety. Through the armory behind us, you'll find a hidden door on the side of the castle. 'Twill look like a statue. Hurry!"*

Though tempted to tell him to be careful, she didn't dare. She did not want to jinx things and lose him any sooner than necessary. So she said, *"Fight well. I'll see you soon."*

"Aye, love," he murmured, already in the thick of it as he crossed blades with several warriors.

Time to get out of here.

Robert shook his head when she tried to pick him up. "Nay, lass. I've two feet. We can travel faster if I run."

With no time to argue, she took his hand, and they raced for the armory with William and Nicole right behind them. They had no sooner entered when an enemy warrior appeared in the next room. Still remarkably calm, everything seemed to slow down. Jackie didn't think but loosened her wrist, aimed her dagger and whipped it hard. It caught the guy in the neck, and he fell to his knees.

But not before he whipped a dagger back.

It was definitely a reflex because his eyes were already bleary. Still, the dagger would have caught William dead on if Robert didn't shove him out of the way.

"Oh no!" Jackie cried when the dagger hit Robert's shoulder instead. Stunned, the boy stared at the blade before he passed out. She caught him before he fell.

"Lair, I need your help," she whispered into Darach's sister's mind, praying that she could hear her. That's all she dared say as they rushed out the backside of the armory and went left. There was no way to know who was listening, and she didn't want to give away their position.

Luckily, nobody pursued, and their route was well covered by trees. Cries of pain rent the air as they ran alongside the castle. Soon enough, she found a statue of a woman built into the stonework.

"Wow," Nicole whispered. "She looks just like you."

She did. How strange. But there was no time to worry about that because she needed to figure out how to get inside. It appeared impregnable.

"Look," Nicole mouthed and pointed. "She even has your birthmark."

Jackie peered closer. It definitely looked like her birthmark except it was slightly raised. Interesting. Drawn, she touched it...and it slid open. "Oh, wow," she whispered as they entered and it shut behind them.

There was just enough light to see up a long, spiral staircase as they climbed and climbed. When they reached the top, they entered a huge chamber tastefully done in shades of deep blue and burnt orange.

"Put him on the bed," Lair said as she rushed in.

Beyond grateful to see her, Jackie made Robert comfortable and took the rag Lair handed her. "As soon I pull the dagger free, press down hard on the wound."

She nodded, sick with worry as Lair started chanting then swiftly pulled the blade out. Jackie pressed the rag against the wound as Darach's sister closed her eyes and kept chanting softly. Meanwhile, William stood at the foot of the bed, brows furrowed and a deep frown on his face as he eyed Robert. Eventually, Lair stopped chanting and opened her eyes.

"He will recover," she said softly. "Remove the rag."

Being extra careful, Jackie pulled the rag back and was shocked by what she found. Though the wound was still there, it wasn't nearly as bad as before. It looked as if it had been healing for days. Lair pulled a pouch out of her pocket and applied a green herbal mixture before she wrapped the wound with a fresh bandage.

Nicole stood by the window with a troubled look in her eyes. "How safe are we here, Lair?"

"'Tis the safest spot in the castle," Lair replied as she pulled a blanket over Robert. "'Tis why Darach wanted the wee King brought here."

Jackie's heart caught in her throat when she joined Nicole and looked outside. Though the enemy had been pushed back, many Hamilton warriors had fallen. Darach and his cousins were with Grant and Heidrek on the battlements as the battle raged in the sky.

"Is it just me or are there a lot more warriors in the courtyard than before?" Nicole said. "And not our enemies but allies."

Lair nodded as she joined them. "Aye, warriors from the Thomson and Broun clans came to help."

"Aye?" William peered out. "The Thomson's are Lilas and Dougal's clan. How did they know to be here?"

"They are an allied clan. Though Lilas and Dougal are from a different era, they came to the aid of their own." Lair glanced at Nicole and Jackie. "As did the Brouns."

"I'll be damned," Nicole whispered.

Jackie looked to the sky when a strange sensation rolled through her. The dragons seemed to be holding their own as they fought the *Genii Cucullati*. But then it looked like Heidrek was helping them. Arms raised in the air, the dragon tattoo on his neck glowed brightly as he chanted. Whatever he was doing appeared to wrap inclement weather around the spirits, making them teeter and twist as they fought.

Meanwhile, Eoghan kept at those on the battlements.

Yet Lair saw it for what it was. "Och," she murmured. "The *Genii Cucullati* are keeping the dragons and Viking seer distracted. Less for the demi-god to deal with."

Fear spiked when she realized what was happening beyond the castle gates.

Death was spreading.

Literally.

The moat had gone dry, and the grass started to die in a wide arc around the castle. Even the trees began turning brown as their leaves fell.

"It's the Otherworld," Jackie and Nicole whispered at the same time.

"How is this possible?" Jackie said. It appeared all the Hamilton warriors and their allies were inside the gates. Thank God.

Lair didn't answer. Hands white-knuckling the windowsill, her eyes were trained on Grant and Darach. Alarmed, Jackie watched as Eoghan continued to battle the wizards. Specifically, Darach and his father.

Yet Eoghan spoke to her.

"Where are ye, my lass?" he whispered into her mind. *"Why will ye no' come with me? 'Twould release all these people from harm. They would forever be protected by my overlord, and we would be free to live the life stolen from us."*

"Och, your ring, m'Lady," William said.

It again twirled with blue and black.

"If I go to him I can save everyone," she whispered.

"Heck no." Nicole shook her head. "He tried that trick on Erin and I, so don't believe it for a sec."

"Yeah, but you weren't actually involved with him in another life," Jackie argued.

"Da told me everything." Lair frowned as her eyes met Jackie's. "Dinnae be foolish, lass. You'd do well to remember who our enemy serves. If ye go to him, the only end that will come is yer happiness and the lives of everyone ye love. And dinnae think for a moment 'twill go any other way once he has yer ring."

Lair's voice grew softer. "The Celtic demon will never let Eoghan keep ye. Tis wishful thinking. You've already escaped his clutches once and have the unique power to resurrect. He will keep you for his own purposes. Just imagine what he could do with such a thing."

Deep down, she knew Darach's sister was right, but that didn't make it any easier. Especially when Lair's gaze shifted sharply to the battlement and she whispered, "Nay, Da."

Eoghan now focused the entirety of his wrath on Darach, and it wasn't going well. Despite how hard he tried to hold up his sword, it fell from his hands. Terrified, numbness spread through her as blackness thrashed at him and he dropped to his knees in pain.

"No," she cried and gripped the windowsill.

She had to help him somehow. There had to be a way. She couldn't lose him. Not yet. They were too connected. Then it occurred to her.

Maybe she could use that connection.

So she tried something different and prayed it would work. She allowed her anxiety and fear to completely take over until she had no sensation. Then she focused hard and willed her numbness into *his* mind.

"*Nay, lass,*" he whispered. "*Get out of my head. Dinnae do this.*"

Lair's eyes widened. "Lass, if ye continue what yer doing, ye will switch yer sensations and take his pain as yer own."

"That's what I'm hoping," she whispered.

"Bloody hell," Lair muttered.

Seconds later, excruciating pain tore through her. It felt like a thousand bees stung her all at once from the inside out. She threw her head back and wailed. Her muscles felt like they'd been separated from her bones and every inch of her skin was being ripped off.

She would have fallen had Nicole and Lair not braced her up. Even William wrapped his arms around her and held on tight. Darach remained immobile, but at least now he wasn't suffering. She tried to focus on that as tears poured down her face.

"Nay, Da," Lair said again, distress twisting her features as her eyes remained on the battlements. "Dinnae do it."

Soon enough, it became clear what Lair sensed. Grant stepped in front of Darach and took the demi-god's wrath. Jackie's pain vanished, and though she knew Darach was no longer immobile, his father still held him back with magic.

What happened next was explosive. Terrifying. Near blinding.

When Grant's magic crashed against the demi-god's, it seemed to do them both a great deal of harm. Bluish gray wind wrapped and twisted around the black cloud and almost seemed to strangle it.

At first.

Then blackness seeped through Grant's blue magic and wrapped like a tornado around it. The ground shook. Darach roared but was drowned out by a loud boom. It was so strong that its shockwave blew Jackie's hair back.

A strangled sound came from Lair as not only the demi-god and *Genii Cucullati,* but Grant vanished. There was nothing left but ashes and a few scraps of plaid blowing in the wind.

"It's okay. Grant's okay," Nicole said, her words stunted. "The same thing happened to Rònan before he ended up in the Celtic Otherworld...alive."

"Nay," Lair whispered, tears streaking her cheeks. "That was true death. There can be no doubt. He is my Da, and I'm a healer. We know things about the human body that others dinnae. How its life force works."

Jackie kept shaking her head, her eyes locked on Darach who remained on his knees, trembling as he stared at his father's ashes. This couldn't be happening. Grant could not be gone. She tore her eyes from Darach and took Lair's hand. "Go be with your family. I'll stay with Robert."

"Nay." Lost, Lair's eyes met hers. "Darach needs his wife. Go to him."

When Jackie started to argue, Lair shook her head sharply. "Dinnae make me ask again." She pulled away and though shaky, sat beside Robert. "All of ye go, please. I need some time alone."

Speechless, Jackie kept staring at Lair.

"Come on, sweetie. She needs space, and I don't blame her," Nicole said softly as she took Jackie's hand and pulled her along. "You too, William. Let's go."

Everything seemed surreal as Nicole led her out a different door. They traveled down several sets of stairs and long hallways before they came to a wide set of stairs that led down to the center of a massive great hall. She'd never seen anything so spacious.

"Dear God...where am I?" she whispered as her eyes floated over the vaulted, cathedral-like gothic ceilings and hundreds of tall, thin stain-glassed windows. It was stunning. Remarkable.

"You're still in your new home." Nicole led her downstairs. "This is the heart of Hamilton Castle. Unbelievable, isn't it?"

Jackie nodded and kept walking as if lost in a haunted fairy tale that mixed a beautiful beginning with a terrible end. In an alternate reality, living in a place like this with a man like Darach would have been magical. A dream come true. But now it was shrouded in sadness. A nightmare. Because dreams didn't begin knowing you are dying, and they certainly didn't come to life with death, be it Grant's or the others who lost their lives today.

Blood stained the ground, and the crowd was somber as they filtered through the courtyard. Her eyes went to the fallen who wore Hamilton plaids. Thankfully, she saw none that matched the Broun or Thomson colors. Still, the further she walked, the more upset she grew. And of course, the more numb she became. She didn't want to find forgiveness in this slaughter. Instead, she allowed rage and heartache to fill her.

By the time she made it to the stairs leading up to the battlements, her feet were tingling, and angry heat filled her veins. A feeling she remembered all too well. And though she started to hear murmurs of amazement filter through the crowd, she never looked back as she climbed the stairs.

Speckled with blood and eyes damp with sadness, Darach's cousin Machara stood at the top. She lowered her head, stepped aside and murmured, "He's over there."

Darach still knelt but sat back on his heels with his shoulders slumped and his head hung. Not only his cousins but several uncles stood behind him with their heads bent. She had met them all before. Colin MacLomain, Bradon, Malcolm and Colin MacLeod. Those who had been part of the Next Generation.

Grant's generation.

But where was Sheila? Jackie's heart broke for her.

Yet right now, all she could focus on was Darach. His immense sadness. *Their* immense sadness. Because his grief was every inch hers. She said nothing but dropped to her knees in front of him. Half a breath later, she was in his arms. Face buried in her hair, he wrapped his arms around her tightly and held on as if she were the only thing grounding him.

He remained silent for a long time as he held her. His emotions shifted and fluctuated rapidly between sadness and anger. Incredible anger. And while she understood it, she refused to let it ravage him. So she pushed comforting thoughts into his mind. Ones that reminded him he wasn't alone. He had his family, his clan and *her*. She reminded him how much love still surrounded him. How his father would want him to focus on that. How his father would want him to be strong rather than embrace bitterness.

Eventually, a soft but firm voice broke through everything.

"Son," Sheila said. "It's time for you to be strong. You're laird now and must be with your people. Your clan."

"I cannae," he whispered into Jackie's mind.

She pulled back, met his eyes and spoke aloud. "But you have to...for your dad."

A different sort of sadness flickered in his eyes and he shook his head.

"What is it?" she murmured.

He stared at her for a long moment. "I dreamt you died in my arms when I was laird."

"That's why you've avoided becoming laird for so long?" Emotion welled, and her throat thickened. "Because of me?"

When he nodded, she pushed aside her emotions and said what needed to be said. "Well, now you know I'm going to die either way." She cupped his cheeks. "So it's time to step up because it's not about me anymore. Not in the least. Now it's about doing right by your clan and being the man your father expects you to be."

Their eyes held for several long moments before he nodded and kissed her palm, murmuring, "Aye then, lass."

He pulled her up and looked at his mother, whispering, "I'm so verra sorry Ma."

Sheila was pale and her eyes red-rimmed, but she stood tall. When he went to embrace her, she shook her head. "Not right now, Son. I'm okay." She gestured at the crowd. "You are the Hamilton chieftain now and need to address your people. Though Jackie bolstered them considerably, they still mourn for your father...for all of us. They need to see that you're well. That you can lead them."

Confused, Jackie said, "How did I bolster them?"

A soft smile came to Sheila's lips. "Though they don't know who did it, you resurrected every fallen Hamilton warrior. Not the enemy...just your new clan."

Shocked, she looked down into the courtyard. Sure as heck, every fallen Hamilton was standing. Some embraced their family while others their fellow soldiers.

"Bloody hell," Darach whispered. "Thank you, Jackie."

"I didn't... I don't..." She shook her head. "What I mean to say is I didn't do it consciously so I'm not so sure you should thank me."

"Nay, these men wouldnae be standing if you didnae feel great emotion for them." He took her hand and met her eyes. "You should be verra proud of your gift, lass. 'Tis part of who you are and brings great joy to those you touch."

Jackie didn't quite know what to say so merely nodded. Darach squeezed her hand and kissed her cheek before his eyes swept over the lifeless, dead land beyond the castle. His thoughts filtered down to two singular emotions.

Determination and a need for revenge.

His jaw clenched as his gaze went to his cousins. They seemed to understand because they nodded, their expressions just as fierce. Then his eyes met his mother's. Sheila stood up a little taller and nodded as well.

He had an impregnable wall of support behind him.

Darach never released Jackie's hand but walked to the edge of the battlement and faced the courtyard. The crowd quieted and a long moment passed before he spoke. She felt the air shift around them and knew he used magic to make sure everyone heard him.

"Let me begin by thanking each and every one of ye for fighting so well this day." His gaze roamed the crowd as he made a point of meeting as many eyes as possible. "Not only my own kin but those of ye who are Broun and Thomson. 'Twas admirable and willnae be forgotten by the Hamilton clan. We are kin and will always help if ye are ever in need."

People cheered, but it was a low, tempered sound. One that bespoke underlying sadness. One that Darach now addressed.

"We lost a great man today." She felt the surge of emotion he pushed down save for a small part. That came through clearly in the huskiness of his voice. "My Da not only led this clan to greatness but he loved ye with all his heart. Ye have been every inch his lifeblood for a verra long time."

There were sniffles far and wide as Darach continued. "For too long now I have wondered if I could ever fill his shoes." He shook his head. "And 'twas not because he was such a powerful wizard but for another reason altogether."

Jackie squeezed his hand when he paused and fought back another wave of emotion.

His eyes met hers and he nodded before he continued speaking. "I might have grown up here, and ye are my kin, but ye didnae know my secret. The overwhelming, crippling anger I felt at how badly my Da was treated at this castle when he was but a young lad." He shook his head. "But it turns out I was wrong and have only just recently realized it. 'Twas never this castle and certainly not this clan that bothered me. 'Twas that monster Kier Hamilton, who festered here beforehand."

"Aye, he was pure darkness," many older clansmen murmured.

"But he isnae here anymore, and I dinnae intend to let any of his ilk infest the Hamilton's again so long as I draw breath. So now I have to ask ye something because I willnae have it any other way..." The crowd grew very silent as he eyed them. "My Da became laird of this clan because he loved ye and ye loved him just the same. So in good conscience, I willnae take his place simply because I am his son." Darach lowered to one knee and bent his head in respect. "I am yers only if 'tis what ye truly want."

It grew so quiet she didn't dare breathe.

She knew the crowd wouldn't shun him but would there be random murmurs of displeasure? After all, he'd just told them he had been angry for years. Though he made clear at whom, you never knew how people would take things.

"I for one would be honored to call ye Laird," a woman called out. "Yer as good a lad as yer da ever was!"

Jackie's brows perked when she spied the woman. Though older, there was no mistaking Kenzie. The teenage girl that young Grant had been so kind to in the cottage.

"Aye!" the crowd roared in response.

"Ye've a kind heart, Darach Hamilton," someone called out.

"None kinder!" another said.

"Aye!" the crowd roared again.

"Ye are loyal to kin and a fierce warrior," a man declared. "I would follow ye into battle always."

Jackie recognized the man as Kenzie's brother, Bryce.

"Aye!" the crowd roared in agreement.

The praise continued then shifted slightly.

"Och, and what a handsome laird ye'd make, Darach Hamilton," a young woman called out.

"Aye, he's mighty in battle and mighty in," another started before Darach stood swiftly, pulled Jackie against his side and interrupted the woman with one simple, awkward word. "Wife."

The crowd went silent and stared at them.

Jackie's face burned as she spoke within his mind. *"Great speech and I know you're going through a lot right now but could you maybe...I don't know...say more than that."*

"Aye, I just didnae want ye to think that..." His eyes met hers and whatever he was about to say trailed off. He cupped her cheek, and though he spoke to the crowd, he never looked away. "I found my Broun, the love of my bloody life and married her straight away. Meet my wife, Jackie."

Then he kissed her hard.

Not a quick, chaste kiss but the kind that made her knees weak and had her wrapping her fists into his tunic. Whistles of approval rang out, and people clapped. Though she knew it was the last thing he wanted to do, Darach eventually ended the kiss and turned back to the crowd.

"I dinnae know what to expect next from the darkness that plagues this land, but I promise ye that my kin and I will get to the bottom of it." Darach looked to his family. "My Da might not be here, but ye've the strongest wizards, dragons and warriors right here to protect ye. We *will* defeat this evil and return the land to what it was."

"Aye!" the crowd roared.

"How else can it be since the gods brought our fallen back!" someone cried.

Jackie bit her lip, grateful they didn't know she had resurrected them. Yet she recognized an opportunity. Before Darach could respond, she said into his mind, *"Don't tell them it was me. Not yet. Maybe not ever."*

When he frowned at her, she continued, *"Don't you see? If they believe the gods are behind this, it'll keep their spirits up. Though mankind has done awful things in the past, they've also done amazing things when they thought God or their gods rallied behind their cause."*

"'Tis a lie, though," he replied. *"And I dinnae want to start as chieftain by lying to my people."*

"Jackie's right, Son," Sheila cut into their mental conversation. *"The land has died around this castle, and they just lost your father. You've done well to rally them so far, and I'm proud. But a person can only take so much. Most have families beyond these gates. If you*

216

want to keep hope in their hearts and stop them from leaving the castle, then they need to believe their loved ones are being protected by a higher power. When the time is right, and all is said and done, then share Jackie's gift and beg for their forgiveness that you didn't tell them sooner."

"Also," his mother continued. *"Though they would mean well, Jackie doesn't need the kind of attention they would show her if they knew the truth right now. It might be worshiping, but it would also be endless. It might also be dangerous. You don't know if someone in this crowd has an ailing child or wife. Imagine what they would do if they knew what Jackie was capable of. She might very well end up beyond these gates in a mob you couldn't control. If you can count on nothing else, Son, it's that humans will always be human. Most are capable of anything if it means saving their loved one's lives."*

Darach's eyes held Jackie's for a long moment before his attention returned to the crowd and he roared, "To the gods! And to God Himself! Might they and He always show us such favor!"

The crowd roared with approval.

"'Twas good council," Darach said into Jackie's mind before he wrapped his arms around her, pulled her close and murmured in her ear, "Ye are already an admirable Lady of Hamilton Castle, my lass."

"Thanks to good advice from the previous Lady of Hamilton Castle," she reminded.

"'Twas your idea to begin with. Ma just followed your lead." His eyes met hers. "But dinnae doubt I know where else your mind was at."

"I don't know what you're talking about."

"Aye, but you do," he said softly. "You weren't concerned in the least about being carried off by a crazed mob. Nay, you are as determined to keep our people at arm's length as you were me because you dinnae want anyone hurt when you leave."

He had hit it dead on. The idea of letting everyone down already hurt and she didn't even know them. What she *did* know was that she cared a great deal about Darach, and they were his clan, his people.

"There's just no point in sharing anything right now," she murmured.

"Aye, you and Ma convinced me of as much but," he tilted up her chin until their eyes met, "as soon as all of this is over, they'll know everything and nobody will be carrying you off anywhere. Not so long as I draw breath."

She almost said, "How could you when we won't be here because of your love for me," but didn't. He had been through enough today. Far too much. So she nodded, stood on her tip-toes and kissed his cheek. "Sounds good."

"I mean it, Jackie."

"So do I." She brushed her lips over his and met his eyes again. "You need to be with your clan now."

"Aye," he murmured. "The wee King is safe enough, and our people are protected. Go to the castle and rest."

"So you know what happened to Robert?" Jackie frowned. "You know that I did a crappy job of protecting him, and he nearly died."

"Nearly died?" Darach said. "Och, lass. He might be a wee bairn but he's strong, and my sister is a master healer. You protected him well by getting him to safety. If our future king decided to save another and take a blade, it shows great strength of character. That which he will someday need."

Her brows perked. "I guess that's one way to look at it."

"He's safe, and that's what matters most." Darach gestured toward the castle. "Go rest, lass. I need to visit with my clan and make sure all is well. It's been a truly difficult day."

Jackie held his gaze, and though she knew he was trying to keep things lighthearted not only for her sake but everyone else's, she felt his overwhelming sadness. Losing a parent was devastating.

"I don't want to rest. I'm worried about everyone," she said. "Would it be okay if I tagged along and kept you company? I'd like to…be there."

"You dinnae need to," he said softly. "'Tis not expected of you."

"I'm not worried about what's expected of me." She squeezed his hand. "I just *want* to…please."

Their eyes held before he finally relented. "Aye then, lass. I would like that."

So they spent the remainder of the day not only with the Hamiltons but the Brouns and Thomsons. Jackie remained impressed by how well liked Darach was and equally humbled by how well she was received. Though sad over losing Grant, a thread of hope had ignited not only because of the resurrections but because of Darach's words. He had touched everyone either with his speech or long beforehand.

When night fell, a bonfire was lit in the center of the courtyard as all paid their respects to the great Grant Hamilton. Sheila had long disappeared, and Lair remained in the castle, unseen and unheard from. Jackie never left Darach's side and did everything she could to keep his sadness from overwhelming him. While they said little if nothing, she noticed his cousins and her friends were always close. Always there if they needed them.

It was a good thing the courtyard and castle were huge because there were an alarming amount of people to house. That, it appeared, was something his aunts and uncles saw to because by the time Darach bid all good night, everyone had a spot and seemed content enough.

"Where are we going?" she said as he led her up the stairs in the great hall.

"To your chamber."

"*My* chamber?"

"Aye." He led her down a familiar hallway then up more stairs.

"I don't understand," she whispered but had a feeling she was starting to.

"Lass, I've been dreaming about ye for years," he said, brogue thickening as they went down another long hallway and up more stairs.

"I know, but you couldn't have possibly," she began but trailed off as he led her up the final spiraling set of stairs.

"Possibly what? Made sure a room waited for ye if ye ever arrived?" he murmured as he led her into the huge bedroom she had been in earlier. His eyes met hers. "This chamber has been yers for well over a decade, lass."

Chapter Seventeen

DARACH HAD IMAGINED this moment for years. That someday he would walk the lass from his dreams into this chamber. What he never could have imagined was that it would end up being a sanctuary to keep her and the future King of Scotland safe. More so, that he would be so bloody sad when they entered it together for the first time.

Rightfully so, Jackie wasn't awed but distressed when she looked at the bed. "Robert's not here anymore." Her eyes went to him. "I take it he's somewhere safe?"

"He is," Darach assured as he touched the small of her back and led her further in. "No need to worry. All is as well as it can be for now."

Her eyes met his. "I sense how guilty you feel for being up here when you could still be downstairs."

"Aye." He tried to fight exhaustion. "'Tis where their laird should be."

"Maybe." She urged him to sit on the bed. "But I think it's safe to say they understand how sad you are right now. That you need some time alone. You just lost your dad, Darach. That's not easy."

He sighed. "Nay, 'tis not."

"You need rest," she said firmly as she untied his boots. He watched her without really seeing. His Da was gone. *Dead.* At first, he hoped he was wrong and what happened was similar to Rònan's experience, but his sister soon squelched that thought. Not just his life form but his essence was gone.

There could be no resurrection.

His father had sacrificed everything to defend Darach.

To keep his son safe.

Jackie pulled off one boot then the other before she took his hands and met his eyes. "Favor?"

"Aye, lass."

"Stand."

So he did, ready for anything she wanted, anything she desired, despite how sad he was. Yet when he stood, she leaned around him, pulled back the blankets then met his eyes. "Now sit."

So he did and rested his hands on her hips, lust flaring despite all they'd been through.

"Nope, not what you need." She patted the pillow. "Lie down."

"Nay," he whispered, pulling her close until he rested his cheek against her stomach. "I dinnae want to sleep."

"I know," she whispered and caressed his hair. "But you need to."

Darach's eyes slid shut. "Nay."

Lost in exhaustion and grief, he had no idea she managed to lie him down until he awoke much later. Fire crackled on the hearth and torchlight flickered against the deep purple shadows of pre-dawn. As he had done to her earlier, she was propped on an elbow, her gaze tender.

"How long have you been watching me, lass?" he murmured.

"For a while." She trailed a finger along his jaw. "You're hard to look away from."

A smile curled his lips at the familiar words before he remembered where they were and all that had happened.

"Och." He closed his eyes. "I slept when I shouldnae have."

"You slept when you needed to," she said softly.

"Tell me it was all a nightmare, that none of it happened," he whispered as her hand slid into his. "Tell me Da isnae dead."

"I can't tell you that," she whispered so softly he barely heard it.

Darach had yet to cry, had yet to shed a bloody tear. Because that would make all of this real. Yet when she rested her cheek against his chest, and her sadness blew through him, a new level of grief made his chest tighten.

He could let go with her.

He was allowed.

So he did. In his own way. He wrapped his arms around her and grieved. Tears likely fell, but he didn't feel them. He only felt her as memories of his father washed over him. She felt like an anchor in a wave of emotions that flipped him every which way in a sea that he couldn't control. He never let go but held on tight no matter how rough the waters.

Needing more, both distraction and release, he pulled her lips to his. Their tongues twirled as he pressed closer to her warm body. There would be no foreplay. He was too desperate. So a chant later, their clothing was gone.

"You should rest," she whispered into his mind.

"I have," he whispered back as he came over her. *"I will."*

Until then, he wanted to be with her...*in* her. There was no need to wedge her thighs apart. She spread them willingly before he buried himself deep inside her. With a breathy sigh of relief and pleasure, she wrapped her arms around him and matched his every move. Not fast but very slow.

So slow.

He wanted to drown in everything she offered.

Escape.

Yet oddly enough it felt like he was, at last, coming home.

She was finally in the chamber he had created for her long ago. Blues and oranges to match what he sensed of her. What he didn't realize at the time was that he had inherently chosen colors to match her transition. Blue...cool, aloof and contained. Orange...changing, warming, blossoming. He had designed this room to welcome and make the lass of his dreams comfortable.

One he never gave up hope on.

How often had he fantasized about making love to her here?

"Darach," she half whispered, half groaned as they moved against each other.

He slowed to a near stop, cupped her cheek and kissed her as though it were their first time. And it felt that way. As if they were just beginning. But then this was the first time he'd had her in his castle...as laird.

Eventually, he broke the kiss and quickened his pace.

When her eyes fluttered shut, a shudder rippled through her, and she arched, he was long past gone. He gripped the headboard and thrust twice more before his muscles seized. Teeth clenched, he made a guttural sound that was part animalistic and part anguished pleasure as he shook hard and released his seed.

After his muscles finally relaxed, he kissed her several more times before rolling them onto their sides facing each other. He gazed at her before he pulled her close then promptly drifted off to sleep. When he woke again, it was to the smell of fresh bannock and to the sight of his beautiful wife standing at the window. She wore a white chemise that billowed around her as she stared out.

His eyes widened at the strong sense of familiarity.

He had dreamt of this moment.

Sensing that he had awoken, her eyes drifted to him, and she offered a soft smile. "Hey there. How are you feeling?"

Sad. Changed. A different man than he was yesterday.

But always happy to see her.

Darach sat up. He should get back downstairs.

"No, Son. You should rest more," his mother said into his mind. *"Your aunts, uncles and cousins have everything under control."*

"Nay, I should—"

"This isn't up for debate." Then she left his mind.

He knew better than to argue with her so remained focused on Jackie.

"I'm feeling a wee bit better," he said in answer to her question. He held out his hand. "Come here, lass."

Though he knew she was tempted, she shook her head. "You need to eat first. Regain your energy."

"I think we both know I've no issues with my energy." He patted the bed. "Join me and I'll remind you."

Jackie shook her head. "I'm sure you will." She brought a tray of food and drinks over and set it down between them. "But first, you'll eat."

Darach sighed and eyed her. "You're pushy."

"I can be," she agreed. "Especially when I care about someone."

He sipped some water and eyed the food. "I'm not hungry."

"You're not supposed to be. You're depressed." She handed him a piece of bannock. "Even so, eat up so we don't have our first fight already."

Darach worked at a pout. "You'd argue with me even in light of my loss?"

"Absolutely." She gave him a pointed look. "You might've signed your death warrant by loving me but I don't intend to let you die beforehand from starvation."

"Och," he muttered and bit into the tasteless food. Though he could think of far better ways to start his day, he was warmed by her concern.

Jackie ate as well, but not that much. Instead, she spent the majority of the time persuading him to eat more. By the time they were finished, he'd polished off several slices of meat, another piece of bannock and a wedge of cheese.

"I never got the chance to thank you yesterday." Darach took her hand. "Not only for your support but for taking my pain when the demi-god attacked me." He pushed down troubled emotions as he remembered it. "You could have gotten seriously hurt, lass."

"It was worth the risk," she murmured. "You would've done the same."

"Aye, I would've, but I'm far stronger." He shook his head. "You cannae do that again."

"Sorry, but I will if I have to." She didn't seem all that miffed by his request but rather matter-of-fact. "My health is only going to go downhill so there's no point in worrying about me."

"Mayhap." He tried to keep his tone light. "But that doesnae mean I dinnae want to keep you around as long as possible."

When she said nothing, he continued. "Several times now I've felt the numbness you experience and have heard you use the word forgive to temper it. Why?"

"Because it helps me move past my anger." Jackie sighed. "Erin isn't a huge fan of the whole forgiveness thing because she sees it as me folding. Giving up the good fight. Forgiving means I'm caving." She shook her head. "But like me at first, she just couldn't accept the truth. This is a battle that can't be won. So I finally decided to forgive the fact I was sick. Once I did, it became easier."

"I can understand where both of you are coming from," he said. "But I stand with Erin. While forgiveness is good, I dinnae think you should give up the fight either."

"I get it. You feel that way because you're new to all of this." Emotion churned in her eyes, but she blinked it away, a determined set to her chin. "Like I said, it's incurable. The numbness and my sense of smell will get worse until they're permanent. Until then, embracing forgiveness seems to keep things under control. I know it sounds weird, but it works. It must lower my blood pressure or something. Which must mean less strain on the tumor and nerves." Her brows furrowed. "You're the only other thing that works."

He frowned. "I dinnae ken."

225

"I can feel you even when I go numb," she murmured. "I'm assuming it must have something to do with your magic."

"Aye, mayhap," he said. "But I would say 'tis more likely because of our unique connection."

"Could be," she whispered. He heard her thoughts. How she didn't want him connected in any way to her sickness. Before he could respond, she changed the subject. "They brought up a tub of water. It's still warm."

Though tempted to continue speaking of her illness, he figured she'd had enough for now. So he fingered a silky strand of her damp hair. "I'm sorry I missed watching you bathe, lass."

"I have to keep some things a mystery." A small smile curled her lips. "Besides, we seem to have started a tradition where we bathe separately."

"Aye." He managed a small grin. "A tradition that needs to end. I'd much rather bathe *with* you."

"I'm sure you'll get the opportunity." She eyed the chamber. "This room is gorgeous. Stately. So did I tell you in one of your dreams my favorite colors were blue and orange?"

"Not any dream I remember directly." His grin remained, and he was never more thankful considering his sadness. "'Twas just a strong feeling so I went with it."

"Interesting." Her eyes drifted over the oceanic tapestries before returning to him. "I'm curious about a few things."

"As am I."

Her brow swept up in response to his words, but she continued talking as she balanced a small piece of meat on its side. "Weren't your parents curious about this room? Why you had it designed?

"Nay." He shrugged. "But then it's been my chamber for years now."

"What?" Her eyes widened. "I thought you had it created for me?"

"I did," he said. "More so, for both of us. But then like you said, 'twould have been odd to create such a space and not reside in it."

"Didn't they question why it was made the safest?" She cocked her head. "I assume that means with magic."

"Aye, both with magic and location," he said. "I told them it was the perfect place for the wee King if he ever ended up here. I've been training my whole life to protect him so 'twas a logical assumption he would eventually arrive at this castle."

"True. That makes sense." She slanted a look at him as she stacked a piece of cheese against the propped up meat. "So my husband's not only a long term planner but clever as well. Not to mention devious."

"I like when you call me husband." He trailed a finger over her idle hand, increasingly amused by her food architecture. "Aye, though I dinnae think I was all that devious. The king would someday come, and I *did* need a larger chamber. If I thought of you during its creation, there cannae be any harm in that."

"I suppose not." She stacked another piece of meat on her wobbly creation before her eyes drifted to their bed. Huge with four posters, it could easily sleep many. "Nice bed. I'll bet it's gotten a lot of use."

Well, she certainly knew how to keep him distracted. He cocked the corner of his lip. "Are you jealous of who has been here before you, lass?"

"Of course not," she said a little too quickly as she took a chance with an extra wedge of cheese on what had become a teetering tower. "It's none of my business."

"Aye, you're probably right." He enjoyed playing with her. "You've lain with other lads, and I've lain with other lasses. There isnae any point in discussing it." A grin ghosted his lips. "Save to say that we're both better off because of our experiences."

There was a compliment in that, but she clearly wasn't interested in praise, sexual or otherwise.

"Right. I suppose all that matters is that I'm on birth control and practice safe sex. At least, I did before we got together." Her lips curled down, and she risked one wedge of cheese too many, toppling her tower. "I just figured because you had this room created…" She stopped and shook her head. "Never mind. Anyway, I'm curious about something else. The statue built into the castle. The one that looks like me." She pointed to her birthmark. "It even has this."

"Aye, 'tis you, lass," he said. "Yet another thing created by Goddess Brigit."

"No kidding." She tilted her head. "I'm surprised nobody in your family thought it was odd when I showed up. You would've thought someone would've mentioned the statue and connected the dots."

"That's because nobody knows about it but me. 'Twas recently created by the goddess in case of an emergency," he said. "She told me 'twould be visible when needed and thankfully 'twas."

"She seems to have an uncanny sense of foresight," Jackie said.

"Aye," he agreed. "But then she *is* a goddess. And one who likes to play games at that."

"Evidently."

Darach studied her. "Might I ask you something as well, lass?"

"Sure."

"What did my Ma say to change your mind about marrying me?"

Jackie considered him for a long moment before sharing. "She pointed out something I couldn't dispute."

"What was that?"

"Like I told you, I connected with your mom at the Viking fortress. We had lots of time to talk so she knew that my parents wanted me to marry before I got my inheritance. That they believed in true love above all else." Her eyes met his. "Not only would they have liked you but they would have wanted me to follow my heart no matter the risk." She grew more emotional. "They would have wanted me to marry you. They would've given their blessing."

"'Tis good to hear." He wrapped his fingers around hers. "I wish I could have met them."

"Me too." Their eyes held for a long moment. "You have a pretty wise mother, you know."

"Aye," he agreed. "I'm verra lucky."

Jackie nodded as her eyes swept over the bed again. Though she was eager to distract herself, it wasn't so easy, and she was back to thinking about who'd been there before her. Darach flicked his wrist and removed the tray. Perfect time to put her concerns to rest.

Her eyes widened when she saw his intent. "Oh no, you don't."

Before she could get far, she was on her back beneath him. She wasn't going anywhere. Propped up on one hand, he wound the other into her hair and made sure her eyes stayed with his. "I know you're still curious about the bed." He dropped a kiss on her lips. "You're the first lass to sleep in it."

"I wouldn't care if I wasn't," she fibbed, a telling light of relief in her eyes. "It's your room."

"*Our* room."

She trailed a finger over his straining bicep, her voice softer. "Our room." Her eyes stayed with his. "So where did you go to—"

Darach put a finger to her lips and shook his head. "Never here, lass. That's all that matters."

He brushed his finger down her neck, pleased by her gooseflesh and the shudder that rippled through her. Before she could utter another word about previous partners, he pulled up her chemise, settled between her thighs and spent longer than intended showing her just how much this bed really was *hers*.

By the time they finished and he dried off from his bath it was mid-morning. As sated as him, Jackie sat at the table and watched out of the corner of her eyes as he wrapped his plaid.

"'Tis cute how you fiddle with things," he mentioned as she appeared to be creating some new design with the left-overs. "First the pebble at the glade, now the food."

She pulled her hand back as though she hadn't realized she was doing it. "I don't know that I'd call it cute. My uncle would call it unbecoming." She shrugged. "I picked it up after I traveled back in time."

He pulled on his boots. "Really?"

"Yeah. Like I hinted at before, life was a lot different back home. I was expected to act a certain way. Always use the right utensils and say the right thing. Be a lady. Fiddling with anything would have been frowned upon." A guilty little grin crawled onto her face. "I guess a new me is emerging here." Her eyes met his. "With you…because of you."

"Good to hear, lass." He winked. "Because this 'you' will be the perfect Lady of Hamilton Castle."

"And here I thought a more refined woman would be better suited as the laird's wife."

"Och, nay, there's no fun in that." He pulled on his tunic. "Ma was in your position for almost three decades. Does she strike you as all that refined?"

When she didn't respond, he looked her way and froze. Her body was limp, and her eyes were rolled back in her head.

"Bloody hell. Jackie?" Fear spiked as he scooped her up and laid her on the bed. "Lass?" He cupped her cheeks. "Can you hear me?"

He called to her telepathically.

Still no response.

"Lair, I need yer help," he roared into his sister's mind. *"Something's wrong with Jackie."*

"Aye, brother," she responded. *"I'm coming."*

He tried to remain calm. This couldn't be happening. Jackie could not be leaving him all ready. He wouldn't allow it. They needed more time. Far more time. Though Lair arrived within minutes, it felt like hours. Thankfully, Aunt McKayla was with her.

"What happened?" his aunt asked as they went to Jackie.

"She passed out." Darach shifted around to the other side of the bed. "She willnae even respond within the mind."

"So she is beyond simply passed out," Lair murmured as she pressed her palms against Jackie's temples and started chanting.

Meanwhile, Aunt McKayla put a hand against Jackie's sternum and closed her eyes. She was connecting to Lair's magic so they could search out the problem together.

"It's grown," Lair whispered between chants. "Influenced by dark magic."

"What's grown?" But he knew. He frowned and squeezed Jackie's hand, his chest tight. "The tumor?"

"Aye," his aunt murmured. "Recently. When she took the brunt of the demi-god's wrath."

"Och, nay," he whispered and pressed his lips against her palm. "When she took my pain."

Lair nodded but kept chanting before she stopped abruptly and pulled her hands back. Her eyes met McKayla's and understanding passed between them.

"What is it?" he asked, more concerned by the moment.

"'Tis something odd about her tumor." Lair frowned. "Has she tried to have it removed?"

"I dinnae think so." He shook his head. "She said 'twas inoperable."

"Aye, mayhap inoperable," Lair said, her eyes still on Jackie's face.

"I dinnae ken, Sister." Darach tried to keep aggravation at bay. He wanted answers. "What are ye trying to say?"

"There is something unnatural about her tumor. Something I sense dark magic can control." Her eyes narrowed on Jackie's ring. "Look, Brother."

"Bloody hell, nay," he whispered.

The stone at its center wasn't blue in the least but black.

He was about to say more when Erin and Nicole rushed into the chamber. Though they were clearly worried about Jackie, that wasn't the sole reason they were there.

"We've got problems." Nicole gestured out the window. "There are some super spooky sounds coming from beyond the castle. Horrible wailing. Good thing I seem to be the only one who can hear them because they'd likely throw this whole place into a panic."

"*There's more.*" Erin stood at the end of the bed and frowned at Jackie. "*I just had another one of my ghostly out-of-body experiences.*" Her eyes went to Darach. "*And you're seriously not gonna like it.*"

"I dinnae like a damn thing happening right now, but I've no choice but to face it." His frown deepened. "So tell me."

"*Whatever is going on with her illness is only going to get worse if she stays here. Or so I assume based on what you're about to do.*" Erin clenched her jaw and shook her head as she eyed Jackie's ring. "*You must put her on Eara and send her out beyond the gates. When you do, life will return to everything around the castle as death fades away.*"

"I would never do such a thing." He shook his head, confused. "Besides, Eara isnae even here."

"*Actually,*" Erin said softly. "*She appeared a few minutes ago beyond the gates.*"

"Nay."

"*Aye, lad,*" Eara said into his mind. "*I am here, and ye must bring Jackie to me if ye want to save her. 'Twill also spread hope to yer clan to see this land alive again.*"

Baffled, defiant, he shook his head. "Where would ye take her? And why would the land heal?"

"*Jackie can only go to the Otherworld now, lad,*" Eara said softly. "*She cannae survive here.*"

It felt like everything dropped out from beneath him. "But she's still alive." His eyes went to the very slight rise and fall of her chest. "She breathes."

"Mayhap." Aunt McKayla's pained eyes met his. "But not for long."

"Hell." Nicole sank down beside Darach. "I thought...I mean...things don't usually work this way with tumors, do they?"

"There isnae anything normal about her tumor. I've dealt with several and this isnae one. 'Tis different." Lair's eyes went to Darach. "I think 'twas somehow created by the demi-god." Her frown deepened, and her voice went whisper soft. "And I think only he can heal it."

"How can that be?" Darach kept shaking his head. "Da or Adlin would have figured it out. They would have told me."

"Nay, Brother, they might have been powerful, but neither were healers," she said. "So they wouldnae have known."

"But Goddess Brigit would have," he said. "And she would have told me."

"*You mean the goddess who likes to play games?*" Erin reminded.

"She wouldnae about something so grave," he assured. Would she? He shook his head. "'Twould make no sense."

"Damn." Nicole flinched in pain and yanked out her hearing aid. "The wails are getting louder."

"Rumor has spread that there's a bonnie horse beyond the gates," Sheila said from the doorway. "You need to go down now, Son." Her sad eyes went from Jackie to him. "You need to take care of your wife and your clan."

He knew what she asked of him. Darach bit back emotion. "Nay, I willnae let her go."

"You will do what you must." Sheila joined them and put a hand on his shoulder. "Not only do the Hamilton's have family beyond these gates, but the Thomson's and Broun's do too. If you've a way to lift the curse on this land, you will." Moisture flashed in her eyes before she grew sterner. "And if you've a chance to save your love, then you must do it."

"Save her?" he guffawed. "Handing her over to evil isnae saving her."

"Neither is keeping her here," she said. "At least, if you send her to where she can survive, there's always a chance you'll be able to find her later. If not, she dies in this bed." Her eyes went to Jackie. "And she deserves more than that. She deserves the chance to fight."

Fight? An odd turn of phrase considering what he and Jackie had recently discussed. Had they been talking about her illness right now he would have agreed. She should fight. She should try to survive.

Then it occurred to him.

His eyes shot to his mother's when he realized what she meant.

Jackie *should* try to fight her illness.

Maybe not in the typical sense because the rules had changed. It seemed the fight would not come from this reality but another. An afterlife of sorts. Because the Celtic Otherworld they all knew thus far was Eoghan's creation. A dead place co-created by Balor. Not Heaven but very much a version of hell.

"But how can she possibly fight such darkness on her own?" he said. "Not even Da could win against the demi-god. How is Jackie supposed to stand up against not only Eoghan but Balor?"

"I don't know," his mother said softly. "But I think she deserves the chance."

"*Eara will be with her, and I'll bet just about anything that she's merged with someone powerful,*" Erin said as her eyes met his. Emotion thickened her voice. "*If there's one thing I know…we both know about Jackie, it's that she wouldn't want to die here with the Otherworld threatening everyone. Not when she has a chance to set everyone free.*" Her voice dropped to a whisper. "*Especially little Robert and William.*"

He knew how hard that was for her to say.

But she was absolutely right.

Darach stared at Jackie. How could he make such a difficult decision? Yet he knew there was only one choice. The one Jackie would make if she were awake.

"I need a moment alone with my lass," he murmured. "Then we'll be down."

"Aye, Brother, of course," Lair said softly, and they all left.

Darach pulled Jackie onto his lap and cradled her head. "I dinnae know if you can hear me, lass, but…" He paused. But what? I'm sending you to hell to fend for yourself. No. It was more than that. "I know you said you were done fighting. That you had accepted your fate." He stroked her cheek. "But I havenae. None of us have. And so you're going to have to fight after all. You're going to have to be verra brave and battle your darkness. Just a different type of darkness than you expected."

He paused again and fought emotion as he brushed his finger over her birthmark. "I believe you have this for a reason. Not only because you were once Gwendolyn but because you're so much more. *We* are so much more. Were you not able to open the door below stairs by touching the mark? And did those stairs not lead you to this room?" He struggled with his words. "'Twas the verra first place I saw you in my dreams. Right here in this room was where it began."

"It means something." He brushed her hair back from her cheek. "And I think whatever has brought you here will be there to fight alongside you." His brogue thickened. "But nothing can help ye if ye willnae fight to begin with, aye, lass? And me keeping ye here in this room will only ensure that ye end where ye began and I willnae have it."

"So 'tis time to fight, lass." He kissed her birthmark, laid her down and strapped on what few weapons he had. Two daggers and his sword. *The* sword. Then he leaned down and whispered in her ear, "But know this," he kissed her lips then lifted her, "I'll not let ye fight alone if I can help it."

By the time he made it down to the courtyard, the battlements were full, and a small crowd had formed around the gate. His family and Jackie's friends were waiting.

"The people only know that yer letting the horse in," his Uncle Malcolm said into his mind. *"Not that ye'll be sending Jackie with her."*

The gates were opened as he strode forward. Murmurs of curiosity rippled through the crowd as they wondered why he carried his wife. Better yet, why she appeared to be sleeping. As soon as he passed through the gates, he murmured a chant, and the gates slammed shut.

"I'll not have anyone put their lives at risk out here," he said into his family's minds.

Eara lowered her head at his approach, her voice sad. *"Put her on me, lad. She willnae fall."*

234

Darach nodded and raked his eyes over Jackie one last time before he swung her up onto the horse and made sure she was draped evenly over Eara's neck.

"I love ye, lass," he whispered before Eara turned and started across the first drawbridge. Darach flicked his wrists and the portcullises rose. Just like Erin said, life began to return in the horse's wake. The moat filled with water and greenery started to bloom on the vines crawling up the battlements.

Life returned in the wake of a lass sent to face the darkness alone.

Just like she had all along with her tumor.

He understood that this had to happen to save his people but the further the horse trotted the more his chest tightened. His clan was not alone. She was. His clan had the magic of wizards, warriors and dragons protecting them. She did not. Yes, he knew that something would be there to help her, he felt it, but that just wasn't good enough.

His lass would *not* face this alone.

To hell with that.

He raced after her.

Chapter Eighteen

JACKIE COULD HEAR Darach. She could hear them all.

But nobody could hear her.

He was letting her go again. Just like he had in the beginning. And like before, it was to keep her alive. Yet this time was different. This time, she was in complete agreement with his decision. She would have made the same choice if she were awake. Anything to save everyone, especially the boys.

Even so, that didn't make any of this less frightening.

When she jolted awake at last, Eara had just reached the end of the drawbridge.

"Hold on tight, lass," Eara whispered. *"This willnae be an easy journey."*

"Nay, it willnae," came Darach's gruff voice as he swung up behind her. "But at least you willnae be alone."

"What are you doing?" she cried over her shoulder. "You're riding straight into death!"

"Aye." He wrapped a strong arm around her. "You knew I'd follow you into the afterlife, lass."

Jackie held on tight when Eara bolted. Is this what Grant meant when he said the man who loved her would die? Because for all intents and purposes, that's exactly what both of them were doing right now. When she glanced over her shoulder, it was just like Erin had said. Far and wide, the land came to life behind them.

Then it all ripped away as darkness swirled around them. Oppressive, dank, their surroundings became something she had long feared. The end. Those final moments when death took her, and she slipped into eternity alone.

Yet she wasn't alone.

She might not be able to see a thing, but she felt Darach at her back. She felt the warmth and security of his arm wrapped around her in the cool, dark void they'd entered. Slowly but surely, shapes started to materialize. Not the Celtic Otherworld but a dark forest. Then something else. Tall standing stones that formed a circle.

"'Tis Brigit," Darach whispered. "We're in ancient Ireland."

Face averted, a glowing woman knelt a few feet away. She dropped something into a small hole. Within seconds, a small sprout shot up, sparkling as its root thickened and twisted and its branches reached out.

"The great oak Chiomara coupled with King Erc beneath," he murmured into her mind. *"Where Adlin was conceived."*

The woman stood and vanished but not before an acorn fell from the tree and landed in her palm. Then the landscape shifted. Jackie narrowed her eyes. It couldn't be. *"Eara, are we at the American Stonehenge in New Hampshire?"*

The horse gave no response but slowed to a trot as they passed through what was definitely Stonehenge. But everything was different. Then she realized. There were no landmarks. No platforms where you could read about each stone and its alignment with the horizon.

"I think I saw someone up ahead," Darach whispered.

Jackie peered through the darkness. He was right. Someone walked through the woods. Slightly aglow, it appeared to be Brigit again. Soon, another woman joined her. Slight of build with long, dark hair, she thought it was Erin at first. But no. Her hair wasn't as curly.

"This will help connect your kin with the MacLomains." Brigit dropped the acorn into the woman's hand. "Place it where ye will, Iosbail."

Iosbail? As in Iosbail Broun…or MacLomain depending on who you asked. She was Adlin's sister, once an immortal wizard just like him.

The goddess vanished, and they followed Iosbail through the forest. Caught in these strange in-between worlds, it was clear they were silent, unknown witnesses to history.

Eventually, Iosbail stopped and crouched. Jackie looked around. Though there were only trees around them, the area felt familiar. "Darach? I think we might be…" she started but stopped when Iosbail dropped the acorn in a small hole. Just like before, a small sprout shot up, sparkling as its trunk thickened and its branches grew.

"Oh my God," she whispered, eyes moist. It was the old oak that would someday sit in front of the Colonial. And based on the location of the tree, Eara had stopped right where Darach stood the first time Jackie laid eyes on him.

Iosbail came to her feet as the Oak bloomed overhead. She put out her hand and one of its acorns dropped into her palm. When a little old woman hobbled out of the forest, Iosbail handed her the acorn. Animals drifted around the woman. A squirrel sat on her shoulder.

"Fionn Mac Cumhail," Darach murmured.

Fionn? But she thought he was a golden Celtic warrior.

"Sometimes seen as an old woman as well," Darach said. "But his animals are always ghostly not solid like they are now."

Jackie swallowed. "What does that mean?"

"That we arenae in the world of the living, lass."

She sort of figured as much but had hoped not.

Eara started walking, and their surroundings shifted yet again. This time, they rode beside a mountain face. The little old woman lumbered along until she began to glow. Seconds later, a tall, strapping blond warrior appeared in her place.

"Oh, wow," Jackie whispered as Fionn crouched next to the mountain and dropped the acorn in a hole.

"Bloody hell," Darach murmured. "I always thought..."

"Thought what?" she prompted when his words died off. "Where are we?"

"I always thought this tree was born directly of the oak in Ireland," he continued in awe as a sprout shot up and thickened into a trunk that grew up the side of the mountain face, sparkling, until its branches wrapped into a cave far overhead.

"Where are we?" she asked again.

"One of the Defiances," he murmured. "'Tis a mountain of many things."

Jackie's eyes rounded as she peered upward. "Are we at the Magical Mountain of Fertility?"

"I forgot Nicole had named it." He chuckled. "Aye, 'tis precisely where we are."

Eara started walking again. This time, woodland didn't appear in front of them but rock and open sky. It looked like they were near the top of a mountain.

"Where are we now?" she whispered.

"The same mountain."

His arm tightened around her as a dragon appeared through the darkness. A man with blond hair stood in front of it with Iosbail nearby.

"Och, 'tis Uncle Colin but much younger," Darach said.

He had two Uncle Colin's. "Based on his build, I'm going to guess Rònan's dad?"

"Aye," he said as colors swirled around the dragon until a young woman lay curled up on the ground.

"Aunt Torra," he whispered as her hand opened and an acorn rolled out of it. Moments later, it took root and sprouted. This time, it blossomed into a small oak. "'Tis the baby oak when born over thirty winters ago."

"You mean the huge oak outside of MacLomain Castle?"

"Aye."

Though everyone vanished, she and Darach remained where they were. She narrowed her eyes. "Do you see that?"

"What?"

"Let me down." She tugged at his arm. "Please."

"Why?"

"I think I see an acorn." She tugged at his arm again. "And nobody's here to catch it." She shot him a look over her shoulder. "Don't you find that suspicious?"

"Aye, suspicious enough for us to stay put."

Eara stomped her foot and neighed.

"What is it, Eara?" he asked.

No response.

Instead, the horse neighed louder and stomped her foot again.

"I'd say Eara agrees," Jackie said. "Time to get off."

Though he didn't seem pleased in the least, Darach grunted, swung off then pulled her down. Jackie strode over and knelt in front of the tree. There it was. A tiny little acorn. "Oh, look at it."

"Where, lass?" He crouched beside her. "I dinnae see anything."

When an all too familiar tingling ran through her, she held out her palm beneath it. She swore she saw a burst of sparkles before the acorn fell into her hand.

Darach's eyes widened. "That wasnae there a moment ago."

"Uh oh." She closed her fist around the acorn as colors started to swirl around the little oak. Darach pulled her away as the tree twisted into a small tornado and wind whipped at them. He wrapped his arms around her but not before the tornado flew into her closed palm.

"Holy crap," she exclaimed but didn't release the acorn. Rather, she clenched it tighter when Darach pressed her head against his chest as the wind increased. It was so strong, he barely kept them afoot as he braced his legs.

When the wind finally stopped, darkness shrouded them at first. Jackie blinked as she tried to adjust to the dim lighting. "Where are we?"

Darach kept her close and narrowed his eyes. "I think 'tis the meadow in front of MacLomain Castle."

Again, he was right. The castle was a dim shadow backdropped by a soupy, dark loch. Like it was outside Hamilton Castle when they left, everything appeared dead.

"What's that?" he whispered.

"What?"

"Come." He pulled her after him. "I think I see someone lying on the ground."

Jackie ran after him. Someone *was* lying on the ground. The closer they got, the odder she began to feel. Almost a sense of trepidation. Darach slowed within feet of the body and shook his head. "Nay, it cannae be!"

He tore away, raced the rest of the way and fell to his knees. "Da?" Jackie bit back tears as he flipped the man over and pulled his head onto his lap.

It *was* Grant.

Darach pressed his ear to Grant's chest. "Nay," he whispered. "No heartbeat." He shook his father a little, his voice strained. "Wake up, Da. We wouldnae be here if there wasnae hope for ye."

Jackie knelt beside them and watched in distress as Darach continued trying to bring his father back from death in a land that was just as dead.

"Bring him back, lass." His bloodshot eyes met hers. "Please, ye can do it."

Her eyes went to Grant. "Of course…I'll try," she stuttered and touched him.

"Focus on anger," Darach urged, face ravaged with grief, "emotion."

Jackie nodded and did just that. Yet nothing happened. No tingles. No heat.

"Please, lass," Darach pleaded. "Ye need to try harder."

"I am. I will." She nodded, upset that she was letting him down. "I'll try even harder."

"Aye." He looked from her to Grant as she tried to relive her emotions. To *really* feel them. The anger she felt when Grant was murdered by the demi-god. The sadness she felt for everyone who lost him. Her anger at young Grant's hardships. Though she felt the emotions, and let them flow through her, nothing happened, and Darach only grew more upset.

"I'm so sorry," she whispered. "Forgive me."

Incredibly sad, Darach's eyes held hers as he cradled his father's head. "There isnae anything to forgive," he murmured. "Ye tried yer best."

Watching him go through this all over again about ripped her heart out.

"Did I?" She shook her head. "You don't know that. Neither do I. Maybe I'm not thinking the right thoughts or doing the right thing."

"Ye did, lass," he said. "I know ye did."

She shook her head again and stared at Grant without really seeing him. No, all she could focus on were her mistakes. On things unrelated to this moment but determined to surface. "I should have gotten a second opinion. I should've seen more doctors. Instead, I just gave up."

"Erin was right." Her eyes met Darach's. "I gave up without fighting. I forgave everyone and everything and just gave in."

He didn't seem to think it odd in the least that she spoke of this right now.

"Ye gave in to what is likely an unnatural tumor." He took her hand. "Ye cannae be faulted for that."

"Can't I?" She frowned. "You're right. I have been a coward."

"Nay, I was wrong." He shook his head. "You made a decision and stuck by it. That isnae cowardly." His eyes held hers. "You found peace in your decision. That is *your* choice and 'tis commendable. Erin and I only argued otherwise because we love you so bloody much."

Jackie bit her lower lip and looked at Grant, not sure how to respond.

"I think you're amazing, lass." Darach tilted up her chin until their eyes met. "But it seems you've one last person to forgive."

"Who?"

"*You.*" His brows shot up. "After being inside your head, I'd say deciding not to fight your illness is the least of it. I think you need to forgive yourself for not standing up to your uncle far sooner and for allowing him to tear away what was once a happy childhood. I think you need to forgive yourself for allowing your uncle to mold you into something you barely recognized and didn't much enjoy. For tearing away the spirit you once called yours."

"Forgive yourself, lass." His eyes stayed with hers. "That's what your parents would have wanted."

Her lip trembled at his words. At how profoundly they affected her. That he said them now with his dead father in his arms—someone she couldn't save though she had saved so many—made it almost impossible to draw breath.

Was he right? Had she forgiven everyone else when she was the one that needed it most? Had she really stopped standing up for herself and become something she wasn't? She had escaped some of it when she was with her friends, but when she found out how sick she was, she'd reverted yet again. Even around them.

But she wasn't that woman anymore.

Not since traveling back in time.

Not since meeting Darach.

"You're right," she whispered. "I do need to forgive…myself."

"Then do so." He cupped her cheek. "Forgive yourself and be who you're supposed to be. The lass I met time and time again in my dreams. The lass you've always been beneath it all." His eyes warmed though sadness remained. "Do that little forgive, forgive chant for *yourself* this time."

"Okay." Her voice grew hoarse as she closed her eyes and did what he suggested.

And she meant it.

She'd become someone else because she thought she had no choice. It was what made sense if she hoped to keep her inheritance. No, that was wrong. It had never really been about the money but about losing her home. Losing the life she once had. She did everything to conform and become someone else for her uncle, her young mind convinced that she did it for her parents.

But they wouldn't want her to change. To become a shell of her former self. They would want her to be exactly who she was now. Fearless. Selfless. Proud. Loving. Kind. Loyal. *Happy.* Wasn't that all they'd ever wanted for her?

So, in the end, she forgave herself because despite everything she was exactly who she should be. More than that, she had everything they could have hoped for her. Good friends. Strength. True love. Happiness.

A new sense of peace spread through her.

Something she had never felt before.

Absolute forgiveness.

When tingling began in her hand, her eyes shot open. "The acorn!"

She opened her fist to find it glowing. When she set it down, it sank into the ground, and a sprout shot up.

"Look at your ring, lass," Darach murmured.

Her eyes widened. The black swirled away as blue shone brighter and brighter and the sprout grew taller and taller.

"Och." Darach grabbed Grant under the arms and started dragging him, but it was too late. None of them moved fast enough to scramble away from the thick trunk that formed as it and its branches shot to the sky. Instead, they rolled a few times before leaves started to blossom.

By the time it finished growing, her ring shined a bright bluish gray, and the tree was full grown. More than that, Grant was propped against its trunk blinking.

"Da?" Darach stumbled closer. "Are ye...alive?"

"Aye," Grant croaked before he cleared his throat and focused on Darach. "Now this has been a wee bit o' magic I hope to never use again."

"Thank, God," Darach muttered before he threw his arms around his father. "You're really alive."

"Aye, lad." Grant hugged him right back. "Thanks to you and Jackie."

Darach helped his father stand. "Are you well?"

"I am." Grant said, and pulled Jackie into a tight embrace. "I'm verra proud of you, lass. My son is lucky to have you."

"And I'm lucky to have him," she said softly. "I'm so glad you're okay."

"Aye." He pulled away and eyed the tree with pride. "What a beauty."

"'Tis," Darach agreed as he took her hand and looked up at the tree. "But I dinnae ken how 'tis here...now." His eyes fell to his father. "Or you for that matter."

"I once told you this tree was born of great love." Grant's eyes went from her to Darach as he grinned. "Great love, indeed."

"But I thought the stories were about Aunt Torra and Uncle Colin's love," Darach said. "Did they not create the baby oak?"

"Aye," Grant said. "But 'twas you and your lass who made sure it ended up here. Exactly where it needed to be."

Jackie frowned, trying to remember what she had learned about this clan. "Forgive me if I'm wrong but how is that possible when this tree was here twenty-seven years ago, but yet it was just created now?"

"Because there is no such thing as the passing of time in the Otherworld. 'Tis like any other supernatural world. So right now can just as easily be twenty-seven winters ago." Grant's eyes fell to her ring. "Speaking of time, we've little left now that your ring has ignited. The demi-god has been tracking you, but thankfully we've stayed one step ahead." He started for the castle. "Good to see you've got the sword with you, Darach. You'll need it soon."

Darach pulled her after him. "What's going on, Da?"

"I'll tell you soon enough," Grant said.

They jogged to catch up.

"Da, there's nothing here but death." He gestured at the castle. "No people. Nothing. We're in the Otherworld."

"Aye," Grant agreed. "The Otherworld."

Darach frowned. "You're reminding me a bit of Adlin right now."

"Aye?" A small smile curved Grant's lips. "'Tis nice to hear."

She and Darach glanced at each other, confused.

"Do you know where Eara went?" Jackie said. "Is she okay?"

"I would imagine," Grant replied as he strode over the drawbridge. The moat was dry, and the portcullises appeared to be rusted open. "But you can ask her yourself."

"I can…" Jackie started but stopped as they headed for the second portcullis. Eara was trotting around in the courtyard.

"*Eara, you're here*," she exclaimed as the horse trotted up to her. "*I don't understand.*"

"*'Tis hard to ken any of this, lass,*" Eara said. "*Worry less about me and follow Grant, aye?*"

"Please do," Grant encouraged as he strode through the courtyard. "We're almost out of time."

Darach nodded and pulled her after him. "But what about Eara?"

When she glanced back, the horse was gone. More confused than ever, she stumbled up the stairs after Darach. They only made it about a quarter of the way before a terrible sound screeched overhead and the land started shaking.

Grant whipped around and eyed the sky. "Hurry up! We cannae use our magic here."

"But the tree," Darach argued as they struggled up the stairs despite the rumbling. "'Twas great magic, aye?"

Jackie glanced back one more time to see if Eara had returned and tripped.

"I've got you, lass," Darach said as he turned back to help her.

Eyes frozen on the horizon and so scared she couldn't move, she whispered, "What the hell is that?"

"What?" he started but went silent when he saw what she referred too. Yes, the three shadows, the *Genii Cucullati*, rushed in their direction. Yes, the massive dark cloud that was the demi-god rushed in their direction. But that wasn't what rendered them immobile.

No, it was something far more sinister.

A wave of jet black shrouded the horizon. A wave that simply ripped everything beyond from sight as it moved closer. It destroyed *everything*.

"That, my kin," Grant said. "Is hell itself."

"Balor," Darach whispered.

"Holy shit," Jackie whispered.

"Let's go," Grant roared. "Now!"

Darach threw her over his shoulder and raced up the stairs two at a time. Terrified or not, she was impressed at how good he was on his feet considering the massive earthquake.

What she didn't expect to hear were so many familiar voices when Darach plopped her down in the great hall beside Grant. They stood in front of the massive mantel that she and Darach had created. Her eyes widened on the various faces in the rock.

They were speaking...no, chanting.

All of Darach's cousins. His sister. Even his aunts and uncles. She peered closer. Was that Adlin? Iosbail?

Grant started chanting as well.

Miraculously enough, the earthquake ceased, and Eara trotted into the chamber seconds before the *Genii Cucullati* twisted in and shot towards Jackie. When Darach leapt in front of her and thrust up his hands, they smashed into an invisible wall.

Then boom. Crash. The floor rocked.

A deep suctioning sensation made her ears pop before the light became so bright she was momentarily blinded. Wind whipped around her as an all-too-familiar voice roared, "She's mine!"

When she was able to see again, the great hall was no longer dark but normal. Everyone she had seen in the mantle except Adlin and Iosbail were alive and well, and rushing to protect her. Jackie leaned against the side of the mantle as pain tore through her head.

She knew what it was.

The tumor.

Better yet, the darkness behind it.

Eoghan half manifested as he tore through the room with his minions in tow. Magic was thrown in all directions as the demi-god and *Genii Cucullati* battled against the MacLomains, MacLeods and Hamiltons.

It was a fight for the ages.

Weakened but still on her feet, Jackie blinked, amazed by what she saw.

Movement in the Viking tapestry.

"Jackie," whispered through her mind.

"King Naðr?" Her eyes widened. Who else could it be? Because that tapestry had come alive and the man at the Viking's feet struggled beneath his blade.

"Do you trust me, woman?"

She had come to like the King very much. He'd been nothing but kind. *"Of course, I do."*

"Then go with Heidrek."

247

How many times would this request be asked of her in a lifetime? Twice was once too many.

"But I love someone else," she said.

His eyes met hers. *"Then trust me and go with Heidrek."*

The fighting became more intense as magic whiplashed across the hall. Darach stayed in front of her the whole time, shifting air every which way to keep her safe. Her eyes shot to Heidrek when he moved closer.

She shook her head. *"I can't leave him."*

Darach's words entered her mind as he battled. *"What's happening, lass?"*

Heidrek put a finger to his lips and shook his head. *"He cannae hear we Vikings unless we allow it."*

"What's going on?" she cried into his mind. *"Why can't you just tell me?"*

No sooner did she say it than pitch black filled the doorway and everyone's magic seemed to compress into a mirage. Darach glanced over his shoulder, and his eyes narrowed on Heidrek as understanding dawned.

Here they were.

All over again.

Her only chance of survival lay with Heidrek.

There was no hesitation. No jealousy. Darach managed to roar two words before all hell broke loose.

"Save her!"

Heidrek threw her over his shoulder and raced toward the tapestry. Blackness swirled around the room, taking half the great hall with it before it rushed after them. But it seemed the Viking was faster as he leapt straight at the tapestry.

Another boom erupted around her before everything slowed down and Heidrek dropped her to her feet. She had a split second to gain her balance before he cupped her cheeks and kissed her. As soon as it began, it ended.

"Did you *not* tell Darach we kissed?" He winked. *"Now* there are no lies between you and your husband."

"Loki's balls, Heidrek," the Viking King exclaimed as he appeared beside them. "I didn't think you had it in you."

"Love is love, Uncle," Heidrek muttered. "Just not mine to have this time."

She suddenly realized where they were.

Inside the tapestry.

"Are you ready, Nephew?" Naðr asked Heidrek.

"More than ever."

The King laughed. "That's my lad. Let's end this once and for all." Jackie's eyes rounded as everyone vanished from the great hall a blink before the *Genii Cucullati* whipped over their head and into the tapestry. Heidrek scooped her up when blackness overtook everything and screams of rage echoed around her.

The air went icy and numbness settled over her moments before fire erupted. Heidrek tossed her and she sailed through the air. Jackie screeched as she landed in Darach's arms. His entire family was chanting and moving closer to the tapestry. When she looked back at it, she shook her head in denial.

Flames ravaged it.

Hell ravaged it.

"Go, Son!" Grant roared.

Jackie had no chance to see what was happening before Darach swung her onto Eara, leapt up behind her and the horse took off.

"Oh no," she cried as the great hall vanished, and they ended up back in the last place she wanted to be.

The Celtic Otherworld in Ireland.

"Aye." Darach swung down then pulled her after him. "But I think we might stand half a chance here this time."

"What do you mean?"

"I mean you kissing Heidrek in the tapestry didnae hurt our cause. Now Eoghan wants you more than ever," he whispered near her ear before pulling away.

Her eyes widened. That didn't sound good. She shook her head and strode after him. "I didn't kiss Heidrek. He kissed me."

Darach pulled a dagger from his boot and handed it to her. "It doesnae matter."

"I think it does."

"Nay, lass." He nodded at the blade. "Use that wisely."

Eara neighed and stomped her foot. *"Aye, fight well. Both of ye."*

"But we're back where we began," she argued. "We don't stand a chance."

"Mayhap not." Darach walked backward, his eyes on the sky as a black cloud rushed over them, then thumped down hard. "But we'll soon find out."

His eyes fell to hers. "Remember everything I taught you." He nodded at her dagger. "Use it only if needed."

"What? Wait!"

But it was too late. Darach spun and raced away. The second the black cloud shifted into Eoghan, he drove a foot into his chest and rushed him. The demi-god flung out his hand, and Darach fell back.

Not that far, though.

Darach leapt to his feet and swiped the blade. Eoghan evaded then came back at him. When Darach thrust at his throat, the demi-god dodged. Darach jumped the blade when Eoghan swiped low. The fighting became so fierce there was no way of keeping up. All she could do was watch closely and be there if Darach needed help.

"Soon enough," a soft voice said.

Her eyes whipped to the beautiful woman who materialized beside her. It couldn't be. Jackie had last seen her at MacLomain Castle before Darach thrust her into Heidrek's arms. The evil bitch had been fighting her own brother Cullen, a Highlander turned angel.

Jackie narrowed her eyes. "Brae Stewart."

"Aye," Brae drawled. "Back once more."

Brae had been Eoghan's sidekick from the beginning. She was every bit as corrupt as him. Jackie kept a cool head and clenched her dagger. "You're not going anywhere near Darach."

Eyes trained on the fighting, Brae offered no response.

So Jackie did what she was taught. She focused on her surroundings, tuned out the fighting and paid attention. To the way wind kept blowing Brae's hair in her eyes. How she seemed to favor her right hand. Better yet, how Brae didn't see Jackie as a threat in the least. If Erin was right, the Scotswoman's magic didn't work here either.

So it was now or never.

Jackie waited for the next gust of wind then made her move. She tagged Brae in the jaw then punched her in the stomach. *Ouch.* Everyone made it look so easy, but that likely hurt her fist as much as Brae's chin.

Brae rubbed her jaw and frowned. "I probably deserved that."

"Are you kidding me?" Jackie held out her dagger and circled Brae. "You totally deserved that for everything you've done!"

"Nay, Jackie," Darach said into her mind. *"She's on our side now."*

She frowned, dagger still at the ready. "Since when?"

"Since now." He dodged another close swipe of Eoghan's blade. *"I'll fill you in later."*

"So she's on your side now, aye?" Clearly having heard their silent communication, the demi-god roared with laughter. "Then Brae Stewart has decided the life of her parents and clan no longer matter."

Some had started to speculate that Brae Stewart was aligned with the demi-god against her will, but most remained unconvinced. After all, she had killed her own brother.

Brae's eyes flickered between Jackie and a nearby hill. "Ye must save yerself, lass. Get up that mountain now."

What? How was running up a mountain going to do any good? Jackie shook her head. "No way. I'm here to help Darach."

"As am I."

"I find that hard to believe," Jackie said.

"'Tis true." Darach ducked beneath a mighty swipe of Eoghan's blade. "The demi-god's power is nearly gone. A power that forced her into slavery in order to keep her family safe." Darach spun and leapt when Eoghan's blade swept low. "She's here to see him to his end. To right wrongs!"

Grunts of pain rippled through the air as the men fought.

"Run, Jackie!" Darach roared seconds before Brae jumped into the fight as well.

Run? That was about the last thing she wanted to do.

"Of course, it is," Eoghan murmured before he flung up his hands and black crackled around him. A sizzling shadowy force field stretched out and encompassed Jackie as well. Though Darach and Brae kept swinging their swords, the demi-god was untouchable.

A second later, he stood in front of her. His icy fingers touched her cheek with affection. "My master might be gone, but ye are not." His eyes focused on her ring then shot to her eyes. "We can be together again. Do ye not remember what we had?"

"I do. *Very* clearly." Jackie gripped her dagger tightly. "You wanted me, and I didn't feel the same."

"But ye did." He shook his head, as deranged now as he had been back then. "Ye must have, lassie."

Maybe it would be better to go about this another way and use his desire against him.

"You're right." She softened her voice. "But do you understand how I might have forgotten?"

"Aye, the bloody ring." He frowned, and his eyes swept over everything before they landed on her again. "This was where we first met. This was everything, Gwendolyn."

Though she started at the use of that name, she showed no reaction. "I know. I'm sorry." She touched her temple. "I just kept forgetting, and I *knew* something was wrong."

Enchantment and insanity mixed in his dark gaze. "Aye. Close. But not quite there." He touched a spot slightly higher than her temple. "I asked him to put it here."

Jackie struggled to breathe as he pointed to the location of her tumor. She tried to remain logical despite the horror. "So you know about it." Bile rose in her throat. "You were there when it…" she started to whisper but trailed off.

Eoghan's brows perked and an unnatural smile curled his lips. "Aye, lassie, Balor made sure the growth took root." He leaned closer, pleased. "So that ye would once again be mine." Lust and promise lit his dark eyes. "And now we will pick up where we left off."

Chapter Nineteen

JACKIE COULDN'T PRETEND to desire this monster…could she?

She might have been cast into slumber at the time, but she heard what Lair said at Hamilton Castle. How the tumor was unnatural. That evil likely put it there. And now evil controlled it…her. Or at least it *had*. Because regardless of what happened now, she wasn't simply accepting her fate anymore. She was ready to fight. To go down fighting. Yet she was careful to keep her anger hidden.

"You're right," she whispered. "I've been blinded to the truth for far too long." Her eyes rose to his as she stepped closer. "But now I remember." Though repulsed, she pressed her hand against his heart. "How much you cared." She hid behind her eyelashes and kept a lovelorn tone. "How much *I* cared."

His pupils flared. "Ye remember now, aye?" He closed the distance, cupped the back of her head and lowered his lips. "There's still time to marry. To restore things to what they should have been…" He leaned closer and whispered, "I love ye, lassie and have come so far to have ye once more."

"I'm so glad you never gave up," she murmured and closed her eyes, tried to remain calm.

"My lassie," he murmured then his lips closed over hers.

This was it.

Her golden opportunity.

So she drove her dagger into his gut.

The demi-god roared with rage and staggered back with disbelief as the cage around them fizzled away. All hell broke loose as Darach and Brae came at him again. Eoghan ripped out the dagger, more furious than ever as he battled.

"Get her up the mountain, Darach!" Brae cried as she went at Eoghan.

Jackie yelped when Darach flung her over his shoulder and ran.

"Put me down!" she said. "I'll run."

"Not fast enough."

The fighting behind them intensified. The demi-god was definitely changing...weakening. His movements were slow and the dark aura that always seemed to shift around him fading.

"He's becoming human, isn't he?" she said.

"Aye." As he had at MacLomain Castle, Darach moved amazingly fast considering the hazardous route up the mountain. "And your dagger is getting him there a wee bit faster. 'Twas quick thinking, lass."

"It was awful."

"I'm sure, but 'tis good you keep dishing out kisses," he said. "Verra helpful."

She didn't take his bait. Not after kissing evil. "Hey, you gotta do what you gotta do."

"You more than most," he mocked.

"Are we really having this conversation?"

"Are you properly distracted?"

Jackie sighed and shook her head. He was doing the same thing he'd done to keep her mind preoccupied when they were in Ireland.

Her gaze returned to what was happening behind them. "He's coming after us!" She narrowed her eyes. "But he's not shifting into a black cloud. He's still a man. That's good, right?"

Darach didn't respond but kept moving. Luckily, Brae was making things tough for Eoghan and battling him as they climbed.

"Really, you should put me down," she said. "You need your strength."

"You dinnae weigh overly much," he said.

"Overly?"

Darach plunked her down, eyed her chest and smirked. "Well, those likely weigh more than most."

She frowned. "How can you joke right now?"

"Sorry, lass. I'm only trying to keep your spirits up," he said. "Because this is where we make our final stand."

Her eyes widened as she took in their surroundings or lack thereof. Though it didn't seem like they had climbed nearly long enough, they were at the top of the mountain. Yet it looked more like a plateau with nothing but a sheer drop on every side except the one they'd climbed. A rock pathway completely surrounded a large, circular wading pool.

"Is that a waterfall I hear?" she murmured, astounded by the crystal clear water considering everything else seemed so murky and dark.

"Aye." His eyes met hers. "If Da's right, we should be at the verra top of the mountain the oak tree grew up."

"The Magic Mountain of Fertility?"

The corner of his lip shot up, and he nodded.

"But how is that possible?"

"I dinnae have time to explain." He led her along the right-hand side of the water. "Stay here, lass." His brogue thickened with urgency. "Dinnae move unless ye've no choice, ye ken?"

"But—"

He put a finger to her lips and shook his head. "Just do as I ask, Jackie."

"But I want to help," she said into his mind.

"And ye will. From right here when I ask it of ye." He pulled his finger away. "All right?"

"Why not let me fight alongside you guys?"

"Because when 'tis time your battle is right here," he said softly. "Promise me ye'll do as asked."

She searched his eyes. "I take it you're not going to tell me exactly what my part is.'

He shook his head. "Not yet. I just need you to trust me."

"I do."

"Then promise."

How could she say no when he looked at her with his heart in his eyes?

"Okay," she whispered. "I promise."

Darach brushed his lips over hers then headed back the way they came. He no sooner vanished over the edge when the sound of metal striking metal rang out. The fighting sounded intense. Fast and furious. Then suddenly ear piercing. But why so loud?

" 'Tis time, lass. 'Tis time to fight just as I taught you," Darach said. *"Close your eyes and visualize your surroundings."*

Jackie frowned. It didn't seem like they had time for that.

"You promised, Jackie."

She had. And if these were their final moments she didn't want to break her word. About to do as asked, she tried not to panic when everything suddenly went black.

She couldn't hear, see, speak, feel or smell anything. It was as if she suffered all of her friends' disabilities at once. Tingles spread through her as anger flared at the difficult journeys each had suffered. So did a renewed sense of pride. How much they had learned. How brave they had been.

Then the tingles faded along with the anger.

And something else got through.

Darach's voice from far away.

"Fight your darkness, Jackie," he said. *"Close your eyes and visualize your surroundings, lass."*

Jackie swallowed back fear. She swore she would fight. She promised. So though already seemingly blind, she closed her eyes and paid attention. First, she saw the flicker of her ring. The blue of Darach's eyes.

Then more.

Bit by bit she started to hear a raging waterfall and lapping water. She began to feel the fine mist of moisture caught on a warm wind. The scent of wildflowers and spruce.

More than that, she began to see her surroundings.

Not as they had been, but what they were becoming. Sunlight warmed her cheeks. Replaced with color, darkness began to fade away. Only when Darach raced over the edge in her direction did she realize her eyes were *open.*

They were no longer in the Otherworld Eoghan had created.

"Well done, lass," Darach said before he spun back and everything happened within the blink of an eye. Sunlight spiked over the staggered, green mountains as he lifted his arms over his head and gripped the hilt of his sword. The metal seemed to flash against his back before Eoghan rushed onto the edge. All dark divinity was finally gone.

The demi-god was human.

Darach whipped the sword.

Eoghan whipped his as well.

Darach's sword lodged hilt-deep in Eoghan's stomach, and he fell to his knees, shocked as he looked down at his own blood. A split second later, Brae came up behind him and drove her sword through his back.

Yet Eoghan was strong enough that he managed to swipe his leg around and catch Brae off guard. She stumbled back, lost her footing then went over the edge. And not the one she had come up but a sheer cliff. There came no scream but a silent drop to what could only be certain death.

But none of that mattered when Jackie realized Eoghan's blade had struck Darach. Her world came to a screeching halt when he yanked a sword out of his stomach and turned. Blood trickled from the corner of his mouth as his eyes found hers.

"I'm sorry, lass," he whispered into her mind before he staggered then landed in the water.

"Darach," she cried and stumbled after him. "No, no, no. This can't be happening." She managed to drag him a few feet until she fell down on the side of the pond and rested his head on her lap.

"I need to drag you further," she gasped as red blossomed in the water.

"Nay, lass," he whispered. "There's no point."

"There is," she said through tears and tried to put a hand over his wound to stop the bleeding. "If I had to fight, so do you!"

"I did fight. We both did." He wrapped his fingers around hers. "And won."

"We need to find Lair…or your Aunt McKayla," she urged, trying her damnedest not to panic. "Someone who can heal you."

"No time," he murmured, struggling for breath as his eyes stayed on hers. "Just be with me, lass. 'Tis all I want in the end. Just ye."

The end? God, no. Not after everything they had been through.

But it was, and she felt it right down to her soul.

She choked back a sob before blinding pain ripped through her head. A thump sounded off to their left as Eoghan finally slumped to his death at the same moment Darach took his last breath.

Pain increased.

Right where her tumor was.

Yet she never let go of Darach. Or she didn't think so. The pain became far worse. Unbearable. Crippling. She lost sense of everything around her.

Then a little bit at a time, the pain faded.

That's when she realized she sat on *his* lap, and he held *her*. The oak that grew up the side of the mountain had apparently continued growing because its branches fanned over them. Colors had only intensified, and the clear water shone a bright, Caribbean-colored blue.

It was stunning. Indescribable.

Darach cupped the side of her neck, concerned. "How are you feeling, lass?"

"Good...I think. What happened?" she whispered, confused, before it occurred to her she had to be hurting him. "Darach, I'm sitting on your wound!"

When she tried to move, he shook his head. "Nay." A smile lit his eyes as he stood, lowered her to her feet and made sure she was steady. "The wound is gone."

"Oh, thank God," she whispered, smiling with relief and wonder as she touched his midsection. The wound had completely healed. "But how?"

"I dinnae know," he murmured before he cupped her cheeks and kissed her so tenderly that all the horror she'd just witnessed drifted away.

"So ye are back where ye began. Beneath the oak," came a whisper on the wind. "Or should I say its offspring."

They pulled apart as a beautiful woman, and tall, blond warrior shimmered out of nowhere.

"Goddess Brigit," Darach whispered. "And Fionn Mac Cumhail."

"Aye, laddie, 'tis us." Brigit eyed Fionn fondly. "It has always been us."

There was no mistaking the great love that passed between them.

"Where are we?" Jackie inquired softly, not quite sure of the proper octave in which to address a god.

"You're in the Celtic Otherworld," Fionn said. "The way it actually looks rather than that demented place Eoghan took everyone."

"A place that was only sustainable with help from Balor," Brigit said. "A hell that does not belong on this plane."

"So...I'm dead?" Jackie's eyes went to Darach then back to Brigit. "We both are?"

"Aye," Brigit said. "As is Eoghan."

"Just like my dream foretold. You died on my lap when I was laird," Darach said. "I just didn't realize I would be dead too."

Jackie shook her head in amazement. "So the tumor got me in the end." Her eyes met Darach's. "And one way or another got you too."

"Nay, 'twas always evil that ye fought," Fionn said. "And 'twas evil that ended your lives."

"Ye do have a flare for the dramatic on occasion." Brigit slipped her hand into Fionn's and offered him a soft smile.

"Me?" Fionn pulled her closer. "Were ye not behind the rings, oaks and the connections through time? And was it not all a wee bit dramatic?"

"Aye." Brigit grinned and nuzzled even closer to him. "And for the most part, great fun with ye there to help every step of the way."

Jackie and Darach glanced at each other. He was thinking the same thing. They better get answers soon before the gods got too wrapped up in one another.

"So should Jackie and I say our goodbyes?" Darach's voice deepened with emotion. "I dinnae see Eoghan so I can only assume we all move on from here."

"Say your goodbyes?" Brigit stared lovingly into Fionn's eyes as she answered Darach. "Why would ye do that?"

Fionn fingered a strand of her hair, enchanted. "They do not understand, lassie, because we have yet to explain."

"Ah…" Brigit whispered as if she just remembered. Her coy eyes turned their way. "Is it not foretold that he who loves she with the power to resurrect will follow her into the afterlife? That he will meet his end?"

"Aye," Darach said. "And so here we are."

"Yet ye forget something, laddie." Her eyes flickered between them. "Three men loved Jackie. One brought her into the Viking tapestry where he was able to use that love to defeat not only the *Genii Cucullati* but Balor. Or should I say ban them from the MacLomains for all time."

"Heidrek." Jackie's eyes widened. "Is he okay?"

"Aye," Fionn said. "His love was strong and his power formidable. 'Twas a lucky thing at the time that Eoghan was more obsessed with ye than saving his son, Keir Hamilton, or Heidrek might have faced a wee bit too much evil to succeed."

Jackie wasn't sure what to think. She was sad that Heidrek evidently loved her so much but happy he won.

"Then there were the two other men who loved ye," Brigit continued. "Darach and Eoghan. And both have loved ye for a verra long time. Now both have followed ye into the true afterlife. Yet 'tis foretold that '*he* who loves' must pay the price of his soul's death. Not '*they* who love'." Brigit eyed Darach with a gentle smile. "Especially not he whose life ended in my healing waters."

"So Eoghan met his final death...the death of his soul because he loved me?" Jackie said. "And because it was foretold that only one man would pay the price, Darach escaped the same death?"

"That is right." Brigit's eyes fell to Jackie's ring. "And because of your ring. Because of love that remained so strong through time."

"Thank God." Jackie blinked back tears as she looked from the ring to Darach then back to Brigit and Fionn. "I mean thank you. Both of you. For everything."

"'Tis all right to thank God as well," Brigit said. "Did Cullen Stewart, one of God's angels, not help everyone along the way?"

Jackie nodded. "He did."

"As did many others." A small smile hovered on Fionn's lips. "Viking and MacLomain Ancestors alike."

Very true.

"No disrespect intended, Fionn," Jackie said softly. "But I was under the impression that you were as baffled as the rest of us by everything that happened since my friends and I traveled back in time." Her eyes flickered between the gods. "If you knew all along exactly who the demi-god was and our story, why not go after him from the beginning rather than put Robert the Bruce through so much? Why have Darach and his cousins been trained from childhood to protect him?"

"A wise man once told me that 'twas all the moments in between that mattered most," came a familiar voice. "Or mayhap *I* was that great man."

Adlin MacLomain, young and healthy, appeared beside the gods.

"Nay, 'twas certainly a great *lass* who said as much," came another voice before Iosbail Broun appeared beside her brother.

Adlin's brows swept up as he looked at her. "Aye?"

"Oh, aye," Iosbail assured and grinned.

"Say what ye will, my wee bairns," came a familiar voice as Eara trotted out of nowhere. *"But never forget who ye learned such wisdom from to begin with."*

Jackie smiled as the horse shimmered then a woman appeared. Lovely, with little beads interwoven in her many braids and a long, white gown cinched at the waist with a gold belt, there was no mistaking Chiomara the Druidess.

"I was right!" Darach grinned. "Eara was Chiomara."

Chiomara smiled softly at him. "Aye, laddie."

A blink later, the druidess stood in front of Jackie.

"Sister," Chiomara whispered as she took her hand, eyes moist. "Or ye once were."

Jackie felt every ounce of love and familiarity with Chiomara that Gwendolyn once did. "And I somehow still am," she managed before she embraced the druidess. "You risked *so* much for me. Gave up so much. I can't tell you how thankful I am."

"I would do it again and again. Anything to save ye." Chiomara's eyes flickered between her and Darach. "Anything to help you reconnect with a love I never should have dissuaded you from to begin with."

"It wasn't just about us, though," Jackie reminded. "It was about keeping our people safe."

"Aye. And we did." Chiomara squeezed her hands. "After ye died and I left with Eoghan in pursuit, 'twas Devlin who rose up against Da in your name. And 'twas Devlin our clan followed. Under his leadership and without the oppression of the dark Druid, our people thrived."

Her eyes went to Darach. "Ye never took another lass but focused everything you had on our clan. A few decades later, your warriors found ye beneath the oak in the dead glade. Ye'd passed away alone where ye'd last held Gwendolyn. This was in your hand." She held out a piece of cloth. "'Twas hers. I held it for ye all these centuries."

It was the handkerchief Darach had found in his pocket in Ireland. The one Gwendolyn gave him when they were married in secret.

"Bloody hell," he whispered as he carefully took the threadbare material. He held it to his nose and inhaled as his eyes met hers. "It still smells like you…in that life and this one."

"Unbelievable," Jackie murmured before her eyes went to Chiomara. "I'm still curious about something."

Chiomara cocked her head in question.

"Your hair. It was blond in Ireland and when Erin saw you in the Otherworld." She fingered a braid. "But now it's dark. How come?"

"That would be because of my magic," Brigit interjected. "'Twas all part of her new life traveling across Eire."

Jackie smiled at Chiomara. "I like it."

Chiomara smiled as well. "Thank ye."

"'Tis nearly that time," Adlin interrupted softly. "Robert the Bruce leaves for home soon and Darach and Jackie should be there."

"Aye," Chiomara agreed as she joined her children then gestured at the horse. "Eara is yours, Jackie. Brigit long foretold that ye would reconnect with your ring in the New World. So the horse was named for the Easterly direction that ye needed to travel to reconnect with your lost love." She stroked the horse's neck. "'Twas her I rode across Ireland after Gwendolyn passed on. And 'twas she who was with me when I started my life with the Dalriada. A clan and king that led to so many wonderful connections through time."

"Aye," Adlin murmured. "But all truly started when a young druidess and her father's first-in-command broke the rules and fell in love."

"Aye," the gods said at the same time.

"It has all been one long bloody good story, aye?" Iosbail said.

"Aye," Adlin and Chiomara agreed, smiling.

"Thank you all *so* much," Jackie said. "But I'm still curious about a few more things."

Fionn and Brigit were already wrapped in each other's arms so Adlin answered for them. "Aye?"

"While I'm glad we're officially done with Eoghan, what about the original price of what Brigit did for Darach and me…or should I say, Gwendolyn and Devlin?" Jackie said. "Am I still doomed to die young in every life?"

"See, that's a Broun right there," Iosbail said triumphantly. "Always looking at the bigger picture." She grinned. "And in an optimistic light considering she assumes she'll meet Darach again in another life."

Darach squeezed Jackie's hand.

Adlin frowned at Iosbail while Chiomara shook her head and sighed. "Oh, my wee daughter, ye always did have a unique way of wording things."

Iosbail's brows slammed together. "I dinnae ken. 'Twas logical enough."

Chiomara shushed her and answered Jackie. "When all of the darkness was at last defeated, and ye found yourself here, the curse lifted and the price was paid in full. In this life and every one to follow."

"In this life?" she asked, confused. "But I thought we were dead. Even if we aren't, I'm still dying."

Brigit pulled her lips away from Fionn's long enough to tilt her head at Jackie. "Ye were in my healing water every bit as much as your lad, were ye not?"

Her heart thumped into her throat. Did Brigit mean what Jackie thought she meant? But it seemed the time for questions was past. Bright light flashed. When it faded, everyone was gone but the horse and Darach.

Yet Adlin's last words whispered on the wind. "Use your magic and go home."

Was she no longer sick? Did she dare hope?

"Do you think…" she started but the words caught in her throat.

"Aye, lass." Darach pulled her close and tilted her chin until their eyes met. "I think you're healed. But I want to know for sure. We need to get home and ask Lair."

"Definitely." She nodded. "That makes sense…but how do we get home?"

"I think I have an idea." He eyed the horse. "But I'm not sure you'll like it."

"Why don't we just head back down the way we came?" she said as he pulled her after him.

"Because it isnae there anymore." They walked to the edge. The path they had traveled up was gone. Now, like every other side, it was a sheer cliff except where the waterfall poured off. And that was a straight drop down too.

"Though I can't believe I'm saying it, poor Brae," she murmured as she peered down. "A fall like that had to hurt."

When Darach didn't respond, she looked his way. "Speaking of Brae, when did you learn that she'd been enslaved by the bad guy?

Things were crazy at MacLomain Castle, so I didn't catch much. What happened? Because you seemed to know a lot more than before."

"'Twas part of a well-executed plan by my Da and likely even Adlin. One that I still dinnae ken entirely." He led her to Eara. "I'll explain what I know once we get home."

"You seriously can't mean to ride this horse." Jackie shook her head. "What about the tree? Why don't we climb down then find a way to come back for her?" She patted Eara. "Or you climb down, and I'll wait with her."

He glanced over her shoulder. "I dinnae think that's an option anymore."

Jackie's jaw dropped when she looked at the tree. The branches were shrinking back down the cliff.

Darach cupped the sides of her neck and made sure their eyes connected before he said, "You trust me, right lass?"

"We already went over this," she reminded. "Of course, I do."

"Good." He rubbed his thumbs along her jawline gently. "Because I need you to do something that you've only ever done in a nightmare."

"That doesn't sound promising."

"Nay," he agreed. "But keep in mind we're in the Otherworld so technically we're still dead. That means, no matter how frightening things might seem, it cannae get much worse."

"That sounds even less promising."

"Mayhap." She had no time to react before he tossed her on the horse then swung up behind her, his words close to her ear. "But I've never met a more courageous lass so this is but one more wee thing to face in a great adventure, aye?"

"I think that card might be overplayed by now," she said warily as he directed the horse until they faced the water. "*Really* overplayed."

Darach tilted her chin until their eyes met and his lips were inches from hers. "Like I told you, I had the strongest sensation when Eara leapt over the cliff in the nightmare that I had done such a thing with you before. It could not have happened in any previous life, Jackie. Only this one...such as it is now caught betwixt worlds." He brushed his lips over hers. "I think 'twas not a sense of hindsight but foresight. I think I sensed what we are about to do."

She shook her head when she followed his line of sight. "Oh, no. That was a cliff in my nightmare, not a waterfall. So that kills your theory."

"Not entirely. There's still water involved," he pointed out. "And this time 'twill not only be part of our magic but Brigit's healing waters. Powerful stuff, indeed."

"Yeah, yeah, *indeed*." She didn't like it. Not a bit. "What about the poor horse?"

"As dead as us right now," he reminded. "And likely willing to take the risk to live again."

"I would think she'd be too spooked."

"Does she appear spooked in the least?"

Jackie eyed the horse. If anything, Eara seemed eager. Her eyes met his. "This is insane."

"Not really considering you possess the power of resurrection."

She flinched. "You mean to say I'm going to resurrect all three of us?"

A twinkle lit his eyes. "'Twould be helpful considering we need to be resurrected."

"You have a horrible sense of timing when it comes to humor, you know that?"

"It depends on how you look at it."

"There's only one way to look at it," she said. "You've got poor timing."

"Are you distracted?"

"Not at all." Her eyes narrowed. "Nice try—"

He cut her words off with a deep kiss. The sort that made everything vanish and her problems fade away. The kind that *truly* distracted her. Then they were moving. And not in the dreamy, lustful out-of-body-experience sort of way.

Jackie ripped her lips away and held onto Eara's mane as the horse started trotting through the shallow water. Darach wrapped his arm around her waist and said, "'Tis time to embrace your magic, lass."

"But," she started and held on tighter as the horse moved faster. She still wasn't entirely sure *how* to embrace her magic. "Oh, hell."

"No more hell for us," he said, his voice urgent. "Now *focus*."

That was easier said than done. But she did her best, focusing first on her fear. Yet fear soon turned to anger when she realized that this might be yet another end for them.

She thought of how much had come between them for so long. All the years they must have lost because of Eoghan and Balor. Darach began chanting, and a tingling sensation started to spread through her as Eara broke into a run.

Close. Closer.

"I love you, Darach," she said, just in case this was the end.

Closer still.

"Aye, lass, in every lifetime."

Then the horse leapt into the air and they went sailing over the waterfall.

Chapter Twenty

"THERE THEY ARE!" someone yelled from the battlements as Eara landed and continued racing along the loch beside MacLomain Castle. The raging waterfall and sheer drop they experienced moments before were but a memory.

"We made it!" Jackie laughed. "And everything looks normal again!"

"Aye!" He laughed as Eara raced around the castle and onto the field. The gate was open, and the portcullises were raised. Everything was whole and beautiful.

When Eara stopped beneath the mighty oak, Darach pulled Jackie down, swung her around and kissed her soundly.

"Jackie!" a familiar voice called.

Jackie's eyes rounded at him as Erin headed their way. "Did she just speak?"

"Aye, lass." He grinned and let her go when Erin about barreled her over.

Jackie laughed when Nicole and Cassie arrived moments later, and all four embraced. He had no time to greet them because one by one his cousins embraced him and clapped him on the back.

"You had us truly worried." Logan grinned. "We didnae think you made it, Cousin."

Rònan offered a broad smile. "Och, I knew he had."

"You knew no such thing." Niall shook his head and grinned at Darach. "But I did."

Soon enough, their lasses greeted Darach with big hugs. Everyone was smiling and laughing as they reunited.

"You can speak?" he said to Erin before his eyes found Cassie again. "And you're wearing your glasses."

"Yup, everyone's back where they started," Nicole piped up and cupped her ear with a wink. "Even me."

"That's wonderful but..." His eyes widened on her swollen belly. "How long have we been gone?"

"Long enough," his Aunt Leslie declared as she and Bradon joined them.

"Look at you two!" Jackie grinned as she touched both Nicole and Leslie's swollen stomachs. "Now here's a moment no one foresaw when we arrived in New Hampshire."

"Yeah, we went home for a bit to close up the house," Leslie said. "Now Nicole and I are both about eight months along."

"I dinnae ken," Darach said. "Nicole should be much further along considering how time passes differently."

"You would think so," Grant said. "But it seems though over seven hundred years still exists betwixt here and there, time is no longer trying to catch up with itself." He eyed Leslie's stomach curiously. "Or mayhap time still passes differently, and there's more to this than meets the eye."

"What do you mean—" Leslie started but got cut off by Darach.

"Och, Da." He embraced his father. "'Tis good to see you alive and well beyond the Otherworld."

"Aye, lad." Grant held him tight. "I feel the same. Ye gave us a good scare."

As soon as Grant pulled away, his mother and sister wrapped him up in a big hug. Then his parents and Lair embraced Jackie in a family hug, clearly as happy to see her as they were him.

"So what's going on?" Jackie asked her friends with tears in her eyes. "How are you all..." She shook her head. "Your disabilities...I don't understand."

When Nicole started talking, Grant shook his head. "Nay, lass, not now. First we need to see off some verra important people then we'll commence in the great hall, and all will be explained over a mug of whisky."

She sighed. "You mean water."

His eyes fell to her belly. "Aye, mayhap for you but not for me." He grinned, linked arms with Sheila and headed toward the castle. "I'm officially retired."

Though Darach and Jackie hoped to get answers beforehand, far too many people greeted them along the way. Not only his aunts and uncles but many allied clans. He was surprised by how many were here. Not only MacLeods and Brouns but some Stewarts, MacLauchlins, Sinclairs and Thomsons.

Yet as he and Jackie made their way onto the drawbridge, he wondered...had any Hamiltons come? He wouldn't blame them if they hadn't considering he abandoned them to pursue Jackie into the Otherworld.

"Darach, look." Jackie squeezed his hand. "I think I see our plaid's colors ahead."

The crowd parted, and he filled with pride when he saw Hamilton warriors lining either side of the drawbridge from the last portcullis to the gate. Their swords were lowered, crisscrossing one another's.

"What are they doing?" she whispered.

"Welcoming us...honoring us." He offered her the crook of his elbow. "Will you walk with me, wife?"

"Always." She slid her arm through his.

As they walked, the men raised their swords and remained silent. When they reached the gates, clapping began. It grew louder until cheering erupted. Hundreds of Hamiltons filled the courtyard. Humbled, Darach greeted as many as possible. Jackie did the same, every inch the laird's bride. Yet his people eventually melted back when Darach and Jackie joined his parents near the bottom of the castle stairs.

"Jackie? Darach?" came a young voice. "Is that really ye?"

"Of course 'tis her," came another voice. "Ye already knew that, lad."

Jackie laughed and crouched as wee Robert rushed down the stairs and into her arms. Darach crouched and hugged him as well. Meanwhile, young William dropped to one knee in front of them and lowered his head. "Welcome back, M'Lady." He met Darach's eyes. "M'Laird."

It seemed he was officially no longer lacking ballocks as far as the lad was concerned. "Good to see ye, William."

"We must go home soon, son," Robert's mother announced as she joined them. "Yer Da misses ye something fierce."

Darach bowed to Marjorie, Countess of Carrick. Jackie did the same. The Countess took their hands and looked between them. "I have already thanked everyone else for keeping my wee bairn safe, now I will do the same to ye." Though she stood perfectly straight and little emotion showed on her face, a tear rolled down her cheek.

"I cannae begin to thank ye enough for all ye've done…so verra much.

Her eyes met Darach's. "Ye devoted yer life to protecting Robert." Then her gaze went to Jackie. "And like yer friends, ye were willing to sacrifice yer own life to save Robert's, a lad ye barely knew." Her eyes swept over his cousins and Jackie's friends. "Might Robert have learned well from ye all and act with the same honor and courage when he someday rules Scotland."

Marjorie stepped away and took Robert's hand as Torra came alongside. Though no longer journeying through time, it seemed she would make sure they got home safely.

"We must travel on as well, William," came a deep voice as Dougal and Lilas stepped from the crowd.

"Aye." William's eyes met Jackie's. "It has been a pleasure meeting ye, m'Lady. I leave ye in good hands now."

"I couldn't agree more." A few tears rolled down her cheeks as she wrapped her arms around him. "I'm going to miss you, William."

"Och, nay, 'tis unseemly," he muttered but embraced her quickly before he pulled away.

"Come, lad," Marjorie said to Robert. "Time to go."

When they turned away, William said, "Wait, Robert."

It was clear the wee king had been hoping for such because he turned and was about to embrace William but the lad stopped him short. Instead, he held out his arm. "Ye've come far in the short time we have known each other. Ye've grown up some." William kept his arm extended. "'Tis time to shake like countrymen…like Scotsmen."

Robert stood up a little taller, his chest puffed out and for a moment some might say he almost peered down his nose.

"Yer not a bloody king yet," William said out of the corner of his mouth. "Yer but a man right now. A wee bit less tilt to yer chin couldnae hurt."

Rather than stammer and regret his actions, Robert relaxed his stance, grinned and gripped William's arm, hand to elbow, then gave a firm shake.

"Will ye tell me yer full name now, William?" Robert asked.

Darach remembered when he asked that same question back in the cave by the glade.

William considered him for a long moment, before he stepped back, sank to a knee, held out his blade and lowered his head. "My name is William Wallace and my blade will forever be at yer back if ye do right by Scotland and love it as fiercely as I do."

William Wallace? *Bloody hell.* No wonder he felt compelled to kneel when he asked William's permission to marry Jackie. It wasn't just the need to win over the lad for her sake but something much deeper.

Small gasps came from Jackie and her friends. Who could blame them? They were witnessing the beginning of a camaraderie that would make history. A camaraderie that explained why William might have ended up on this journey. What better way for two people from different stations in life to form a connection than when still bairns?

It seemed Adlin and his Celtic gods were always up to mischief.

"I accept your blade, William Wallace," Robert said softly and went to take William's dagger.

"Och, nay, ye cannae have my blade right now," William muttered as he stood. "I meant if ye need my sword at yer back someday, 'twill be there."

Robert eyed William's dagger. "'Tis a fine piece, though."

William eyed it with pride. "Aye, it truly is."

Jackie smirked. They might be witnessing history, but bairns were bairns and would act as such until they grew up.

"Time to go," Marjorie repeated.

"Aye." Robert smiled at William. "I look forward to seeing ye again someday, friend."

William cocked the corner of his lip. "I could say the same, Robert the Bruce."

"We must go as well," Lilas said but stopped short when she spied something on the ground in front of Darach and Jackie. She scooped up Gwendolyn's handkerchief, the very one Darach thought was tucked safely in his plaid. She slowed, staring at the material with an odd look on her face. When he went to take it, and their eyes met, he knew. He finally understood why she seemed so familiar. Why Dougal did as well.

Lilas had been Jackie in another life.

And Darach had been Dougal.

In tune with his every thought, Jackie figured it out at the same time and inhaled sharply.

"What is it, Lilas?" Dougal said when he saw the confusion on his wife's face.

Jackie and Darach's eyes went from Lilas' to Dougal's. Now he could truly appreciate how strange it must have been for his Da to meet his younger self.

"All is well," Darach said as he took the handkerchief. "Yer good wife but returned something I dropped."

Dougal eyed Darach with a frown.

"It was wonderful meeting you both." Jackie took the handkerchief and handed it back to Lilas. "Please, take this as a small token of our appreciation. You've done well by William. He was very brave on our journey, and we're thankful." Jackie's eyes fell to the handkerchief. "It's not much, but it holds great meaning."

Lilas and Dougal stared at the material, drawn to it in a way they would never understand.

"'Tis time that all return home," Torra announced. Her eyes went to Lilas and Dougal. "Some to our new homes here in Scotland."

There was no chance to say another word as magic started to swirl around everyone. When it faded, Torra had vanished with William and his parents as well as Robert and his mother.

"No wonder we were so drawn to each other," Jackie whispered. "We raised William in another life...or this life. He was ours."

"Aye, lass." He wrapped his arms around her, well aware of her sadness. Her sense of loss. "Though I dinnae quite ken how we can co-exist at the same time."

"'Tis simple." Grant came alongside. "Though William is from this era and his birth parents died here, Adlin somehow made sure he ended up at the Highland Defiance. In *Lilas and Dougal's era.*" He shrugged. "Now they are here and so are you." His brows perked. "Though 'tis probably best that you dinnae see them again. 'Tis bloody odd, aye?"

Jackie's eyes shot to Grant. "So Lilas is going to die young?" She frowned. "William is going to lose another mother? And Dougal is going to lose the love of his life?"

"Nay, not now that they have the handkerchief." Grant's eyes softened. "It was something returned to you in the land of the gods *after* the curse was lifted, so now their fate mirrors yours. Like you, they are free of the curse. Free to live and love a full lifetime."

"What a relief," Jackie whispered.

When his father smiled, Darach realized how happy and free his Da finally felt. How truly long his journey had been. But now his son was laird and all was well. "So 'tis time to meet in the great hall so that you and Ma might enjoy your retirement?"

Grant nodded before he headed up the stairs, whispering into Darach's mind, *"Ye should hold yer lass's hand when we enter the great hall. 'Twill be...difficult for her."*

"Aye, Da."

The only people in the great hall were Darach's cousins and Jackie's friends. Darach didn't have to look to know what had changed. He stopped and met Jackie's eyes.

"What is it?" she asked.

"Change," he murmured and looked at the Viking tapestry.

~Passion of a Scottish Warrior~

Chapter Twenty-One

WHEN JACKIE'S EYES swung to the tapestry, Darach wrapped his arm around her lower back for support. Her jaw dropped when she saw what it now depicted. Not the Viking King but someone entirely different.

Heidrek.

He wore a red jerkin with a brown fur draped over his shoulders. A bronze medallion hung around his neck, and he held a sword. His expression was calm, firm and unafraid as the sky burst brilliantly behind him and Viking ships sailed on calm seas.

"He really did it," she whispered. "He defeated them."

"Of course, I did, woman," Heidrek whispered into her mind.

Emotion swamped her as she thought of all the times they had spent together. A Viking who had become a better friend than most. A man who was now frozen in a tapestry.

"I can hear him," she murmured to Darach.

He nodded.

"Where's Naðr, Heidrek?" She kept staring at the tapestry. *"Where's the Viking King?"*

A long silence passed before Heidrek responded. *"My King is safe."* Then another pause. *"As are you."*

"Yes." She blinked away tears, remembering what was said about three men loving her. *"Thanks in big part to you."*

"I did what needed to be done," Heidrek said.

She nodded, inhaled deeply and asked a question she wasn't sure she wanted the answer to. *"Will I see you again? Or are you somehow trapped...in the tapestry?"*

"It is unlikely we will cross paths again," Heidrek said. *"Be with your kin now, Jackie. You have nothing to fear. Not for yourself or for my well-being."*

"Why do I feel so heartbroken then?"

"Because you are saying goodbye to a friend." She heard the gruffness in his voice. *"It is never easy."*

Though tempted to apologize for not loving him, she got the sense they were beyond that. He wasn't mourning for what might have been. And if he were, he would never admit it. Rather, he seemed to find solace in knowing all had ended well. Everyone was safe and happy.

"Goodbye, Heidrek," she whispered. *"Thank you so much."*

"And thank you, Jackie," he said. Though it might have been her mind playing tricks on her, she swore she heard him whisper, *"Now I know what to look for,"* before his voice died away entirely.

"He's gone." Jackie rested her cheek against Darach's shoulder. "What a good friend he was."

"Aye." Darach wrapped his arms around her. "Heidrek is one of the best men I've ever known."

"I couldn't agree more," she whispered and eyed the tapestry for a few minutes, sad that he was truly gone.

"Come join us," Grant said at last. "So that we can enjoy each other's company in peace at long last."

"That sounds like a great idea," Jackie murmured as her eyes met Darach's. "Peace at last."

"Aye, lass," he said softly. "Peace."

When they joined everyone in front of the fire, Grant finally explained things.

"Though not entirely cured, your friends willnae suffer the totality of their affliction anymore," Grant said. "Cassie willnae go blind, Nicole will never go deaf and Erin willnae lose her voice."

His eyes met Jackie's. "And then there's you, lass."

"Right." She had forgotten about her sickness. "Me."

Lair sat down beside her and met her eyes. "Your tumor is gone, Jackie. I knew the moment I embraced you earlier."

"Seriously?" Jackie whispered.

"Aye," Lair assured. "The darkness is gone. And with it, your illness."

Jackie rested her elbow on the armrest, put her hand over her mouth and stared at the fire. The tumor was gone. She had been suffering the symptoms of it for years and then the diagnosis. She had long prepared herself for death. And while she'd certainly seen and experienced enough since traveling back in time, including death, nothing could have prepared her for this moment. She didn't know what to say. She needed to process this…to let it sink in.

Thankfully, Darach simply held her hand, and Grant kept talking.

"Your friends are partially cured because something happened in the Otherworld that affected them," he said. "Something that included not only Eoghan's death but your magic and Brigit's healing water."

Jackie's eyes shot to him. "What do you mean?"

"It had to have been a moment only you could have controlled." His voice grew softer. "Did you think of them when you were there? If so, they benefitted from the same healing powers you experienced."

"Of course I thought of them." Her eyes went to her friends. "I thought about how angry I was because of what they had to face. And how proud I was of them." Her eyes turned to Darach. "It was when you asked me to visualize my surroundings, and I closed my eyes." She frowned. "Why *did* you ask me to do that to begin with?"

"Because I asked him too before he made his final stance against Eoghan," Grant said. "I told him the demi-god would likely whisk you back to where it all began. That dark Otherworld."

She shook her head, confused.

"You see, I played a trick on my son," Grant said. "One I couldnae share."

Before she could reply, Grant continued. "It needed to seem like I died at Hamilton Castle, that I buckled beneath the power of the demi-god and even Balor. Darach needed to believe it." He shook his head. "But I didnae. Nay, I called on Goddess Brigit and harnessed magic that nearly killed me."

Having communicated with his father since they returned, Darach continued. "Da called on Brigit in an unexpected way. One she couldnae stop. 'Twas the power of the trees...the oaks." His eyes met hers. "'Twas a spell that carried him through the memory of our oak, lass. From her conception then straight through every acorn it released. Though it might seem simple, you have to remember how many acorns a single oak sheds in its lifetime. So Da was pulled through the life of every acorn as his magic tried to stay the course and follow ours."

"'Twas truly dangerous," Torra said upon her return as she and Darach's aunts and uncles joined them. "Even Adlin MacLomain might not have dared such a feat."

"Aye, but he would have." Grant looked at Darach. "If he was protecting his bairn." His eyes went to Jackie. "And his one true love."

"So how did you end up at the foot of the oak outside this castle in the Otherworld?" Jackie asked.

"'Twas the last acorn," he said. "I was lucky that you and Darach brought it to me. I was even luckier that you ignited the magic needed to pull me free."

"You took a big chance." Jackie grew upset. "And you mean Eara…or Chiomara, because she took us every step of the way."

"Nay." Grant shook his head. "Only the love betwixt you and my son could have brought you so far. A love that helped you find true forgiveness, aye? Eara…Chiomara, simply helped."

"You had that much faith in us?" Jackie said. "In me?"

"Aye." Grant's eyes stayed with hers. "From the moment you vowed to deny your love for my son to keep him safe." His eyes went to Darach. "And from the moment I knew you would give your life to be with her."

Silence fell over the hall except for the crackling of the fire.

"Ohhh," Nicole finally groaned, clearly unable to help herself. "So touching. That's the most romantic story *ever*."

"It *really* is," Leslie added, wiping away several tears, hormones getting the best of her. "And I can't stand being sappy."

"Me either," Nicole moped, wiping away tears of her own.

"What about Balor and the *Genii Cucullati*? How did they end up in the tapestry?" Jackie shook her head. "And what about Cullen Stewart? Does he know what happened to his sister?"

"As we recently learned, Balor wanted you and the ring from the verra beginning, Jackie," Torra said. "When Brigit stole you away in Ireland, it marked the start of his fury. He tracked Chiomara, then her lineage after that…the MacLomains. Anything to get his hands on another Claddagh ring that might somehow lead him to you." She shook her head. "If he and Eoghan got you and your ring at the same time, he intended to travel back to Ireland and destroy Chiomara first, hence there would be no MacLomains. That in itself would have changed Scotland's history."

"Aye," Grant agreed then continued. "When Jackie was born, the long lost ring reappeared, and Brigit knew the time had come. Though someday it had to find its way back to its rightful owner, she hid the ring until the time was right for Jackie to wear it. Before that day came, she needed to be one step ahead."

"So she whispered the prophecy of the wee king." Grant's eyes flickered over Darach and his cousins. "Four MacLomain warriors would protect Robert the Bruce when evil sought him out. She did this knowing all in the Celtic Otherworld would hear. 'Twas a means to draw out Balor. Because if one thing remained true above all else, 'twas that Balor still held a grudge against Brigit for interfering in Ireland to begin with. Therefore, when the MacLomain name was mentioned, he took the bait."

"Little did Balor know that Brigit was using him to fulfill her own prophecy," Torra said. "In his lust for revenge, it never occurred to the demon how ironic it was that the ring turned up at the same time the prophecy unfolded. No, he was too focused on his plan. He helped Eoghan's soul reincarnate once, but that ended poorly. Then he tried again through the druid's influence over his son, Keir Hamilton. That failed as well."

"But evil is vigilant and doesnae give up," Torra continued. "So when Brigit's prophecy unfolded, Balor played right into her hands and offered Eoghan's soul a chance to return as a demi-god so he could get his lass back. Hence, he once more became Balor's conduit to our plane. Because unlike a demi-god, a god can only meddle but so much in the affairs of mortals."

"When we traveled back in time to MacLomain Castle and Heidrek saw the potential in using Jackie as bait, he and I concocted our plan." Grant said. "We would lure the beast to the tapestry once again. Just a different beast this time. And while I knew Jackie and Darach would eventually cross over and hopefully find me, I never could have anticipated things going as they did." His eyes met Jackie's. "You taking Darach's pain and your tumor growing. How connected to evil it was." He shook his head. "'Twas verra brave of you, lass."

"I would have done the same thing even if I knew the demon had put the tumor there." Her eyes met Darach's. "Even if I knew it would grow as a result."

"Aye, lass," Grant murmured, his eyes still on her. "As I surmised, evil followed you both here to the great hall. 'Twas then that Brigit told me Eoghan would pursue you back to where it all began in Ireland and that your final battle must be fought in the

Otherworld. That when the time was right, you must visualize your surroundings in order to return to the world of the living, no matter how brief." His eyes went to Darach. "And naturally, my son was determined to stay by your side every step of the way."

Their eyes met, and Darach squeezed her hand.

"But let's get back to what happened before you left," Grant said. "Through the use of the mantle and the magic of all our kin, we were able to breach worlds and return to this reality." His eyes went to the tapestry. "When we did, it was enough to make Balor act without thinking and follow you and Heidrek into the tapestry. Always eager for your soul, the *Genii Cucullati* were right behind."

"So what happened to them?" Jackie frowned. "All I remember seeing before Heidrek threw me to Darach was fire."

Grant was about to respond, but Torra shook her head. "That is another story entirely. One born of our dragon ancestors and the length they were willing to go for us."

"Heidrek said he was okay." Jackie's eyes narrowed on Grant. "Is he or was he just saying that so I wouldn't worry?"

"He is," Grant assured and gestured at the tapestry. "Does it not look peaceful?"

It did. Yet looks could be deceiving. Though inclined to seek more answers, she was well aware of how tired everyone was. And how they wanted to relax and celebrate the fact that they were safe now, especially Robert the Bruce and William.

Jackie still couldn't believe she had met *William Wallace* as a boy. Someone who would one day become a leader in the Scottish Wars of Independence. A brave and loyal man who would lay down his life for his king, Robert the Bruce, so that Scotland might rise up against tyranny.

"What about Cullen Stewart?" Erin asked. "He's important to me...to all of us. What happened to him?"

Grant and Torra looked at each other and smiled.

Grant explained. "As the story goes, a brother embraced forgiveness, spread his wings and saved his sister before she plummeted to her death."

"The last time I saw them they were battling it out here at MacLomain Castle. And then they just vanished." Erin frowned. "What do you mean, Cullen saved that evil bitch?"

"She wasnae so evil in the end," Darach informed. "Da gave me the message before Jackie and I went off to fight Eoghan."

He explained what happened.

"So after everything she did, he still saved her?" Nicole scowled. "I'm not sure I would've been so forgiving. Not at all."

"I agree," Cassie murmured. "But then it seems like she might've been trying to tell us what was happening sooner." She looked at Erin. "Didn't you see her ghost at Stewart Castle? Wasn't she trying to reach out?"

"Yeah." Erin frowned then looked at Nicole. "And didn't you say Brae acted strangely when you came across her in the Otherworld?"

"Yup." Nicole frowned just as heavily, shook her head and eyed Grant. "So what happened to them after Cullen saved her? And why did she kill her brother to begin with?"

"The stories are wide and varied. Some say she did it because she had no other choice. Killing him kept her parents and kin safe. Then others say her magic was so great that she knew his death was around the corner, and so she killed him first so that he would ascend and keep the blame on her...hence following her pre-destined path into all this," Grant said. "As to the end? From all reports, the Stewart clan has found closure, happiness, and peace. All is well."

Jackie cocked her head at Grant. "Can't you just chant a little something and travel back to their time to find out exactly what happened?"

"He could. He might have already." Darach's mother chuckled and winked at Jackie. "But you'll likely never know. Hamiltons are very talented at being evasive for the greater good."

Jackie smiled. "Yeah, I'm getting that."

"What about the horses?" Darach's eyes met his father's. "We know they merged with ancestors but who delivered them to New Hampshire?"

"I still dinnae know. But I suppose every Scottish clan deserves its mysteries." Grant grinned and nodded at the mantel. "May future generations forever wonder who was at the heart of protecting our clan so well."

Everyone smiled as their eyes went to the mantel.

Four horses were carved into the stone over the center of the hearth, running free and wild. Content with a job well done. Two happy faces were carved on either side. Faces nobody could mistake.

Adlin and Iosbail.

"Why does Adlin's face seem less defined?" Bradon asked.

"Funny you should ask." Grant kept grinning as his eyes landed on Leslie's stomach. "Where was it you conceived that bairn, again?"

Leslie put her hands over her belly protectively. "Why?"

Grant chuckled as he stood and pulled his wife into his arms as people streamed into the great hall. He responded then winked before he and Sheila twirled away to the pipes. "Was it at the Highland Defiance then?"

Leslie's eyes narrowed on Bradon. "What did he mean by that?"

Jackie shook her head and groaned, "You two were *so* loud when we stowed away there."

"No surprise." Nicole grinned. "Remember how loud they were in New Hampshire?"

"Yeah, so what, we had sex...a lot of sex at the Defiance," Leslie grumbled, her eyes narrowed on Bradon. "But what does that have to do with Adlin's face being less defined in the damn mantle?"

"My guess?" His eyes fell to her stomach, a little wondrous. "I'd say he meant Adlin's soul is fading from the Otherworld and returning to this one."

"Aye." Torra smiled at them. "After all, the original Highland Defiance was the most powerful place Adlin created ...and a portal at that." She shrugged. "It's supposed to move people from one spot in Scotland to another but who knows what other kind of doorway it might be..."

Everyone's eyes rounded on Leslie's stomach as they contemplated the possibility that Adlin's reincarnated soul might be in there.

Though interested in the conversation, Jackie had no chance to follow the rest of it before Darach pulled her into the happy crowd. Jackie laughed as he spun her once, twice then pulled her against him. They spent a long time like that. Swaying against each other...grateful that they were together and everything was over.

Then they joined their friends and family in celebration. There was so much happiness. Lightness. And while she knew it was partly because she was accepting her illness was gone, it was so much more.

"We've come a long way," Jackie said as she and her friends stood outside later that night and stared out over the moonlit loch.

"Have we ever." Nicole looked at Cassie. "I never would've guessed any of this when we pulled your Chevette up to the Colonial in New Hampshire." She chuckled. "What a ride."

"I know," Cassie agreed.

"I thought you were full of bullshit," Erin reminded, an easy smile on her face.

Jackie bumped her hip against Erin's and smiled. "Glad you were wrong?"

"Very," Erin confirmed.

Everyone's eyes turned Jackie's way when Erin said, "How about you, Savior? Thrilled as the rest of us?"

Jackie shook her head and scowled. "Please don't call me that."

"But we mean it," Cassie said. "If it weren't for you, we'd still be disabled."

"I…" She shook her head, not wanting the dynamics between them to change. "I didn't mean to…"

Their expressions softened when they saw her struggling. They understood.

"Listen." Erin gripped her shoulder and met her eyes. "I shouldn't have said 'savior'. That was too intense. We're just grateful." She notched the corner of her lip. "If we're sharing a happy ending together and you played a part in that then way to go, Sweetheart."

Jackie nodded and whispered, "Anytime."

"I for one am glad that I experienced blindness. It gave me a deeper understanding of so many things," Cassie said. "There are others in the village. Those losing their sight or are already blind. I've been working with them and will continue to do so."

"Same here," Nicole added. "Though they're all elderly, I've been spending a lot of time with those losing their hearing."

When Jackie's eyes met Erin's, her best friend shrugged. "It's sort of rare to go mute, and I haven't been here long so cut me some slack." Then she pulled her into a hug. "But I'm opening my heart and learning about an amazing clan." Erin grinned. "The MacLeod's will never be the same after having me as Lady of their Castle."

Jackie chuckled. "No, they won't."

Her eyes encompassed them all. "I love you guys." She fought back tears. "Thanks for sticking by me every step of the way."

"Hell yeah," Nicole murmured as Cassie said, "Where else would we be?"

"*Braveheart* came to life," Nicole echoed as they all embraced.

Right. Their love for movies. A way to bridge the gap when they all lost their sight, hearing and what not.

"William *Wallace*," Nicole mumbled as they hugged tighter. "Like holy shit, *right*?"

All nodded in agreement.

"Mind if I steal my lass now?" Darach said.

While she loved being with her friends, since the moment they separated, she was eager to be with him again. Some might say she suffered the romantic affliction of new love, but she knew how very old it was.

"Darach Hamilton." Nicole grinned as she hugged him the best she could with her big belly. "You *always* wanted Jackie." She shook her head and half sauntered, half waddled away, proclaiming, "Let it go on record that when I think two people want each other, I'm right."

Cassie hugged him next then murmured, "I'm so glad you found each other," before she left.

Erin squeezed Jackie's hand and met her eyes. "Are you okay?"

There was only one way to answer, and she meant it with all her heart. "I'm better than ever."

Erin eyed her for a long moment before she nodded and headed Darach's way. She embraced him and whispered in his ear. Something Jackie heard because of her and Darach's connection. "I love you both, but you better be good to her," she said. "Or I'll use your own weapon against you."

When she strode away, Darach frowned, patted his side and muttered, "My blade's gone. Bloody hell, how does she do that?"

Jackie chuckled. "The woman's talented."

"That's one way to put it," he muttered before he swiftly closed the distance between them. "I missed you," he whispered as he backed her up against the railing and kissed her.

"Me too," she murmured between kisses. "Missed you too that is."

His lips closed more firmly over hers before she could say another word. It was astounding but not quite perfect...not quite what she needed.

Something was missing.

Her heart wanted more.

Aware of her discontent, he pulled back and frowned. "What troubles you?"

"Nothing that should..." She frowned, trying to understand. "But don't you sense it?"

His eyes searched hers before he nodded and whispered, "I think I do...you want to go home."

"Yes." Her brows perked and her heart fluttered. "I do."

Though he tried to hide it, distress flashed in his eyes. "Back to the twenty-first century?"

"Yes." Jackie shook her head when she realized what he said. "No." Her eyes stayed with his. "I want to go home...to Hamilton Castle."

Relief flashed in his eyes. "Aye then, lass. I learned a wee trick from Brigit along the way."

"What's that?"

"Another way to get you home." He cupped her cheek and brushed his finger over her birthmark before he pulled her close. Magic swirled around them before darkness descended.

"Oh no, not the Otherworld again," she mumbled against his chest.

"Nay." He turned her. "*Home.*"

Jackie blinked as she acclimated. A full moon cut through the trees and lit the statue of her carved into Hamilton Castle.

"We're back," she exclaimed, smiling.

"Aye," he murmured in her ear as he reached around and touched the birthmark on the statue. "We're back to where it all began."

"What about the rest of the clan still at MacLomain Castle?" she managed, breathless as he pressed against her back.

"We'll get them home on the morrow," he managed before he spun her and kissed her again.

"How?" she whispered between kisses as he lifted her and she wrapped her legs around him.

"Magic," he said as he ascended the stairs with her in his arms.

"But we're home," she managed between more kisses. "We should call the clan together. Have a celebration."

"Yer out of yer bloody mind," he growled seconds before she ended up on an all-too-familiar bed. "I chased ye into the Celtic Otherworld. We died. Several times." His body covered hers. "The only way I intend to celebrate right now is with you on this bed." He removed their clothes with a flick of his wrist, settled between her thighs and whispered in her ear before he thrust and everything spun away in pleasure.

"Welcome home, Lady of Hamilton Castle."

Later that night as Jackie cuddled against Darach, she reflected on everything that had happened as a result of preserving the passion first born between Gwendolyn and Devlin. Everything Goddess Brigit began in ancient Ireland and saw through thanks to careful planning and the help of her greatest love, Fionn Mac Cumhail.

A large tapestry had been woven, in more ways than one.

Evil had at last been defeated.

Robert the Bruce was safe. He had learned much from his adventures and now understood things most never would experience at his age, never mind in their entire lifetime. From Cassie, how to see things more clearly and pay attention to what was going on around him. From Nicole, how to listen closely, especially to things unsaid. From Erin, how to appreciate the value in choosing his words wisely and using less of them to make his point.

And from Jackie?

Hopefully to see the bigger picture and remember that everyone did things for a reason. Get to the heart of a person and learn what those reasons are before judging.

But she knew he had benefitted in so many more ways.

Darach and his cousins had made an impact, showing Robert firsthand what his countrymen were willing to do for him. The lengths they would go. That he was beloved enough that four warriors would devote their lives to protecting him long before he became king.

Yet when all was said and done, it had taken many to protect the future of Scotland.

Courage had been rallied.

Fears had been faced.

Some might say in the end that a single Claddagh ring started it all, but Jackie knew better.

It had not only been the passion found between her and her Scottish warrior but what took root so long ago when a Celtic goddess saw how strong love could truly be.

How it had the potential to withstand time.

How it could affect so many others.

It was the perfect foundation for everything to come.

The true birth of Clan MacLomain and Clan Broun.

The End

Nothing is ever as it seems. Though Heidrek showed Jackie one thing when she looked at the MacLomain tapestry, something else altogether brews in Scandinavia as a result of his time in Scotland. Certain gods are unhappy and new enemies threaten his people. What's worse? Heidrek knows women from the distant future will once more be amongst them. Though he suspects his heart will be tied to one, it's now in everyone's best interest that he keep her and her kin away.

Find out what happens next with Heidrek in *Rise of a Viking*, The MacLomain Series: Viking Ancestors' Kin, Book One.

Previous Releases

~The MacLomain Series- Early Years~

Highland Defiance- Book One
Highland Persuasion- Book Two
Highland Mystic- Book Three

~The MacLomain Series~

The King's Druidess- Prelude
Fate's Monolith- Book One
Destiny's Denial- Book Two
Sylvan Mist- Book Three

~The MacLomain Series- Next Generation~

Mark of the Highlander- Book One
Vow of the Highlander- Book Two
Wrath of the Highlander- Book Three
Faith of the Highlander- Book Four
Plight of the Highlander- Book Five

~The MacLomain Series- Later Years~

Quest of a Scottish Warrior- Book One
Honor of a Scottish Warrior- Book Two
Oath of a Scottish Warrior- Book Three
Passion of a Scottish Warrior- Book Four

~The MacLomain Series- Viking Ancestors~

Viking King- Book One
Viking Claim- Book Two
Viking Heart- Book Three

~The MacLomain Series- Viking Ancestors' Kin~

Rise of a Viking- Book One
Vengeance of a Viking- Book Two
Soul of a Viking- Book Three
Fury of a Viking- Book Four
Pride of a Viking- Book Five

~Calum's Curse Series~

The Victorian Lure- Book One
The Georgian Embrace- Book Two
The Tudor Revival- Book Three

~Forsaken Brethren Series~

Darkest Memory- Book One
Heart of Vesuvius- Book Two

~Holiday Tales~

Yule's Fallen Angel
+ Bonus Novelette, Christmas Miracle

~Song of the Muses Series~

Highland Muse

About the Author

Sky Purington is the best-selling author of over twenty novels and several novellas. A New Englander born and bred, Sky was raised hearing stories of folklore, myth and legend. When combined with a love for nature, romance and time-travel, elements from the stories of her youth found release in her books.

Purington loves to hear from readers and can be contacted at Sky@SkyPurington.com. Interested in keeping up with Sky's latest news and releases? Visit Sky's website, www.SkyPurington.com to download her free App on iTunes and Android or sign up for her quarterly newsletter. Love social networking? Find Sky on Facebook and Twitter.

Made in the USA
Middletown, DE
02 April 2018